HYSTERIA

HYSTERIA

A NOVEL

Elisabeth de Mariaffi

HARPERCOLLINS PUBLISHERS LTD

Published by HarperCollins Publishers Ltd

First edition

HarperCollins Publishers Ltd
2 Bloor Street East, 20th Floor
Toronto, Ontario, Canada
M4W 1A8

www.harpercollins.ca

The author wishes to acknowledge the support of ArtsNL, which last year invested
$2.5 million to foster and promote the creation and enjoyment of the arts for the benefit
of all Newfoundlanders and Labradorians.

Library and Archives Canada Cataloguing in Publication
information is available upon request

ISBN 978-1-44345-340-0

Printed and bound in the United States of America

LSC/H 9 8 7 6 5 4 3 2 1

For my grandmother,
Marcella Neufeld,
and especially for her grandmother,
Maria Sieber—
a girl who walked a very long way

A little child died, and its mother fell to weeping. Then the child came to her and said, "Mother, do not cry so much. I am deep in water. If you cry any more, I will drown.
— from *Niederlausitzer Volkssagen (Folktales of Lower Lusatia)*, compiled by Karl Gander, 1894

1 9 4 5

The dog was standing at the edge of the clearing, hackles raised. It lowered its head, watching her, but made no warning sound. Heike crouched where she had fallen, on her hands and knees, maybe twenty-five feet away. For a moment she froze, fear dropping low into her body. She was used to worrying about soldiers, but there were no people with the animal. It might have been a wolf.

No: a wolf would not be so purely black, and its fur would be matted. She sat up, moving slowly. Twenty-five feet is nothing for a dog.

She'd come hard through the bush, her arms and hands badly scratched, and her throat raw from calling out, despite the danger of being heard. Her braids loose and tangled. When a root caught her foot, she'd pitched forward, slamming her shoulder against a stump. She hadn't slept for two days, her bones heavy with exhaustion.

A village dog. She'd been calling for Lena and the dog had heard her. The dog would have heard her coming from some distance. It took a step toward her now, still in the shelter of the forest.

It was early, the sky a light violet. Heike gathered her basket from where it had fallen and rose to her feet. She had no kind of bribe, no treat to throw. The bread she'd been carrying was long gone; the girls living on what they could find, chewing on hay to fool their stomachs, pinching the snow off evergreen boughs and rolling it around on their tongues.

They'd avoided the road, instead making sure to stay half-hidden in the bushes. Two sisters hunting for berries at the edge of a wood. Winter berries. Relentless as little sparrows. Heike told stories to distract them as they walked: the one about a raven that turns into a golden bird, the one about the twelve sisters who disappear every night, dancing through the soles of their shoes by morning. Lena repeating the words in her sleep, *Once there was a king who had twelve daughters, each more beautiful than the other.*

In the end, they'd wandered too far west. At night, Heike could hear the echo of artillery fire rolling out through the hills, and she'd led Lena deeper and deeper into the woods.

Now she began to skirt the edge of the little clearing, keeping her eyes low. Where the hill descended into valley the earth broke up, rocky, and the trees changed. She gripped a branch for balance, the new buds rough against her skin. Down farther, there was a stream. She could hear it running freely, the water no longer trapped under ice. It was late March, colder in the hills than it would have been at home. She knelt by the stream to drink, and her knees got wet, her skirt soaking through.

On the other side, the forest rose up into another, steeper incline. There was a sound behind her and when she looked, she saw the dog again, maybe fifteen feet away this time. Its eyes on her, unwavering. Whether it was following her or hunting her, Heike could not be sure.

In Dresden, her mother had often taken them walking by the river at night. The stars came out, one by one, and they rushed to count them where they reflected in the Elbe, a game between the three of them. This seemed so long ago now that Heike no longer knew if it was a real memory or only another story she told, a way to pass the time on the long days of walking.

On a clear night, the river glittered like heaven.

This is what she thought of now, kneeling by the stream. If her mother was looking at the water when the firebombs came down, the whole city sparkling, the river rising up to meet a massive star. Like a shower of suns.

Heike got to her feet. She had on a pair of leather boots and a man's overcoat, her father's, and a kerchief around her hair; Lena had worn boys' pants and shoes with laces. They didn't have any gloves, and sometimes she'd taken off the kerchief and wrapped it around Lena's hands like a muff. The tips of her own fingers had suffered, bleaching white now at the touch of any cold. The blood remembers: what's lost to the mind is not lost to the body.

She clambered up the bank. She'd been circling the same area since Lena was lost—five days, or six, she'd lost count—widening out the search a little each time. At night, she sat with her back against a tree and worked to keep her eyes open. Just in case, in case Lena was somewhere close by, crying. She didn't want to call out in the nighttime, a girl's voice, lonely in the dark.

Once she thought she saw a fawn, was sure of its shape and the spindles of its legs, but when she looked again it had only

3

been a fallen branch. She followed any noise, any rustle or crack of twigs, but the sounds never led her to Lena.

Alone now in the woods, she found herself checking again and again for the dog. Anxious. Willing it to be another trick of exhaustion, a vision she could blink away—but it was always there, close by, its paws soundless on the hard ground.

ON THE OTHER SIDE of the rise there was no forest. The dog let out a low growl; it was right beside her now, huge and panting. Taller at the shoulder than Heike's waist. There was a trace smell of smoke in the air.

She could tell what had happened by the emptiness, by all the paper in the field. What remained after the fighting: every soldier with a picture of his sweetheart in his breast pocket, every soldier with a photograph of his mother. And when they were hit, *pfoum!* Like confetti.

There were no people left. There were not even bodies. Just bits of paper.

At the edge of the village she found a barn, its door not fixed, the latch batting lightly in the breeze. Heike went inside, shutting the door behind her. If the soldiers had already been through here, then it was a safe place. She hoped that the dog, shut outside, would tire of waiting for her. She climbed up into a corner hayloft and closed her eyes.

Halfway through the night, she heard them come through again, but it was only a handful of voices and some random gunfire, a cleanup crew or a few angry survivors, the dog outside kicking up a fuss and waking her. She pulled herself into a darker corner, holding her breath.

In the morning it was very quiet. She came out from where

she was hiding. There was a girl on the barn floor: the soldiers had dragged her in during the night.

When they'd first come in, Heike hadn't moved, hidden away up near the rafters. But the sound of the girl's voice, crying out, made her sick with fear, and she crawled to the edge of the loft to see her face, to at least make sure it wasn't Lena—it wasn't, this girl tall and lean with copper-coloured hair, sixteen years old at least. Heike pulled her hood tighter, deep in the back corner of the hayloft. Her arms wrapped around her head so that she wouldn't hear.

Now the soldiers were gone, but the girl was still there. She was dead, her skirt wrapped tight around her face.

Heike looked at her from the hayloft, lying there with her neck at an odd angle, and then climbed down the ladder to the ground. There was no sound from outside. The girl's body scared her in its stillness, her skin almost blue. She had no boots on, only a pair of house slippers, worn through, not meant for the snow and the outdoors. *Once there was a king who had twelve daughters, each more beautiful than the other.* Heike left the barn as she'd found it, with the door half open.

It had turned cold again in the night: outside, the ground was white with frost. On the other side of the barn she found the dog, shot in the belly. Its fur was so dark you couldn't see the wounds, but blood soaked the earth around it.

She crossed back the way she'd come, faster now, her feet sliding as she ran, and all the paper, paper everywhere. Tissue-thin pages from tiny bibles, melting into the ridge of snow. A sound from behind her, the low creak of a half-dead tree moving sharply in the wind. She turned back to look. Beside the dog's body stood a single crow, its black eye shining.

THE RAFT

One just expects it will be used properly. There is no warning on scalpels,
"This is sharp, don't cut yourself."
—Dr. Frank Milan Berger, creator of Miltown,
the first mass-market psychiatric drug

1.

Heike had seen the raft the day before. Just a glimpse of it through the trees on her way out, and then again when she was hiking back, the stream sparkling now in the sunlight. It was anchored about forty feet from shore. She'd been following the little river down to where she knew it must spill into open water and was surprised to see it suddenly give way to a pond instead. Wide and flat, an inlet slip of lake. From where she stood on the beach, she could see beyond the tree line to the open glint of Cayuga, the lake formal and civic and plain compared to the closeness of the woods.

Three days of rain had left the ground soft but resistant, and it gave a little under each step. There was ten or fifteen feet of beach, hard-packed and marked with driftwood and the odd fallen log, and here steam rose up off the ground like a thin and expansive curtain, separating woods and pond. Sunlight caught the mist and turned everything to prisms. Too-bright. High summer.

Heike squinted. It was a wood-plank raft, maybe six by six, or a little bigger. Grey-green in the light. To the left of it, there was a bank of young reeds, just the green knife-tips pushing above the waterline, but the raft bobbed slightly and the water looked clear and deep on the far side. Good for swimming. She could bring Daniel here, the next day even, if the rain didn't come back around. This was the summer of the downpour, the summer of indoor games and puzzles and painting-by-the-window. They were lucky to be on the lake instead of stuck in a city apartment. Eric had been offered a summer of teaching at Cornell that had quickly come to include a position at Willard Asylum. His old stomping ground, in a way: he'd worked some little portion of his residency there. The hospital was one lake over, on Seneca. Eric spent a lot of his time driving and teased that Heike would get jealous. When he'd met her, overseas, she had briefly been his patient.

His sister, Arden, found them the summer house, a rental, close to their own place. Heike's heart in her throat at the offer. Eric was not one for family connections. But he'd been caught off guard, Arden's husband suggesting the idea in a way that seemed to leave no room for debate.

She turned back to the forest and let her eyes adjust. She'd been picking her way through the woods in high rubber boots and an old pair of man's work shorts, belted tight around her waist. There was no set trail. When she stopped and turned around, she could watch the moss spring slowly back into shape where the crush of her boots had pressed it down. Her knuckles and bare thighs scraped against the trees as she made her way through, and she had to grasp the wet branches with her hands to avoid losing her footing. Her hands were damp with bark grit.

Inside the tree line it was cool and damp, but Heike's feet were hot in the rubber boots. She stood back, just within the shadows. Out on the water, the sun was in full force. She took a moment to gauge where it sat in the afternoon sky. Three o'clock, if she had to guess. Maybe another half-hour before Daniel would be up from his nap and looking for her.

She'd put him to bed late the night before, the way she used to do in the city, the two of them cuddled close in a hammock on the back veranda until the sun was down and the mosquitoes made it impossible. Swaying there as the stars came out. Daniel counted them, one by one, then grew cranky with heat and jumped out to sit next to the table lantern and count instead the moths as they bumped against the glass. Heike told him how she'd learned to count the stars, reflecting off the river, when she was a little girl, and then later at home, to count the corners of the bedroom where she slept as though they were stars. Her own mother's instruction: if you count the corners of your room and then make a wish, it will come true.

By nine-thirty they'd lost the light entirely. She gathered Dani up for a bath.

Where Eric often sat nearby in the evenings, watching as Daniel set up a course for his wooden trains—each piece of track linking up with a click—this time he'd surprised her, lost to his work. The lamp in the office burning and a bottle of brandy within easy reach. With Daniel sleeping, Heike kept to herself, curled on the couch in the white room at the back of the house until she lost track of the hour, a sketchbook on her lap. The breeze and night sounds through the French doors, an owl just where the yard ended and the forest began. The mosquitoes most interested in her bony parts: clavicle, shoulder, knee.

A bite at the outer edge of her elbow thrummed away now at her patience. She was wearing thin socks and the left one had slipped down below the heel, the skin at the inner edge of her ankle rubbing away like wet tissue. There was a rise just beyond where she was standing, and a kind of clearing that opened out to the pond, and she followed it over and sat down on a stump to take the boot off. The ankle stung. Heike reached into the boot to see if there was anything in there—a piece of bark, a pebble, some little sharpness that might be exacerbating the damage—and in doing so, her body twisted so that she saw the house. Green-roofed and hidden away just beyond the rise. Easy to miss.

She'd walked right by it, twice, without seeing it at all.

— WHAT WERE YOU DOING OUT THERE?

Arden picked up the knife she'd just placed, held it to the light, then polished it furiously with a napkin. They were laying the table for dinner. Heike and Eric, John and Arden. Only the men were both outside.

— I thought these were public lands, Heike said.

— There's nothing public here, Arden said absently. She laid the knife down again in its place. All the land was handed out in big swaths, she said. After the War of Independence: bounty land in great big bolts, rolling out to the brightest and shiniest, you know. John likes to say his family's been splashing about here for almost two centuries.

— But you didn't know you have a neighbour?

Arden swept a hand over the fold of the napkin, then picked it up and sharpened the crease more deliberately between her fingers. She cocked her head.

— Does Eric know you're just out wandering around in the woods like that?

Heike reached back and untied her apron.

— I was looking for birds, she said. Eric says a hobby is good for the soul. Besides, I couldn't stand to be cooped up for one more day. She folded the apron over the back of a chair. The sun was low in the sky now, and she thought of Dani, tucked into her own bed upstairs, the puff of white sheets around his face. There's a raft, she said. I thought I might go back tomorrow. For a swim.

— Good, Arden said. I'm into souls. Let's eat. I've had nothing but grapefruits and hard-boiled eggs all day. She was a tall girl, handsome rather than pretty, with sturdy shoulders and a strong waist. I wish there was no such thing as a reducing diet, she said, stopping in front of the hall mirror to fuss with a capped sleeve.

Heike relaxed, her shoulders softening. The truth was that Eric considered her solo hiking expeditions somewhat ambitious. Arden, on the other hand, found such independence alluring. She had herself been the star pitcher in her girls' softball league at college—Heike had seen the team photograph—but dropped out of athletics for a different kind of competition, and met John Wyland just before he wrote the bar exam. They'd been married in December, in the city, Arden wearing long sleeves and a white wedding coat with a fur-lined hood over her dress, flanked on either side by pretty bridesmaids.

Behind her now, in the mirror, Heike herself might have been a child. Slight and blond, a full head shorter than Arden, but with a long neck and slender wrists and fine, slim fingers. She rose high on her toes and watched her reflection grow taller, almost tall enough to match Arden's height, then sank back down again. As though in response, Arden teetered up on her own toes a moment. Catching Heike's eye, she stuck out her tongue and winked.

Like they were old pals. In fact, Eric had not told his family he was married at all—Heike appearing as a surprise in the receiving line at Arden's wedding, Eric's hand soft on the back of her neck. They'd spent hardly any time together in childhood, Arden told her later: Eric a full ten years older. Their mother, a widow, had passed on suddenly a few summers before. Since then she'd barely seen him.

In the weeks after the wedding, Arden had sent a blitz of invitations: to tea at the Waldorf Astoria, then again to lunch at Schrafft's. Eric regarded the new friendship with suspicion: his sister's enthusiasm, he said, founded merely in housewifely boredom. When John's firm bought a table at an Easter charity gala, Heike received their tickets directly. John had blanched, Arden said (Eric could be single-minded—strident, even—in party conversation), but she'd reminded him that her brother was her only real relation: the reason he'd turned up to her wedding at all. Besides, they could afford it.

It was at this Easter party that the summer plan had been hatched. John planned to make the long weekend commute back and forth from the city for the season and Arden, faced with the prospect of loneliness during the week, itched for something to fill her dance card. She badly wanted a job writing the society column for an upstate paper out of Syracuse—more occupation, John had announced to the table, than was strictly required.

— You've already got two deadlines: Drop me off at the station on Sunday, and pick me up again on Friday night. There's women who'd kill for that kind of leisure! Make some friends, why don't you? What about Heike here? Didn't you say your brother had an offer from Cornell?

John's idea, almost: the girls hadn't even had to do the work. Eric, unprepared for once, reticently agreed. Arden had an estate agent within the month.

Now Heike watched her fussing in the hall mirror: she couldn't make the damn sleeve cooperate. Arden let out a breath of frustration, and her bangs lifted and fell. Heike rose high on her toes again.

The men had been out on the veranda with rocks glasses, and as Heike carried the meat through to the dining room it was suddenly decided that they would eat *al fresco* instead. Eric had hired a man to install a new trellis at one end of the rail, and within the trumpet vine he'd hidden a hummingbird feeder made of blown glass. For Heike, Eric said. He was hoping the hummers would give them an evening show. She diverted course and set the platter on the outdoor table, wedging it between a couple of fat candles in brass holders, not wanting to tell him that the noise of their dinner party would almost certainly defy his efforts. Eric followed her back inside and gathered the cutlery from the set table, jangling it in his hands and scrunching the folded napkins.

— Heike's been ransacking an abandoned house, Arden said when they'd all sat down.

Eric looked up from salting his greens. He had dark hair, close cut, and high enough cheekbones. The sort of skin that tans easily in sunshine. The overall effect was dashing, especially in summer, but there was some problem around the eyes, something Heike could identify but not name. Disloyal, to think it.

—What house? John said. He leaned to Arden: Your brother's been trying to hook me with his research propositions again. I need a change of subject before I'm compelled to turn state's evidence.

Eric turned from Heike to look at John:

—Any decent doctor tries his own scripts. The whole thing is about opening the mind. Too progressive for you?

—Oppenheimer was also progressive.

John said this with his usual pleasant manner and shook out his napkin before tucking it in over the top button of his shirt.

Arden took up the salt shaker.

— I'm afraid John is quite a Continental theorist, Eric. Mad on the French, you know.

— The French? The French are still obsessed with Freud. What I'm doing is strictly twentieth century.

— Like the Fox, John said. Only less foxy. Heike, what's this house?

She'd been moving a baby potato back and forth with her knife, half-watching the new feeder, and now picked up her fork to give the meal her attention.

—It's not so much a house, Heike said. A fishing cabin. Maybe a mile up the lake. Mile and a half or so.

— Funny, she never mentioned a breath of it to me, Eric said. He laid a hand over Heike's on the table and stroked the soft place between her thumb and forefinger with his own thumb. Then, to Arden: You ladies and your tales.

— I was out walking, Heike said. And I stopped to fix my ankle. I'm sure I told you. She turned away to take the bread-basket from John's hand. You've probably passed by it ten times before. You can't see it from the road. It's hidden, kind of.

— But you went inside, Eric said.

— I knocked, and there was no one. The door was unlocked.

This was a lie. The deadbolt wasn't engaged, but there was a doorknob lock, and Heike had tinkered with the knob and smacked hard against it with her hip until the door swung open.

— I could tell no one was there, she said. It has that look. There are dandelions growing right in front of the doorway.

— Squatter? John said. If it's well hidden. He scooped up a pat of butter and used the back of his dessert spoon to spread a firm circle of it inside a roll.

— I think a squatter wouldn't have so many nice things, Heike said. Would you? If you're just staking a claim?

— What kind of things? Eric said.

Inside, the house had had a feeling of casual disuse: the cupboards lined in newspaper and all the cups stored upside down, but a thick layer of grime on the stove. No drop cloths over the furniture. Heike had picked up a corner of the coiled rag rug and let it fall, releasing a little storm of dust. But it was the presence of the raft outside that made it feel most like a home. Something extra, with no purpose other than a bit of recreation. A raft for a sunbather, for children to practice their deep dives.

— Whoever owns it, they thought they'd be coming back, Arden said.

— Whoever owns it died in the war, Eric said. He sawed at the chop on his plate. Died without family. Or they all died, who knows. He speared the meat with his fork. So long as no one knows you were there. We don't want any trouble.

It was a three-room house, just a big kitchen and living area and one room with a bed, the coverlet pulled tight over the mattress. Heike had sat down on the edge of the bed, leaned over to peer into the crack under the highboy in the corner. Windows with their winter storms on. In the kitchen drawers there was real silverware, though, and she'd almost slipped a coffee spoon into her pocket, running the pad of her thumb in and out of the dull bowl. The newspapers lining the cupboard were from Rochester rather than New York. She let the spoon clink back into its drawer and opened up a glass cabinet instead, fingering the abandoned souvenirs before choosing a porcelain figurine of a girl, her round white hat tied under her chin, holding the corners of her apron out wide. Heike flipped the figurine over to check the bottom. Two swords. Meissen.

A destroyed place now, but Heike's corner of the world, near to Dresden.

Bombed and scattered. She ran her fingertip down the smooth finish of the girl's skirt. She'd been only three days away by foot when they came.

Lena sleeping next to her in a field. The sound of the planes overhead and suddenly it was morning, but in the east somehow two suns rising, instead of just one. Firebombs from Dresden and a red herring target, Böhlen, less than sixty miles to the north, lit the sky in two points. She'd thought she was crazy or dead.

Heike turned the figurine over in her hand again.

The connection seemed too much for coincidence. She pulled a single sheet of newspaper out of the cupboard and wrapped the girl up for the hike home.

— No risk of trouble, Heike said now. There was a cucumber salad on the table, and she spooned a little onto Eric's plate before serving herself. No one's been there for years, I'd say. You're probably right: whoever owned it died overseas.

From the corner of her eye, she caught the sharp glint of a

wing flickering in the trumpet vine, and for a moment she froze, unsure of whether to call attention to it. The little bird hovered at the feeder, neither drinking nor taking its leave, its tiny, furious body suspended. A held breath.

Heike set the salad bowl down and turned her own body to Eric.

— I walked all the way around the property, she said. No tire tracks, even. No trace.

THE NEXT DAY was clear and bright, with a high sun, somehow even early in the morning. Heike shifted in bed. Light flooded in strong through the sheers and caught the cut-glass vase on the vanity, spangling between the vase itself and the mirror behind it. She draped a hand across her eyes and tried to settle. John and Arden had stayed late—later, Heike knew, than Eric had originally wanted. But their attention had been too fawning for him to resist. His sister was committed to matching her own family's camaraderie to John's. They were all to be great chums, Arden said. Like the Wylands.

Heike had crept upstairs to check on Daniel twice, watching his eyes roll and twitch beneath the closed lids. She'd tucked him snugly into their bed, a pillow on either side of him to stop him falling out. The second time, Eric had found her there, sitting quiet in her vigil, and whispered to her harshly to come back downstairs. She'd been gone too long; his brother-in-law had marked it. Ungrateful, to hide away like that.

The words came out with an abruptness that made Heike stiffen: the real problem was that her absence had forced Eric to host his relatives alone. He dropped to a crouch beside the rocking chair. After all Arden had done, he said. Imagine how it looked to others. Disappearing like a witch at midnight.

Heike said she thought it was witches who came out at midnight, and Cinderella who disappeared?

She could see by the taut corner of the bedsheet that he'd slept the night in his office. A lazy pang of regret ran through her: she could have apologized, hurried back downstairs, and saved herself what might now be a tiresome start to the day.

To the other side, Daniel curled against her, bum wriggling. Heike peeled out of bed and began to raise the blinds, one by one, crossing the long wall of the room. The front garden was in full light, English roses glowing coral-coloured where they wound high around their arbour, then the chamomile and low-lying thyme pale against the fringe of rock roses with their wilder look, a deep red. Heike paused a moment, surveying the landscape. She could see now that she'd overslept, the sun casting only the slimmest of shadows. It was not, in fact, early morning at all. To the west side of the lawn there was a bank of raspberry canes, and part of her songbird project taking shape— Eric's idea, a few colourful houses on stilts. Berries being, he said, a lure for birds and children. Around the back, out of view, was the kitchen garden. Then only the shade trees, and beyond that the grass ran down to the stream's edge, too shallow in this place to swim or set a boat down, the one failing of the house.

She spun and pulled the covers up high over Daniel's head, covering him completely.

— Hey, wake up in there!

He shrieked and curled lower in the bed, his knees tucked underneath him.

— Who's inside? Heike gave the little mound a preliminary

tickle, the lilt of her voice leaning more German now, as it always did when they were alone: Is it Mr. Snail or Mr. Turtle? Who lives always in his bed?

There was a creak, and she looked up to where the door was suddenly standing open, Eric half inside the room with them. Heike straightened and moved toward him.

— Oh, Eric, I'm sorry we fought. Don't be angry. Let's not fight this morning.

He had a glass with him, balanced on a tray, and he stepped farther into the room and set the whole thing down on the dressing table.

— I'd hardly call it morning. He held his arms out to her, but she'd stopped a few feet shy of him, and after a moment he let them drop to his sides. I don't know what you're talking about, he said. There's no reason to fight. Is there? Have you been up to something?

He was almost smiling.

Heike pulled her dressing gown off the chair and wrapped it around herself.

— No, of course not. Not if you don't think so. She fussed a moment with the tie on the gown. I just want to have a happy day, she said. With no problems. I'm sorry I slept so late, I don't know what's wrong with me. The light is beautiful.

She pulled the tie into a bow and let it drape off her hip.

— I brought you a tonic, he said. Something for your head.

She looked back to where Daniel lay, bunched up under the covers, still again, as though he'd fallen back asleep now that the game was done. She turned to Eric:

— My head. How did you guess?

— You complained of a headache last night. Eric nudged the

tray with the back of his hand to settle it more securely on the vanity. It sat centred now, in front of the mirror. He adjusted a perfume bottle, and then the tray again. Symmetry was satisfying to him.

— Did I? Heike said. I have a headache now. Or maybe not quite. She pressed her hands to her temples and closed and then opened her eyes again. I can feel it there, underneath. She let her hands drop. Like it's waiting, she said.

— You were sitting up here in the rocker, Eric said, and I came to find where you'd gone. I thought maybe Daniel had had a nightmare, or you'd heard him call out, but you said you had a headache. Remember? He reached out, not for her hand but for her wrist, and used it to pull her closer. You remember now, don't you? A terrible headache, you said. He drew a line with his thumb across her brow, temple to temple.

Heike worked to remember if that was the excuse she'd given. She'd been half-asleep in the chair when Eric came into the room, her eyes soft and only a bit of moonlight casting the room into grey shadows. It wasn't antisocial, not really: Dani looked so calm and lovely when he was sleeping, his breath rising and falling like a quiet tide.

— I didn't mean to disappear, she said. I was so tired.

He let his hand drift from her temple down along her jawline and cupped her chin a moment.

— Perhaps you should stay inside today.

— Oh, no. Eric, it's a waste to keep indoors. Look at the sky! And the garden is so charming. Really. I slept very well last night.

He leaned in as if to kiss her, then spoke low into her ear instead:

— I wouldn't want you to tax yourself.

He bit her cheek, gently, teeth pulling at her skin.

Heike touched the place where his mouth had been. The cheek was warm. She left her palm there, covering it. Eric stepped back and held the glass out to her.

— Come now. Drink up your tonic like a good girl. Did you see I've added to your bird village? There's a new house, a blue one.

Under the blankets, Daniel gave a squawky yawn. Heike swivelled to watch the rumple of bedding rise up and flop down again. It grew limbs, stretched like a starfish under the white sheets, and then lost them, returning to its former hunched shape, and bounced there to some rhythm of its own device.

She looked to Eric, her eyes a mix of amusement and quiet pride, and then back to Daniel. Eric leaned to one side so as to follow her gaze.

— Will you trust the good doctor, or won't you? I'm sure Daniel wants his breakfast. He called over her shoulder, toward the bed: Don't you, Dani?

Heike watched the bedding perform its dance, her head to one side. Eric laid a hand on her shoulder to try to draw her attention, then slid the hand along her back, his fingers playing at the knob at the top of her spine, a tiny massage.

— You've got fresh eggs in the icebox. The neighbour's girl brought them over this morning.

Dani sat upright, the sheets falling away.

— Eggs and soldiers?

Heike turned back to face Eric, mimicking Daniel's wide eyes:

— Eggs and soldiers? She had an easy smile now.

Eric held the glass.

— You know I'll always take care of you. You do know that, don't you, Heike?

— I know. Heike slipped the tonic out of his hand, repeating the phrase: I know you'll always take care of me. She swallowed the liquid down, making an exaggerated face. Ugh. It tastes like baking soda.

Eric picked up the tray and took the empty glass back again.

— I think the fresh air does you good, he said. Perhaps it's not such a bad idea to go for a little walk today. You'll be alright all by yourself?

Heike gave the back of her head a scratch. Then, sitting down at the vanity mirror, she wrinkled up her nose and began to fix her hair, moving it this way and that. Her eyes flicked to Eric's reflection, pausing there for a moment to read his expression. A softness in his eyes.

— We'll just play in the garden this morning, she said. And maybe later on, a little hike in the woods.

THEY SET OUT IN the afternoon heat, on foot, Heike carrying a pack across her shoulders. For this and that, she said. The pack clanked in a gentle way as she walked, the sound of glass jars knocking against each other in the cradle of the fabric. Maybe a few peaches are in there, she told Daniel. Maybe something else, too.

Daniel had strapped on a lifejacket and rain boots, although she'd explained to him that they couldn't take the canoe the whole way. First they had to walk in the shade awhile.

— You'd get a sunburn at this time of day. Besides, don't you want to see some rabbits?

The launch was farther downstream. She pried the rubber boots, heat-damp, off his bare feet and made him wear sandals.

Daniel played with the straps of the lifejacket, pulling them tighter over his T-shirt. His swim trunks had blue stripes.

The earth at the edge of the woods had begun to look sandy again, granular. A whole day without rain. Heike picked up her own trail through the trees, boot prints still marking out a path where the ground was shaded from sun, but she wore sandals now, too, and short sleeves, the halter of her own swimsuit teasing at the back of her neck, and they stopped to peer down holes cut into the ground, tunnels hidden under brambles or tree roots. Daniel right down on his hands and knees, Heike behind, holding him by the shoulders.

—What do you call rabbit babies?

—Kits, I think, Heike said. No. Kittens?

—What about bunnies?

—*Bunnies* is maybe a cute word.

—But not real?

—Not scientific.

— It's kits, Daniel said, nodding. Then, wiggling out of her grasp and lurching forward: Maybe we could catch one!

— It might not be bunnies in that hole.

— Kits!

—Kits, okay, she repeated. But maybe it's not. Rabbits or mice. It could be badgers. Or a rat! Heike gave his shoulders a squeeze, and Daniel jumped. So we don't try to catch things, she said.

Daniel considered this. From above them came the solitary, persistent knock of a woodpecker. He looked up, suddenly distracted from what he might find under the path.

— I'm hungry a little bit.

— Wait till we get to the raft. Then you can have a peach and put your feet in the water, yeah?

— Okay. How about in the canoe?

— To eat in the canoe, or put your feet in the water?

— To eat.

— Okay.

— Okay, Daniel said.

At the launch, Heike threw her pack into the boat, then hauled him up into her arms and swung him over the side.

— Now let's see if I can make this thing go, she said. She tapped at the gunwale with her paddle.

Daniel unzipped the pack and pulled out two peaches. He weighed them back and forth in his hands.

— That one is for you because it's a Mommy peach, he said, letting her peach roll back into the open pack. This one is mine because it's a Superman peach.

Heike didn't question this. She paddled out of the shallows and down to where the stream met the lake, and then followed the shoreline, stroking smoothly but switching sides a little more often, she thought, than you should really need to. The canoe waggled its way along like a duck on land. It was a longer trip than she remembered, the shore maybe thirty feet to the east of them and a little island clouding the view to the west.

Daniel pointed.

— Who lives here?

— No one does, Heike said. The water is for everyone. Anyone can come.

It was hot, and she searched ahead for a break in the tall grass at the shore. Could they have passed the entrance to the pond without noticing?

— But someone used to live here, Daniel said.

— How do you know that?

— Because you said there's a house. And the raft. Someone built the raft for kids to jump off. So there was kids, Daniel said. This satisfied him, and he took a bite of peach.

A new stream opened out into the lake, and Heike manoeuvred the canoe around the bend and dipped the paddle deeper to propel it up against the current. Surely this had to be right. A little way upstream, the channel widened out into a pool, lax and clogged with river plants, and the current stilled. Daniel leaned against the edge of the canoe, trailing one hand in the water. It was a brief moment of shade, and she let them drift, pulling the paddle up and resting it across the boat and closing her eyes.

— I have a friend, Daniel said. He's a tadpole. I have a tadpole friend. He's on me, Mami. See? He's just little and nice.

Heike peered at him with one eye to make sure he wasn't leaning too far over the water. From behind her came the quick, repeating *splish* of the swallows, beaks and wingtips nicking the water's plain surface again and again. Daniel thumbed at something on the back of his hand.

— Mami?

She shut her eyes again. His voice rose higher:

— It won't get off! Mami! My tadpole won't get off!

Heike jumped forward, upsetting the paddle and grabbing it just before it slipped into the water.

— Here, give me your hand. Give, now, she said. Daniel.

She pinched the leech with her thumb and forefinger, tugging it sharply up, then flicked it back into the stream. A little droplet of blood sprang up on Daniel's hand.

— Put your hand in the water, she said.

— No! What if it gets on me again?

— You have to wash your hand. Heike grabbed his wrist

and crawled forward, careful to keep hold of her paddle, then swished his hand in the wet two or three times before letting go.

— Now, she said. You see? All done.

Daniel took his hand back and glowered at her.

— Oh, you don't have to be so sulky, Heike said. You put your hand in his home! Maybe he was trying to be friends.

Daniel touched the sore place on his hand, and the little dot of blood thinned and widened.

— He wasn't a tadpole friend, he said. Then, putting the trauma behind him: Will we go in the house?

— No, Liebchen. It's not our house. No one lives there anymore.

She took the paddle in both hands and steered out to where she could see that the stream opened up wide again. The sun felt all new. Heike squinted into it. There was a younger bank of reeds ahead, the green tips barely breaking the water's surface, and hidden just beyond that, she saw the raft.

— I found it, Daniel said.

2.

Heike pulled the canoe up against the side of the raft and held it steady, hooking the tip of the paddle into the notch between two slats of wood.

— Go on, now. She nodded to Daniel and then gave a flick of the chin, gesturing for him to climb out. Give me the peach. She took a hand off the paddle and held it out, the boat wavering slightly.

Daniel took three bites in succession, then tossed the pit overboard.

— It's gone, he said. Heike brought the canoe tight against the side again, both hands back on the grip, and Daniel clambered up onto the raft, his fingers digging into the boards. There was a mooring line attached to the stern deck behind her and Heike laced the yellow rope through a metal ring on the raft, cinched it, and tied it off before getting out herself.

— Alright, now look what's in the bag for you.

Daniel drew the zipper down and brought out three more peaches, lining them up in a row; then a knit blanket, two towels in tight rolls, and two canning jars, one full of lemonade and the other stacked with almond cookies, thin and uniform and lacy-edged. He'd managed to wiggle out of the life jacket without unclipping any of the buckles, and it sat upright on the raft, boy-shaped.

Heike shook the blanket out into a loose square.

— The corner is wet. Did the jar leak?

Daniel rolled the jar of lemonade between his hands.

— It's still full, he said. *Swish-wish-wish*.

— Give it here and I give you a drink.

— How about a cookie?

— Okay, then give me that one.

Heike popped the lid and passed a cookie to Daniel, and then, after a moment's pause, a second one. One for each hand. A little wave of pleasure rolling through her as she offered the treats: Eric often so strict about sugar, what they should or shouldn't eat. The almond cookies almost but not quite the same as the ones her grandmother used to make at home, when Heike herself was small.

She twisted off the top of the second jar and took a long drink, then leaned forward to ruffle Dani's hair.

— Where's your hat?

Daniel held a cookie up and peered at her through the filigree.

— It blowed off.

— When? Heike looked around.

— A while ago. It went in the lake. He took a bite of cookie, then examined it to see the shape his mouth had made. You were paddling, he said. It was before my peach.

Heike drew the blanket up close to the edge of the raft, and they dangled their feet in the water.

— I can't reach! Daniel straining to get more than his toes wet.

— Here, come here. Heike hauled him up onto her lap, then between her knees, dipping him into the water, on and off the raft again: Hoppa! Hoppa! Ploomps!

Daniel kicked his feet in the water.

Heike sang:

> *Hoppe, hoppe Reiter*
> *Wenn er fällt, dann schreit er*
> *Fällt er in den Graben*
> *Fressen ihn die Raben*
> *Fällt er in den Sumpf*
> *Dann macht der Reiter plumps!*

She dipped Daniel low, leaning so that he was wet to the belly. He shrieked and wriggled in the cold water and Heike grabbed at him, her nails digging in a little.

— Hey! Stay still, I'm going to drop you! She squeezed him in tight against her lap again, nuzzling his neck. I don't want to lose you! Here. Let's swim.

Heike sat him down next to her on the raft and stripped off her shirt and shorts.

— Do you want your shirt off?

Daniel nodded.

— Okay, here, I help you. She pulled the T-shirt up over his head and folded it next to her own clothes on the blanket, then lowered herself off the edge of the raft. The water deep enough that her feet didn't touch.

— Come. Now you can jump. She held her arms out, treading water with her legs only.

Daniel danced on the raft, one foot to the other.

— What if there's a turtle?

— There's no turtle. I promise. You can come.

The splash and force of his jump caught her off guard, though, both their heads ducking under the water before they came up, Daniel sputtering.

— It's okay, it's okay. You're bigger every day, makes it harder for Mami to catch you! She bobbed him in the water a little before easing him out of her arms. Hold my hands. So, like this: you make your legs like an egg beater, like we are making a cake in the water. Daniel's face turned up to the sun, chin and ears barely breaking the surface, legs pumping. His fast breath. That's it! Heike beamed. Kick your feet! Kick your feet! She caught him up again just as he started to tire, his mouth and nose slipping under. The two of them treaded together for a moment and then Daniel wrapped his legs tight around her waist. The little wet lick of blond hair behind his ears.

— You're holding me like a monkey! Are you a baby monkey? Heike pinched gently at his toes: Look out, it's a turtle! What's under the water? Look out, a turtle gets your toes!

When her legs began to tire, she helped him pull back up onto the raft, guiding his hands and heaving from behind, then pulled her own body up and collapsed in the sun. She closed her eyes. It seemed impossible that she should feel so sleepy after rising so late in the morning. Daniel sat upright and pinched at her toes:

— Who got your toes, Mami? Something got your toes!

Heike threw her arm up over her eyes and listened past Daniel's chatter. They were just far enough from shore that the general noise of the woods was muted, only a few clear notes reaching them. The high, true song of a warbler, and then the mockingbird's poor counterfeit, a slim set of repeated tones. Ducks setting up shop back in the reeds. From somewhere far off, a solitary loon called and answered to its own echo. Out on the lake, Heike thought. Or around the other side of the bay.

She crooked her elbow up and peered at Daniel. He was on his belly, a cookie in one hand. With the other, he traced a path between knots in the wood with a solemn finger: a car on its way to the city, or a school bus heading out into a field. A garbage truck. He made a low humming sound that increased in fervour with the speed of his travelling finger. She closed her eyes again. There was so much freedom in a day like this. Just her and Daniel, no one else. No Eric.

Heike let the guilt and pleasure of this thought wash over her. Then, for a moment, allowed the imagined possibility of a life without him to drift into her mind. As though she were telling herself a little story: What if there had been a car accident on the road to Ithaca, a morning drunk crossing the line, Eric too distracted by his own thoughts to notice until it was too late? She called up one version after another, in a daydream way. He'd taken an unexpected detour and hit a place where the road was washed out, the car rolling and tumbling down a steep ditch; out running at noon hour in the July heat, he'd suffered a freak young man's heart attack.

These things happen. Heike had read something like it in *The New York Times*, a thirty-year-old marathon runner who fell down dead.

The truth was that being with Eric often felt like work. Was this a private honesty, or was she simply disloyal, too demanding?

He just required so much of her energy. Was he bored, or

tired? Had he eaten recently, had Heike packed enough food, and the right kind? Had she brought a radio. Was it too hot, too cold, too buggy, too wet. Was Daniel too chatty, too quiet, too nervous in the water, had Heike taught him to be nervous. Did Heike not look happy enough. Had something unnerved him, or, better, could she catch that thing before it happened? Prevent him from going sour, or sulky, make everything just right, perfect. Above all, keep the day from seething within him, ward off an evening argument early. Block the blow-up.

Of course, there were rules to this kind of game. Ways that Eric couldn't disappear: No abandonment. No gory accident, or at least, not an accident Daniel might see. No suicide, obviously, although she didn't think Eric the type. Nothing that might follow Dani into his own life.

Heike sat up suddenly, shocked at herself for letting it go this far. The sun blinded her, and she held up a hand to shade her eyes and scan her surroundings, as though making sure this musing of hers was only that, a moment of intimacy, that it hadn't somehow careened into the real world. Daniel needed a father.

And Eric loved her. He took care of them, Heike and Daniel both.

Daniel with his cookie, with the sun in his hair, continued driving his truck along the boards, unaffected by this conflict. Heike lay back again, her hands against her belly so she could pay attention to the rise and fall of her breath.

Eric had simmered three eggs in their shells for their breakfast, stood close behind her as she buttered and cut the toast into little strips, one hand rhythmically stroking her arm. He had a new idea, something glorious and untested that he began to explain before waving off her questions. He was looking for

a nomination, a prize: that part she understood, and in a way
it was the best part of him, boyish, half-bouncing on the balls
of his feet over a moment of greatness that was sure to come.
Heike listened, heating the milk for his coffee before he got into
his car and left for the day. The summer house far enough from
the hospital to make commuting a chore. This house she had
wanted, Heike, and the few times she'd come along for the ride,
Eric hadn't even dragged her into his office to make polite small
talk with the nurses but let her sit outdoors in the sunshine
or sipping a coffee in the diner down the road. She reminded
herself of these kindnesses; they counted for something. She
counted them out.

This calmed her, and she forgave herself again and shook off
the last traces of anxiety.

She dozed a little. Stretching out one leg so that her foot
rested on the back of Daniel's thigh, keeping track of him that
way. The loon calling again, a little closer, the tune broken and
lonely but far enough away that the ducks weren't bothered. Not
close enough to be a threat.

DANIEL WAS TALKING to her now, and Heike realized that his little
leg was gone from under hers, the wood plank hard against
her heel. She sat up and opened her eyes. The sun was strong
enough to make her vision spotty. The light washed everything
out. She squinted and Daniel came into focus. He was on hands
and knees, at the raft's edge, talking away. Not to Heike. She sat
up taller, drew a leg in, one arm supporting her from behind.

There was a little girl with him, down in the water, one hand
gripping the side. As though she'd swum up to the raft. She held

something in her other hand, a paper. A drawing, the bright crayon catching the sun.

Heike looked around. There was no other boat; no one, that Heike could see, standing on shore. She brought a hand up to shade her eyes, looking off toward the cottage roof in the distance, looking for a car, any sign of people. Was it possible that she was wrong about the place being abandoned? She thought back to the click of the doorknob lock opening against the force of her hip, the dust on the windowsills, the absence of any track, tires or shoes, in the warm, wet ground. After all that rain.

The little girl pulled up onto the raft with both hands now, Daniel crawling back to give her room. She'd abandoned her drawing. It wavered, white against the surface of the pond. Heike thought how quickly it would take on water and be lost to the bottom; a gift, perhaps, that the little girl's mother—wherever she was—would fail to receive.

— Come, let me help you.

Heike reached out her arm, but the girl was up on the raft on her own by now, sitting high on her knees. She was a sweet thing, about the same size as Daniel but perhaps a touch older. She'd already lost her babyness. Heike saw that her face was slim and almost sculpted, where Daniel's cheeks still puffed out round. She had the same blond hair, the wisps near her face shining almost silver in the sunlight, pulled back neatly in a ponytail, and wore a blue-patterned one-piece bathing suit with a ruched top and little gathered bloomers. So there was a mother, somewhere. Someone to brush and comb her hair, look after her, send her out into the world well cared for. Her skin, too, had nice colour, although she was certainly fair. A rosiness to her cheeks. Heike thought she looked a bit thin compared to Daniel. She guessed she might be as old as seven.

— I am Mrs. Lerner, Heike said. She held out a hand still, but the little girl didn't move toward it, looking instead at Daniel.

— This is Tessa, Daniel said.

— Tessa, where are your parents?

The girl gestured vaguely behind her, and Heike glanced up and scanned the lake again. How long had she been dozing? At some point she must have drifted deeper asleep, had heard nothing of the girl's approach. Not a splash. Where had she come from?

She looked for movement in the reeds, the nudge of a row-boat. Maybe the parents were hidden, fishing quietly, unaware of how far their daughter had gotten in a short time. When they lived in New York, Daniel had often hidden inside the big round racks of dresses at Bloomingdale's. Or Heike would find him standing, stone-like, in a boutique picture window with the mannequins. She'd lost him more than once.

— I'm thinking your mother is going to be very worried.

— I always swim here, the girl said, but she was talking to Daniel, not Heike. The water isn't so deep on that side of the raft.

Heike watched her in profile, the sharp lines of her cheek and chin. She tried again:

— Do you live here?

The two children had gone back to chattering quietly together; he was showing her something wedged deep in a knot in the wood. Heike looked up toward the cottage a second time, then searched the shoreline with her eyes. Surely someone had to be missing this little girl. Soon they would hear a woman's voice, her mother or grandmother, calling out and rising in panic: *Tessa! Tessa!*

But the call didn't come. Tessa's hair was already dry in the sun. Had it ever really been wet? It was so light that Heike couldn't see a difference. But now not even the tip of her pony-tail hung damp. The children had risen to their feet, and she was teaching Daniel some kind of clapping game, their fingertips moving together and apart, together and apart.

Perhaps the parents were hiking in the woods and Tessa had run ahead for a swim without telling them. By now they would be frantic. Heike pictured Eric, thrashing in the brush, furious, and her chest tightened up so that she had to take a breath and expel it.

Out on the water, the girl's drawing was floating away. She could see the colours in it, the childish wings of birds, an indiscernible scatter of letter *m*'s littering a cloudless sky. It had somehow failed to become waterlogged and sat, pristine, on the surface. An unseen current pulling it slowly to shore.

— Oh! Your picture is there!

The words slipped out as fast as Heike thought them. Tessa looked up from their game. There was something there, on one side of her face, something Heike hadn't noticed before. She peered at her. If she hadn't just been in the water, Heike might think she had a bit of her breakfast there, stuck on her cheek. A little errant porridge. As she looked closer now, she wondered if it could be mud.

— Come here a moment. Reaching out to her. Tessa turned her head, looking for the paper she'd left floating away. The smudge on her cheek now looked not so much like mud as like vomit. Heike recoiled.

— My birds! The girl stepped lightly off the raft and seemed to skip, weightless, across the water, her feet barely skimming the surface of the lake.

Heike lurched forward and grabbed onto Daniel, pulling him

against her. He tried to squirm free, and she locked her arms around him.

— Something is wrong.

How could it be so shallow? Were the reeds so matted there, just below the surface? The girl was a tiny thing; the reeds might hold her up. The water looked clear and clean. Heike thrust a hand into the water off the side of the raft. There were no mud flats that she could see.

The disturbance had created a band of choppy waves across the veneer of the lake, and now one corner of the picture tipped, as though a drain pulled at it, the whole sheet suddenly sinking fast. Heike watched as the girl dove down after it, her feet and ankles disappearing under the water. Then nothing. The pond flattened, instantly calm.

At some point, the woods had gone still. Heike loosened her grip around Daniel's middle and then let go altogether. Not even the loon was crying.

She counted to five in her head. Neither the girl nor the drawing resurfaced.

Heike turned and grabbed Daniel by the shoulders, shaking him.

— Stay here! You don't move, you understand? Stay right here! She dove off the raft, long and shallow, making the distance to where Tessa had gone after her picture, then duck-diving down, her eyes open and searching. The pond had little depth on that side of the raft. Eight feet at most to the bottom, the water clean and clear. She dove again and again. No sign the silt had been disturbed, and only a few fronds waved gently from the sandy floor and caught in Heike's fingers. The bed was still.

Heike came up for air, her heart moving fast and heavy. There was no little girl, no Tessa. She inhaled and oriented herself, turning her back to the shore, looking for Daniel. Her head was spinning. She could see him, now, crouched on the edge of the raft, toes curled over the side, looking down into the water. He reached out with one arm, the tips of his fingers. Heike called out to him, but he didn't turn his head, instead leaning farther forward until suddenly his body tipped off the raft. He disappeared with a splash.

— Daniel! Heike charged forward, stroking with her head above water, and then dove again, arms out in front of her, the pond suddenly deeper and silt stinging her eyes. She could see him there, already ten or twelve feet down, a little compact ball, his knees in tight to his chest, pink and yellow against the green-grey of the water. She grabbed him by the arm and tugged, hauling him up and kicking hard to get back to the surface. They broke the water line, Heike's head spinning again as she struggled to take in air herself and push Daniel's head above water.

She propelled them forward until her feet found bottom, only then realizing how far they'd travelled from the raft: in her panic, she'd made more distance than she would have imagined. Daniel's eyes wide with fear and the long moment of silence before he finally gasped and let out a long, choking wail. His body registering shock.

She waded out onto the beach, holding his body against her and calling out.

— Hallo? Hallo? Is anyone here? Please! Hallo?

There was no movement from the house or the woods around it. Daniel thrashed against her and pummelled her chest with his little fists, a panicked temper tantrum, still not fully able to take in air, his wet trunks plastered against her stomach. Heike dropped to the ground, rolling him onto his side and rubbing his back. He was crying, and the sound came out broken, stilted, between bouts of coughing.

— It's okay, Mami's here, Mami's here. Cough out the water. Just cough out the water. You're alright. I am here, I am here.

She stroked his cheek, his hair, his brow. Daniel coughed a little more, his breath coming quick and shallow, then deeper. Heike leaned over him.

— Just stay lying down nicely. Mami's here, just lie down a moment longer. Catch your breath.

She left a hand on his back for comfort and sat up slightly, looking out over the water to the raft and then beyond it, to where she'd last seen the little girl, Tessa, before she disappeared below the surface. There was no change in the weather, the sun as high and hot as it had been when they first tied up the canoe. No breeze, a wetness to the air, the woods still and humid. The birds were as quiet now as they'd been the moment the little girl went under. Somewhere back in the trees Heike heard a cicada start up. Its weird song rising, louder and louder against the silence.

3.

Daniel stopped coughing and pushed himself up, hugging Heike's legs a little. She pulled him close, leaning back on a log with their feet in the damp sand, and ran a hand through his hair, her other arm wrapped tight around his chest. By now, it was clear that no one was looking for the girl: no voices shouting her name from the woods, no magical appearance of a rowboat from the reeds. Heike twisted around to look behind her. The little house sat dark and indifferent, the windows shut tight. Her breathing was shallow, and the action of stroking Dani's head calmed her a little. She did not want him to be afraid. They needed to get home.

The canoe was still tied up out at the raft. She could see her pack, the jars of lemonade and cookies, their clothes all heaped together where they'd been sitting, before the girl appeared. The towel she'd been lying on when she fell asleep stretched flat in the sun. The pond was not quite still. The canoe lifted and fell with the swell of the water.

Daniel turned and clambered onto her, his arms tight around

her neck, and Heike struggled to see over his shoulder, scanning the far shoreline for any sign of movement, the splash of a child's kicking feet, or her fingers at the edge of the raft. He pressed his face into hers, demanding her attention, and finally she pulled back and squeezed his two hands and swung them, rubbed her nose against his, trying to soothe him with playfulness. Pretending nothing was wrong. She turned to look at the cottage again, sure now that she'd made a mistake. She must have missed something, the girl surfacing at the beach and running inside while Heike was underwater.

Daniel tried to climb up against her again and she stood up, setting him firmly on his feet and taking his hand.

— Come, let's see if someone is home. Come on.

They picked their way up to the clearing, on tiptoes where the sand mixed with sharper shingle and driftwood, then old roots and weeds nearer to the cottage. At the side of the house, Heike put a hand up against the windowpane and peered in. Everything looked as it had the day before, undisturbed. No dishes on the table or kitchen counter, no shoes kicked off by the door. The house was orderly and unchanged. She tried the door and it gave easily, the latch still sprung from where she'd given it her hip. It swung wide but they didn't go in.

— Hallo? Hallo, is someone at home? Her voice broke off. The sound of her own calling made the space lonelier, empty. She had the urge to check over her shoulder, the woods behind them, to slam the door. Her head hurt.

She led Daniel up and around the other side, and then beyond the house in the other direction, through taller grass and some low brush, until he whined about his feet.

— The ground is all spiky here!

Heike stood still for a moment, tightening her fingers around his hand. Her heart felt high in her chest, jerky, uneven. There was no car; not even a place where the plants were pushed down, no kind of driveway at all. Daniel pulled at her. She squatted low to pick him up, held him against her hip.

They came back around the other side of the house like that and down to the beach again. The trail she'd cut through the trees two days before was just to their left, and Heike heard a chattering off in the woods, chipmunks, and then the bleating call of a nuthatch. The warmth of Daniel's body against her and the noise, a break in the silence, gave her some comfort. The pond lay flat and wide as an open mouth.

— We're going to walk back through the woods, she said.

— What about the canoe? Daniel said. And my cookies?

For a moment she didn't answer. Her arm ached from holding him.

— Mami comes back for them tomorrow.

His body slipped down against her thigh, and he kicked his legs:

— Don't put me down! Don't put me down!

Heike, suddenly frustrated, twisted and dropped him to the ground. She crouched to his level, his hands tight in her hands.

— When Tessa came to the raft, and Mami was sleeping, where did she come from? Did you see her parents, or a boat?

— She swimmed.

— And then what happened?

— We played a game. Then she swimmed away.

— Did you see her swim away? When Mami was under the water?

Daniel hopped on one foot.

— It's hot here. I'm too hot. I want to go home.

— Did she tell you anything, when you were talking? When she told you her name, did she say where she lives?

— She didn't tell me her name.

— Yes, she did. She said her name is Tessa.

— She didn't tell me her name. I just knowed it.

Heike let go of his hands and turned to look out at the lake. Then:

— Hold onto my shoulders. Come on, we do a piggyback.

When Daniel was holding tight, she started to run.

THEY WERE IN THE LONG WHITE ROOM at the back of the house, curled up together on the daybed, when she heard Eric come home. Not alone: Heike heard the car door slam, then laughter—Eric, that much for sure, but she couldn't have said how many others—the key turning in the front door lock, chairs scraping the kitchen floor. She left Daniel sleeping and walked to the front of the house in her bare feet. She hadn't bathed, and her calves and ankles were still spattered with dry mud from the walk home through the forest.

Arden and John were there, the chairs pushed aside to make room for a bushel basket of groceries Eric had brought in with them: apples and two bottles of milk and a green frill of lettuce, wilting in the heat. There was a wildflower bouquet on the counter that looked like the kind of thing you'd buy from a child at a roadside stand. He seemed in a golden mood. Heike hung in the doorway, watching.

The maid, Rita, had arrived at the same time, a signal that Eric meant for them to go out somewhere and leave Daniel behind.

Heike's fingernails dug into her palms. She'd wanted a quiet evening in, an early bedtime for Dani, some way to counteract what had happened at the pond. When Rita stayed with him something always went wrong: she forgot to bathe him, or left him without a warm blanket at bedtime. Eric had a soft spot for waifs. Rita was a kind of charity case, a patient sent to him by the local doctor. She had some little family in town—her uncle caught and sold fish house to house—and Eric had offered to keep an eye on her outside the hospital. This little job the perfect amount of occupation for her, he said, brushing off Heike's complaints: the girl was certainly in fine enough form to put a child to bed and do a few dishes. Heike could see now where she had one of the flowers from the bouquet tucked into her cuff like a corsage.

The flower stem bent but did not break as Rita dragged the basket back toward the pantry. She was a short girl with thick wrists, and knees and shins that almost surely betrayed an absence of good food in her childhood: they bowed out heart-shaped. She was usually silent in Heike's presence, avoiding her eyes and often looking to Eric for instruction instead. Heike suspected that he'd designed it this way, offering Rita an easy excuse to avoid her. *Madame is prone to nerves and tires easily*, or something else of the kind. She'd heard him say such things before. Try as she might, Heike had not managed to make of her anything like a friend and often found her staring, reproachfully, when she looked up from buttoning Daniel's jacket or shoes. She did not always answer when Heike called. Eric said the last thing they wanted was a talky Tina, anyhow.

He had his back to her now, at the counter with a brown bottle in his hand, riffling through the drawer for a church key.

— Eric.

Heike crossed the linoleum and pulled the opener from the draining rack.

— Oh, you're here. Eric popped the cap off the beer. What did you have the door locked for?

Heike shook her head slightly.

— I don't know. I don't remember locking it. Then, reaching out a hand to touch his arm, fingers squeezing where the bicep curled into the elbow's crook: Eric. I need to talk to you for a moment. Please.

He glanced over her head, to where John was standing, then back down at Heike.

— Stop. What's eating you?

She pulled at him gently, hoping he would step out of the room with her, but he didn't move.

— Are you alright? Arden stepped forward to look at her. You don't look well.

— Too much sun, Eric said. I told you not to go out on the lake today. He flexed the arm to shake her off a little, then looked down at her legs and let his eyes stay there.

— We're going up to Skaneateles, Arden said. To Leo Dolan's house. You've met him before, haven't you? The playwright.

— I don't think so, Heike said. She could see now that Arden was dressed for a party, with her short string of wedding pearls and a light crinoline under the skirt of her dress. She turned to Eric again, tugging at his arm: Eric, listen to me. Something happened today. Out on the water. There was a little girl there, but no parents, I couldn't find her parents. And she went into the pond, and then—Heike stopped for a moment, as though she were unsure of her words. And then, she said. Then I couldn't find her, either.

Eric glanced over to John again.

— I'm sorry about this. Give us a minute. He pulled Heike back toward the doorway, irritated: What are you talking about?

— I'm saying we met a little girl, we saw her, Daniel and me. And she went into the water and she disappeared. I dove after her, but she was gone. Heike let her voice drop. Like she didn't exist, Eric. And then, when I came up, Daniel fell into the water. Only it wasn't quite a falling. It was like something was pulling him. She was almost whispering now, frantic: Eric. Something was pulling him under the water.

Eric shook his head.

— Sounds like a bad dream, he said. He looked over his shoulder at Arden: Your party may be too much for her, he said. We'll have to bring her around a bit. Then, to Heike: You're black under the eyes. He patted her cheek. Just look. The colour's draining out of you.

Arden swished in Heike's direction:

— Don't! Don't listen to him. Dolan's a whopping lot of fun, and the house is gorgeous. No idea what to do with money, so he just spends it however he pleases. Champagne all night! Go get dressed, would you?

— That seems terribly extravagant for just a writer of plays, Heike said. She still had her bathing suit on, under a red beach coat meant to look like a Chinese jacket.

John stood up and swiped at his lapel, brushing away some invisible crumb or remnant.

— I thought you Europeans loved artists, he said. Isn't that why they all moved over there, before the war? Of course, they soon scurried home, didn't they, when the clubs caught fire. He said this absent-mindedly, more concerned with the state of his jacket than with making conversation. To Eric: I'd take a whisky soda if you had one lying around.

Arden said Dolan was fun *and* an artist because now he wrote for television.

— Tele-plays. He used to do radio, but the whole future is in television.

Heike looked at Eric.

— But, Eric, she said. Eric, the girl.

Eric set his bottle down and watched her. She could see his mood slipping; her insistence was making him stiffen. She crossed her ankles, one foot tucked lightly behind the other. Her bare legs made her feel like a child.

She turned back to Arden.

— I don't know, Heike said. I don't think I should leave.

— For Christ's sake, Eric said. He turned briefly to Arden and John: This is about the kid. He leaned back against the counter and gestured at her with the bottle, forcing a more lighthearted tone: He's not an infant, you know. He'll be fine without you.

— I don't want to leave, Eric. I don't think it's a good idea. You said yourself, I look tired. She turned to where the maid was setting canned goods onto a pantry shelf: Rita, I'll put those away myself, later. You can go home, after all. I'll do it.

The girl paused, looking first at Eric, then to Heike and back to Eric again. Eric shook his head.

— Stay, Rita. I know you like to line up the jars for us. He leaned to Arden and John, some odd mix of paternalism and something else: You see how she does it? By colours and by size, both. So the tomatoes and then the peach preserves. Then the little arti-chokes beside the green peas. And now the beets. That's right, isn't it, Rita? Look, I've embarrassed her!

The girl hadn't blushed, exactly, but her fingers played at her apron in a nervous way.

— You go on and keep working, Eric said. Madame has had a tiring day, that's all. Then, to Heike, his tone less playful: Where were you just now?

— Sleeping.

Eric looked at her legs again.

— You're filthy.

— I had to come back through the forest. She dropped her voice and reached out to touch his shoulder but stopped short, her hand wavering just near it instead: Eric, I think it's better if I stay here.

He caught her fingers, mid-air, and squeezed them.

— You'll need a moment to clean yourself up. He drew the hand down and squeezed again before letting go, then turned to John and Arden: Come on, help yourself to a drink while she gets herself together.

He strode off toward the back of the house, carrying the beer with him.

IN THE WHITE ROOM, Daniel had already been up and locking wooden track together on the carpet for his trains, but now he was gone. Hiding on the stairs, Heike supposed, and she leaned to look back down the hall. Only his hands were visible, gripping the spindles of the rail about halfway up. She could see the little white fingernails.

Heike turned back to face the windows. She'd drawn the sheers when they first got home, and now Eric pulled them aside, sunlight streaming into the room and playing off the walls.

It was a large room with high ceilings, running the width of the house, the back wall entirely done in glass windows that gave onto the deck through a set of heavy French doors. Designed to catch the light, every piece of furniture was colourless: eggshell walls, sheepskin carpets. A pure white grand piano in the far corner, its black keys punching holes in the brightness. Even with the sheers drawn, the sun had reflected and refracted through the glass, beaming into the room with them, kindling Daniel's honey-coloured hair where he'd lain sleeping. Without them, it was bright enough to frost the pearly white daybed so that it shone almost silver. Outside, the lawn stretched back to a sudden drop where Heike knew the stream cut through, gleaming, a shining vein hidden by the tall summer grass.

Eric was over at the bar now, scooping ice into lowball glasses. Arden lowered herself onto the couch, her skirt forming a wide, navy blue poof from which her legs stuck out like two rolls of paper towelling. She crossed her ankles this way and that. Heike suspected she was worried they were too thick.

She tried to think of something nice to say and tugged at the clasps on the beach coat. She still had not gone upstairs to wash.

— Where's Daniel? Arden said.

— I think he's playing hide-and-seek with us, Heike said. On the stairs.

— Well, send him down while you're dressing. I never get to see him; we're always here too late. I can dandle him on my knee while you bathe.

Heike turned to Eric:

— Will you make me a gimlet? Not too strong. Or whatever you're giving Arden, I don't care.

Eric glanced up at her, his hand on the ice tongs.

53

— You don't need a drink. You need a bath. And get Daniel into bed while you're up there.

He came over with Arden's drink, and she took it from him and swished it around, her eyes moving only once in Heike's direction, then down again. Eric stood behind Heike, a hand on her shoulder, but it was Arden he spoke to:

— If you get the kiddo involved now, we'll never get out of here. Heike is incapable of leaving him as it is.

Heike half-turned to him, shifting her weight from foot to foot. His look had changed again, as though, now that he was used to the situation, her grubbiness filled him with new affection. He gave her shoulder a playful squeeze:

— And no gimlet.

— Oh, you're a menace, Arden said. Never mind then, Heike, I'll spoil him rotten the next time I'm over. Go on and get ready. Wear your boatneck, with the little bluebell pattern. You always look entirely charming in that dress. Like a little shepherdess, up in the mountains somewhere.

— Like a Dresden doll, Eric said, turning now to make a drink for John. He stood and looked at Heike: Get a move on, would you? I'll need to shave, myself.

HEIKE TOOK THE STEPS to the second floor lightly, trying not to grind her feet too hard into the pale carpeting. The dirt on her legs was almost flaky by now. Bits of dried mud caught in the carpet fibres anyway, sticking there like weird crumbs, and she perched on the landing and bent low to pick them out. A house designed for servants, with its long white room and creamy rugs. She crouched there a moment longer, listening for the murmur of conversation below, but she couldn't make out more than a word here or there.

She scrubbed off her arms and legs under the running tap of the bath but didn't fill it. The water hot enough to turn her skin raw, the bathroom door left wide open. She strapped her hair back and scrubbed her face the same way, over the sink, then pawed through the closet in her underwear and pulled out a wide-strapped silvery grey dress, with a tight waist and large white print. The back cut low. About the furthest thing from a shepherdess. She cast the dress out over the bed and then stopped and turned back to pull open the drawer where she'd hidden the little Dresden figurine from the cabin.

She wondered if Eric knew. A Dresden doll: the turn of his face when he'd said that downstairs—as if he'd somehow stumbled across it. But it was untouched, still wrapped in the newsprint from the cottage cupboard, the whole package tucked into a long sachet pouch. Heike unwrapped it, and bits of dried lavender spilled out into the drawer, slipping between the camisoles and panties. It was cool and smooth in her hands, her fingers playing over the face and resting for a second over the blue eyes. She wrapped it back up and buried it at the back of the drawer.

The dress was barely over her head when she heard Eric coming up the stairs, but it was Daniel who came into the room. The bathroom door shut, and then the sound of water running in the sink—Eric getting ready for a shave. Daniel clambered up on the bed behind Heike. She leaned into the mirror and pinched her own cheeks to give them some colour.

— There you are! She turned around. Well? Do I look pretty?

Daniel's mouth opened and then closed again.

— You look like a lady, he said.

—So, that's good?

—You don't look like you. I like you better when you look like you.

—Well, this is also me, Heike said. Here, let me put on some shoes. She went over to the bed and drew a shallow wooden rack out from underneath it. There were five pairs of high heels resting on it in a long row, and Heike hooked the slings of a pair of silver sandals with her index finger and drew them up around the backs of her ankles. She hitched her skirt above her knees and posed for the standing mirror. After a moment she realized she was holding her breath. It spilled out in a quick puff and she took in air, ribs expanding. The waistband of the dress a bit tight.

—Who will stay here and protect me? Daniel kicked his legs in a rhythm against the side of the bed. Just Rita?

—What? Heike shifted her focus and caught the movement, his dirty legs, in the mirror. Oh, Daniel! No. You're filthy!

Daniel hopped down, a spray of sand coming with him. Heike thwacked the coverlet to clean it off.

—Yes. Of course Rita will be here. *Thwack, thwack*. We won't leave until after you're in bed anyway. She drew in another breath.

—Promise?

—I always promise, Heike said. Don't I always promise you?

—And you tell me a story.

—Okay. A story.

—*Es war einmal ein Mädel.* That one.

—*Schau, so gut sprichst du.* Once upon a time there was a girl. Named Gretchen, yeah?

—What happens to Gretchen again?

—Don't you remember?

— I some of it do. I some of it remember. Gretchen has to live with the witch in the forest. And then the Golden Bird wants to save her, but his head gets chopped! And Gretchen's finger, too. But then she makes her old finger into a flute, and the bird can sing out of the flute. And that's how it still saves her.

— I thought you wanted me to tell you the story!

— That's not the story. That's only a *bit* the story.

Heike sat down at the vanity.

— I think Gretchen is saving herself, she said. She added a few pins to her hair, one by one. Because it's her own finger, after all.

Daniel thought about that.

— Okay. We can say she saves herself. And we can say she lives in our house with the witch!

— Here in our house?

— The little house we found today. That's the witch's house. The witch likes to go swimming, too.

Heike stopped for a second, looking at Daniel in the mirror. He was standing behind her, tracing a dusty pattern on the coverlet with his thumb.

The bathroom door opened again. Eric came out into the hall, a razor in one hand, half his face still covered in shaving cream.

— I want a bath now, Daniel said.

Heike stood up and swiped at the bedclothes a final time. Eric was saying something to her, but she found it hard to focus. Daniel pulled at her skirt, and she brushed his hand away, suddenly irritated by all the dirt. She gave the skirt a tug herself to straighten it.

— I'm sorry, what was that?

Eric paused and took a breath.

— I said, Do you want to put him in the bath while I shave? It's all poured in here.

Heike thumbed the hem of her dress, rubbing away any bit of leftover grit. She looked up before answering.

— I'd rather stay home with him, Eric.

— What's the matter with you? He lay a heavy hand on the door frame. You can't very well send me out to a party alone. People talk.

— Eric, you know what's the matter.

Daniel twisted around, grabbing Heike's hand and pulling her past Eric, into the bathroom. She crouched down and touched his chin.

— Okay, okay. So, you want a bath now? Let Mami help you. She began to tug at the little shirt buttons, working fast to keep her fingers from shaking. Eric stepped back into the room and stood over them, watching. Heike glanced over her shoulder to the door.

— Don't close it.

Daniel's clothes fell around him in a rumple. When she was done, he clambered over the edge of the tub, the water warm and frothy, bubbles to his chin. Just his face stuck out. He took an empty shampoo bottle from the ledge and sank it under the water, air bubbles blubbing up as the bottle filled.

Eric's hand on her elbow, spinning her gently toward him.

— I got you something, Sport.

He was talking to Daniel. He pulled a hand out from behind his back and held out a blue plastic boat. The boat had thin white racing stripes painted along its sides, and a wheel of some kind on its bottom.

— It really goes. See? Eric worked the grey rudder with a

thumb. He looked at Heike expectantly, then pressed the boat into her hand.

— It won't rust?

— Stop worrying! Go on and give it a whirl, he said.

Daniel was already standing up in the tub, hands outstretched. Heike wound the dial on the boat's underside and crouched low to watch the toy chug along the water's surface, cutting a path through the foam. Aware of Eric's presence behind her, almost gratifying despite the argument. Daniel moved to pick it up, the mechanism still whirring. Heike straightened and stepped back, the boat's rudder spraying in her direction.

Eric had turned back to the mirror, stroking cleanly at his jaw with the long edge of the razor. In her slingback heels, Heike was still five or six inches shorter. She reached out and touched his arm.

— Eric.

He jerked the razor away and pressed a facecloth to his cheek.

— Jesus Christ, Heike. He dabbed at the spot but there was no blood, and after examining himself in the mirror, he threw the cloth at the sink. She could see that it would have been more satisfying if she'd managed to cut him.

He lowered his head and closed and opened his eyes before taking up the razor again. Heike started over, keeping her hands well back from his body.

— Eric, listen to me. It wasn't a dream. I saw a girl, she disappeared under the water. I saw it, I know I did. And here we are going to a party.

Eric went back to scraping at his face.

— Are you still talking about this?

— Because you won't listen!

Eric wiped his face with the cloth.

— You didn't see it, Heike said. Dani. It was like something took hold of him.

— You go swimming today? Eric turned to face the bathtub, his back to Heike.

— Yep.

Daniel was pouring water from one empty bottle to another. Bubble bath foamed over the slim mouth of the receiving bottle. His eyebrows lifted in concentration. Heike put a hand out to touch Eric's shoulder and then withdrew it.

— Out at the raft. Eric, you're not listening.

— I made a friend, Daniel said. But then she goed home.

Eric turned back to Heike, lifting one hand in dismissal. A half shrug. She stepped in close, taking his facecloth and twisting it nervously in her fingers.

— It's more than that, Eric. She was whispering now, a kind of desperate hissing. Please. He was sinking in the water; I had to pull him out. He was like a half-drowned boy. I had to pull him to shore. And the girl. I can't explain it. I don't want to leave him tonight.

— Stop. Eric yanked the cloth back. You're scaring yourself. What are you doing? Just because you didn't see the parents doesn't mean they weren't there.

He raised his arm and threw the cloth down at her feet. Heike stepped back quickly, drawing her hands in against her body. She turned to look at Daniel. He had paused in his play and was gazing at them quietly over his bottles, each one a little more than half full of water.

— Go get some air, Eric said. Whatever you need to do to get yourself together. I'll bring you a pill.

He was standing over her, and she pulled back again to give herself some space, her elbow bumping the wall.

— Do you think? Maybe that's all I need.

— Of course that's all you need. Everything's fine. You've scared yourself, that's all. Too much sun.

— I just want to make sure he's safe. I'll tell Rita to sit with him.

— I'll get you something. And don't worry about Rita: I'll talk to her. Now go on.

Heike looked from Eric to Daniel and then back again.

— You have to watch him every moment, she said. Her voice plain and resigned.

He took her by the wrist, twisting it around to guide her out the door, and shutting it after her. Heike heard the latch bolt slip, miss its catch. She turned back and pushed it open a crack.

— Don't lock it. Please.

She shut the door again herself, turning the knob with a quiet hand.

JOHN WAS OUTSIDE ON THE VERANDA, the French doors standing wide behind him, his back to Heike as she came down the stairs. The cooler evening air flooded the room. Arden handed Heike a swizzle stick shaped like a lightning bolt.

— For the forthcoming cocktail, she said. I can tell when a girl needs a drink, no matter what my brother has to say about it. What can I make you?

— Just something cold.

When Arden handed her the glass, it chinked with ice.

— Drink up, kid. You say you were out on the water today? I'd never guess it. You haven't got a bit of colour.

Heike held the cold glass against her wrist.

— I don't know. Maybe it's sunstroke.

Arden glanced out at John and then stepped closer.

— Don't let Eric's moods get you down. I really think you'll be much happier out here in the end. Than you were in the city, I mean. She clinked her glass lightly against Heike's. Bottoms up, yes?

The New York apartment had been three rooms at the top of a tall walk-up on 86th Street. Hot in summer, thin-walled and permeated with the neighbours' cooking smells, but she could imagine a view of the park from her rocking chair, and it was only a walk to the German bakery. In fall she'd fed the sparrows with crusts.

— Every place has its charms, Heike said.

Arden looked down into her drink and stirred it lightly with a finger. When she spoke again, her voice was soft:

— He was terrible to me when I was a child, you know.

Heike said nothing for a moment. There was a drop of condensation on the outside of her glass, and it ran down and pooled against her skin.

— I thought he was so much older, she said.

— He was, Arden said. He was, but he'd come home from college on holidays. You have to understand, his picture was all over the house. I'd brag to my friends about this big brother I had. So I'd beg him to play hide-and-seek, and he'd just leave me hiding forever. One time he found me crammed into the bottom of a wardrobe and locked me in there. He teased me from the other side of the door while I cried for him to let me out. Keep in mind that he was nineteen years old and I was nine.

She paused, twisting her glass back and forth in her hand.

— That sounds petulant, she said. So many years later.

— You were a child. Heike let her eyes flick briefly to the stairs, and then back to Arden. Children remember such things.

It wasn't a conversation she particularly wanted to have.

Arden's brow furrowed slightly. She let her hand with the drink in it fall to her waist.

— And I had this doll, she said. Penelope. She shook her head. It's funny. I hadn't thought about her for years. I suppose I haven't seen Eric for so long, and being with him these last few days, suddenly she popped to mind. My father gave her to me, just before he died. A birthday present. Arden's forehead relaxed, cheeks lifting a little. She had the loveliest crinolines, she said. A white porcelain doll—you can imagine the kind. Anyhow, I'd been building a flotilla of sailboats out of newspaper for the Girl Scouts, you know, some sort of badge, and Eric bet me that they wouldn't float. I kept trying them out in the bathtub, one after another. He taunted me about it, kind of. One day he said a boat isn't seaworthy if it can't carry a passenger. So he wouldn't honour the bet, even though they floated just fine.

But she'd insisted. Indignant the way a young girl can be, she said. It was Eric who suggested they use Penelope.

— Off we went to Coney Island. With the Ferris wheel going and the noise of the barkers and every other child sticky-chinned and laughing, and me kneeling down on the board-walk, casting Penelope out to sea in a paper boat.

She pushed a hand out in front of her, fingers splayed, then, catching herself, stopped and fixed her hair instead.

Heike dropped her gaze, almost motherly.

— But a porcelain doll is so heavy, Arden.

— Oh, she floated for a while. Arden shrugged, her voice flatter now. The tide was going out. It's just as you say: a porcelain doll has that heavy head. I watched the boat curl up around her until she slipped into the ocean. Gone.

She downed the last of her drink.

— Anyway, she said. That wasn't the point. The point is, I see so little of that left in him when he's with you. You must be a good influence.

Heike frowned.

— I'm not sure I have any influence on Eric at all.

The image of the little doll, tipping into the ocean, had upset her. She could imagine the doll's hair, fine and soft, fanning out all around her in the water. She looked out at the veranda. John still stood with his back to them, his glass resting on the railing beside him.

— Do you remember yesterday when I asked you about that little cottage, up the way?

— The squatter's place?

— I think maybe someone is there.

Arden popped a heel out of her shoe and flexed her foot. They were high shoes, meant for sitting or dancing, but painful to stand around in.

— Eric doesn't seem to think so, she said.

Heike bit down on a piece of ice with her molars. The cold of it sent a jerking pain high into her cheekbone. A delicate nerve. She was imagining Daniel at the pond, as she had seen him when she first came up for air, his body folded tight on the edge of the raft, leaning in close, peering down at the water in the moment before he fell.

Daniel upstairs now, chin-deep in bath water while Eric dressed in the next room. Slipping beneath the surface of the bath, silent and sinking. Or Eric there with him, his back turned to the bath. Eric, his hand pushing down on Daniel's head, pushing him under.

Arden pressed the foot back into her shoe.

— But of course, you're the only one who's seen the place.

The ice cube cracked in Heike's teeth, and a shard slid to the back of her throat, edges smoothing in the new heat. She felt it there like a cherry stone, a moment's almost-choke before it melted clean.

— I have to go.

She turned and ran up the stairs, slipping and catching her own fall, fingertips brushing the carpet. Hand over hand on the knob, shoulder hard against the bathroom door.

She swung into the room. Eric stood at the counter, absently making a notation in one of the black books he kept stashed all over the house. The bath full and still: bubbles thin and used and floating there listlessly in cloud formations. No sound. Not a hair of him. Heike felt her stomach turn. Her breath locked in her throat, choking her.

The blue-striped boat rested on the edge of the tub. Eric tossed the notebook back into an open drawer and pushed the drawer shut.

Daniel, wrapped in his hooded towel, just behind the door, the thing Heike saw last. She almost cried out: air rushed into her lungs all at once, her body flooding with relief.

He lifted his face to her. The little fingers and toes bare and wrinkled with damp.

4·

The living room of Dolan's house already had the look of a midnight buffet the morning after a long party. A solid oak table ran down the middle of it, the colour of its cloth unknowable except where the trim hung down, pulled unevenly by the placement of platters, packed edge to edge. The platters themselves were by turns fresh and full or else ravaged. Cold meat and salty, lurid shrimp with their springing eyes still attached, great wooden boards of bread ends and the smeared remains of creamy white and blue cheeses, little ramekins of mousse, spoons of all sizes, and everybody's crumpled napkins left behind to decorate the blank spaces, abandoned to their fate. There was a bowl of fresh figs and another of oranges already scooped from their shells and left resting in them, in that way that's meant to make them look like jewelled castles. This was a trick that Heike performed herself when she wanted Daniel to get some vitamins, on a day she was making his pancakes in the trinity shape of Mickey Mouse. The couch and chaises had all been pushed over to one side in a hurry. They pointed in different directions and pressed up against each other, bawdy, front to front or back to back. In some cases you'd have to climb over the back of one to get into the seat of another. This hadn't stopped guests from using them; on the contrary, it created a squall of loungers on one side of the room, bordered by a dangerous-looking pile of discarded shoes. Spiked heels aimed every which way.

It was only nine-thirty when they arrived. Dolan himself was standing in one corner of the kitchen, eating an apple.

— He's a divorcé, you know. Arden lifted a tiny white pot-de-crème closer to her face and dug around in it with a silver spoon. They were standing at the edge of the kitchen themselves, near to the living room passage, next to the pile of shoes. When Arden brought the spoon to her mouth, Heike saw that it left a blackish stain against her lipstick. So, not a pot-de-crème after all. Caviar. Arden handed the container to Heike and shook the spoon in Dolan's direction.

— His wife ran out on him, she said. From Barcelona, I think. Very dark about the eyes. I could never understand a word she said, but then I don't suppose they spoke much. Arden sucked on her spoon for a moment. With her other hand, she squeezed Heike's elbow and leaned closer. What I mean is, I don't suppose it was a meeting of the minds.

You could see that she was pining for the vetoed society job. Heike touched her forehead to Arden's.

— You would have made a terrific newspaperwoman.

— A reporteress, Arden said. The world will never know what it missed.

She tapped the edge of the spoon against her wrist and then passed it, clean and wet, to Heike.

— What was she? A political refugee, or a movie star?

— She had the most amazing round breasts, Arden said.

She said the wife's dresses had always been too high- or too low-cut, but you can get away with that if you don't talk.

— Silence made her seem pristine. Like a dark dolly. I bet she never owned a girdle.

Heike took a lick of roe off the spoon.

— But surely if he only wanted to sleep with her he could have left her in Barcelona?

— Did I say Barcelona? Maybe she was Mexican. I know she ran off with someone else. A prizefighter. She followed him back to Europe.

— To Barcelona!

Arden's forehead creased up.

— England, I think.

— So he didn't care much for words, either, then. Heike jangled the spoon, scraping the last of the caviar out of the little jar.

— I suppose not.

There weren't any children, or at least, none that Arden had ever heard of. She wasn't the kind of woman to get caught like that, Arden said. By *caught* she meant *pregnant*.

— Spain is a Catholic country. Heike took a last lick off the spoon and set the little empty vessel on a side table.

— Catholics can be tricky, Arden said. Believe it.

Heike shrugged her cardigan down off her shoulders and let it hang like a scarf around the small of her back. The crush of bodies moving to and from the kitchen made it hot in the passageway. Arden twitched her head, distracted for a second by a loud whoop somewhere to the left of the living room. Otherwise, both women aimed their attention over the crowd, to where Dolan stood in the kitchen, apple still in hand. He was maybe ten or fifteen feet away, just off-centre of a noisy group, but Heike couldn't tell if he was engaged with the conversation or if people just liked standing near him. Greatness by proximity. Leo Dolan was a captain of his own industry. Radio plays, sure, but he also owned a small chain of stations. John classified Dolan's move into television as breakneck.

This in the car on the way over. A moment later, Eric had turned sharply into the driveway and pulled up hard on the brake, leaving even the usually dignified John to jounce against the window.

— Breakneck, Eric had said. Don't you just love it?

Heike said that Eric always acted like a child when he was jealous, and a shot of silence ran through the car, electric. The words had just slipped out, off-hand almost; even Heike was surprised. Her head felt clear and light. John began to laugh. Eric told Heike to settle down before she embarrassed herself.

Arden said it was a well-known fact that the house was empty half of last year, Dolan working the whole winter in California.

As punctuation, she'd swung open her door and climbed out.

Dolan had some colour to his cheeks. Looking at him now, Heike thought that might be booze. His hair was a little longer than the fashion, with a mark of grey at the temple. He'd been wearing a grey pinstripe suit, but the jacket had come off and been lost before they'd arrived, so that he was in his vest and shirt sleeves, the cuffs rolled almost to the elbow. He was possibly the tallest man in the house. Certainly he was taller by three inches than any other man in the room.

There was almost no red skin left on his apple now, and Heike watched as Dolan took a bite off the bottom of the core.

— I'd better find Eric, she said, already turning away from where Arden leaned against the wall. He'd stayed with them for the first fifteen minutes, long enough to wrap a hand around Heike's champagne glass and guide it back to the table, giving her a stern shake of the head. She'd only picked it up again after he'd left them alone.

Now she abandoned the empty glass and picked her way out of the living room, weaving to avoid a few wayward limbs that stuck out of the clustered lounge chairs. Her cardigan, still hanging loose across her back, caught on someone's hand and rather than stop and disentangle herself, she simply let it go, walking out of the garment with her fingers trailing behind her. In the other direction was the hall leading back to the front vestibule where they'd first come in, and the tall door to what she remembered to be the study. A few low men's voices, and the door standing halfway open, as if to discourage less diligent guests. Heike curled a few fingers around the edge of the door and pulled it a little wider but didn't quite look in. She could hear Eric talking, vehement and almost rough. The hall near the door smelled of cigar smoke and she wondered if he was working up some kind of a deal, even here, angling for new donors to fund his work. He was always looking for interested parties. Backers, he said, who might "smooth the rough edges" of his research project: a new medicine that worked to calm the nerves.

There was a burst of harsh laughter. Cards. In which case he wouldn't be missing her at all. If he was gambling, he wouldn't later want to know where she'd been all night, who she'd been with, why she'd embarrassed him by avoiding standing next him even for five minutes. She didn't need to check on him.

From inside the study, there was a woman's voice.

Heike leaned into the room.

The furniture had indeed all been pushed back against the walls to make way for card tables, five or six of them set close enough together that the chair backs almost touched. Games of four men at a time. The woman laughing was the caterer's girl, passing out highballs from a tray. She closed her mouth again and tucked a bill inside her blouse and then moved toward the door, her body brushing up against Heike in the doorway. Eric was there, but he didn't look up. The girl stopped for a moment and rolled her eyes at Heike.

— Get two drinks in 'em and oh brother!

Heike inclined her head in the not-unfriendly way she'd cultivated before learning to speak English. The girl dropped her arm and walked off toward the kitchen, swinging her empty tray as she went. Eric still hadn't looked up, and Heike could see by the shape and size of his glass what he was drinking: straight rye, or maybe bourbon. No ice, no twist. Every reason to think he might still be working the table, playing name-dropper over and around the game. Put it all together and it meant she was off the hook. She started to turn away. There was a pile of money on his table instead of chips, and smaller piles to the right of each player. She couldn't remember if John and Eric had talked about it as a gambling party on the drive over. Where had Eric come up with the buy-in if he hadn't known in advance?

Suddenly anxious, Heike moved past the door and out into the vestibule, where her coat and purse were hung on a rolling rack. She unsnapped the purse and slipped a hand down into a slit in the lining where she kept her own billfold, whatever she could put away without Eric noticing. The money was there; he hadn't found it. She counted it by feel, with the edge of her thumb, then snapped the clasp together and sank the purse down into the sleeve of her car coat. It made her feel almost giddy. For a moment she imagined telling Arden about this, Arden's delight at the very idea of a secret stash. Relieved, she leaned against the coats on the rack.

The weight of her body set the wheels moving and Heike stumbled backward into the soft rustle of fabric as the rack rolled and then stopped hard against the wall. There was the sharp bang of a wooden ornament hitting the ground, and then the hall was quiet again. She sat back into the coats. The ornament rolled to a stop somewhere to her left.

For a moment everything was still and then, quick footsteps. A maid. No: this woman was too senior to be only a maid, matronly in her uniform, her grey hair pulled back. Practical shoes. She arrived so quickly it was almost as though she'd been just around the corner, watching to see what trouble Heike might cause. The shoes stopped in front of where Heike sat, ensconced in the coats. The woman leaned down and reached for the ornament, a kind of mask with a new notch now chipped out of the top corner, pausing to look Heike square in the eye as she did.

Heike hadn't moved. She could hear the men talking in the study and over that the broad noise of the party in the kitchen. Dolan did not rush in to assess the damage, as she had feared he might. The housekeeper stood waiting, her face blank and somewhat hostile.

Heike drew herself taller, tilting her chin to return the stare. After a moment she slipped off her shoes and, rising nobly to her feet, carried them in one hand past the woman standing there, back down the hall, and out the open doors to the lawn.

THE GRASS WAS COOL against her bare feet. There were fairy lights strung along the edge of the house and railings, and they blinked and shone, reflecting off the windows. Pockets of revellers sprawled out in lounge chairs or piled up on the ground with their tilting cocktail glasses. Two men had carried the hi-fi console outside, and a couple of girls were dancing together at the edge of the veranda, their arms straight out like Argentinians. Heike walked away from it all, toward the darkness at the back of the property.

It was quieter the farther she got from the house, the voices flattening out into a faraway hum, pierced only now and then by some woman shrieking. Her skirt brushed against her knee, and she bent to fix it, thinking for a second it must be Daniel, tugging at her. A child's needs such a constant thing, her reflex automatic. But Dani was fast asleep at home, the blankets tangled around his feet or thrown off the bed entirely. Heike pictured him there, his little chest moving in sleep breath. The hair at his brow still damp from the bath and the heat of the upstairs bedroom.

There was a gardener's shed shaped like a little barn set back against the fence line. A greenhouse domed out of one side, its door not quite shut. Beyond this, only the blackness that she knew must be open water. Another lake, the idea of it giving her a chill despite the warmth of the evening. Heike looked back over her shoulder at the house for a moment, to make sure Eric wasn't out on the porch, trying to find her, but nothing had changed. She pushed the greenhouse door a little wider, until the edge of it grated against the wood floor and it stopped.

Inside, the place smelled of soil and manure and wet ferns. The floor was damp and gritty—she still had her shoes in one hand. There was a little light coming through the panes of the greenhouse wall, moonlight and whatever glimmer stretched there from the house, and the leafy stems and fronds of plants reached out of their pots, organized more or less by size on shelves that graded up toward the roof like stairs. Everything seemed sharper than usual, heightened: the pale strand of light, the wetness in the air, the smell of damp earth. Or she was more than usually aware of it all, the roughness of the floorboards beneath her feet. The night air had left her feeling focused. At home inside her skin.

Toward the back wall, the workshop fell into deep black, a darkness that felt soft from where Heike stood. Too dark even for shadows.

She leaned her temple against the glass. It was an old greenhouse, or made from old fixtures, and the panes were thick and rippled, distorting the view. She could see the deep green of the lawn and the shape of the house beyond that, queer somehow, like it was a model house set on the pebbled floor of an aquarium, next to a chest of sunken treasure.

Heike thought suddenly of the little girl with her clapping game, fingers stretched wide to press up against Daniel's, only a moment before she disappeared into the pond. The way she'd spoken only to him, never to Heike, answering Heike's questions only by talking to Daniel, touching Daniel's hands. Daniel, as he had been on the raft that afternoon, toes wrapped tight around the edge, leaning in to see something under the surface before he fell. Reaching: as though something below the water also reached up for him. A mirror image, the surface rippled, distorting the image of whatever hovered beneath. Heike's stomach turned. She closed her eyes and took a slow, cool breath, as though it was the wavy glass that was making her seasick. It might be hours before she could get home, lay her hand on his back, curl up beside him while he slept.

She opened her eyes. The light inside the greenhouse had changed. Something moved in the dark, just a few feet away. Heike jumped back.

— Who's there?

There was a scuff against the floorboard and the figure moved closer, then stepped back against the shelf.

— I'm sorry. I didn't think anyone would be here.

A match flared and Heike could see the serving girl from the study, holding a cigarette to her mouth, her eyes pale blue in the sharp light, almost transparent. She stepped forward again and moved to push past Heike toward the door. A trickle of blood from one nostril dark against her skin, cheekbone swelling out purple. The match puffed out, all at once.

— Stop, wait. Heike leaned closer and caught the girl's arm. What happened to your face?

— Just let me go.

The smell of the cigarette in the damp of the greenhouse made Heike feel sick again. In the dark, just the red tip of it flashing as the girl moved. From outside there was a new brightness and they both turned.

The beam from a lantern lit up the doorway, skimming across the girl and Heike both in a quick sweep.

— I thought I saw someone out here.

It was Dolan. He stooped a little to get past the transom.

— You can't smoke in here, he said. It's a greenhouse. You're killing my roses. He shone the beam at each of their faces in turn. And who are you? Oh, the German girl. *Heil, heil.*

— Not *heil*. Heike. She's hurt.

— Hikey, then. Who's hurt?

Dolan moved the lantern so the beam fanned out wide and bright, and Heike stepped back, wincing in the glare.

— Jesus. Look at that shiner! Prizefighter, are you? He turned to Heike. My aura is chock full of prizefighters, you know. I can't get rid of them.

The girl looked at Dolan and then over to the doorway.

— So it wasn't you, then. Heike let go of the girl's arm.

— Me? Dolan gestured to himself with both hands and then blinked violently against his own light. I didn't even hire her. You come with the cook, don't you? With Mickey?

— Please!

The girl pulled away, skimming past Dolan.

— Wait a minute, Heike said. You dropped your cigarettes.

The pack had fallen in the girl's desperation to escape. Heike bent down to retrieve it, but she was already gone, out across the grass.

Heike stood there, holding her shoes.

— She thinks she loves him, do you imagine? Dolan said.

— Some men are bad to you.

— Some men are very good. Dolan got down on his hands and knees and cast the lantern around. There you are, he said. He pulled a brown glass bottle out from under the rose shelf. He was on his knees, looking up at her.

Heike grabbed her skirt and held it tight against her hips.

— I'm only here in the summers, he said. I never know what the gardener will find and what will stay hidden. He stood up again and pulled the stopper out of the bottle. Could you ever love a bad man like that?

Dolan swayed slightly on his feet as he poured liquor from the bottle into a pocket flask. He'd set the lantern on the shelf to free up his hands and it shone an arc of light across the floor.

— People are never just one thing. Heike flipped her chin sharply toward the door where the serving girl had run out into the night. I can't tell you what makes love tip into control.

This was a somewhat bolder statement than she'd meant to make, and it surprised her. Her eyes widened, then relaxed again. It was not untrue.

Dolan drew a swallow of whisky off the top of the flask.

— You're Lerner's wife, he said. He capped the flask and tucked it away in the pocket of his vest, suddenly reformed.

Heike stepped back.

— Hikey, he said.

— Heike.

— Either way. I saw you yesterday, walking. You were on your own up on the road, right where the trail leads down into the woods. Near Union Springs. Isn't that right? I don't have you mixed up with some other creature? He leaned back on a heel. Seemed a far way out for a girl on her own.

— You were far from home yourself if you saw me.

— I'd been down to Ithaca.

She looked at him, more cautious now, and moved slightly to one side.

— I like to be alone in the woods.

— Aren't you afraid?

— In the woods?

— In the woods, Dolan said. Or anywhere. Here. Now. Aren't you afraid, hidden away here with me? Who knows what I might do.

Heike glanced out at the lawn, but the light from the lantern glared against the glass, casting a reflection instead. She couldn't see the deep green or the house in the distance; instead, another Heike, another Dolan, his flask back in his hand now.

— All the best stories start with a girl alone in the woods, Heike said.

— Interesting. He took a slow and thoughtful drink. And occasionally true, he said.

— Only occasionally?

— I don't know about *all*. Occasionally, I can agree with.

She turned back to face him.

— You're a terribly agreeable man.

— A minute ago you thought I'd punched a girl's lights out, Dolan said. He offered her the flask: Between storytellers, he said. Just a capful. Just a swish.

For a moment she put out her hand, then hesitated.

— I'd better not.

— I thought you weren't afraid?

Heike reached down and slipped a foot into one shoe, hooking the back strap around her heel. She could imagine by now that Eric had noticed her missing, and the idea made her nervous.

— I don't think we ever met before, she said.

— I was paying attention when you arrived, Dolan said. She leaned forward with the other shoe and Dolan took it from her, catching her hand in his. He said: You think I've been drinking.

— Drunks don't make me afraid.

— I wouldn't say *drunk*. Would you say drunk? Really? You're hard on me, Heike. I've barely met you, and you're awfully hard on me. He crouched low with her shoe in his hand and touched her bare foot. Come on now. Give it here.

Heike pressed the foot against the ground.

— Don't be silly. I'm getting my trousers dirty so you don't have muss up your dress and have your jackass husband ask you a bunch of uncomfortable questions.

— You shouldn't call him a jackass, Heike said. But she lifted the foot.

— I've met Lerner, Dolan said. He straightened up, bringing the lantern with him. I wish you'd take a drink.

— You should turn off that light, Heike said.

— Place is probably glowing like a UFO, is that what you think?

— You should turn it off so I can go back quietly.

— You think I'm a drinker, but you're wrong.

Dolan shut off the light and stepped forward, matching the toes of his shoes almost to hers. He stood a foot taller than her, even in her heels, but she looked down instead of up, and took a step back, making space. Her hair curling now in little tendrils at her forehead and neck.

— I don't think anything of you, Heike said.

— You must have been a kid when you left. He set the dead lantern back on the shelf and stepped in toward her again, closing the gap between them. They airlift you out? Or Red Cross brought you over. Yeah? And now here you are, another New York housewife in charming shoes. Charming shoes and clean fingernails.

He was talking to her in a careless way, disappointed, as though they were under the bright light of a kitchen potluck and she was holding a jellied salad instead of something better, as though the dark and the close air of the greenhouse and the line of her hip in the thin dress meant nothing to him. He put out a hand and let it run back along her waist and wrap the exposed skin at the small of her back.

— I could do more of this, Dolan said. His voice pulling cleanly along. Like he was peeling an orange.

— No, Heike said. She didn't move but looked down and waited for him to drop the hand and let it trail away along the flare of her skirt. I told you: I'd better go.

She stepped backward and to the side to get around him. At the doorway she turned back.

— I walked, she said. From Germany. Nobody airlifted me out.

— You walked to the USA?

— To Switzerland. I was fourteen. I walked through the forest.

— Alone in the woods, were you? Dolan said. Funny. I hear that's how all the best stories begin.

There was a little dip off the floorboards at the doorway that made it feel like she was falling back out into the world. Her heel sank into the soft lawn immediately and stuck there, and she had to take the shoes off and carry them up to the house anyway.

ON THE WAY HOME in the car, Arden slumped against her in the back seat and stroked her hair, like sisters, and Heike stayed back there for the rest of the drive, even after Eric had dropped the two of them, Arden and John, off at their own house.

— And where were you all night? Eric said once they were gone.

— Talking to people. Walking around. Like at a party, she said. Then, catching her own tone: I stopped in to see you playing cards, but you looked busy.

— What's that supposed to mean?

Heike tightened her shoulders and the small of her back against the seat behind her. He'd had some luck at the table and it should have made him genial, but she knew that he'd been drinking, too.

— Tell me, she said. How many games did you win, exactly?

Eric dropped one hand off the wheel.

— Eight, he said. Eight! It's not right; it shouldn't be that easy. His shoulder moved slightly with a bend in the road. He spoke again, and his voice was loud and low: That whole party was full of pseudo-intellectuals. Dolan wasn't even in there playing, he said. What kind of man won't gamble in his own house?

— Maybe he doesn't want to be accused of stacking the cards.

— Why do you have to argue with everything I say? Why can't you ever be on my side?

The car turned sharply off the main road and onto the gravel drive that ran close along their part of the lake, wheels spinning for a moment against the loose ground.

— Eric, be careful.

He threw both hands up in the air.

— You want to take the wheel? Go ahead!

— Eric, please! I only said to be a little bit careful. It's so dark.

He brought his hands back down and glared at her in the mirror.

— He's a moping drunk. Your friend Dolan. Did you see that? Head on him like last week's helium balloon.

Heike hesitated, unsure if she was meant to answer him or not.

— I suppose.

— You suppose what?

She dug her fingernails into the vinyl seat cover. It was late. She wondered if Daniel had woken, looking for her. The girl, Rita, was meant to have slept in the same room with him. She wasn't supposed to leave him alone.

— It means I don't know. I wasn't paying attention.

They were close to home. She could see the dark shimmer off the water on the other side of the trees, forty or fifty feet in. They passed another house, set close to the road, where Heike sometimes saw a lone man smoking on the porch. Tonight he was not there, but there was a light in an upper window, and the curtain blew in and out of it. She felt a warmth at the base of her spine where Dolan had laid his hand.

— Funny thing about you, Eric said. You never have a thing to say. Not a damn thing interests you, is that right?

She could see part of his face in the rear-view and watched him, hoping for his brow to soften. The road had twisted away and uphill from the lake proper. Their stream, wider here, snaked between the trees. She caught a glint of light in the mirror and turned to see out, suddenly afraid. A flash, the glare of flames reflected in the water. The white house on fire, windows popping like fat drops of oil in a hot pan. Daniel locked inside.

But it was only the clearing where the drive began, the open lawn down to the stream, the headlights of the car revealing the band of dark water below. A clear night. The stars spangled the little river like floating candles, as though someone had lit a thousand tiny lanterns and set them adrift.

5.

Eric stayed in bed through most of the next day.

He'd been easier again once they were home, his own house, half-smiling as he walked up the steps at the crooked set of the car where he'd parked it:

— Maybe I ought to have quit while I was ahead.

Heike scurried to catch up.

— I don't think the sheriff has a drunk-o-meter balloon for you.

She'd seen the contraption on the cover of a magazine the year before, but there was little risk of running into a patrol car on a country road in the middle of the night, and even less of Eric being stopped.

He liked that and laughed aloud and took her by the hand to the kitchen and fed her bits of cured ham from the icebox. There'd been a parcel on the front stoop as they came in—something he'd been waiting for—but he set it aside on the counter, just within sight, while they ate. She was itching to see Daniel, but Eric drew her along with him, like they were tied at the hip.

— The house is still standing, isn't it? He teased her, playing at a mosquito bite on her knee with his fingers until she managed to slip away, saying she wanted to change out of her dress. His hand on her leg irritated her.

She came back downstairs later, in her nightgown, and found him no longer in the kitchen but hunched over his desk in his undershirt and dress pants, comparing one notebook to another. The stack of money, his night's take, sat neatly to one side, and the parcel, now open, was emptied out on the floor.

— It's so late, Eric.

— Did you check on Daniel?

— He's sleeping. She didn't stay with him, though. Rita. He's in our bed, and she's in his room. I thought you told her to stay with him.

— I don't want the maid in our bedroom.

He spoke without looking up at her. She waited for him to finish his notation, taking her own quiet inventory of the space. She didn't come into the office often. On the wall over his desk there was a type box, each square home to some souvenir or keepsake: an arrowhead he'd found as a boy, a Pro Juventute Helvetia stamp worth a single Swiss franc. He had fussy habits, almost feminine. Heike was not a trinket collector. In school in Dresden, before schools shut down altogether, she'd been best at mathematics, scored worst at *Mädchenhandarbeit*, needlework things.

On the other side of the room, a tall bookshelf loomed, and she let her gaze drift along the spines: Hegel and Kant, Erikson, Kinsey, Skinner. It seemed to her now that Eric had described Skinner's work to her once, but she could not remember much beyond rats and electrodes. One of them had observed his own children as part of his experimentation. Piaget? Not Skinner, surely, with his little treats and electric shocks. Or was it? Heike pushed the thought from her mind.

Eric pulled open a drawer, and there was a clink of bottles knocking against each other. She almost told him he'd had enough to drink but then thought better of it. One of the windows was open at the back of the house—she could hear the breeze as it made its way through the garden, a creak from the wood-plank veranda as it settled in the cool of night.

He pushed the notebooks to one side and spread a small handful of paper tabs across the desk in front of him, then riffled through the bottles in the drawer. He pulled out two of them: small and brown, like iodine bottles. With eyedroppers. Heike pulled a stool over from the corner of the room and sat down. She was tired, but it was worth a few extra minutes to end the night on an agreeable tone. He didn't like it when she went to bed without him.

—Are you hurt?

He didn't respond right away but lined the paper tabs up in two rows, five per row, and unscrewed the top of one of the bottles with his thumb and middle finger.

—You're getting a real scoop here, you know. A new project. You're the first to see it.

—What is it? A serum?

— Sure. Kind of. Call it a medicine. He squeezed the little bulb, and a single drop of liquid hung from the tip of the dropper, held there for an instant by its meniscus, before spreading into the tab below. Mustard-coloured. It's not what I was planning on, he said.

He nodded in the direction of the empty parcel. She could see

85

now that one side of the box was caved in, as though it had been kicked or stomped on.

— But I can work with it, Eric said. They give you lemons, you make lemonade.

He moved his hand along the row, then stoppered the little bottle again and selected a different one for the second row of tabs, the liquid milky this time, and viscous, but invisible when it soaked into the paper. He screwed the lid back onto the second bottle and set them both in the drawer again and shut it, then held his hands up off the table as though he didn't want to interfere with his own handiwork. He looked like a woman waiting for her nails to dry. Heike leaned in for a closer look.

— But it's not a medicine. You're making it yourself.

— Only a trial. Something new, like I said. He pinched one of the tabs by the corner and held it up the way a magician might present a prop to his audience, careful not to disturb the circle of colour on it. Go on, he said. Lift up your tongue.

— Me?

— Go on.

Heike moved her body back, just a little. Her hands came together in her lap.

— I don't think it's a good idea. What's it for? What if Daniel wakes up and needs me?

— What, you're worried? One hundred percent safe. Guaranteed.

She didn't answer, and Eric leaned in, regarding the tab. Then he opened his mouth and slipped it under his own tongue.

— See?

Heike blinked. This wasn't what she'd expected. He pressed his lips together, like a child who's just taken a sweet from the candy bowl without asking.

— I ought to sleep like a demon tonight.

He cocked his head at her and picked another one of the tabs up by its corner, as he had the first one, and held it out to her. A priest offering communion. Heike moved farther back in her seat, almost without thinking about it.

— Eric. I'd rather not.

— Don't you trust me? He leaned forward again, no longer looking at the little tab but keeping his eyes locked on hers. His face was kind. She thought for a moment he might kiss her. He reached out with one hand and cupped her breast.

— Come on, now. Let me see your sweet tongue.

Heike didn't say anything, didn't open her mouth. His hand stayed where it was, stroking her, the tip of his thumb catching her nipple.

— Or did you want to stay awake for some reason?

There was a sound on the stairs, and she jumped back a little.

— Eric, the girl.

She crossed an arm over her chest, brushing his hand away as she did so, but he only leaned closer. His lips almost on her neck. Heike, half-turned in her seat, heard the little footsteps start and stop again. Her body tightened, as though her arms were stitched to her sides. Daniel. She pushed Eric away, and he moved easily, her hand against his shoulder. Her throat hurt.

— Dani? Is that you? You should be in bed, my love.

He came shuffling into the room on his bum, sliding along the wooden floor. His blue pyjamas with race cars on them. Heike brought a hand to her forehead and rubbed it, a kind of relief. He clambered up into her lap and circled his arms around her neck.

Eric sat back in his chair, palms up in an expression of res-ignation. He looked to the ceiling and then back at Heike, an almost-laugh.

—I give.

She bit her lip.

—He's still so little, Eric.

—He is so little, it's true.

He leaned forward again, but it was casual, one elbow on his knee, one cowboy talking to another at a saloon:

—Shouldn't you be in bed?

—I heard Mami talking.

Heike gathered him closer against her hip before standing up with him like that, his arms still wrapped around her neck.

—Come. I take you back to sleep.

Eric took up a pair of tweezers and began to carefully stash the paper tabs into two small brown envelopes.

—Aren't you going to say goodnight to your father?

Daniel buried his face in Heike's chest, then peeked out to whisper each word on its own before hiding again:

—Good. Night.

Eric set the little envelopes in the same drawer and shut it again.

SHE'D BARELY GOTTEN DANI back down when Eric made it to the bedroom: eyes slightly reddened, both happy-looking and oddly mistrustful of her. He pulled her away from where she was curled around Daniel, over to his side of the bed, and she lay quiet next to him, her hand against his back while he snored, unable to sleep herself. When she was sure he wouldn't wake, she got up, taking Daniel along with her in her arms.

The house was still but not silent. It was just past three in the morning.

She stood at the top of the stairs and listened to the tick of the kitchen clock, the sound rising from the hall below. Daniel lay against her shoulder, deadweight. The girl, Rita, slept curled on the little bed in Dani's room. Heike was glad enough of that now, glad there had been no witness, especially to Eric staggering up the stairs. She peered into the room. In her sleep, the girl moved a thumb to her mouth. At sixteen, her face looked not much bigger than Daniel's.

Heike shut the door and walked down the stairs with Dani still on her shoulder, and lay down with him on the daybed in the white room. There was a crocheted blanket folded at one end, and she drew it up and around her shoulders; when she touched her lips to the back of Daniel's neck, she found he was cool, not sweating at all. His breath came in little puffs. It calmed her, and she slept there for a few hours, until she heard the latch of the milk door opening and catching shut again.

She got up then and pulled the car into the garage and shut the door and went and got dressed in the laundry room. Daniel woke up, and Rita also, and Heike made pancakes: they ate them outside, so as not to wake Eric, and then she and Daniel watched Rita walk up the drive toward the gravel road, with her green satchel slung over her shoulder.

— Is she sweet to you?

— She makes popcorn, Daniel said. We made popcorn in the big pot and mooshed it with melty marshmallows in our fingers. Heike was holding onto his hand, and he yanked it up and down. I want to go swimming, he said. And play water-spiders with Tessa. I want to go in the canoe. He wrapped his other hand around her wrist now and pulled down with both arms.

Heike dropped down to crouch in front of him and shook her hand free.

— What did you say?

Daniel picked up her hand in his own again and squeezed. He jumped up and down on his toes.

— I want to go swimming, swimming, swimming with Tessa, Tessa, Tessa.

Heike pressed her lips together. For a second the sky stretched tall and bright above her, and she squinted and put a hand on the ground to steady herself.

— I think today we work in the garden, Heike said. No swimming today.

SHE WAS LOOSENING UP the earth around the tomatoes with a hand rake when she heard the sweep of tires on the dirt drive. Daniel was sitting underneath a pole bean teepee, snapping off the young green beans and eating them with dusty fingers. She had her blouse open at the neck, and a pair of high-waisted shorts on, peach-coloured, and she stood up and brushed the dry soil from her bare legs. It was past two. The sun beat off the brick path that led between vegetable plots. There was a thickness to the air, the scent of the fruit off the tomato plants, and this made it feel hotter. She heard the engine cut in the driveway, and then the slam of a car door. She thought for some reason of Dolan and looked up to the bedroom window to see if Eric had also heard. Her hands were too dirty to fix her hair, even. A little curl fell along her brow, almost in her eyes.

She caught herself thinking this and shook off her vanity. Probably the milkman, coming to collect. The upstairs curtains were still drawn. She called to Daniel to stay put and walked around the front of the house alone.

— I was hoping I'd find you home.

Heike started.

The car was a long red Eldorado, its roof peeled back in the sun. Not the milk wagon at all. Leo Dolan leaned against the hood with his hands in his pockets. He began walking toward her, but she waved him back and hurried up the drive. She did not want Eric waking to find another man in the front yard.

— Is there something I can do for you?

— All on your own again? Dolan leaned in and offered his hand.

— My son is in the backyard, playing. Heike regarded the hand, suspended more in beckoning than in greeting, and knotted her own hands behind her back.

— Eric Lerner, Junior? Or what kind of family names does a German girl have?

— It's Daniel. But I think it's better if you're not here right now, Mr. Dolan.

— Daniel. That's a fine name. A Bible name. You know who Daniel fought, don't you?

— Mr. Dolan, Heike said. I'm pleased to see you, of course, but my husband is quite busy right now.

He stepped in close, and Heike tilted her head up and lifted a hand to shield her eyes.

— You can call me Leo. Dolan took hold of her other hand and pressed something into it: a card. You really should, too. Call me Leo. He gestured to the house. Lerner seems an odd duck. I've heard a few things, here and there. That card is in case you ever need a pal.

Heike glanced up to the second-floor windows again, and then to the front porch. She slipped the card into the pocket of her shorts and held it there, flat.

— It's very nice to see you, Leo, but this isn't a good time. I wish you would come back later.

Dolan threw a look around past her, toward the back of the house.

— You got a ball or something we could throw? With your boy?

Heike braced her feet against the ground a little more stiffly. She could imagine Daniel, in the backyard, chewing in his bean tent with the sound of a grasshopper.

— Why don't we walk around and find him?

— Mr. Dolan. Leo. I'm afraid I really must ask you to leave. Please.

— The buck stops here, huh?

She felt a pinch against the back of her leg and twisted to brush away an earwig that was crawling up in the soft place behind her knee. Dolan didn't say anything more, but watched her do it. She still had the garden fork in one hand. When she moved, little clumps of dry earth shook off it to the ground.

— I'm afraid I offended you last night, Dolan said.

— It was your party. Heike brushed the hair out of her eyes with the back of her wrist, streaking her forehead with dust. You have every right to drink in your own home.

— You think poorly of me. I can see you think poorly of me.

— I shouldn't have been hiding in your greenhouse, Heike said. She took a step away and leaned out to see if she could catch sight of Daniel in the backyard, but the garden hedge rose up high against the corner of the house, blocking her view.

— Did you learn anything? Dolan followed her lean, as though they were both looking for the same thing.

— What do you mean?

— In the greenhouse. Dolan reached out and took the hand

rake from her. He hoed the air a little. Didn't you learn any little thing?

There was a sharp chattering from the other side of the front garden, and Heike flicked her head toward it without thinking: a blue jay pecked at the ground near the cluster of birdhouses. What Eric called her bird village, the houses and feeders a gift for her, a kind of special treat. It wasn't the jay but a little wren making the noise, from inside one of the shelters. Warning the jay off. Its beak just visible now, peeking out of the red-painted house.

Heike straightened and turned her back to the noise, oddly ashamed, unwilling for Dolan to notice or ask her about the birdhouses sitting high on their posts. A dryness in the back of her throat.

From the front porch, the slap of the screen door.

Eric came out and down the front steps, dressed in summer whites. Dolan's jaw tightened and released. Heike grabbed the hand rake back.

— I told you, she said.

— In fact you didn't.

Dolan said this without taking his eyes off Eric. He sank a hand into one pocket and sent up a high salute with the other:

— Lerner! Just the man I came to see. Dolan stepped away from Heike and walked on down the drive.

Eric had on a white linen jacket and shirt, and he slouched forward, the soles of his loafers brushing against each step. Heike could see that the shirt collar was half-popped under the jacket. He hadn't shaved.

She slipped around the side of the house. Daniel wasn't in the garden, but the back door to the garage was open, and she found him in there, kicking at a soccer ball that was wedged beneath the bumper of the car. It was dark inside compared to the brightness of the day and it took her eyes a moment to adjust to the change. She heard him before she saw him. There was a ringing sound as he knocked over a tin sand pail, and then the ball bouncing free.

At the front of the house, the Eldorado's engine started up again, revving onto the road and away. Heike's stomach tightened. She stood quietly, waiting.

Eric came to the doorway in his white suit.

— I thought you said you never talked to him last night.

— I didn't, Heike said. She picked up the tin pail, avoiding his look, and began to sweep the old sand out with her fingers.

— He wants us over on the weekend. An old-fashioned clambake, he calls it. Dinner on the lawn and cards after.

The edge of Heike's fingernail caught inside the pail, and she winced.

— But not just us? she said.

— Us and some radio people. A couple of dancers, show people. Says he's going down to Cornell and has a few writers there he might ask.

— Sounds like a big party.

— He calls it dinner, Eric said. He picked up an edging tool and tapped the blade against the concrete floor.

— And you want to go?

— You don't think it's strange he wants you there?

— I think it's more likely he wants *you* there, Heike said. Cards after dinner. You see?

She had her back half-turned to him now. Dani, she said, not so close to the car.

Daniel dribbled the ball off the back tire, then ran after it and kicked it again. Eric stopped playing with the tool and leaned it up against a wooden seed cabinet.

—Where did you sleep last night?

The question was hostile.

— I lay down with Daniel, she said. Downstairs. I couldn't sleep. I walked around first.

— You sound guilty. Something troubling you?

There was a pause as Heike regarded him for a moment. He seemed dishevelled, unpredictable in his rumpled suit. She beckoned to Daniel.

— Dani, we go back out in the sunshine, yeah? She bundled him along toward where Eric was standing.

—Wait, my ball! Daniel balked and dug in his heels.

Heike turned and saw the edge of the ball, stuck again now, this time well under the chassis.

— Go on out. Mami brings it for you.

She watched him skim past Eric and then got down on her knees to unwedge the ball. She heard Eric move closer.

— Are you feeling quite well today? Her back was to him, and she turned her head only slightly to ask the question, guarded, over her shoulder. It's so strange for you to stay home like this, she said.

— Look at me for a second.

Heike pulled hard at the ball to free it and sat up a little taller. She tilted her head slightly but looked out past his body, to the grass beyond the doorway.

— You think you're smarter than me? He lifted a foot and touched the toe of his shoe to the ball in her lap, tapping it.

— I don't know what you're talking about.

— Asking Dolan to the house when you know I'm sleeping.

— I didn't ask him anything, Heike said. He came to invite you to dinner. You just told me so.

She pressed a hand against the ground to push herself to standing, but he held her there, his foot hard against the ball.

— Eric, you're being tiresome. She looked up at him but didn't say anything more for a moment. Then: You're hungover. Let me make you something to eat. You'll feel better with something in your stomach.

He took his foot off the ball, and it rolled away from her. She followed it with her eyes but didn't get up right away, keeping tabs on him instead from where she was. He seemed sharp at the edges. An entirely opposite effect from the soft sedative of the night before. She thought for a second of the way he'd swallowed the dose, blithe and easy as a cough drop.

— Maybe your sleeping medicine wasn't a good idea.

He walked over to where the ball had landed and hooked a toe under it, kicking it sharply to one side. Heike winced. The ball smacked off the side wall of the garage, then bounced a few times, the sound of it tinny against the concrete floor.

— You need to get that canoe this afternoon.

— I can't. I have Daniel, and I don't want to take him back so far. Yesterday he almost drowned. We'll go tomorrow. She pushed her hair back out of her eyes. Let me make you some breakfast, Eric.

— So, then, what? Your canoe floats down to the lake? Someone will take it. Go today.

Heike watched him, considering whether to keep arguing.

— Eric, she said. Eric, he talked about her today.

— About who?

— The girl. Tessa. The girl we saw.

— The girl you saw.

— I'll go tomorrow, Eric. I promise. I just want to stay with him, nicely home today.

He came back to where she was sitting, crouching down to look her in the eye. She could see even in the low light where a crease cut into his cheek from the pillow. He'd slept all night without moving, the little iodine droppers doing their work.

— You should have stayed in bed last night. He reached out a hand and cupped her jaw, turning her head to one side and then the other, as though examining her skin tone or the movement of her eyes. This is just a lack of sleep, he said. You should have taken something when I told you to. The hand shifted: he used his thumb to tip her chin up and hold it there. You always think you know best, he said. It's emasculating, you know? The way you are.

Heike sat still and kept her eyes on the ground and watched his feet. Eric patted her cheek. He stood and turned his head toward the doorway, out to the garden.

— He keeps you so busy, doesn't he? Little Daniel. He turned back and looked down at her. If you want to stay home, that's fine with me. I'll give you one of those new sleeping tabs. Something to calm you down.

Heike's head fluttered.

— I'm not your patient anymore.

— You don't have to be my patient for me to want to help. He stepped in, watching her. Heike, he said. You're my wife. Remember?

She nodded slightly, still looking down but trying to keep her face easy and pleasant. He stood directly above her now.

— If you're so anxious, the poor canoe will have to wait.

— No. No, I can go, she said. You're right, I'm just being silly. She tilted her head back to look at him. If you're home anyway, I can leave Dani with you, for his nap. I'll go today.

Eric held out a hand, to help her up.

— Dolan's clambake, he said. It's Friday night.

Heike stayed where she was, her hands resting on her thighs. When she didn't reach for him, he drew his hand back, sharply enough to make her flinch. But he only used it to pick a gardening tool from where it was hanging on the wall. A dull spade. He flipped it in the air and caught it again. Then:

— No man wants to be your friend, Heike. Keep that in mind.

He left the garage, but she still didn't move right away. From the front of the house, the sound of the screen door slapping shut.

6.

An hour later Heike was in her own closet, picking out a thin, long-sleeved shirt in jersey that would be better for the long walk, and a pair of cotton ankle socks. The house was silent: she'd left Daniel in his room, the blinds drawn low to darken it for his afternoon rest. Outside, it was holding at eighty-five degrees.

The long sleeves were against the sun on the road and biting insects in the woods. Under the shirt and shorts she had on a bathing suit and, for a moment, as she slipped the top over her head and pulled it smoothly down, she let her hand rest against the satin finish on the suit. She'd have to swim to the raft to get the canoe.

The carpet was soft under her sock feet. She pressed her toes down into it, then without thinking pulled open her top drawer and swept a hand back past the silk-and-wire bras to find the paper-wrapped Meissen figurine. Her fingers closed on the newspaper, and she felt the little china doll underneath it, hard as bone. Heike pulled the package forward and curled the paper back.

The doll stared up at her, cool and vacant. Someone else's nostalgia. The ridge of the girl's round hat, her tapered neck, the wide sweep of her apron, held out as if mid-curtsey. She moved a thumb over the eyes.

There was a sound from out in the hall and Heike started and glanced up, tucking the figurine back into the drawer by reflex. The door stood, as it had before, just slightly ajar. But was the gap wider now than it had been? She turned so that her back pressed flat against the dresser. Worried, for a moment, that it was Eric come up the stairs from the office, peering in at her. The doll a secret thing, her own.

But the noise did not come again. She turned back and drew the shepherdess toward her for a final look. The light fell, a shift in the clouds, and the doll's features came up sharper, shadowed. Some current of air from the open window brushing the back of her neck and catching also the bedroom door, which yawned open. The tap of the doorknob as it knocked back against the wall. A wave of nausea washed over her. Suddenly she didn't want the thing anymore; she thought of smashing it, or jamming it somehow into a pocket and taking it back to the house, back where it came from. Her hand tightened on it.

From the first floor, she heard the clink of ice tongs against a glass, then Eric's heavy step, pacing and stopping at the foot of the stairs. Waiting for her to come down.

She looked down at the figurine again, and pushed it to the back of the drawer.

Outside, the sun was still high. Heike blinked hard against it after the semidarkness of the house and tied a blue kerchief behind her hair on her way up the drive. She had about an hour before Daniel woke up, maybe two in the heat. At the feeders, the little wren she'd seen earlier was now out of sight, and there was no blue jay, but a solitary crow stood guarding the fallen seed beneath the red house.

She turned onto the road: a faster route, but hot in the sun. She'd left her walking sandals in the canoe and so was wearing only espadrilles, the gravel underfoot biting through the rope soles. A car skidded by, throwing pebbles against her calves, and then a few minutes later another one slowed down behind her, pacing her for a while before the driver changed his mind and hit the gas again. Heike kept her eyes forward. Where the road curved, she turned down into the woods.

The embankment was soft and sloping, but down on the path she found the earth hard-packed, and she stamped her feet to shake off any loose soil. Where the trail met the stream, she turned east and away from the lake, retracing her own steps and wiping the damp from her forehead. A thin column of trees separated her from the water; one of these leaned out, almost perpendicular, so that on the landside its roots levered up out of the ground. She held onto the trunk and swayed out over the stream herself, to get her bearings.

It was a clear day, hot and shiny and clean-skied. At the water's edge there were ox-eyes blooming and some swamp milkweed and those little white and yellow butterflies, what her mother had called cabbage butterflies. Ahead, the stream opened up and a weave in the trail took it farther into the woods and then back down again. She tried to imagine how you could lose track of a child for five minutes, ten minutes, enough time for her get out across the water and back again. You might not look first in the pond. You might look in the forest.

There was a game she'd played with Lena, her sister, to entertain her on the long days of walking at the end of the war. To distract them through the hard climb. A kind of scavenger hunt where each girl kept track of her own collection of animal sightings: owls and eagles, chipmunks, foxes; near the end, the very first of the early caterpillars. Deer, always deer. Lena arguing every time that she had seen it first, whatever it was, large or small, and Heike showing her how to stand still and wait for the birds to reveal themselves. Once, they heard the sound of a pig rooting and stood back to avoid a boar. Once, a lone sheep surprised them in its stillness, at the path's edge, separated from its flock.

Sometimes she wondered if it was this game that had taken Lena, if she'd wandered off to follow the sound of some little animal. Heike liked to picture her safe, living up in the Allgäu with a shepherd and his family and braiding edelweiss into a crown for her hair, as though she had followed that lost sheep home. As though she had stayed seven years old forever.

It was quiet. The butterflies played at a black-eyed Susan near the stream bank. For a moment, she imagined Daniel lost without her and then blinked hard to chase the image away: Daniel was home safe, napping. It was only herself, Heike, out here alone.

From where she stood now, she could see the tall reeds ahead, and just beyond them, the younger bank, where the raft must be. She could imagine the tail of the canoe throbbing back and forth, caught between the current and its tether. The shortest distance between the shore and the raft wasn't at the house. It was here, through the reeds.

Heike steadied herself on the trail. She would walk around, down farther to where the cottage was and the easy grade of shore, and swim from there regardless. She was a strong swimmer but not interested in fighting off a drake or feeling her ankles wrap in the lurid tendrils of some underwater plant, no matter how much shorter the distance.

She did not want to swim at all.

When she got down to the clearing, she took off her shoes and crossed the rough beach. The canoe was there, just as she'd left it, cherry red and lost in the sunlight, like a dog someone had forgotten tied up outside the grocery store. She stripped off her shirt and shorts and wrapped them around the shoes, using the shirt sleeves to tie it all up into a bundle, and left it on the log where she'd rested with Daniel the day before, Daniel spitting up water to catch his breath.

She would swim out to the canoe, but she would not put her head in the water.

There had been a breeze when she set out, but it was gone now, the air heavy and still enough that she checked the sky for a coming storm, but it was clear and blue and cloudless. The beach no different than when they had left it. She'd half-hoped to find some evidence of people: a forgotten picnic blanket, or the remains of a sandcastle at the pond's edge. She stood in the sunshine but did not get closer to the water, turning instead to look back at the house.

A shadow wavered in the doorway. Heike pulled back, then caught herself. Of course. There had to be someone there, someone who would know about Tessa, who could explain the girl's strange appearance and disappearance. She walked up over the tall grass.

The door was standing open. Not much. About a foot. She called out.

— Hallo?

There was a stillness to the place, the doorknob cool against her fingers when she touched it. She pushed the door a little farther open. She could see the dull linoleum in the entranceway, unmarked by dirt or mud that might be tracked in at this time of year. Could the open door be her fault? Maybe she hadn't latched it securely—although she could remember pulling it closed.

But there had been some wind at night. She called again:

— Hallo?

Then:

— Tessa?

The name caught in her throat—for a moment she thought she heard something, a voice crying back, high and far away as a bell. She listened through her own silence, but the sound seemed to disappear. A new breeze, or some echoed birdcall from deep in the woods. Heike swallowed and called the girl's name a second time, stronger.

The door wavered slightly, or her arm did, holding it open. She looked down at the threshold and saw for the first time a thin line at the sill, a kind of joining mark, as though someone had held a match to the flooring and let a strip of it burn. The thought of a fire made her draw back, and she turned to look out at the raft, at the canoe where it waited, but just then she heard the thing again, the same call. Not a bird, but a song. Someone singing. Heike hesitated in the entryway, then stepped inside.

In the house, the sound did not echo but seemed to come

from somewhere deep within. Ringing high and sweet, but too faint to make out any words. She came in a little farther, step by step. It was a tune she knew. Wasn't it? Her own song, the nursery rhyme she'd sung to Daniel at the raft, bouncing him on her knee: *Hoppe, hoppe Reiter*...

She pulled up, suddenly afraid. The door was still open behind her. Heike scanned the room, her eyes falling on the kitchen cabinet, the empty space where the Dresden doll used to stand—the doll itself hidden away now, home in her own dresser drawer. The tune kept on, muffled and tinny. Outside, there was the rougher pitch of the wind, picking up speed through the trees, and something else, too, closer by this time: low and coarse, an animal sound. Heike looked toward the darkness at the back of the house, panicked. Something using the old cabin as its den, the door pushed open not by a hand but by a shoulder, a snout. The noise fell away, though, even as she searched for it, leaving only the same high, ringing song in its place, oddly rhythmed now, faster, off-key. There was a glint of something at the kitchen window, and Heike started and jumped back, grabbing for the door.

A wind chime. She could see it there, dull and dangling from its rope, on the other side of the dirty glass. Not a song, but the sound of the wind, a string of tin bells. The tune only in her mind. It lifted and rang again as she watched, spinning slightly on its hook. She wondered that she had not heard the chime before—but the other days there had been no breeze, the air hanging heavy around her.

Heike turned away. The place still empty as before, no voice, no girl, no Tessa at all.

She came back outside, wary, drawing the door closed behind

her. The sky had darkened now in one corner, a far-off edge. She did not hear the animal sound again, but from the other side of the pond there was a low rumble, a truck moving slowly along the upper road, or else thunder. The breeze came through from one end of the beach to the other, lifting the branches as it went, the chime rising with it, and another sound, too, a steady beat. She turned: the door batted at its frame. Hadn't she already closed it?

Something played at the back of her neck and she started, but it was only the breeze again, ruffling the knot of her kerchief. Heike pulled the door shut a second time, strong and tight.

SHE LOOPED THE BUNDLE of clothes over her head, using the tied-up sleeves as a strap, and moved out into the water with the makeshift pack resting against her shoulders. She could hear the ring of the chime in the distance, even now. She wanted noise, some kind of commotion to cover the sound of it, still mimicking a tune in her head, and she dove forward without thinking. Her arms pulling cleanly through the water. The canoe was out there: as she got closer, she could hear the dull knocking where the bow end was beating against the boards of the raft. She kept her head up until that also made her nervous and she began to dip her face on every third stroke, and then on every second, eyes wide, the pond greenish and the floor of it far down below. The bundle at her neck dragged with the weight of the water it took on and choked her. At the raft she heaved herself up, pulling the waterlogged clothes off her shoulders and throwing them against the bulkhead in the canoe. The paddle still lay there, flat against the boards, along with the pack; her towel in a rumple next to the two glass jars. She loaded all these into the boat with her wet things. She could see her sandals where she'd left them tucked under a seat.

A streak of white caught her eye from shore, and Heike stopped and stared, searching, her breathing heavy. A flash of blond hair. There: some shimmery movement. The girl, Tessa, half-hidden in the trees. Heike froze, sure of her. The child's grey eyes shining pale and clear, unwavering. But a moment later she was gone: it was only the tall grass, swaying where the forest broke into clearing, wheat-coloured and seedy. She looked away, blinking hard. She was only spooking herself, hearing a song in the peal of cheap bells, seeing things that weren't there. The house itself still as she'd left it.

There was a long, crackling roll in the distance: the coming weather moving toward her in a line now. She took the paddle in one hand and stepped into the canoe, staying low and working her cold fingers to untie the knot. The rope was wet. It threaded as she worked, a wiry strand pulling sharply under her finger-nail and drawing blood. The high, constant ring of the chime in the wind. The light fell low all at once, and Heike checked over her shoulder to see where the clouds were and sucked on the finger. A shadow flickered in the window of the little house, the sun moving out from behind its shade and back in. She felt a wave of cold rush over her, the prick of pins across her brow, the back of her neck.

The door stood open again, as it had when she arrived.

She pushed off hard and started paddling. The pond was wide open, and the wind sent licks of water slopping up over the gunwale, the current carrying her to the narrow and down-stream quickly, then out onto Cayuga. She leaned into her stroke, aiming for open water. It would be calmer and safer against the shoreline, but she didn't want to get mired in the reeds. The light dimmed again.

The wind came across the bay in a wide sweep, hitting the canoe sharply on one side. Chop swelled up and flooded the bow deck. The rain hadn't reached her yet, but she could see the line of it moving down the lake. The next burst of wind picked up the bow and spun the canoe on its stern end, sending her back against land. She fought hard with the paddle, cranking the canoe around and pushing back on the reeds, then stroking deeply to put some distance between herself and the bank, her shoulders aching. She got the canoe out into deep water, and a new gust of wind swept her around again.

She was losing ground. The wind was now strong enough that it seemed possible it would push her back up into the stream, against the current. A hundred yards back, almost hidden from view, she caught a glimpse of the raft, bobbing on the surface of the pond. Her grip tightened on the paddle: on shore, she could see the house with its door open, stubbornly banging against the frame, and down at the water's edge, the girl herself, standing out in the weather. Her hair streaming, as though she had only just surfaced.

Heike thrashed at the reeds, desperate to get back out into the lake. As the canoe swung around, there was a low roll of thunder and the rain caught up to her in a sheet. Upstream, the girl seemed to lean in, moving across the water to the raft in a fluid line, then disappearing altogether in the downpour. Replaced by just the same high grass, battered in the storm. Heike pushed off the bank, her hair soaked and sticking to the back of her neck and the kerchief funnelling water down the sides of her face. There was a voice, loud over the beating of the rain, and she realized she was screaming. She was on her knees in the bottom of the canoe, hacking at the reeds with the paddle. Water sloshed up over her thighs. Heike dipped the paddle low and stroked hard to get free. There was nothing behind her except weather. She imagined being hit by lightning and Daniel left alone, and she blamed herself and kept moving forward until she found the mouth of their own stream, their own launch.

She jumped out and pulled the canoe in by hand, wading through the rocky shallows in her bare feet and dragging the boat up onto the shore instead of tying it fast. The rain slacking off now, mud flecking her legs and arms. She ran up the trail. The stream ahead grey and empty, and the woods to either side no longer lively, but wet and heavy and dark with harm.

HEIKE CAME UP THROUGH THE GARDEN and along the drive to the front steps, relieved to find everything normal, in its place. The rain had come and gone here with the same ardour, and she stopped, listening for a moment. There was a knocking at the back of the house. Repeated, but not patterned. She put down her armful of wet clothes and walked around to the yard. The back door to the garage swayed a few inches in the last of the rain and sank softly against its frame, then swayed out again. This gave her an odd turn: she watched the heavy air drawing at it like breath, then reached out and shut the door.

She found her housecoat where she'd left it that morning in the laundry room and stripped off her wet clothes and leaned over the wide sink to wring out her hair. She straightened, pulling her fingers through the damp curls a few times, and glanced up at the clock. She'd been gone almost two hours. There was no sound of playtime from either the white room or anywhere else in the house, and Heike padded up the stairs to see if Daniel was still sleeping.

The blinds were still down, and she opened them, one after the other, to let the afternoon light into the room. She turned, expecting to see him still asleep within a mess of blanket, but he wasn't there.

— Daniel?

She said his name softly, not wanting to bother Eric if he was working or wake him if he was asleep. The closet was standing open, but she peered inside anyway, and then under the bed, in case he'd heard her come in and decided to play hide-and-seek. Heike called out to him again, louder this time. She shook out the blanket and folded it before leaving the room, patting it down as though to make sure he was not somehow stretched and tangled inside.

She went back down the stairs and walked a fast circuit, calling louder now, but no one answered. At Eric's office she drew herself up and took a breath before knocking.

— Eric?

She eased the door open. There was a lowball glass on the desk with a trace of water at the bottom of it, and the window was open just enough for the breeze to make a flickering noise in the blinds. No one was in the room.

— Eric! Daniel!

Heike twisted in the doorway. The car was still in the garage; she'd seen it when she went around back to shut the door before coming into the house. She ran back upstairs, frantic now,

everything lying still and neat, even the towels folded and resting on the counter at the edge of the bathroom sink.

— Dani!

She grabbed the handle to her own bedroom door to push
through, but her shoulder slammed against it instead. Locked.
The knob rattled in her hand.

— Dani! Are you in there?

The handle refused to turn properly. It was not a room they
ever locked, although there was a copper key, missing now, that
normally sat in the latch on the outside of the door. A decora-
tive feature. Heike got down on her knees and called through
the keyhole.

— Dani, are you in there? Are you in Mami's room?

She cranked at the knob again, pushing hard against the
door. The action felt no different from the way she'd hacked
at the reeds with her paddle to free herself, and she again felt
trapped by the dark water, the current pulling her in. The room
was dropping out; her vision crowded with tiny pinpricks of
light. The back of her hand touched her cheek, and she realized she was in tears.

She lay the hand on the doorknob again and this time it gave
way, Eric pulling it open from the other side and now crouching to meet her, help her up, quizzical.

— Heike. Heike, whatever's happened?

He reached out for her hand, lifting her properly to her feet
and holding her there. Heike shook her head.

— Why didn't you open the door? I was crying to get in.

Eric's brow furrowed as though she were telling a story he
couldn't quite understand. Daniel was sitting up against her
pillows on the bed. He had something, a toy of some kind, but

he looked up as soon as she came into the room.

—Mami! Mami's home! He dropped his plaything and crawled forward. Heike rushed toward him and grabbed him up, then sat with him on the bed, her lips in his hair, rocking.

—Why didn't you answer me, Dani? Why didn't you say something when you heard me calling?

Eric stepped closer, following her in.

—We played hide-and-seek with you, Daniel said.

—Yes, I see that, Heike said.

—Me and Daddy hided in here.

Heike looked at Eric. He was somewhat neater than earlier in the day, as though he'd spent the afternoon on his own care. If it hadn't been so late, she'd think he was on his way to the clinic. His shoes were on and polished. There was something curious, gentle, in the way he looked at her.

—The bedroom door has no lock, Heike, he said.

—It was locked, she said. You heard me!

—Heike. Eric crossed over to where she sat on the bed. Do you need something to calm you down? You're soaking wet. He touched her forehead. You're raving, Heike. Let me give you something.

She stood up suddenly, leaving Daniel behind.

—You already gave me something: you gave me a heart attack. You locked the door! How could you be so cruel?

He raised a hand and let it fall against his own hip.

—I just told you, that door doesn't lock. Calm down now, Heike. Or I could drive you over to the hospital. Would you like that better?

Heike turned back to Daniel on the bed. He'd picked up his toy again, and now that she looked closer, she saw what it was:

the little shepherdess, the Meissen figurine she'd hidden in her drawer. He tilted his hand, left to right to left, walking her along the coverlet.

Heike dropped onto the bed beside him and reached out to touch the doll.

— Where did you get this?

— I finded it, Daniel said. Daddy helped. When we were hiding.

7.

Out on the road, the late-afternoon light was unfiltered. Only a thin film of water shimmering off the telephone wires and the puddles in the ditch, deep and almost clean-looking, left a trace of the rain that had come through. The asphalt itself was pale and dry.

Daniel lay against the bench in the back seat. Eric lit a cigarette, his window down and the wind whipping at the crumbling ash. They had the radio on, and Heike rolled the dial between her thumb and forefinger, looking for something you could dance to. It was warm in the car, and she tucked her dress under her legs so that her skin wouldn't stick against the vinyl.

The look on her face when she saw that porcelain figurine, Eric had said. He knew he'd gone too far. He'd brought her a glass of ice water in the bath. Daniel played in the next room so that she could hear him.

— I had no idea you'd brought anything with you out of Germany, Eric said. You're full of secrets.

Heike had sipped at the water and said nothing.

Then, thinking better of the silence, she set the glass down and tried to smile.

— How long was Dani awake before I got home?

— Oh, I don't know. Twenty minutes? Not long. We had a little time together.

— Did he show you his drawing?

— What do you mean?

— This morning, while I was making breakfast, he was very busy drawing at the kitchen table. He made a Mickey Mouse. You should see it; it's so cute. He's really very good for his age.

The corner of Eric's lips curled up, just on one side. Amused by her.

— That's funny. He told me you sent him outside to play with Rita this morning.

— Why would I do that?

— He said he wanted to stay inside, but you shooed him out the door. Are you sure you're remembering correctly?

— Of course I remember. Don't be silly.

Heike had picked up the glass again and held it against her lips, not drinking from it. Eric reached out and tucked her hair behind one ear.

— Maybe you're thinking of a different day. You're more delicate than you know. We have to take care of you, he said.

He'd suggested a little dinner out, just the three of them. An apology, he said, for riding her so hard all day long.

She was surprised when they passed through Ithaca without stopping.

— It's early yet, Eric said. He passed her his cigarette to hold and she relit it for him with the red ember of the car lighter. She was looking out the window at the houses, white and wooden and barely set back from the road. There's a particular taste to a cigarette lit for the second time.

They were between the lakes. He'd bought himself a new hat a few days earlier and fit it onto his head in front of the hall mirror before they left, admiring the angle of it. When it was satisfactory, he'd pulled his billfold from his pocket and counted out twenty-five dollars.

— Here, he said. Why don't you buy yourself a new dress. Or two of them. Pair of party shoes. He held the bills out for her to take. I just want you to be happy, he said.

Heike folded the money in her hand, two tens and a five. Eric took a last look at himself. He'd caught her eye in the mirror:

— I only spent fifteen on the hat, you know.

She nodded, and closed the hand tighter.

These houses belonged to poor people, Heike decided now. Landlocked little properties with zigzag fences, pretending to be farms, and the people in them mechanics or cashiers or girls like Rita. Now and then you could see a vegetable plot set to one side, where the fence rails were missing or fallen down. There was a dog lying out on a tether in one driveway, lapping at a puddle, and at the next, another dog, loose, chased along beside the car, its paws battering the rough shoulder of the road. The dogs looked matted and forgotten, and she wondered if they were fed properly or just sent out into the woods. Eric was talking to her. The dog chasing them turned back. They had reached the end of his domain.

It wasn't the hangover so much as the gambling, Eric said. It made him reckless. It made him feel like he could spit on the world. He'd meant to bring her some flowers, but perhaps the new dress would do.

— Why are we going to the hospital? Heike still held the cigarette, but it was burnt down to the filter now and she threw
it out the window. She'd recognized the turn near the bottom
of Seneca and sat up a bit smarter, remembering his earlier
remark. Almost a threat. His new jovial mood too hard to trust.

Eric pulled a case out of his breast pocket and flipped it open
with one hand, offering her a new cigarette to light.

— For me, he said.

He let the cigarette case slip onto her lap. Heike gave the
lighter a slow push to heat it up. The lake spread out ahead of
them, and if she leaned just slightly out the window, she imag
ined she could still see Cayuga in the rear-view mirror. Or the
light off the water, anyway.

— I've been waiting for a certain package to arrive, Eric said.
Research chemicals.

— Yes, you told me. Remember? Your little bottles. But it
wasn't what you wanted?

— Wrong stuff. Interesting, but no, not what I wanted. The
details would bore you. I'm afraid that's why I was such a bear all
day. The hospital pharmacist is a skinflint, but there's another
doctor. Someone I knew in the army. I just need enough to finish
this project, and then maybe we'll go back to the city, yes?

— Back to New York? What for?

Eric switched hands on the steering wheel and reached over
to pat her knee.

— Don't worry, everything's fine. Look, I'm cheered up! You
can go for a little walk in the gardens. You and Dani. Then we'll
drive back into Ithaca for supper. What do you want, a steak?

He pulled up next to an outbuilding. They could see the main
hall from where they sat.

— All gone in to have their dinner, Eric said. You'd think the place was abandoned.

He let the engine die.

— What's in there? Heike said.

— Nothing. Workshop building.

— A workshop. Like for crafts? Or real working? She twisted around to look at Daniel in the back seat. His eyes were closed, and she could see movement under the lids. Dreaming. He had a stuffed bear in one hand, half-tucked under his leg for safe-keeping.

The grounds stretched out warm and glowing in the low evening light. Eric had told her once how they used to keep patients chained up in the basement. Like a French prison, he said, and now it was all Heike could think of when she looked at the place.

She tapped a finger against the cigarette case.

— Eric? Let's go. Dani is already sleeping, and it will be hard to wake him up for dinner.

Eric seemed suddenly at peace, intent on watching the sunset behind the hall. The lighter popped out and he reached for his cigarette, the paper browning at the edges with his inhale.

— There he is.

Eric hunched into the windshield. Heike followed his gaze. There was a man walking across the field, toward the building. The light was still strong enough behind him, his silhouette curving at the shoulders. An old man.

— Who is that? she said.

— Marek.

— And he is a doctor?

— Patient.

The man moved steadily along, his head down, following the walking path.

— What's wrong with him?

— Nothing.

Eric's body relaxed and he leaned on the steering wheel with one arm.

— What do you mean?

— Nothing, Eric said. I like to watch him.

— Why don't you let him go? Heike squinted.

— He's been here since the twenties, Eric said. Or earlier. Must've been sick sometime. I asked him if he came here after the war, and he said he fought for the Kaiser. Older than you think.

— So he's German?

Eric didn't answer. He held up one hand, thumb out, like a painter judging perspective. Heike realized what he was really doing: blocking the old man out. Erasing him.

— They call it the bughouse, he said. And there he is, cutting his little path every day like an ant in an ant farm. He closed the hand and brought it away from his eyes, as though he were checking to see if the old man was still there. Spend your life under some other man's thumb, he said.

The heavy door swung open and Marek disappeared into the building.

— Surely you have to send him home. You say he's not mad.

Eric started the motor again, and the car crawled down the drive toward the main parking lot. He tipped a little ash out the window.

— What's home? He says he fought for the Kaiser; maybe he worked at Kaiser Deli in Brooklyn. How should I know? Some of them get brought in by train, all the way from California. He eased into a spot and killed the motor. Madness follows you like a dog, he said. These people, who knows where they're from. That's why we say *committed*. No way out once you're in.

Heike leaned down to tuck her purse under her seat, pausing there for a moment to look at him. She reached back and gave Daniel's leg a little shake.

— Dani. Hey. Naptime's over.

Daniel kicked his feet in a kind of protest, but his eyes opened. Eric took a last look through the windshield for Marek, but the field was empty. He leaned back and tapped the rear-view so he could see himself and adjusted the new hat.

— Besides, Eric said. He digs all the graves. What would we do without him?

HEIKE OPENED THE BACK DOOR of the car, and Daniel swung his legs toward her. He'd kicked off his sandals on the ride. He wiggled his toes.

— Daniel, stop. Let Mami buckle your shoes.

But he wiggled some more, until Heike grabbed the toes with one hand and jammed the sandal on with the other.

— I want to go with Daddy.

Eric was off across the lot already, two hundred feet away, his briefcase swinging.

— No, we go for a little walk. Then supper. What do you want to eat? You want some ice cream?

— I want a shrimp, Daniel said. I want shrimps in a cup with cold sauce.

She tugged his hand, and he hopped down out of the car. The door swung its wide arc and shut heavily. They stood there for a moment, holding hands and watching Eric walk away. He climbed the steps to the main door, and then he was gone.

— Now, Heike said. Which way do we go? She pointed ahead

to where two trails cut through the grass. Daniel let go of her hand and ran up between them. Heike followed, the soles of her shoes sliding a little on the wet path. She swung her arms up into the air.

—Look out! Here comes the monster! The monster is chasing you!

Daniel shrieked and disappeared behind a bank of shrubs. They played at this for a while, Heike hurrying along behind him whenever he got too far away. On either side of them were lilacs, out of bloom now, arched and leafy. She could see the orchard from where she stood, and the farm to the south of that. The path was not quite paved but beaten down with time and had been layered with gravel, although not recently, Heike thought. The grounds were maintained in a good-enough way by the patients themselves, who worked for free as part of their rehabilitation.

It's good for them to have an occupation: Eric's explanation when he'd first told her of the practice. Plenty of fresh air to be had working the gardens and livestock. (And in the sewing room? And the slaughterhouse? Also fresh air? Heike said. This made Eric sulk, and he'd ignored her for the rest of the evening. At bedtime he'd held her gently from behind and pushed her thighs apart with one hand, moving into her fast and hard and leaning close to whisper that her kind of people should never make jokes about work camps. *Arbeit macht frei*, Heike. Don't forget what you come from. Don't forget what you did.)

Daniel disappeared into a lilac bush and suddenly cried out:
—I'm stuck!

Heike pressed a branch down and held it with her foot while he climbed out and ran on to the next one. The branches were full and green, and she combed at the leaves with one hand and wondered if the flowers had been white or purple in the spring.

— The little one is full from energy.

The voice surprised her. She turned toward it, and the branch jerked up from under Heike's foot, thwacking sharply back into place. She stepped back. The old man, Marek, stood a few feet away from her. He was not much taller than Heike. Mostly bald, with a whitening fringe of hair over his ears and a thick grey moustache. Apart from a few deep lines, his age didn't show. He wore a striped shirt, buttoned to the collar, and a dark jacket over top, also buttoned. His arms hung at his sides.

— It's not so often we can see children here, he said. His English was practiced but broken.

— My husband is a doctor, Heike said. She gestured with an arm toward the main hall. We are just visiting. Then, testing him: *Mein Mann ist hier Arzt. Hier im Spital.*

Marek tilted his head back in understanding but didn't say anything in German or English, and Heike wondered if she'd set him on edge. Or if Eric was wrong about him: his mind was gone. Daniel was calling to her, and she let him call, watching Marek's face.

— You live here? she said.

— *Ja, hier, hier.*

— *Hier im Spital?* In the hospital?

Marek shook his head. He lifted a hand and looked at her almost affectionately, as though she also were a child, then pointed out into the field, away from the farm, out past the workshop building where Eric had first stopped the car.

— *Im Spital nicht, nicht. Nicht! Meine Wohnung. I' hab' meine eigene Wohnung g'baut, i' selbst.*

He had his own house. Heike looked around, following his gaze.

—Where is your house? Here?

But Marek had stopped talking. He rocked back on his heels and put his hands in his pockets. Heike checked on Daniel over her shoulder. He was crouched low in the grass, playing with something there.

—A little friend, *ja*? *Noch ein Kamerad, das Kindlein da*?

Heike turned back to Marek. His meaning was a little lost to her. She wondered how often he got a chance to speak to another person, someone from outside.

He gestured again with a hand, this time toward Daniel and then back to Heike, adding a slight bow of the head in her direction: A little friend.

—*Nein*, *nein*, no friend. He's my own, my son. She touched her belly. *Mein Sohn, mein eigenes Baby*.

The old man's eyes clouded for a moment, as though he were perplexed, but then he crossed his arms and his mouth opened to laugh. He tipped his head in Daniel's direction:

—*Jawohl, haben Sie so ein Kamerad. Kamerad, Kamerad.*

Marek muttered the words over again—a friend, a friend— low enough that Heike had to step forward to hear. He seemed on the face of it no worse off than any other man his age, but his language had suffered, and perhaps he had never picked up enough English to compensate. Isolated, she thought. A bit lonely. She started to call to Daniel to come over and say hello, but Marek waved her off. He was tired, he said. An old man. He was going to bed.

—*Nach Hause! Ins Bett!*

Heike watched him walk off along the path, then up over the hill until he disappeared beyond it. At the last second she called out:

— *Schlafen Sie gut!* Sleep well, Herr Marek! He didn't reappear, and she couldn't tell if he'd heard her.

She felt something at her side and looked down. Daniel was there, his hand sliding cleanly into hers. He wanted something.

— Now you hide! Mami, you!

Heike shook her head a little. Daniel linked his fingers in hers and squeezed, insistent.

— Okay, I hide. I hide. But you have to count—can you count to ten? She took his hands and moved them over his eyes. You have to close your eyes, see? His fingers were pink and clean and damp from touching the wet grass. He screwed his eyes up tight. Heike started counting out loud and let him follow. When he got to five, she backed away and tucked herself behind the closest bush, crouching down into the branches. She called out to him:

— Seven, eight, nine, ten!

— Nine, ten! Daniel's high little voice: Here I come!

Heike hugged her knees. She braced her heels back against the low, thicker branches of the lilac, where it was dry, and waited. Daniel ran up and down, swishing at the leaves.

— Are you here? Are you here?

Then he was quiet. Heike waited. She counted to ten in her own mind before straightening up and peering around the side of the bush. The sun was low now. Where the grounds opened up, flat along toward the farm, the sky was shadowed but still warm. The path had a violet cast to it. She squinted to find Daniel in the shade around each lilac bush.

— Dani?

Heike came around into the little clearing where she'd been talking to Marek. Daniel was maybe fifteen feet away, close to where he'd been playing in the grass. He stood next to a ridge of smaller flowering shrubs, batting his hands at the petals. He wasn't looking for Heike. His mouth was moving, and she realized he was talking to someone. As she came closer, she could hear him, his voice a sing-song. She strained to see if there could be someone there, hidden by shade. The old man, come back around. Suddenly she recognized the song: her own rhyme again, truly this time, the song she'd thought she could hear at the pond. It made her feel cold now, something in it strange and ruined.

> *Hoppe, hoppe Reiter*
> *Wenn er fällt, dann schreit er*
> *Fällt er in den Graben*
> *Fressen ihn die Raben . . .*

It was an old rhyme, gory the way folklore can be. An anxious rider falls in the ditch, cries out; the ravens pick at him. Heike listened. He wasn't batting at the petals. He was playing a clapping game, his hands coming together and then smacking at the air. The fingers, so pink and clean a moment ago, suddenly dark. There was no one with him.

Heike stopped moving and watched him, a stitch tightening across her chest. His little voice clear in the sunshine. She caught herself looking over her shoulder, then shook it off. She was ridiculous. Spooked by the hospital and tired from the long day. More than one long day. She was hungry and tired, and it made her jittery. Any little child sings to himself. She wiped her hands on her skirt and called to him:

— Daniel! You forgot about me!

She moved forward to take his hand, and he stopped the game and turned to meet her. His eyes were bright; there was no reason to worry about him. They would go and meet Eric and drive to town, and she would order him shrimp. Shrimp cocktail and an ice cream sundae. He reached for her hand, and she rubbed it in hers.

— How did you get so dirty so fast! The muck streaked her own hands, and Heike suddenly took hold of his and opened out the palms.

Not garden muck, but blood. Each little hand scratched open. She looked at him, and his face was placid. He stretched his fingers wider.

She dropped his hands and wiped at her own, the blood making a blush, a thin stain, as she rubbed it in.

— It was the game. The game hurt me.

Heike looked down at the ground near them and then up to where he'd been playing. He'd knocked the flowers with his hands. Shrub roses. The branches all full of thorns.

She took hold of him by the wrist only, her fingers shaking a little against him.

— Come on, we wash you up. Before your father sees.

There was a garden hose at the exterior of the workshop building for the groundskeepers to use. Heike led Daniel over to it and held on to him with one hand, working the tap with the other. It stuck, the handle rusty along its grooves, and then gave suddenly, and she let the water stream out over his fingers. Heike held each hand flat and wide to clean it out. The shock of the cold water surprised him, and Daniel's face screwed up tight. Heike cranked the handle shut and let the hose drop and showed him how to shake off his hands.

— Now let's see what they look like. So. Much better! Just some scratches.

She blew on his palms. Each hand was a mess of little lines. She crouched down, drawing the hem of her dress up so that it wouldn't drag in the mud near the tap.

—When I was a little girl, Heike said, I played hide-and-seek with my sister. We were on a picnic, and we went into the woods to play. I wanted to be very clever, so I crawled right underneath a raspberry bush. Wild raspberries. I was picking them when I was hiding there. But raspberry bushes also have thorns. My arms and legs looked just like this, just like your hands now. She lifted the edge of her skirt and patted his hands dry, holding them in hers. She gave the fingers a squeeze. But it hurt to crawl under that bush, Daniel. Tell me, didn't it hurt to play in the thorns?

He rubbed the hands together and then opened them wide again.

— Do I need Band-Aids?

She watched him a moment, then looked up to gauge the dying light.

— I think you need ice cream, Heike said. She pushed up to standing.

— And shrimps, he said.

— And shrimps.

— With cold sauce, Daniel said.

— Yes, shrimp cocktail. But listen now: Next time if you are playing and it hurts, you need to stop that game. Okay?

She laid a hand between his shoulders, and they walked back along the path to the parking lot. Eric was leaning against the side of the car. He had his hat in one hand, and he tapped it lightly against his thigh. When he saw them, he fixed it back on his head.

— What happened to you?

— Dani got hurt. There are some rose bushes there, and—

Daniel held up his hands like little fans on either side of his face.

— I had to sing the song, he said. The thorns hurted me, but I had to do the game.

Something caught in Heike's throat.

— I already cleaned up his hands.

— What are you talking about? Eric said. He was looking at the ground, at her feet. The soles of her shoes coated with muck, and the peekaboo tip showing off her first three toes, the softly rounded nails painted a delicate pink, with a slick of mud rising between them.

— Oh, Heike said.

— You look like you've been running through a sprinkler.

— It was the hose. I just grabbed the first thing I saw. Heike stepped forward to touch Eric's shoulder, but he twisted away and walked around to the driver's side.

— I can't take you to dinner looking like that.

— Eric. It was only a little water. Here, I'll wipe them off. Everything's fine.

Eric stopped at his own door, and she heard the click of the handle as it sprang open in his hand, but he didn't get in. He looked at her across the roof of the car.

— Everything's not fine. You're a mess. You look like you've been mucking out a farm stall in your dinner clothes. What did you think was going to happen?

— You told me to go for a walk.

—You could have chosen to wait in the car. Use some sense!

—It's only water! Eric, this is easy to fix.

Heike opened the back door and held it for Daniel to climb in. She watched him crawl over the seat until he was square on the bump in the middle. Then she opened her own door and slid into the seat, leaving her legs outside the car and knocking her feet together, twice, three times, to clean them off. Eric flung himself in next to her and slammed the door.

—We're going home.

—What about your package?

—There was no package. The supplier didn't come through. What makes you think it's any business of yours, anyway?

Heike pulled in her legs and shut the door. She'd left her hat and gloves on the bench between them, and now she picked them up and drew the gloves smoothly over her hands. Eric turned, one arm along the seatback behind her shoulders, and spun the car into reverse.

She pulled a compact from her handbag and pinned the hat smartly above her brow, fixing it into her hair despite the jostling of the car as it turned off the gravel lot, back out onto the road. In the back seat, Daniel opened his mouth and began to howl.

8.

Dolan had written a play for television in the spring, and from there things had gone terribly wrong.

— The play about the old Jew, Paulsen said. Only maybe he wasn't a Jew. I don't know. You saw it, right? Sunday night teleplay?

Heike made a noncommittal shake of the head. They were standing on the back lawn at Dolan's house. She wanted to say both yes and no at once, or else neither, and let her eyes drift down toward the greenhouse, then to the water beyond the lawn. Two long tables were set up nearby, under the chestnut trees, outfitted with cornflower blue cloths. Heike rested her hand on the back of a chair. It was cool in the shade. She could feel the flesh on her shoulders prickling. Renny Paulsen was a man she'd just met in the gin lineup. She wondered, if they moved into the sun, would he pay less attention to her nipples, the line of her brassiere, visible under the cotton voile of her dress. She tried a sidestep in that direction.

Paulsen stood with his chin tilted down. It was a Jew play, he told her. Only it wasn't. Surely she'd seen it? No?

— I'm afraid I'm not much for the television. She sidestepped again, her torso shifting at the hip like a tomato plant straining for the light, and Paulsen followed her.

— He sat down to write a play about that kid, Paulsen said. (Here his voice dropped, and he leaned into Heike's collarbone.) That was the thing of it. About the Negro kid that got lynched; you know the one I mean. He straightened up a bit and looked around. But of course that's not going to fly on the television, he said, so he swapped things up, made it an old Jew who gets killed instead of a Negro. Made it Boston instead of Mississippi. You think even with all that cloak and dagger he could get it past the network?

Think again, Paulsen told her. Quit thinking and forget about it.

Paulsen was a writer, too. Only he wasn't. He taught. He'd given up writing for the teaching life, he said, and look at old Dolan, tearing his heart out for the television producers when he could be hawking Ionesco with his feet on his desk and a bunch of lovely young coeds with more money than brains to follow him around.

— Pardon the expression, he said to Heike.

— I never had any money, Heike said.

— Good. It wouldn't suit you. But, like I was saying. He held his empty glass a little higher, and the top half of him swivelled around, looking for a tray of fresh drinks to appear. There was a cigarette girl moving from group to group, and Heike looked at her eye to see if she was the same girl as the other night, but this one had a wide-open look and a mouth that was too small for her face. There was nothing sharp or delicate about her. When she came over to them, Paulsen tapped the cigarettes to one side of her tray and set his empty glass down in their place.

— Does he throw a lot of parties? Heike said. Normally.

— He's cracking out of a funk, Paulsen said. With the glass taken care of, he had nothing to do with his hands, and they danced around, in and out of his pockets, like sad fish hoping to escape a dip net. He's better now than he was. Good to see him opening the place up, seeing people again. Last few months he's been all fight, all tooth and hammer.

— After his wife left, you mean?

— His wife? Where'd you hear that? I mean with the network, kiddo. Paulsen settled one hand on his hip and leaned back against it. He's been back and forth for a year, he said. Best work of his life since then. Now he's really rolling, you know what I mean?

— I thought you said he should quit, Heike said.

— Well, sure he should quit, Paulsen said. But so long as he's working, may as well keep knocking 'em out of the park.

Another girl walked by slowly with a tray of martinis. The girls all wore the same striped dresses, with a blue sailor's tie at the breast. She was walking slow so as not to lose control of the tray, her kitten heels sinking slightly into the lawn with each step. Paulsen spun around to follow behind her.

— Say, where do you think you're going with those?

Heike took a few steps backward until she'd been swallowed up by the low, looming boughs of a willow tree, then turned and walked into the house. There was a little nook in the hall outside the bathroom with a mirror and a small table, and she set down her empty glass and leaned in to take a good look at herself, her eyes and skin. The phonograph was set up near the veranda doors, meant for outdoor listening, and the music reached her in a distant way: the Platters, or maybe the Ink Spots. She pinched her cheeks and watched the colour flood into them.

The door swung open and shut behind her, and she heard the click of heels against the wood floor of the hall.

— Occupied?

There were two of them behind her in the mirror: older than Heike, other men's wives. Old enough to wear jewellery well. The taller of the two with her hair wound back in a twist, the glint of a diamond at each ear.

Heike leaned out and wagged the door handle. It chicked in the lock.

— Occupied or off-limits, she said. She tripped on the words, enough to make the shorter woman raise an eyebrow at her accent. The woman opened her mouth to comment, but seemed to think better of it and turned away instead.

Heike shifted over a little to make room. Only the tall woman moved in close, unpinning and repinning the sweeping front curl of her hair. A silver bracelet slid up and down along her arm and caught on the edge of her glove, a single charm hanging off it and making the tiniest of noises as she worked. Her hair was almost black, and Heike glanced at the line of her part, checking for grey. Her friend flanked Heike on the other side but kept her distance, watching her closely and only pretending to fuss in the mirror. When she noticed Heike looking, she wound a strand of hair around her finger in a bored way and then let it go, the hair really too short to play with. All three of them with white gloves, rather than any colour.

The tall woman shook her bracelet down to her wrist and picked at the edge of its round decoration with a fingertip. Heike peered at this in the mirror, expecting it to crack open and reveal a tiny photograph, a fat baby or grandmother, or both, like a locket. The little door swung back and the woman shook a couple of tablets into her hand. She stretched an arm across Heike to her friend on the other side and handed off one of the tablets.

— I only have two with me, she said. That's all that fits. The woman caught her eye in the mirror, and Heike realized this was meant for her.

— Do you have a pain? She looked from one face to the other.

— No, sweetheart, it's just Miltown.

Heike knew the name. A medicine for nervous ladies. To ease the mind and heart: there was a sign in the pharmacy window in Ithaca, advertising whether or not the druggist was sold out. The selling out was the important part, a hundred scientists just like Eric watching the success of the thing and turning up the burner under their own research.

— I think it's mostly for pregnancy, isn't it? Heike took her handbag off her arm and picked through it with her fingers, looking for something indiscernible. Busy work. The short-haired woman made a face and tossed the pill to the back of her throat, then clapped her mouth shut. There was a cut-glass dish on the little table filled with cigarettes, and she ran her hand over them as though she were evaluating a bolt of fabric.

— I hate not sharing. It feels so rude. The tall woman snapped her bracelet shut. I might have a few extra out in the car, come to think of it. Stir one into your drink, see how you feel.

Heike thought of the tablet Eric had given her when they'd

arrived home from the Willard two nights before. Something of his own making: for her nerves, he said, although it was not Heike but Eric who'd fumed and raged through the long drive back to Cayuga. He'd kept at her, long after Daniel fell back asleep. She couldn't be left alone for even ten minutes without some childish disaster. How could he ever bring her out as his wife? He'd lose his position. People would think she was feeble-minded, slow, subnormal. Heike sat with her hands quiet in her lap and her voice low, refusing the medicine over and over until finally, exhausted, she screamed for Eric to leave her alone. In the end, she swallowed the pill. Frustrated first by the argument and then by the humiliation of her own tears.

Round and blue, with a powdery aftertaste. She'd woken the next morning with dead legs, unable to walk until noon. Because she hadn't had supper, he said; a miscalculation on his part.

He brought her a single garden rose in a bud vase to keep her company and asked Rita to bring up some coddled eggs and a plate of buttered toast fingers. Fresh strawberries, sliced and sugared. There had been a bluebird on the window ledge, and Heike watched it devour a beetle, tossing it up and letting it fall against the wood slats of the house, waiting for its back to crack open like a shell, the tender gauze of its insides to foam out.

Now she leaned forward and took a cigarette from the dish and fit it neatly into a silver holder she'd pulled out of her purse.

— I really feel fine, Heike said.

Unimaginable that she'd volunteer for more pills.

In that moment, snared in her bedsheets, she'd decided to stop arguing with Eric. It was almost the argument itself he wanted, more than any result. When he brought her another tonic later that night, she set it down a moment, to slip off her dressing gown, then poured the liquid into the soft carpet at her bedside while he was turned away. And again early in the morning. The empty glasses lining up on her nightstand, a casual mark of compliance, meant only to be observed and cleared away.

In Dolan's house, the bathroom door swung open and a man walked out: the short-haired woman's husband. They touched hands and exclaimed, and the man took a lighter from his pocket and tossed it around while they talked. He was wearing seersucker, and a white shirt that had lost its crisp look in the heat of the afternoon. The jacket hung loose and open, and his wife tugged it closed and played with the buttons.

Heike went into the bathroom and shut the door and smoked her cigarette down to the filter, leaning against the wall by the vanity mirror, the rising smoke just part of her reflection.

WHEN SHE CAME OUT, the two women were gone. She'd filed away the little cigarette holder and doused the stub before tossing it in the basket, then bent down to take a drink from her cupped hands, leaning over the sink. Now she walked out into the garden. Her mouth and throat thrummed with cold from the water. She had a high, bright headache coming on, as though the day were piercingly cloudless and sunny, a squinting headache; in fact, it was humid and overcast, the weather tracing a prickle of sweat at the nape of her neck.

She held up a hand, as if in salute, and searched the small crowd for Eric. He was deep into a funding pitch, speaking to a black-haired man with a greying moustache and a cane he didn't seem to need for balance. She circled behind them in a dutiful way, hoping to be only peripherally noticed. Eric was on high alert, his hands moving energetically as he spoke.

—Something to beat this man Berger at his own game. There's seven million Americans got a script for Miltown in their pocket right now. Seven *million*. And it's only a year old. Think of the possibilities. And let me tell you, Miltown's nothing. Miltown's only a start. It's a tranquilizer. He's just putting their brains to sleep.

The man shifted and tapped the cane against the shiny leather toe of his shoe. Eric drew closer:

—What if I told you that I could distill a medication that actually changes the way people feel?

Heike turned away. There were maybe thirty people on the lawn, and no children. The headache was entirely behind her eyes. She felt otherwise open and clear-minded. For a moment the situation amused her: an upstate garden party, the women all trapped on the green, their pretty shoes sinking into the soft earth, and the men all trying to sell each other things. She was ready for a drink.

A sailor-suited waitress floated by with an empty tray, on her way up to the house. There was a tug at Heike's waist that guided her around toward the tables.

—Come. You disappeared again.

Eric's face was close to hers, but he spoke so gently that Heike softened her eyes and allowed his hand to rest against her cheek. People were taking their seats, the white wooden chairs filling up.

They sat at one end of the second table, facing the water. The short-haired woman from the hallway pulled her chair in just across from Heike, but the man Heike had thought of as her husband was far off at the other table and another man took a seat with her instead. The stiffness between them explained everything: he wore a dull navy; she did not bother to adjust the line of his collar, although it was skewed. There was a fire down at the shore, and men in white jackets carried steaming pots of mussels and clams up to the lawn, their shells almost blue against the spray of lobster claws, and the sailor-girls brought bread and hot cobs of boiled corn and leaves of butter lettuce. Dolan himself paced the tables, offering a bowl of salt. He sat down finally at the head of their table, next to Heike, and used a corn skewer to stuff clams into a buttered roll.

— It's you, he said. Hasn't anyone had the sense to give you a drink? He pushed his glass along the table toward Heike. When she didn't pick it up immediately, he pushed at it again, in little staccato thrusts. Go on, now. Take mine. I seem to have an unending supply. She curved a finger around the base of the glass, and Dolan lifted a hand to wave a server over, although there wasn't anyone near them and he didn't look away from his plate.

Eric had been turned in conversation with the navy-suited husband and now leaned out across Heike's body to take a cut of butter from the dish at the end of the table.

— You'll find my wife is not a drinker, he said. He spread the butter along a stub of yellow corn and then used his knife to hook the glass away from Heike and pull it down the table. She let her finger fall away and rest on the cloth.

— Lerner, I'm mystified. Dolan took a bite off the end of the roll and chewed at the clams inside. It doesn't make sense to me, he said. That a man who works on the edge of Seneca should make a home for himself on a different lake entirely. You must love your car.

— One could say the same of you, out here in cottage country.

— Ah, but I've got the Thruway now. Thoroughly modern

living, up here. Dolan paused, fingering the sharp end of the skewer. I mean, the country roads are nice, he said. I just don't know why you'd prefer to spend your time driving when you could be in the company of your lovely wife. He put the skewer down and returned to his clam roll, picking it up in one hand. I guess I figured the doctor is never far from the asylum.

Heike looked around the table. The short-haired woman dandled a bit of lobster over top of her own roll, then shook it off her fork. Her husband leaned back in his chair. Down at the other end, she could see Renny Paulsen gesturing at a freckled woman with an empty glass in her hand. Heike turned her attention back to her plate. Paulsen's laugh expanding and carrying up over the hum of other voices.

— I'm not sure who told you where to find us, Eric said.

— Not a lot of secret mansions in New York, Dolan said. Perhaps in comic books.

A striped sleeve sailed down from above, the hand bearing a fat rocks glass, half full, no rocks. The hand went on its way. Dolan picked up the glass and held it.

— You seem happy enough to have been found, he said. There was a lick of wind, rippling the chestnut leaves above them. Dolan held the glass but didn't drink from it.

— This is a pretty piece of land you've got. Eric had taken off his jacket in the heat, and his sleeves were unbuttoned and rolled just once. He looked like a stockbroker, like they were talking cattle futures and he'd been up all night working the numbers. At the fold of his cuff there was a streak of colour. He'd been eating olives, his fingers not quite clean when he'd gone to adjust the crease. He pushed a plateful of mussel shells off onto the table with the side of his hand before continuing: But I prefer to keep my family life private. He wiped his hands on a napkin and unrolled his sleeves and buttoned them at the wrist. Enjoy your dinner, Dolan. I think I should find my wife a drink of her own.

Heike looked up. She had been sitting, poised over the orange claw on her plate as over a drafting table, a lobster cracker at the ready. From the beach came the smell of burning coals; the cook's assistant was down there, dousing the fire. She flexed the cracker, unsure of whether to set it down. She had been about to take on the task at hand.

Across the lawn they heard the slam of a door, a kind of wild shouting. Eric pushed his chair back. The waitress from the other night came out of the house, backwards along the grass, tripping over herself.

A few of the men stood up. The girl had something in her fist. It caught the light as she turned, stuck out between her fingers. There was another slam, and Heike watched as a short man crossed the lawn after her, grasping at the hand. They were the same height; from a distance it looked like a child's game of keep-away. The thrum and squeak of conversation fell low all at once, as though the lights had come down at the start of a performance. Those still in seats forgot to put aside their forks and sat spearing the air around them. Dolan was out of his chair and taking the yard at a light jog. The man reached out and held the girl by one shoulder, his open hand drawing back.

Heike turned to face the water. Her fingers curled around the cloth napkin over her knees, and she wound it into a tight cigar. The lake reached shore in little lapping tongues, the cook shovelling sand over the place where the fire had been. She expected to hear shrieking, but none came. When she turned back, most of the table was up and moving around. Dolan strolled down toward her, tossing and catching a silver thing in his hand. As he got closer, she could hear the thing jangling.

— She had his keys, he said. He swung them once around his finger by the ring, then curled them tight into his hand in a gesture of finality. He's a Buick man, but also a whisky man, and she tells me those two don't mix.

This was meant as a kind of announcement, a cue for the crowd to settle back into their supper, but the spectacle had galvanized them and people moved now from chair to chair. There was a general call for another round of drinks. The tall woman with the silver bracelet had taken off her shoes in the grass; two men nearby began to pick at the plates closest to them. Relief had thrown them into a public house cocktail hour. At the very least, there was now no lack of intimacy. The short-haired woman and her lover stood elbow to elbow; her navy-suited husband sat with his back against a tree and picked his teeth. Only Heike seemed aware of a change. Renny Paulsen wound an arm around the redhead's waist, and together they wandered off toward the willow trees.

She had expected Dolan to return to his seat, but he stood instead at the next table, talking and cracking pepper onto the cloth. In time, the plates were cleared and there were strawberries and whipped cream and brandy served in the dark, with torches. Eric slung his jacket over a new chair and accepted a cigar. Heike picked up Dolan's drink, the one he'd pushed at her, and traced a line along the shore, with its smell of wet wood and muskgrass, rounding the gardener's shed, and eventually finding her way back up to the house.

IN THE KITCHEN, there was a crew of Negroes working the sink in a line: one to suds up, one to rinse, one to dry and stack away. The drunk, Mickey, slumped in a chair by the table. He was wearing workboots under his trousers, suspenders to hold up his waist. He had a belly in the way cooks often do, with skinny, caving shoulders. He looked hungry, a man for whom the ache of wanting is never done. The girl sat near him, fanning and closing a pack of cards. In the light of the room, Heike could see she had not much of a bruise left. She had large eyes and a mouth that turned downward and sat wide across the bottom of her face. A schoolteacher's face; a mouth that belonged on an older woman. The car keys that had been the source of their earlier skirmish were clipped to a bracelet on her wrist. Heike wondered when Dolan had brought them back in to her: she had not seen him as she'd approached the house, outside with the throng. There were cigarettes on the table, and an open bottle and the dirty plates left over from the staff meal: chicken bones, bits of mashed potato stuck in the fork tines. The Negroes did not sing, as they would have in a movie.

She came out into the hall. There was a little alcove in behind the kitchen, and Heike was just leaning in for a look when she caught sight of the housekeeper from the first party. The woman was stationed in the living room, her back to the indoors, her glare now following the progress of a cocktail waitress across the veranda and down the stairs. The alcove turned out to be a kind of elevated pantry; Heike ducked inside to avoid being seen. Shelves stretched to the ceiling: wide-mouth jars of green peas and pickled eggs, and higher still, cardboard salt shakers for picnic season and tin cans of beef stew and Campbell's tomato soup. She stayed there a moment, unsure of what to do next, her body tucked into a corner cabinet stacked with glass that clinked whenever she tried to shift position.

The housekeeper made no appearance. Heike waited.

Her head throbbed. It was a dull pulse now, as though someone had wrapped a cloth around her skull and the pain could only be felt beating through this softness. To one side of the pantry there was a door. Back to the kitchen? It occurred to her that whatever this door led to, it was likely to be a better option than being found here, crouched in amongst the canned goods. She put a hand on the doorknob.

It opened, not into the kitchen as she'd imagined, but rather to a narrow room with a high, wide window giving onto one end of the lawn. There was a small bar with a few bottles and an ice bucket and a tumbler filled with bamboo swizzle sticks, and beside it, Leo Dolan himself, swizzling a drink and looking out through the glass. So he'd come inside, after all. She'd let a triangle of light from the pantry into the room, but as the door closed behind her, the shadows deepened. She had to stop and let her eyes adjust. Dolan's face was half-lit in profile. She could see the line where his cheek met his jaw and the barest trace of a beard; she guessed that he hadn't shaved since early that morning. The only light in the room was the muted glow coming through the window.

Heike hopped up higher to look out. Outside, the torches were burning and the dinner guests had arranged their chairs in small circles. The tables were clear; a few of the men were sitting down to cards. Eric was there already, his jacket on the ground beneath his seat. She came down off her toes.

— So you watched me coming.

Dolan had not turned away from the window. He nodded in agreement.

— I saw you. You went down along the water first, and then you disappeared, just there, behind the greenhouse. He held the little stick in the air over his glass and shook a few droplets off it. You came up again by the side of the lawn, near the trees.

— You don't even have a chair, Heike said. She leaned lightly against the bar with one hip.

He inclined his head toward her.

— Don't you think you ought to ask if you've a right to be here?

— I'm quite sure you would have locked the door if you wanted to be alone, she said. She set her empty glass down on the bar and ran the tongs through the ice bucket, picking and choosing. Offer me a drink. Haven't you got your little flask?

Dolan tilted a bottle of rye, but only briefly.

— Your husband will miss you, he said.

Heike played with her drink, swirling it. The liquid muted the sound of the ice.

— Will he? I think Eric doesn't want a wife.

— The good doctor? What does he want?

Heike held up her glass and let it clink softly against Dolan's.

— A little test tube, of course. She had a child's explosive laughter, one hand over her mouth. Her own flippancy surprising her.

— I heard the sales pitch, Dolan said.

— Of course you did. His work is very important to him. I can't think of anything more important to Eric.

There were some cushions scattered around. Dolan stacked them up in the bare corner, and they sat on the floor like harem girls.

— This is the best I've felt in a long time, Heike said. Except for the headache. And I almost don't mind it. She drew her legs up under her chin, her skirt all around.

— Aren't you nervous at all? Hidden away like this?

— Did you know that half your lady friends are living on little white pills? Heike leaned sideways, toward him, and made a ring around her wrist with her thumb and middle finger. They carry them in their jewels, she said.

— Like Lucrezia Borgia!

Heike dropped one hand and wrapped an arm around her knees.

— You amuse me, she said. You remind me of someone I used to know.

HE ASKED HER to tell him how it was she'd managed to walk out of Germany in the middle of a war, and she told him they'd trained her for it, unwittingly, in the *Jungmädel*. A compulsory club, as she explained it, where little girls got to live like boys: camping and playing sports, away from the watchful eyes of their parents. Himmler had disapproved.

— I'd been hiking all over the forest since I was ten years old, she said. With my rucksack. I don't think they knew they were teaching so many of us how to run away.

— Most people weren't so lucky.

— In Dresden? No.

She told him what she knew of it: that the sirens had started, and twenty minutes after that, the bombing began. Superflamers. Firebombs creating a wind tunnel in every street, a burning gust. People were blown back into their houses, like being blown into a torch. Adults burnt down to the size of children. Pieces of bodies, arms and legs. She'd had to imagine all of this: the details she read about later, in books and magazines.

She'd read an account in *Life* magazine, much later, in New York. Before that, she'd read about it in *Signal*.

— But you weren't there.

— No. No, three days before, my mother sent me to the bakery to see what they had left. She told me not to come home. She told me to keep walking, out of Germany, to Switzerland.

Her mother had hidden false papers and a small roll of money in a breadbasket, under a clean cloth, a week before. Hoping for any chance. The papers to use at checkpoints. The checkpoints to be avoided at all costs. There had been some bombing in the railyards already, Heike said, once in the fall and once in January. So they knew it was coming.

— She wanted us all to go, years earlier, Heike said. But it's not so easy, you see, to give up your home.

He'd been in Europe at the same time, he said. They'd dropped him from a plane over Sicily in 1943, but by the end of the war he was laid up in a British military hospital.

— Show me your scar, Heike said, and Dolan pulled his shirt from his trousers. She ran a finger along the mended places. It must have been hot in Italy, she said.

— Things get infected.

— And you didn't have a sweetheart here waiting for you?

He said he'd stayed in Europe after the war. First in France— Avignon—and then farther west in Spain. He came home to finish his education, but it didn't take.

— So this is how you met your wife, she said. In Barcelona.

— I met my wife in a television studio in California, Dolan said. She was someone else's wife at the time.

— It's no way to start a romance, Heike said.

— Didn't do much for my career, either.

Dolan got up to refill his glass and stretched a long arm out for hers. Heike reached it up to him without leaving her cushion, then, thinking better of it, got to her feet and peered out the window. Nervous, after all, that Eric might be looking for her.

There was a neat crack as Dolan uncapped a fresh bottle.

— So how'd you end up married to the mental?

Heike twisted her body toward him but kept her eyes on Eric at his card table outside.

— What?

— Where'd you meet the brain doctor?

— I lived in a convent in Switzerland, she said. After the war. I was sixteen years old, and they dressed me as a boy so I could drive back and forth to town to make deliveries. We had a big garden, and grapevines. I drove vegetables across the border to Austria, and sometimes even to Germany. The priests handed them out. The war was over, but the winters were very bad, two or three times in a row.

She turned cautiously away from the window and sank back onto her cushion. Perhaps it was better to stay out of sight altogether.

— People had no food, she said. There were no potatoes. In Austria there was a man who made a business selling the leftover breakfasts of French soldiers. He had almost a shop.

— They let you drive a truck? Dolan stood over her, a drink in each hand. There was just a crack of light showing under the door, from the kitchen. The glow from outside filtered in through the high window and made the glasses shimmer.

— The nuns taught me.

— I'm not making fun of you.

— Give me a truck, Heike said. I will drive it right now.

— I wish I had a truck, Dolan said.

He sat down cross-legged, and she took her drink from his hand. His shirt was still untucked where he'd pulled it up earlier. There was a noise outside the door, footsteps in the hall or else the clack of jars being moved about in the kitchen. Heike raised her eyebrows, but Dolan waved it off.

He said he was surprised she got across the border so easily, and she said nothing was easy.

— But it was one thing we could do. Maybe a small thing.

In the bottom corner of the American zone, she met a pilot. His job was mostly flying supplies between American bases.

— It was only 1946, she said. They weren't really supposed to speak to us. Germans, you know.

— But he thought you were Swiss.

— Maybe in the beginning. But at the end of the year, the rules all changed, anyway. I left the nuns, she said. We got married in January, in Munich, and from there we took the train to Vienna. He had three days leave, and the American zone was there, too.

It wasn't until they were at the train station that she realized she'd left something behind, in his room: the billfold her mother had given her when she left Dresden. Tucked in with the false papers, there had also been a childhood photograph, Heike and her sister, together.

— It was a night train, she said, and we'd booked the sleeper car. We had a first-class compartment. But I had to go back. It was a picture of Lena, my only one.

By the time they got back to the station, the train was gone. They sat up half the night and took the next train in the morning. There were no compartments and only one seat.

— So he stood all the way from Munich to Vienna. Her eyes

flitted up to a high corner of the room; after a moment, she looked back at Dolan. Hours and hours. With his hand up here, she said. She lifted her own hand, as though pulling a bell. Holding on to the little rail.

Outside, there were a few whoops and calls. Not laughter, exactly. The sound of someone winning their hand, gin all around. Heike glanced sharply at the window.

— Lerner as gallant, Dolan said. It's not what I might have guessed.

— Oh, no. She crossed her legs and leaned forward, hands on knees. That's not Eric. She rocked back again and drew her hands up through her hair. He died, you see. My first husband. After a year. And not even flying! Imagine, you fly a plane back and forth across a war for four years, and in the end, a car hits you in the street. *Bam!* she said.

There was a little silence, her nostalgia and the sweetness of the previous moment gone.

— I'm sorry.

She nodded but didn't say anything. Dolan waited for her to speak. She stared straight ahead of her.

— But, she said. That's what made me think Americans were good.

— Makes sense to me.

Her eyes flicked up to meet his.

— Harry, she said. She pronounced it *Hah-ry*. That was his name. Harry Foster.

— So you were Heike Foster.

— Only for a short time.

He leaned toward her, but it was a cautious thing.

— Did they treat you well? The army, I mean.

She didn't answer, and after a time he tried again.

— I mean, if you were living on a U.S. Army base. Where, in Munich? Must have been strange, to be back in Germany as an American. He tried to catch her eye. They're usually very good to the widows.

Heike nodded again once or twice, then stopped and looked up at him. Her vision felt watery, and she was embarrassed.

— That's just it, she said. The surge of brashness that had catapulted her into the room was gone now. I don't know. I don't know where we lived before the accident. I suppose it must have been on an army base, yes. But I don't remember it. I don't have a picture of it in my mind. There are a lot of things I don't remember from that time. After the accident, I mean.

— So you were hit, too.

— Yes. Yes, I was. Or I think I was. She turned her head, as though the answer were written down somewhere just to her left. And then . . . And then somehow I went back to the convent. When I met Eric, he was studying in Switzerland. He was my doctor, for a little while. I came across the ocean with him on the boat.

— Ah. Dolan downed the rest of his drink. And the rest is history, he said. Your Harry, he didn't want children? Or I suppose there wasn't time.

She was still for a moment. Her head had stopped its pulsing, but the pain was there, dully, a band that stretched under her eye sockets from temple to temple. The ice in her glass was all melted, and she stirred the bit of water with a finger. She had the sense that she was forgetting something. There was something she was supposed to do; something she was meant to be thinking about. She sucked on the finger thoughtfully.

— I have a son, she said. Then, after a moment: Daniel. I can't stay here much longer.

THERE WERE SHOUTS OUTSIDE.

From the kitchen, they heard the scraping sound of chairs pushed back quickly. The sky looked softer than it had a few moments ago, the topmost branches of the trees sharply black against the blueish glass of the window. Neither of them stood up.

— Do you think he's hit her again? Heike said finally.

Dolan got up on his feet to take a look.

— It's Lerner, he said.

Heike brought a hand up to cover her mouth, then let it drop again, the hand wrapping across her body and coming to rest just under her breast. It did not occur to her to stand up. She could feel the soft pressure, almost liquid, of her heart under her ribs.

— How long have I been here?

— I'm afraid he's quite upset.

Dolan looked down to where she was sitting.

— I'd better get out there, Heike said. For another moment neither of them moved, then Dolan stepped forward and extended an arm, to help her up.

She came down through the kitchen and out into the garden on her own, but Eric was already gone. The car was gone. The handful of remaining guests stood around, a staggery look to them. Dolan came out of the house and went to pick up the card table where it had been pushed onto its side. Renny Paulsen smacked him sharply across the shoulders, and Dolan turned with his elbow drawn back, but he only pumped Paulsen's hand. The evening had been a success.

Heike stood in the grass, with the dew seeping into the toes of her shoes. Around the front of the house, the last few cars started up. The sweep of headlights against the new greyness. There was a suspicion of dawn. No real light, but a softness to the dark. She thought about walking down to the water, wading in, her dress floating out from her body on all sides.

Dolan appeared at the side wall.

— Are you coming?

— What do you mean?

He had his hat ready in one hand, a straw Milan with a black cherry band wide around the brim.

— I need to get you back to your own bed, he said.

Heike stepped forward through the damp grass.

— Before the neighbours get ideas, she said.

— Something like that.

9.

They peeled back out of the drive in the red Eldorado. Heike had asked him to roll the top down so that she could see the night sky ending all around them, and the wind whipped at their shoulders and her hair came down and flicked around her face. She kept tucking it back, behind her ears. They weren't driving particularly fast. Dolan was quiet.

Then:

— Will this be a lot of trouble for you?

— That he couldn't find me, or that you're driving me home?

— Any of it, Dolan said. Yes. All that.

Heike drew a pin from her hair and then another. They weren't holding anyway. She held them out over the road and let them fly away in the wind.

— Yes, she said. Her hair blew across her eyes, and she pushed it back.

They were driving west to Cayuga across the top of Owasco, the smaller lake somewhere to the south of them. A long enough trip: Heike had the better part of an hour to figure out what to do when she got home. She could hear water before she saw the bridge. As they were crossing, she asked him if this was the tip of the lake, but Dolan said it was a river that ran down into it, the river also called Owasco. They were driving through the town, Auburn. There was a stainless-steel diner car over the river, too, propped on stilts. A neon sign out front called it not a diner but a *dinerant,* the second *n* for some reason unlit. Heike folded over to take off her shoes, and when she came up again the town was gone. She curled up on the seat with her feet tucked underneath her skirt and leaned on the door, one arm outside the car. Dolan reached over and pressed down the lock button.

— So, she said. Are you going back to California?

— Undecided.

— Your friend Paulsen says all you do is fight, fight, fight.

— With him? I wouldn't bother. He's got a lousy left hook.

Heike played with the lock button, pulling it up—*click*—then pushing it down again.

— But the network is your boss, no?

— No.

— I see.

She pushed the lock button down into place a final time and leaned out the window and looked at herself in the side mirror. Dolan kept his silence for another minute or so.

— He's talking about the Till story, he said. Kid from Chicago who got murdered visiting his Mississippi relations. I wrote it up as a play for the *Steel Hour*. Not just murdered, he said. Not just lynched. Atrocious things. But the town stood up and protected its own. The very act of violence was the symbol of this, this social evil. He paused for a moment, and his eyes moved up to the rear-view mirror and back down again. The point of the thing was to show exactly that: it doesn't matter how bad your villain is; if he's yours, the whole town will circle the wagons. I knew they'd never let me write it black and white; they wanted nothing to do with it. So I made it about an old shopkeeper, a Jew, and that was still no good. I kept changing it. By the time I was done, it was some unidentifiable foreigner in an unnamed town, and it was lukewarm, it was nothing, it was a bunch of shouting with nothing at all to be shouting about. And still at the end of the day, there they were, running around the set, pulling the Coca-Cola bottles off the tables. Dolan slapped the steering wheel with one hand. Because Coca-Cola reads South, they said. The viewer might figure it out.

— They're afraid of a bomb, do you think? The way they bombed those churches in the wintertime, in Alabama?

— They're afraid the show's going to bomb, that's what they're afraid of. No one's going to set fire to a television studio full of blond starlets.

There was a little moment of quiet.

— They can't take the heat, Heike said.

— In Los Angeles? It's murder.

— In the South. That's why they drink so much Coca-Cola.

She tipped her head back against the seat and pressed her lips together hard. It was a gesture of restraint, but she looked at him, delighted, all the same.

— Continental on the outside, Dolan said. Wiseass on the inside.

— I put it all behind me, she said. What are you writing lately?

— What makes you think I'm writing at all?

— You're not? This is all you do, drink whisky in your hidden room and drive Continental ladies around the countryside?

— There's a script, he said. Sitting on the shelf at Desilu. A pilot. You know what that means?

— I'm afraid I'm not really much . . .

— For television. So I gather. A pilot is episode one. It's the first show in a series, a series I'm thinking of. Something I'd control. *The Mind's Eye.* That's what I'm calling it. Many stories, a different story every week: fables, moral quandaries, things that can't be explained.

— Like a fairy tale? Is it for children?

— I guess it could be. But I think it might also be frightening. Or some of the stories, anyway.

— Some children's stories are very frightening.

— I guess you Germans know enough about fairy tales.

— My mother told me so many stories when I was growing up. We never had books; just stories. Once you learn the rhythm, you can make them up yourself. I do. It's easy.

Then:

— Daniel's favourite stories aren't even from Grimm. They're from me. She thought about this, and her mouth curved. Not really a smile. It's how we learn to understand ourselves, she said finally. By telling stories. So they must be frightening. You see that.

— I see that. You might even say the best stories all start with a girl alone in the woods, Dolan said. I feel like I've heard that somewhere before.

— You remember!

— I remember. This one's about time, though. The pilot episode, I mean. Someone who can appear years after he died, then disappear again.

They had reached the top of Cayuga. Dolan turned the car

south down the lake. Heike turned to look at him, and the little fingers of light that had been behind them now came into view, just beyond his jawline. On her side of the car, the trees lining the water stood heavy and tangled.

— I should have offered to let you drive, he said.

— No, Heike said. You are too afraid of me. She laughed, then mimicked steering with both hands, humming a little tune before dropping one to pull sharply on an invisible gear shift. I would get us there much faster, she said.

They drove along without speaking, aware now of how close she was to home. Heike turned more firmly to the window. After a while she asked him to slow down.

— I thought you liked fast drivers, he said.

— Yes. But I'm looking for something. She leaned on the edge of her door, into the darkness. Can you turn here? Just for a little while.

The car came almost to a stop before turning. It was a dirt road, pitted from the rains, with a thin stream running not far from it. You could hear the movement of the stream but couldn't see it. After a few minutes Dolan asked where they were going.

— Just here. Where the trees are.

The key clicked in the ignition, and there was a new stillness.

— You must need a lot of stories, Heike said. She didn't look at him, her face lit in outline only by what was left of the moon. It was still mostly dark in the woods.

Dolan turned his body toward her.

— Got something for me?

— Can it be anything?

— Sky's the limit. Time, space. Whatever's unknown.

— You see? You do want to make people afraid.

— Maybe. Sometimes. I want to make people stop. I want them to think.

— What about a ghost?

— A ghost story, sure. But there's got to be more to it than that. The ghost has to connect, has to link up to a present situation.

— A ghost story, for the television.

He turned back to the wheel, both feet flat down, and looked out his own window for a moment before looking back at her. What light there was caught the light of her hair, the line of her cheekbone, her jaw. He set his hand back on the ignition but didn't turn the key.

— You're laughing. That's fine. That's alright. I'll take my lick. The stories are mine, and I'll write them the way I want them.

— I'm not laughing at you.

— The idea has promise.

She lifted her face.

— You want me to tell you a ghost story?

— Only if it's a good one.

Heike got out of the car and shut the door, walking forward to the edge of the gully. Her feet were still bare, but the gravel of the road gave way here to softer stuff, the ground sandy and mixed with pine needles and fallen leaves. The little house stood somewhere below them, maybe two hundred feet down, and behind it, the stream disappeared and opened out into the pond. The raft, too, would be there, although she could not see any of it in the darkness. There was a softer thud, Dolan's own door closing.

— I keep thinking someone must live here, Heike said. But there's never anyone in the house when I go looking.

She stepped back and against him, and he laid a hand high up on her back, between her shoulder blades. Almost brotherly, she thought. They stood looking down into the gully until her eyes adjusted and she was sure for a moment that she could make out every detail, the shingles overlapping on the roof. The light changed again, and the shingles turned to aspen leaves, shimmering like dark coins. She was aware that Dolan was watching her.

— You must have been terrified, he said. Walking so far all alone. In the war, I mean.

He let his hand slip down her arm until just their fingertips were touching.

— I wasn't alone. He jarred a little at that, and Heike leaned in toward him, a reassurance. I had my little sister with me, she said. Lena.

— From the photograph?

— You see why I couldn't leave it behind. I pulled her by the hand to the bakery that day. While we escaped. She rode on my back.

She'd promised her mother. If she had to leave, she'd wanted to save Lena as well.

— But I didn't save her.

— She starved, Dolan said.

— No. No, we were hungry, but she was okay. I kept her quiet when the soldiers came. I put one hand over her mouth, and another over her eyes.

They'd moved cautiously, to avoid the fighting and because Lena was so small. It was March and the nights were still cold.

— We were almost in the Allgäu, and I was afraid all the time that we would accidentally knock into the Austrian border. So I made sure we kept going up, up, to avoid this. We were high up in the hills, and far below we could see the lake.

She meant the Bodensee, Lake Konstanz, and Switzerland to the other side of it. Heike aimed in this direction, keeping the lake always in sight. They had been walking for almost two months when Lena disappeared.

— I looked for seven days for Lena in the mountains, and then for her body, frozen or fallen off the trail, she said. But I never found her. I never saw her again.

A few weeks later Heike crossed Lake Konstanz in the night. There is an upper arm of that lake that is narrow enough to row across, if you can steal a boat. Even for a girl. In Switzerland she found the convent in a valley and collapsed.

Dolan said nothing for a moment. There was a susurration from somewhere down below, hidden away.

— Do you think the house is whispering to us? Heike said.

But it was only leaves. The aspens rustling papery in the breeze off the pond. She turned and let him lead her back to the car. He opened the driver's side door. Heike slid in first and linked her hands in her lap.

— You must find me entirely bizarre, she said.

— No. He got into the car but didn't pull the door shut. Not yet. He was half-turned toward her, one arm along the seatback, as though he might look over his shoulder to throw the car into reverse. His hand resting nearby but not quite touching her; she imagined she could feel the heat from his fingers. There, just at her neck, her collarbone.

— I have a son, she said. You remember I told you that.

— It's no way to start a romance.

— I could say, Don't start the car, or, Start the car and let's drive on. We'll keep driving, into the morning, we'll go right to New York and eat pastries for breakfast, out of a paper bag. I won't even put on my shoes.

— Is that all you want? Dolan said.

— But I have a son, she said. So I have to go back.

They were parked close enough to the gully that she could see where the tree roots came out of the earth and the land dipped down. The green roof of the house was down there, and the pond in its silence. Something shifted beneath her, the ground dropping out. Daniel's body, curling off the raft, sure as a heavy stone. She didn't even have to shut her eyes to see them: Dani, his skinny chest in the sun, and the girl stepping off the raft and skipping across the pond. Her feet sinking only an inch into the water, as though there were something there, under the surface, carrying her forward.

Standing on the shore in the storm as Heike paddled away, her hair wet and matted, her stare fixed, unfaltering.

A quick disequilibrium, the world flipping backwards. She turned to Dolan, her hand catching his shirt front as though to right herself. Something solid.

— You remember when I met you, in the greenhouse?

— I was drunk, Dolan said. You told me so.

— You held onto me, she said. You put your hand around my back, where my skin was bare. Just here. She arched forward a little and curved one arm behind her, resting the hand on the small of her back. Can you do that again, she said.

WHEN THEY DROVE BACK out to the road, the sky had gone lavender and bright all around them, and they turned down through

Union Springs with the sun burning through the mist. In the village there was a bundle of newspapers sitting on the curb outside the bakery. Heike leaned forward and switched on the radio. It was almost too late for deer, but they saw one, just off in the woods, near the narrow road down to the house. The car rolled by, the gravel crunching and Fats Domino laid down over top of that, and the deer didn't run but stopped chewing and froze, waiting them out. It was a doe, or else young; Heike didn't know.

— Here, she said. Let me out just here.

She didn't want his car in the driveway, the added problems that would come with that. As she opened the door, a glint of light caught in the mirror and she thought of how she'd once imagined the house on fire, driving home with Eric, that instant fear. Daniel locked inside. It had been starlight then.

She watched the Eldorado disappear before turning to walk, her shoes dangling from one hand, down the drive. It was the moment before true sunrise, oddly quiet, without the birdsong usual for that hour. There were three pearl buttons at the side of her waist, and she'd missed one in the woods, straightening herself up. She fingered it now.

The light flashed again.

At the side of the house, she saw two cars: Eric's hardtop green Buick and a black-and-white state patrol car with a single red emergency light mounted in the centre of the roof. The light spun around and around slowly; the flash Heike had caught in the mirror.

— Daniel, she said.

The front door swung open, and Eric came out onto the porch. The cop followed just behind him in his uniform and hat. He was grey-haired but civil-looking, neither fat nor thin, a man who'd spent years working with his hands but now mainly sat behind the wheel of a car.

— Aha! This your wife? the cop said. Ma'am? Are you alright?

Heike flew up onto the porch.

— Calm down, ma'am. Slow down. Your husband's got you all looked after. I'm only asking if you're alright.

— Dani! Where is Daniel? Heike looked from the cop to Eric and back again. Where is my son?

— I can take it from here. Eric put a hand on the door as if to hold it shut, but then flicked it open for her after all. He was talking not to Heike, but to the police officer.

Heike heard the screen door close gently behind her. The air in the house was still. Back in Eric's office, the phonograph was playing, and from where she stood in the hall Heike recognized the strange echo of the same Fats Domino record she'd just heard in the car. There was a shift, a moment of dizziness, and she caught herself against the kitchen door frame.

The girl, Rita, was in there, wiping down the table with a wet cloth. Seeing Heike, she straightened up and held her hands, with the cloth in them, behind her back.

— Where is he, Rita?

The table was wet where she'd been cleaning it; not just streaky, but puddled, as though she'd pulled the cloth from the dishwater and forgotten to wring it out. Rita stood very still.

— I don't know, ma'am.

— What do you mean you don't know? How can you say *I don't know*?

Heike ran to the back of the house, the music growing louder and then waning as she passed Eric's office, the door standing open. She didn't call for Daniel as she had other times. Her feet sank into the soft carpet in the white room. The French doors to the back porch also stood open, a coffee pot on the table outside. She ran her fingers along the wall to steady herself and pushed back out of the room and up the stairs, the rooms clean and bare, her bed made tightly, the coverlet pressed and laid flat and tucked neatly around the pillows. Heike did not call his name, but she whispered it: *Daniel*.

Downstairs, the screen door hinge creaked as it opened and shut. A car engine started up, and there was the sound of tires against the gravel drive, the policeman taking his leave.

— Dani!

She yelled it out.

The window was open in the bedroom, and the sheers puffed out and sucked back against it, a breath taken and released. The figurine, the little Dresden girl, stood upright on the vanity, her reflection repeating in the three-way mirror. Heike stood in the doorway. Her head was cloudy but did not hurt anymore. There was a noise she couldn't get rid of, a rushing sound that started and ended and started again. She went halfway down the stairs. The record had ended, back in Eric's office. The static sound just the needle hitting the centre label and bumping back and hitting centre again. She saw that Eric was at the bottom of the steps, looking up. Waiting for her. Heike wrapped her hand around the banister and squeezed.

— Eric. She said the name in a soft way. Eric, please. Where is he?

He held up a hand, two fingers beckoning to her. She did not know if they were alone, if the girl was still in the kitchen. She went down another three steps and stopped again and let her eyes drift up and down the lower hall, as though Daniel might suddenly appear, dirty from playing outside, his bare feet making no sound on the carpet.

— Eric, she said.

He made a movement with his head, a shake, almost imperceptible. A tight "No."

— Now look what you've done, he said.

WAIT UNTIL DARK

There are elements of time and space more infinite than we can know. Beyond the boundaries of our waking hours lies another place, limited only by the roiling expanse of the subconscious mind. Somewhere between intuition and imagination, between the darkness of dread and the bright scythe of salvation, the true nature of a man's fear is made manifest: Here, in the shadowland we call the Mind's Eye.
— Leo Dolan's opening narration, season 1,
The Mind's Eye (1959 1963)

I went down fighting, as most television writers do, thinking, in a strange, oblique, philosophical way that better say something than nothing.
— Rod Serling, creator of *The Twilight Zone*

The Bone Flute

There once was a King who so loved to hunt that it was all he thought about morning, noon, and night. One day he was hunting in a thick wood when he caught sight of a Hind the likes and size of which he had never before seen, and he pursued the deer so eagerly that none of his men were able to keep up to him. When evening fell, the King stopped and stood stock-still in the forest, looking around him, and he realized he had lost his way. The Hind appeared then from between the trees, and as the King raised his bow and took aim, she fell on her knees and supplicated him to spare her.

"I have been enchanted by a terrible witch," the Hind said. "And if you kill me, you will never find your way out of this forest again. But if you spare my life, I will show you the way out of the woods and your own life will be saved."

It was growing cold and dark, and although the King wanted nothing better than to mount the Hind's graceful head upon his wall at home, he agreed to this condition. Secretly, though, he thought: Ho-ho! I will let her show me the way out of the forest, and as soon as I see the edge of the trees I will raise my bow and shoot her.

The Hind led the King through the darkest part of the forest until at last he was able to see a glimmer of light beyond the trees. When he was sure that the edge of the wood was in sight, he drew his bow and again took aim, but as he did so, the trees closed in around him and the Hind turned into a witch herself, and the King could see that he had been caught in his treachery. He began to beg for mercy, but his cries fell upon deaf ears until at last the witch said she would let him go on one condition only: that he trade places with his only child, a little girl of such pure heart and pale beauty that her parents had named her Gretchen, which means "little pearl." No sooner had the King agreed than he found himself back in his own castle, but all that greeted him was the weeping and wailing of his wife and her ladies-in-waiting, for his daughter was indeed lost and gone.

For her part, Gretchen grew up wandering the forest and cooking and cleaning for the witch. One day, the witch trapped a Golden Bird with a broken wing, and when she brought it home, Gretchen could see that the witch meant to eat it. In one corner of the little house stood a trunk that was so white it might have been carved out of bone, with many books of witchcraft piled upon it. When the witch went out into the forest, Gretchen urged the Golden Bird to hide in the white trunk.

But, alas! The witch overheard this plan and dragged Gretchen, with the Bird in her arms, out to the chopping block, where she raised her axe and chopped off the Bird's head in one swift motion. Gretchen still held on to the Bird tightly, and when the axe came down, it took not only the Bird's golden head, but Gretchen's finger as well. The witch took up the Bird's body and went off to the house to roast the thing over the fire, but the head lay on the ground next to poor Gretchen's finger, and it spoke to her:

"I am all but gone now from this world. But take your finger where it lies on the ground and make from the bone a little flute, and you

shall always hear my voice. Be careful to hide the flute well, for I shall guide your escape from the witch, and if she finds out, you will never get away."

With that, the Bird shut its eyes, never to open them again. Gretchen dried and peeled the flesh from her own finger, and carved from the bone a little flute. This took many days.

As soon as she put the flute to her lips, she heard the Bird's voice:

"Quickly, now! Hide me away, and when the witch falls asleep tonight, I will help you to escape." Gretchen did as she was told, and hid the bone flute away in the white trunk.

Then Gretchen started the fire and made a heavy stew, rich with red wine, and that night the witch ate heartily and fell asleep in her chair. When she was sure the witch was deep in her slumber, Gretchen opened the trunk and put the flute to her lips.

"Do not forsake me and I will never forsake you," sang the bone flute as it led her out of the house, but they had gone no more than one hundred feet when they heard the witch coming after them.

"Surely she has seen my footprints!" Gretchen said. She hurried back to the house and hid the flute once again in the white trunk.

The next night, Gretchen started the fire again and made another rich stew, and once again the witch's eyes grew heavy as soon as she had eaten. No sooner was she fast asleep than Gretchen opened up the white trunk and the bone flute jumped into her hands.

"Do not forsake me and I will never forsake you," it sang. "This time you must put your boots on backwards, so that the witch sees only a set of footprints leading to the house and not away from it." But they had gone no more than two hundred feet when Gretchen stumbled and the bone flute fell out of her hands, and they once again heard the witch coming behind them.

"Surely this time she has heard us fall to the ground," Gretchen said, and she scurried back to the house so as not to be caught. Once again, she hid the flute in the white trunk.

On the third night, Gretchen lit the fire and cooked a really wonderful meal, and for a third time the witch ate heartily and began to doze before she had even left the table. As soon as she was truly asleep, Gretchen opened the white trunk and the bone flute jumped out.

"Do not forsake me and I will never forsake you," sang the flute. "This time you must swallow me whole." So Gretchen swallowed the flute, which was, of course, really her own finger, and tiptoed out of the house and began to run to the edge of the forest. When she was able to see the glimmer of sunrise beyond the trees, she stopped to cough the flute up, but when she opened her mouth, the flute sang, "Run faster! The witch is close behind us!"

So Gretchen ran along until she could see the light of the sun shining through the leaves, and there she stopped, meaning to cough up the bone, but the flute sang, "Run faster! Even now I can hear the witch's footsteps gaining speed!"

So Gretchen ran along until she reached the very edge of the wood and could feel the long grass and soft buttercups beneath her feet. Just as she was about to pass the last tree in the forest, the witch appeared before her.

"Do not forsake me and I will never forsake you," sang the bone flute. "Now you must cough me out!"

Then Gretchen coughed up the flute, but as it came forth, it turned into a thousand ravens. The ravens fell upon the witch and pecked her to pieces in the forest—but Gretchen ran out into the meadow, and if she is not dead yet, she lives there in the sunshine still.

1951

Why don't you tell me where we are.

The doctor sat in a stiff chair set by the window. He'd offered her the softer one, its velvet rose upholstery only a little worn. This had seemed gentlemanly in the moment but now Heike squinted, facing him. The sun slanting in at an afternoon angle. She put a hand up to shield her eyes.

— We are in the *Kloster*, of course.

— Now, Heike.

— In Thurgau. In Switzerland. Better?

— How do you know this? He paused, watching her eyes shift slightly. His face lightened. Humour me a little, Heike. I have this script to go through, you know. The university is terribly rigorous about these things.

— Where else would I be?

— That's a fair answer.

He reorganized the papers in his lap. Usually he had a pencil, but today he did not.

She turned her head to look around the room, her eyes making little spots until they adjusted to the lower light away from the window. The door to the hall rested against its frame without being quite shut. She could see the latch where it lapped at the strike plate like a tongue.

— There was an accident, she said. That's what you want me to talk about, isn't it?

— That's what I'm trying to help you with, yes.

— I'm sorry, I don't remember. I still don't remember.

— You came here to recover. He got up from his chair and walked over to shut the door tight. It closed with a click, and he turned and leaned against it, but it was a casual gesture. It's — alright if you don't remember.

Heike lifted her face.

— It's not alright. I was all of a sudden a widow. How can I forget this?

He came back across the room, and she stood up to meet him. He had a habit of standing over her chair that made her nervous.

— No, don't get up. Here—

He took her hand and tugged gently downward, but as she sank back into her seat he crouched beside her. Still nervous-making, but not entirely unpleasant.

To one side of the room, she could see her bed with its white sheets and the white curtain to pull around for privacy. They had housed her this time not with the novices, as when she had first arrived here during the war, but in a larger room with three elderly nuns.

— Because you were so sick.

— I was terribly sick. I almost died. So they gave me a bed here, where it's quieter.

Only it wasn't quiet. One of the old sisters often screamed out, and another sometimes wept in her sleep.

What she knew of the accident: The car had come out of nowhere. They were crossing the street, her arms were full of something, flowers or floury rolls from the bakery, she couldn't remember which. He'd died before she woke up. Most likely he died when his head hit the ground. Her injuries were minor; she was concussed. When the ambulance arrived, they found her sitting in the road, his head in her lap. A lot of blood; she remembered that part. Her skirt soaked through. She could not stop crying, and they sent her away from the hospital and brought her here, to a place she knew and a doctor she didn't.

To begin with, she had not been able to remember returning to the convent at all. They met twice a week; then three times. The doctor was helping her to fill in the blanks.

He let go of her hand and patted it where it lay in her lap. She leaned toward him, just a little.

— Doctor Lerner.

— Eric.

She paused.

— Eric.

Now they met every day. He came to see her on Sunday afternoons, and brought her presents: chocolate, or squares of pastry with marzipan filling. The last time, a collection of fairy stories, hard-bound, with coloured illustrations.

— Have you been doing any reading?

— Sometimes I make up my own stories, she said. Reading still hurts my head.

From the hall there was the sound of a tea trolley passing by, and Heike paused, waiting to see if it would stop, if the door would swing open, but it didn't.

— That's not so useful, Heike.

She glanced at the door again. He lifted a hand to touch her face.

— Sometimes we need a new start.

WHEN IT WAS TIME to leave, he watched her settle herself into the back of the car, then shut the door behind her before climbing into the driver's seat, one arm thrown over the seatback as he shifted into reverse.

She studied his face. He was capable of such kindness, but now he was looking past her. Her red woollen coat was folded in two on the bench next to her—she could see the edge of the velvet hood tucked away inside, and the pinpoint gleam of rhinestones set into each round button. There was a breeze, and she brushed a piece of hair away from her face, where it was playing at her lip. The car spun softly out to meet the road. Eric turned back to face the wheel.

There was something in her hand, the wood worn smooth, and she turned it over and over in her fingers. When she looked down, she saw it was a little cross that she was holding.

— From over your bed, Eric said. He'd been watching her in the rear-view mirror. She could see only his eyes and part of his brow. We took it down for you. Remember?

The brow furrowed slightly, but the eyes were warm enough. Heike ran her thumb up and down the vertical bar of the little cross.

— There's a lot of travel ahead, he said. Maybe this wasn't a good idea.

He often told her how much she worried him.

— Don't say that. I'll feel better when I've had a sleep. I promise. Let's talk about something else.

The trees on either side of them went by in flashes. She sat back and let her hands fall into her lap, the cross also falling, caught in her skirt, in the dip where her thighs came together. They drove on for a moment, Heike looking out the window. It had begun to rain very slightly. There was a split-rail fence separating the road from the field, and on the other side of it a few horses milled about, undaunted in the wet.

Eric turned the wheel, and the car rolled to a stop on the dirt shoulder.

— Tell me again.

— I've told you twice already.

— I want to make sure you remember it.

— But it's silly. Let's talk about where we're going instead.

— Once more, tell me. Reassure a man.

Heike swung her feet up onto the bench next to her and slid down to rest, her head in her hand, elbow propped against the red coat as though it were a pillow.

— It was two weeks ago, April third. For flowers, I had lily of the valley, because they were your mother's favourite and you found so many growing in the woods behind the chapel. Father Alphonse married us.

Here she paused a moment, and her head tilted a little in concentration. In the mirror, he lifted his chin.

— I wish sometimes I wasn't a doctor.

— Eric.

— You have no recollection. You were so sick.

There was another car approaching, dark blue, but it didn't

slow down as it passed. To the side of the road the meadow stretched out long and wide and greenish-gold. Eric turned the engine off and twisted in his seat to look at her properly. Heike shifted and lay back flat.

— It's a long trip, Eric said.

— I know. She reached up and ran a fingernail along the car's headliner. Somehow I feel I know exactly what the boat will look like, she said. I can picture it.

The little cross had spilled onto the floor.

— I'll give you something to help you sleep. Then it won't feel so long. Eric leaned over to the passenger seat and unclipped the latch on his bag.

Heike turned her head to look at him.

— And what about my suitcase? You must have sent it ahead to the boat. Did you? It's not in the trunk?

Eric held a glass ampoule up to the light and shook it. Heike sat up.

— Oh no, Eric. Not again. Just give me a pill. I'm really so much better now.

— Who's the doctor, me or you? He pulled the liquid from the ampoule into a syringe and flicked the tip with a fingernail. What do you want your suitcase for, anyhow? He turned in his seat and held out a hand as though offering her a dance. You know I'll always take care of you, Heike. We'll buy you some new dresses when we get to America. A whole closetful of new dresses. You won't recognize yourself.

Heike's hands stayed folded in her lap.

— Be a good girl and give me your arm now.

She inched forward a little, and Eric took her hand, pulling it toward him.

— It's just that it's mine, Eric.

She looked down. Her arm stretched forward, her hand in Eric's, the pale inside of her elbow opening up clean and sound-less. Eric rubbed it with a bit of cotton. He took a handker-chief from his breast pocket and tied it tight around the arm. It was a white handkerchief, silk, with blue anchors on it. Heike thought: Anchors. Because of the boat.

— It's just that it's mine, Heike said again. So I'll be glad to have it back. She looked from the arm back to Eric. My white suitcase. When we get to New York.

10.

1 9 5 6

When she woke, Heike could not tell if it was early or late, and she lay blinking for a few moments and looking around her. Somewhere it seemed to her an axe was falling, a steady rhythm: the soft *thunk*, and then the *shush* of the cut wood being swept away off the chopping block. The sound was both near and muted. Down in the yard, maybe, only the wood must be half rotten to make so dull a noise. No good to burn.

She expected her pillow to be white, and white sheets on the bed, and a white curtain to pull close around at night, and she expected the bells from the convent chapel and wondered that they had not woken her—or if they had, but she had been so deeply asleep that the sound did not register. But after a moment her eyes focused, and Heike saw that the pillow was robin's egg blue, and the coverlet a deeper navy, and there was no curtain save for the sheers over the window, and the sound was not an axe, after all, but the breeze as it came in, batting at the blinds. The blinds swinging inward and then falling back against the frame.

Thunk.

Shush.

She pushed up on her elbows and worked the pillows higher. Her limbs were elastic. Her limbs were wet rope.

There was a cut-glass tumbler on the nightstand with a single deep red rock rose floating in it, the stem stretching straight down like a rough ladder to the tabletop beneath. She felt for a moment as though she had been travelling. The room was strange to her. She felt she was supposed to know it.

She turned slightly to the left and reached out for something by instinct. Not something. Someone. Daniel, so that he wouldn't get too close to the edge and roll off the bed. Her fingers following the coverlet's quilted stitches like text, like words in a reader.

She blinked. Downstairs she could hear a kind of commotion, shouting. Eric's voice, a controlled rumble, and then a woman, too, the higher register cutting in crisp and distinct:

— How could you? Why would you keep this to yourself?

This is what had woken her, this argument. She remembered now. She had been dreaming of the bed by the window in the noviciate sleeping quarters, a dream that held on.

On the vanity, her little bottles and powders were all laid out, the silver-plate brush and mirror lying face down, and in the large mirror above she saw a woman, blond hair across one eye, tucked loosely behind an ear. Her hand flat and searching against the coverlet, itself still tucked smooth around the bottom corners of the bed. Her own reflection.

What was she searching for again?

Dani. But she was alone in the room.

The door burst open.

— Oh! You're awake now. Thank goodness, you're awake.

Heike started. It was Arden in the doorway, hesitant, then rushing forward:

— I've only just found out what happened.

Heike blinked again. The room a little sharper now.

— Where is he?

She peeled back the coverlet to loosen it.

— Eric's only just told me. About Daniel. Arden dropped onto the side of the bed, a hand on Heike's arm, the grip tight.

— Daniel. Heike repeated the name, nodding, and then shifted back, startled: Daniel? What are you talking about?

Arden pulled a bit closer on the bed.

— Try, sweetheart. Think. Eric says he gave you something to help you sleep that first night. He says you had a breakdown. She took Heike's hand and squeezed it. But golly, darling, that must've been some crazy sleeping pill. The maid says you've been in bed for three days. You had a reaction of some kind, I guess.

Heike let her hand rest in Arden's hand. Arden's cool thumb pulsed against the inside of her wrist.

— Three days?

The words seemed to float away from her. She couldn't connect to them.

— I came up to see you earlier, but you were out cold. He wanted you to take something else . . .

— I don't remember.

Arden gestured to the flower on the nightstand.

Heike looked more closely at the tumbler. A kind of effervescence in the base of the glass, the remnant of some little white thing dissolved slowly away. Eric was always giving her such tumblers. She'd lined them up along the edge of the nightstand once, a quiet row.

—We went to a party, Heike said.

—Yes, exactly. At Leo Dolan's house.

—There was a fire on the beach.

Arden waited.

The setting sun and the chestnut leaves and the blue table-cloths all coming back now, prismatic, like an odd dream. Dolan giving her a drink and a cushion to sit on. Driving in an open car, the wind whipping at her shoulders. The gully: the aspen leaves whispering all around.

Then no sound but silence, and that awful heaviness pressing down on her in the dark, high over the woods, the pond and the little house hidden somewhere below.

There was something else, too: something she couldn't put her finger on. She'd been terribly upset. What was she worrying about? It slipped away again.

She pushed up and fought at the covers.

—I have to get up. I have to find him.

—Whoa, whoa. Slow down. You're still recovering. Arden shifted back on the bed a little and then stood up, gesturing to the doorway with a sideways nod. He's downstairs, she said.

—Dani. Dani is downstairs? He's here?

Heike stumbled up, half-tangled, the bedsheets dropping to the floor around her. She had a cotton nightdress on, and she wanted to strip it off. The little buttons moved about under her fingers and refused to go through their holes.

Arden bit her lip.

—No, darling. I meant Eric. Eric is downstairs. I don't know where Daniel is. I couldn't get anything out of Eric, and he told me you were up here and I just ran to see you instead. He says you were raving.

Heike pulled the nightgown over her head and sat hard against the footboard, gripping the fabric to her breastbone with both hands, as though it were something precious. Her hands wrapped in the cloth to stop them trembling.

— Look, let's get you on your feet. You need some strong coffee in you, that's all. We'll figure this out. Arden went to take the rumpled nightgown, but found that Heike would not or could not let go of it. She took both of Heike's hands in hers and held them still. I don't know much more than you do, she said. I was hoping you'd remember something. Three days . . . Her voice was shaking, and she stopped, her eyes flicking briefly away, then back to Heike again. She started over: Three days is a long time. Let me help you.

— No, no! Heike pulled her hands away and held them up like a fighter or a traffic attendant. Give me any clothes, anything. There is no time!

— There is time. Of course we'll find him. The police have been here, yes?

Heike stood up for a moment and then, head spinning lightly, came back to rest on the end of the bed. She looked down to still the dizziness.

— The police. She said this almost like it was a question, then tilted her head up to look at Arden before answering. Yes! Yes, is he still here? The policeman? What did he say?

Arden shook the nightgown out and folded it over her own arm. Her face was both drawn and somehow plaintive, like someone who has stayed up through the night drinking and reading bad news.

— Heike. You haven't heard what I'm saying. Daniel went missing days ago. You've been in bed ever since.

— No. No! I don't believe you.

Heike stood up again, and the blood rushed through her arms and legs. She could hear the *whoosh* of it, a sudden heat in the back of her neck, her cheeks. The breeze came in through the blinds, and they swayed and fell and made their noise, and she wrapped an arm around her breasts. The fresh air made a little goose-flesh rise along her belly.

— It can't be three days. It can't.

The sunlight through the sheers, the cool air on her skin; everything was sharp and getting sharper. She could see herself, her own reflection in the vanity mirror. She stepped forward and noticed then the little Dresden girl, still there, her colours more pastel in daylight. Almost hidden in the brightness. Caught in the three-way mirror, like Heike herself, paler and paler in each repeated reflection.

She reached out to touch the little doll, then froze in place. The heavy stillness that night at the gully: she'd felt the same odd quiet pushing down as she'd come along the drive, alone, toward the house, to find Daniel gone. And the birds. She remembered that now: sunrise, and no birdsong, no sound at all. Her hand hung in the air, suspended. In the reflection, another hand, a hand leading Daniel away, down, down, to the stream, slipping into the tall bulrush, into the cattails.

Something caught in her throat, and she gagged.

Arden watched her in the mirror. There was a sudden commotion outside: the crows in the yard taken by surprise, rising up, moving farther off into the woods.

Heike drew in breath all at once, gulping at it, as though she were surfacing.

A LONG WHITE CORD snaked from inside the house out to where Eric stood on the veranda, his back to her, leaning on the rail. He'd brought the telephone out with him, for privacy, his voice low and hard-sounding the way it often was when he spoke on the phone: I think you don't understand me . . . a significant test . . . years of research at stake . . .

She'd come down the stairs alone, slowing only at the sound of Eric's voice—wanting, then, to know who he was talking to, if he was talking to the police. Half the week she'd lain sleeping, and Daniel out there, missing, without her. The first day or two surely the most likely time to find a child alive.

Either Eric had heard her footsteps and did not turn around, or he did not hear her coming. The receiver smacked into its cradle.

He had a jacket on, smoke grey, that must have been open by the way it hung loose at one side, and black wingtips. She could see the stitching where it tapered off near the back of one shoe, and a gleam off the leather, even close to the heel. This is what he'd done with his morning, with Daniel lost and gone and Heike lost to sleep: driven to town for a shoeshine.

She hadn't simply lain sleeping. Eric had made certain of it, had kept her locked away.

For a moment she imagined herself gaining speed. She glanced over her shoulder. Was Arden still upstairs?

Pushing him over. A quick shove.

It was not a real wish. It was only a moment. She had sometimes imagined herself free of him, walking up the drive, up the road, and away, perhaps down to Ithaca, and from there to the South; or jumping the coal train that ran now and then along the Cayuga shore, over to Geneva and beyond. This felt hardly different.

Heike stepped over the threshold.

— Eric.

She waited for him to turn. She had a dress on, and stockings, but the hook at the back of her neck was still unfastened; she'd torn away from Arden's efforts to help her dress. When he didn't respond, she raised her voice.

— Eric!

He turned and started, seeing her there. She thought at first there was a meanness to his look—he disliked surprises—but he hid it quickly enough.

— I wondered what Arden was up to, up there.

— Eric, where is he? Where is Dani?

Eric cocked his head slightly but didn't answer. He stepped to one side, and she followed him around.

— Eric! Tell me what's happened. The police, what are the police doing? Take me to town, Eric, I want to see the sheriff myself.

— Don't talk nonsense. He stopped in the doorway, looking down at her, his voice low and calm. You've had a breakdown, Heike. You've been in bed for days. Come inside now.

The back door to the garage was standing open, and from within it she could hear a metallic sound, a grinding, and she realized the man was down from the hardware store in Auburn to sharpen the garden tools, his foot riding the pedal of the sharpener. The noise stopped, and the man turned to whistling and the whistling to a song: *In a cavern, in a canyon, excavating for a mine . . .*

She stepped back abruptly, almost tripping herself.

— I don't want to go inside. Did they search the woods already? She pointed through the garden, toward the stream. How far back into the forest? Who is looking?

—You're in a state, Heike. Eric stepped forward and took hold of her arm, turning her toward the house. Come. Let's have a drink. I'll get you some ice to suck on.

—No! No, Eric! Heike shifted hard into the ball of one foot to avoid being moved, and Eric's fingers tightened around her arm. Her voice went up a register: Where is he? Where is Dani?

—I won't drag you.

—Let's go to the police. She grabbed his shoulder, half supplicating, half working to keep him at bay. Please, Eric, I want to know where they've looked.

—I know you're upset; I know you are. That's why I let you sleep. You have to trust me, Heike. The police have been here. I am taking care of everything.

—You let me sleep? My son is missing!

—Stop arguing with me; the gardener can hear you. He had been speaking in an even tone, steady and almost melodic, but it dropped now to a rough whisper. He pried her fingers off his shoulder. Christ knows you were in no shape to speak to anyone, he said. Hysteria. Dropped at the side of the road by a strange man, in the early hours of the morning. He paused and pressed in closer: Infidelity is an offence in America, Heike. Remember? I'm willing to forget all about that night. You ought to be grateful. Now come inside.

This was meant as a threat. She looked past him, into the house, and didn't move.

—And his things. All his things are gone.

Eric said nothing but just looked at her.

—His toys, his trains! She broke out of his grasp but stepped inside anyway, back into the white room. She picked up the crocheted blanket and hurled it against the couch. Everything is gone!

Eric stepped slowly in over the threshold.

— I'm sorry, Heike. I put his toys away. Me. I thought they would upset you, seeing them all strewn around. I was trying to protect you.

— Please, Eric. There is nothing to protect. Please. I am so afraid.

— I tell you I have dealt with the police.

— But I haven't! I am his mother. That counts for something. It counts; it must. Where did you look? Can you tell me that, at least? Where did you look for him? Did you look in the water?

— Take yourself in hand, Heike. You're becoming hysterical again.

Eric turned and walked to the bar and began tossing ice cubes into a glass with his fingers. She followed him, her eyes tracking the trim along the walls as though the room itself might hold a clue.

— Anyone would think you were trying to keep me prisoner.

She said this and then sucked in her breath. He turned suddenly and grabbed her by the shoulder and shook hard.

— Take yourself in hand.

His voice no longer kind.

There were footsteps, someone in the hall. Arden appeared in the doorway. She stayed back but did not take her eyes off Eric.

— Hey, sport. Her voice cool: Unleash the flesh, would you?

Eric released Heike's shoulder, and she stumbled back slightly. He turned away again.

— Go to the police if you want. Go on. I've spent quite enough time with the sheriff. Eric took up the glass and threw in another handful of ice, plus a quick shot from the decanter. His hand slipping a little, a slosh of liquor spilling out over the lip of the glass as he poured. How will you get there? On foot? It's a long walk. He's no friend to Deutschland, I'll tell you that right now. Spent twenty minutes telling me that he didn't lose the best of his unit at Aachen to come home and help Americans with Kraut wives. I had to tell him you were half-loopy to even get his sympathy. I said, "That's why I had to hire a girl to look after things. Madame is prone to fits." He looked at Arden: And then guess who saunters in? Strolling barefoot down the drive from another man's car.

Arden twitched, looking from Eric to Heike to Eric again.

— Everyone's upset here, Eric. Everyone. Not just you.

— I don't have time to stand here answering to a bunch of hysterical women. He turned to Heike and pointed: It's you who lost him. You. His mother. You think we'd be in this mess if you hadn't been gallivanting all over the countryside that night? We'd have been home in bed.

Heike's stomach tightened. The weird silence that had wrapped the house the night Dani disappeared closing in on her now, only the tinny grinding of the sharpener cutting through.

Eric shook his head and moved closer.

— You know I'm right. Don't you? Go on to the sheriff. Go on and tell him yourself what an unfit mother you are. You'll never find Daniel without me on your side. Careless. Carefree. You want someone to blame, just look at yourself. It's your fault he's gone.

He turned back to Arden and motioned for her to take Heike upstairs, and then made for the hallway. There was the smack of his office door.

ARDEN DID NOT MOVE after Eric brushed past her. There was a quiet moment, Heike staring after him as though she expected the office door to open again. Then, suddenly, fists clenched and shaking, she let out a howl:

— Where is my son?

For a moment she saw herself beating at his door, but instead her body caved in, the fists coming down hard against her own thighs instead.

— Where is he, where is he?

She was crying, hollow now and lonely-sounding. Her fists would not unclench, and her fingernails dug into her palms. After a little silence, Arden stepped toward her.

— Heike.

Heike didn't respond but lurched forward, still off-balance, and ripped off her shoes. She'd already imagined Dani waking without her and wandering out into the woods. Calling for her, his voice growing thin and panicked. Or moving silently through the trees to the stream, pulled there by some unseen hand, disappearing into the arrowhead and the ox-tongue, then down into the water below. Dogs searching the stream bank and divers out in the lake. In a moment she was back out on the veranda, then down the stairs and into the yard.

Arden chased after her, catching hold of her elbow just where the lawn descended into forest.

— Heike, wait— maybe Eric is right. Maybe you ought to lie down for just a bit longer.

— I thought you were the one who saved me from that. Heike wrenched her arm away and swished through the high ferns. She could hear the stream running down below, just a little farther on. She shouted back over her shoulder, not a call but a cry: The long stupor of Heike Lerner! Didn't you help me out?

Arden pulled off her own shoes and ran to catch up.

— I don't mean more sleeping pills. I mean, maybe a bit more recovery time. She grabbed hold of Heike's arm again. You see how strange Eric is; he's hardly himself. Spilling booze all over the place and grabbing you like that.

Heike paused, gauging whether this statement rang true. She shook her head.

— A child can drown in nothing, in a puddle.

She moved forward until she was in the stream proper, the water cold around her calves, then held her skirt up out of it and followed the current, slipping a little where the rocks were wider and flat, but recovering herself again.

— This is how I lost my sister, she said. Eric knows that. Lost in the woods. Heike stopped moving and looked around her. What god there is can only be cruel.

Arden stood on shore.

— Let me help you, Heike.

There was the repetitive sound of the grinder from the garage, faint here, and Heike shifted her gaze to search the woods on either side of the stream. The water rushed fast around her legs. She turned back to face Arden.

— He is here somewhere. I feel it. I know he is here.

Arden stepped in, her foot sinking a little into the mud at the side of the stream. She looked over her shoulder before turning back to Heike, her eyes fixed and sharp with concern.

— Let's go to Auburn. I have John's car, up on the road. I'll take you.

— Auburn?

— To the sheriff's office. Let's go. It was the sheriff who was here that night, wasn't it?

— Eric . . .

Heike stopped.

From inside the house, the sound of the phonograph came

up, the music expanding out into the afternoon heat. Mahler. A particularly cheerful beginning. No composer is so completely happy or completely sad as Mahler.

— He's not himself, Arden said.

Heike glanced at her and then twisted around again, staring fiercely toward a rustle in the trees. Her collarbone had a knife edge to it.

— I have lost my son. She turned away from the stream abruptly, wading back out onto shore. If he went into the water, then he is dead. I won't leave him, Arden. I won't give up. Not this time.

— At least we can find out what's been done. That's what you wanted, isn't it? To find out where they've looked? What they know?

The door to the garage was still open; the machine sound cut in now and then over the music from the house, but only in short bursts. She could not hear the man's whistling or his song. Just the pitch of the blade grinder, on and then off again. And then on.

— Heike?

Heike didn't answer but started back up through the garden. At the garage door, she stopped and glanced toward the bean teepee, looking for Daniel's dump truck, but Eric had put that away, too: only the little garden hoe lay there, dirty, where she'd left it last.

11.

rden pulled into a spot a few car lengths down from the courthouse but didn't take the keys from the ignition. She'd had a crimson silk scarf knotted under her chin for the drive, and now she untied it, shaking her hair loose. A solitary mosquito bumbled back and forth at the corner of the windshield.

Heike rolled the window lower on her side and tried to wave the insect out a few times before flicking it sharply against the dash, then leaned into the windshield herself for a better look. They were facing south, the sun off to her side. She already had a hand on the door.

There was a uniform cop standing up on the courthouse stairs, in the shadow of the columns. He reminded her of the officer who'd been at the house the night Daniel went missing, and this made her draw the hand back again, into her lap. She tried to recall what the cop that night had looked like, but could only remember his voice. Indulgent, or paternal: *Calm down, now. Your husband's got you all looked after.*

— I don't know if I should do this.

The officer came down a step or two, and Heike pressed back against her seat. His hat shaded his eyes.

— That's what we're here for. Remember?

Heike turned from the window to face Arden.

— Who knows what Eric has said to them? What if he's right: they call me a careless mother? What if they want to take Dani away from me forever? Before I can even find him? How can I tell them this: Someone took my child in the night. Not even someone. Something. Something took him.

Arden looked at her own hands, still resting on the steering wheel.

— You're afraid of him, she said. Eric. He makes you afraid.

Heike pulled her knees up high under her chin, a protective measure, despite the closeness of the car. Now that they were no longer moving, the heat and the stillness settled in: her skin was damp, the fine hair along her brow curling in little wisps. There was the vague noise of other cars moving by them. She shut her eyes.

— Eric has a mind that reaches into everything, she said. He remembers. I don't mean in a cloud or a wave or as a picture, the way you remember a day you spent on a picnic, or how it looked on the top of a Ferris wheel. Specific conversations. A wording, a phrase. Every marker. She opened her eyes again but did not turn back to Arden. This is his pride, she said. He takes note of your movements, habits you do not know yourself. Which tiny hole in a shoe's leather strap is most worn, the colour of teacup that most appeals to you, the way you wipe your face with a washcloth at night, right to left or left to right. As though his eye were a camera.

She did not say: He collects your moments of quiet pleasure. She did not say: Until you learn this, no part of you is safe.

Heike turned to glance at Arden, then back to the courthouse. The officer had not moved. She wondered if he recognized her, if he was watching their car.

— Sometimes it seems he knows me better than I know myself, she said.

— There are people who'd tell you that's as it should be for a husband.

— In the beginning, it was charming. You think you must be very special, for someone to pay such close attention to you.

When they'd first come to New York, after the blur of travel, he'd wanted to whisk her off somewhere new every weekend. He was still calling it their honeymoon. They called it a honeymoon for months, weekends at Montauk, or spent strolling the boardwalk in Atlantic City. Or leaving a party early to walk home through the park at dusk, eating hot chestnuts from a cart. Or skipping the party altogether (more likely) to sit close against a silver-railed bar drinking Campari. He didn't want other people. He only wanted Heike.

There'd been a moment when she could feel the change, when Eric's attention had moved from sweet talk to something heavy, a hand on the back of her neck, but she could not remember when exactly this had happened.

— Like with the maid that day.

Heike stirred a little.

— You remember? Arden said. His thing about the way she lines up jars. She was so embarrassed. It was like he'd caught her at something, some little illicit thing. I thought it was a strange sort of exercise. Or a test.

Arden took her hands off the wheel and pressed them into her temples. There was very little air. The car was still running.

— The police are meant to help you, you know.

— I have a bad feeling, Heike said. She sat motionless, watching the cop on the stairs, as though any movement might be the thing to betray her.

— Tell me about Leo Dolan, Arden said.

Heike's shoulder twitched.

— What do you mean?

— I mean, what happened that night? When Daniel disappeared.

— It was a party. Eric was gambling. I was alone. We had a drink together. Maybe a few drinks; I wasn't paying attention.

— But you didn't come home with Eric?

It was so late. Eric made a scene. Heike leaned carefully into her seat, curling her legs up beside her. I didn't want to come home at all. I only came back for Daniel.

— Dolan brought you home.

Heike half-turned to look at her.

— I'm not going to ask anything private, Heike.

— This has nothing to do with Dani.

She turned away quickly, though, and fussed first with her waistband and then with the toe of her stocking. For a moment neither of them said anything.

— Yes, alright. She finished with the stocking and looked up. If I hadn't gone to the stupid party, or if we'd come home early, this wouldn't have happened. You think I haven't thought of that already? It's true. Of course it's true. Dani is gone because of me.

But what might she have protected him from, or how? She

could imagine lying with him, close in her arms. But what next? A voice, calling to him? Or just a small hand, slipping into his, coaxing him, a finger pressed to his lips. Tessa, her pale skin catching the moonlight, drawing Daniel out of the room. Heike sleeping on.

This suspicion, that the little girl was somehow involved, her disappearance at the raft some kind of warning, Heike could not even speak out loud to Arden. Explaining such a thing to a room full of policemen was impossible.

Arden gave the scarf in her hand a little shake and laid it out in her lap, smoothing it.

— The thing is, she said. The thing is, three days is a long time. It's hard to imagine a child surviving that long. If he was missing. If no one ever found him.

Heike felt her stomach cave in. As though Arden had thrown a low punch.

— Don't say that.

— Wait. It's just—back at the house, watching Eric, I had this thought: What if Daniel isn't really missing?

Heike looked at her sharply. Arden leaned closer:

— What if Eric has him? To punish you, kind of. The words hung there, heavy in the air around them. Or to teach you a lesson, Arden said. It fits. Doesn't it?

— You mean because of Dolan?

— Because of who knows what, Arden said. Yes, because of Dolan. Because of any number of things. Because you came back from the pond with dirty legs and didn't want to go to a party with him. Because Eric is who he is. I don't know. Mostly because of Dolan. To keep you in line.

Heike looked down at the floor of the car, considering this.

Inside her chest, something was swelling up, like a soft fruit that's been left too long. The skin splitting. She opened her mouth to relieve the pressure, but no breath would come.

— He told me he could have me arrested. For infidelity. Or committed: he's told me that many times.

She raised her eyes again, to where the police officer had been standing. He was gone now. Heike started.

Arden kept on, speaking almost to herself:

— Is it crazy to think this? That my brother would kidnap his own child? I don't know if you could even call it kidnapping.

Heike looked around. No: not gone after all. She could see the officer down on the sidewalk, leaning in to some other cop's cruiser. She turned her body back to Arden but kept her eyes on the courthouse steps.

— I used to dream all the time that we were fighting. Eric and I. We're fighting and I'm trying to tell him something, something important, but he won't listen. I am so frustrated that I start beating him, beating on his chest, but it does nothing. He only smiles. Like I was beating on a glass wall instead of a man. Heike's hands, resting in her lap, curled now into fists. She peeled her eyes away from the courthouse to look at Arden properly. People don't ask men like Eric a lot of questions, she said. You must know this, Arden. Look at John: it's just the same. They move through the world, and the world steps aside, to open the path.

Arden cut the motor and pulled out the key. For a moment she was quiet, the clink of the keychain the only sound between them.

— You're saying people will listen to him if he talks.

— They will.

— They won't listen to you?

— You are listening to me. But the sheriff? Heike indicated with a thumb out the window. The police?

— I don't know. I don't know anymore. Arden tapped her fingers against the steering wheel. I suppose you have a point, she said. It depends what Eric has told them. She dropped her hand off the wheel: And what if you don't go back?

— I can't. I can't leave without Dani, Heike said. I know I can find him, Arden—

Arden shook her head.

— I don't know what use you are to Daniel if you can't get out of bed. That's what's at home for you. Or so it seems. She paused. Then: Has he ever wandered off before? Dani.

Impossible not to think of Lena, also disappearing in the night. Heike pushed the thought away. Daniel usually followed after her, tugging at her skirt, his hand wrapped in her hemline. Quite the opposite. Always at her feet.

— Only if he was looking for me.

Lena perhaps also scared in the dark, looking for Heike.

Arden tipped her chin at the cop on the sidewalk, matter-of-factly.

— He'll never have you arrested, you know. Eric. That's an empty threat. People would talk. He couldn't tolerate it.

— But he will use it against me. If I leave him. He'll say I'm an unfit mother.

— You can go back if you want.

Arden's voice still a little flat.

What Heike wanted was to go back and find everything reset, Daniel in the white room, clicking a little train along the track. For them to never have found the pond, or the raft, never seen the girl. For Heike to never have set foot inside that house. She thought of the little Dresden figurine, her cool almost-smile, stiff and unmoving, her reflection fanning out in the bedroom mirrors. Smiling again and again. A cold current moved through the car.

Arden reached out for Heike's hand, but found it curled tight. They sat there for a moment, Arden looking at Heike, almost fierce, and Heike looking out at where the cop now climbed the courthouse stairs, escorting someone to the door.

— This is your brother, Heike said. So why are you helping me now?

She hadn't turned her head. Arden leaned out to try to catch her eye anyway.

— I never had a sister, I suppose.

Then:

— I wonder if there hasn't always been something wrong with him. I've always wondered. Since I was a child. Her voice was hard-edged. You're right, she said. He's my brother. It's hard not to feel somehow responsible.

It was late in the day. There were a few clouds in the sky, and they had begun to take on colour, the barest flush, the sun low but not yet setting. Heike focused on the stream of light through the trees, the shadows denser now. As though the trees overhead were drawing their veil around. Hard to say where any one branch began or ended.

— If Dani is with Eric, at least that means he is safe, Heike said. The words rhythmic, a rosary: Eric would never hurt him. He'd never hurt his own son.

— I think it makes a kind of sense, Arden said. I think it makes more sense than anything else. Something didn't match up, when I saw him. Eric. He didn't look worried when I arrived. He looked angry. He was angry that the maid had let me in. I know men react differently. I know that, but . . . his child is missing. Missing. For three days. You know? How is it possible that his child has disappeared and he doesn't seem half as worried as you do right now? She wound the scarf around her wrist and pulled it tight. And there you were in bed, and your eyes were all black. There was no blue in them. Just soft and black, and he only wanted to rouse you to give you something else to drink.

— And if you're wrong? If he's not with Eric?

— We will find him. No matter what.

Heike swung her legs down off the seat and sat straight up, feet flat on the floor. Her head was clearing; she watched without squinting the glint of sunlight where it flared in the side mirror. Her hands on the seat, to either side of her, arms pressing strongly into the vinyl.

— I can't go to the police.

Arden hesitated.

— Do you want to come home with me?

— No. No, I'd only make trouble for you there.

— But you're not going home, are you? Is there someplace else you can go? To clear your head. A hotel or something. She wrapped the red scarf over her hair again, the ends of it batting at her throat as she wound them back into a knot. She stopped and turned, a sudden thought hitting her: Do you even have any money?

Heike reached down for her purse where it sat on the floor of the car.

— I've been skimming it off the top of the grocer's bill, she said. It's not much. Every week I tell Eric we've ordered something we haven't. An extra chicken, or some eggs, or a couple of quail.

The thought of this painstaking weekly operation struck her as suddenly ridiculous, shameful, and she pressed her lips together.

— It's not really funny. I've been hiding it in a ripped seam in my purse for a year. She slipped a hand into her bag so that she could widen the secret compartment, ripple the edge of the bill-fold hidden there. If you'd asked me, I couldn't have told you why.

— I guess we know why.

— Imagine having to lie about chickens just to get a little spending money.

There was a silence. Arden finished with her scarf.

— It's your nest egg.

— My chicky bank. Is that it? She looked at Arden sideways, just out of the corner of her eye. A poultry subterfuge, Heike said.

— You've been quailing it away for a rainy day.

They rhymed this all off with serious faces, and for a moment it felt like a reprieve. Heike's vision blurred, and she realized she was crying.

— It's not a lot of money. But it's some. It's something.

She set the bag back on the floor. Then:

Eric keeps his car key in the drawer of the hall armoire.

The words came out soft and slow. A risk, to go back at all, but he would not expect her to take the car.

Arden picked up the key where it lay in her lap and got the motor turning over again, then moved the gearshift into reverse, one arm along the seatback, looking over her shoulder. Down the way, a light had turned green, and she waited for the hum of a few cars to pass them by.

For a moment, Heike tried to picture Dani, or feel him there next to her, as she sometimes did if she were out for an evening and bored, or Daniel was asleep and she felt lonely. His feet kicking the seat, the warmth of him curling into her. The image came slowly, somehow. How much wave to his hair? His eyes a flecked grey, or more blue? She ran through details as though she were taking inventory, but they broke apart like bits of china and lay separate the moment she tried to put them together. Even with her eyes shut, she could not quite see him.

This alarmed her. She needed to picture him pristine, perfect, so that she would know for sure he was safe. It was like she could harm him by slipping up in her imagination. She looked over to Arden and then down at herself, counting out her own shoulder, her arm, then her thigh with a careful hand, as though checking to make sure she herself was still there.

The officer had gone inside now. There was no cruiser waiting for them, no one left on the courthouse steps. Arden pulled the car out into the road.

— Better to wait until dark, she said.

When they reached the top of the driveway, Arden stopped the car without turning in. They were pulled close against the ditch, a few tree branches scraping the roof. Heike swung the door open and left it that way. It was dark enough that she would have liked a flashlight. Halfway down the drive she stopped and looked up to where she knew Arden was waiting, hidden in the trees at the side of the road, but she could not see her or the car and had to believe that she had not driven away.

The sun was most of the way set, a brilliant streak on the west side of the lake, but the house, north-facing against the stream, was privy only to a dull sort of ambience, well filtered by trees.

The front door was unlocked, and Heike went in, carefully rather than quickly, turning the knob in its latch as she closed it behind her so as not to be heard coming. Her movements still at risk of a leftover sedative clumsiness. There was no music on. Her ears felt full of cotton, and she strained to listen through the quiet. In the kitchen, the wall clock beat out the seconds, and her heart kicked too, so that it hurt to breathe. The girl, Rita, was not there.

Heike eased the armoire drawer open. It was a neat little space and held only a few things: a long matchbox; a silver shoehorn; a set of handkerchiefs, corners embroidered (Heike's own; she was surprised to see them there); a single key on a plain ring. She withdrew the key and slipped it into her pocket and left her hand on it, the key head wide and flat and cool. It was what she had come for, and she left the drawer open, not wanting to risk the sound of it sliding closed. She went to turn away, but something stopped her and she froze. There was someone there, behind the door.

No sound, but she'd seen the light change, just to her left. A twitch. Heike pulled the hand from her pocket and left the key in there, her shoulder blades drawing back as she turned. Behind her was the door and then the entrance to the kitchen and a long strip of wall; on the wall, the hall mirror where she and Arden had stood a week or two earlier, Arden fussing at her dress.

She was alone. The movement she'd seen just her own hair in the mirror, from the corner of her eye. She stared in at herself, eyes adjusting to the dark. Her reflection a pale shadow.

If Eric was home, he had not heard her. She slipped a hand back into her pocket. The key was still there, safe. Her body was so tight that she could feel the bones of her hips curving up to meet her breasts, as though she were folding in on herself. She stepped outside, onto the front stoop, but left her hand on the knob.

Arden was standing in the open now, at the top of the drive; Heike could see her there. She decided that they were caught: Eric had returned from a walk and found his sister waiting, was waiting now himself for Heike to come running up the drive with the key. But Arden merely waved to her. Impatient. *What are you doing? It's time to go.*

For the first time it occurred to Heike that Eric might not be at home, that Arden's theory could have weight. If Arden was right, and Eric had somehow taken Daniel himself, was it possible that he'd hidden him away inside the house? What if Dani were there after all, alone? Had been there the whole time. Locked in a closet and frightened, and his mother walking away.

She shouldered the front door open again, stepping backward over the threshold. Either Eric was home or he was not. He had heard her come in, the click of the door and now the small creaks of the floorboards, or he had not. She went up to the second-floor landing in the dark.

There was a thin strand of moonlight in the hall, and Heike used it to paw through the linen closet, the cupboard under the bathroom sink. In Dani's room she got on her knees and pulled his little bed out from the wall, as though his body could have flattened itself into that space. The act of hiding or being hidden almost the product of a magic trick. The bed frame rumbled across the floor, and she did not dare to push it back into place. She crawled to the back of the closet and swept her hands against the corners, the baseboards, flat out on the back wall. There was the soft click of her tongue against the roof of her mouth: *Daniel, Daniel. Daniel, Daniel.* An incantation.

In her own bedroom the blinds were still drawn, and there was no light. What was shadow and what was solid rubbed up and ran together. As Heike crossed the room, something caught her ankle—not strong enough to be a hand, but twine, a trap, some flimsy thing that twisted and pulled tight, and for a moment she lost her breath. She tugged gingerly at her foot, and whatever held her gave in. Not a hand. Not Eric. The coil of bedclothes on the floor, untouched from when she'd run out earlier in the day. She kicked them away.

She could see her outline in the vanity mirror, a bare silhouette, and remembered waking to her own reflection: a stranger, she'd thought. A strange woman, her hair over one eye. And something else: the little Dresden figurine, shining at her, pale in the afternoon light. Jarring somehow. She had not expected to see it there, posed against the three-way mirror, the figurine in multiplicity, not one Dresden doll but three, six, nine.

Before everything: before the girl in the water, before Daniel's game in the thorn bush. Before he disappeared. The girl, Tessa, nothing so much as a bad omen. And yet. Now Daniel seemed to have been swallowed up the same way Tessa had vanished into the pond, the surface closing over her, a smooth seal. The silence of the little house matching the stillness of the water. A sign, and the figurine somehow related.

Heike had hidden it away, a treasure, a china pet.

She wanted it now. She made her way across the room and waited for her eyes to focus, all the muffled shapes of things becoming clearer, her fingers finding every standing thing: the cut-glass bottle of perfume, L'Heure Bleue, the stopper cut to the shape of an upside-down heart, or else a spade; some small bottles of talc; a puff; her hairbrush; a glass bulb of cold cream.

The thin cloth of the runner always there, spanning the length. She found herself peering, not down, but into the mirrors themselves, each item a false version. Her own hair, pale and loose around her face. Unkempt. She lifted a thumb to touch the line of her cheek in the glass. These few cosmetics, a tiny brush for her eyelids, a discarded scarf, blue silk. But no shepherdess. The figurine was gone.

This gave Heike a jolt. She'd seen it just a few hours ago. Before she left with Arden. Hadn't she? Standing in the curve of mirrors, the doll's reflection moving out in three directions, over and over, like something pulled out to sea. The little waves lapping her away with the tide.

Or something she thought she saw, before she was truly awake. She went to the wardrobe where she'd hidden the doll away on that first day, wrapped in the newspaper from the cabin's cupboard, but her hands slipped through the drawer's contents—underwear, a few silk corselettes—too easily. The thin straps of camisoles ran through her fingers like hair. At the back of the drawer she felt something rougher: the newspaper wrapper, empty now. Heike pulled it out, wincing at the scraping sound. She folded the paper and slipped it into her pocket with the matches and the key.

Outside, the breeze had picked up. Heike could hear it in the aspen leaves, a silver sound, shimmery. The house made its regular mild creaks. She went back down the stairs, only somewhat cautious. It seemed to her now that Eric could not be home, would have heard her by now: her movement on the stairs, or pulling out Dani's bed, tripping over the bedclothes, her urgent whisper, calling Dani's name. In the front landing the floor was cool under her feet. There was the swish of the wind in the trees again, and a light knocking. She'd left the front door standing open when she came in the second time; the wooden screen beating gently against the frame, unguarded.

She turned and followed the hallway back to Eric's office, one hand trailing on the wall. The barest glow, a slim band of lamp-light, showed beneath his door. She stopped and shrank back against the wall across from it, watching for a flicker in the light, a movement, a shadow. Her hips pressing into the moulding on the high edge of the wainscot, the woodwork sharp against her tailbone. The light left on, absent-mindedly—or Eric himself in there, waiting in the wingback chair?

Waiting for her. He'd known she would come back. Or come looking. She imagined him there, in his chair with a Scotch and soda. He curled his lips at her meanly. Or, if not quite mean, imperious. Like a man waiting for a dog that's tired itself out.

Heike closed her eyes and opened them. She was still in the hall, and she stepped forward and stopped again. Her hand lay on the doorknob and stayed there, the other hand on the wood frame close to her face. She counted breaths: three, four, five. When she turned the knob, it was slow and silent, and she pushed the door in.

There he was. In the wingback, as she'd pictured, the reading lamp with its green glass shade shining down. But he did not sit staring. His head lolled back, nestled against the cushion. One hand sullenly hanging over the edge of the chair, and an empty tumbler lying on its side on the floor below.

Heike drew her arms in close against her sides. Eric's eyes just thin crescents of white, almost but not entirely closed. A sleeping giant.

For a brief moment she thought he was dead. The plank

floor in the office was polished smooth where it was not covered by a red hooked rug, and Heike stayed slightly on her toes, watching him as she moved closer, then back again. The silence made everything seem false. She felt visible within it, as though there were a camera on her, or a real Eric hiding just behind the door, this unconscious, failed version only a lure. One arm hanging off the chair, one arm across his chest, and on this hand the finger gave a twitch. He was dreaming. She could see his eyes roll back under their lids. She had an urge to look over her shoulder.

He had shelves with books on them, and bookends, and a file cabinet that she knew from the past was kept locked; a wide oak desk with three drawers. She eased these open now, one after the other, her back dangerously close to the chair, but the top-most drawer held only pencils and some notecards, and the other two were mostly empty. But they had not always been so: thin metal file hangers spanned the depth of the drawers' sides. The files were missing.

In the lowest drawer, she found two kinds of glass containers. The drawer chimed as she opened it, the noise of it sending a quick shot of tension up her spine. The little iodine bottles she'd seen Eric using the first night they went to Dolan's, but also another set of vials, filled with powder, resting in a wooden rack. Each stoppered tube marked with a name: Ledyard, Canoga, Moravia, Locke, Lodi. The names of villages on either side of the lake. She noticed now that there was one vial open on the desk. Aurora, the village down the road.

She glanced up at him, quickly, then back again. Impossible that he did not see her doing this. There was no figurine here, either, unless he'd locked it up, although she had not realized until this moment that she'd expected to find it here, hidden from her as Daniel was hidden. She did not dare move farther into the room. She leaned a hand on the desk and flicked at the pages of his notebook, lying open, Eric's smart penmanship tracing its lines around her fingers. A hospital journal, his own set of notes on the patients housed there:

> *February 12, 1956. Patient sleeps as normal, with-*
> *out interruption, but engages in limited somnam-*
> *bulance in the early part of the rest period before*
> *settling into a heavier phase for the final two to*
> *three hours . . .*

Eric's hand twitched again. Heike closed the book and lifted it off the desk, tucking it against her side like a schoolgirl. She did not want to turn her back to him; at the same time, she was almost afraid to back out of the room. As though he might also be behind her, the other Eric. Out in the hall, the darkness was thick, the office door arcing slowly closed on its hinges and seal-ing off the lamplight within. She stepped sideways, her finger-tips curled under the brass doorknob, coaxing it along with her.

It was not until she stepped over the threshold that she felt it. Something brushing by her, the hem of her skirt swishing against her calf. Heike froze, waiting to feel the breeze from the doorway against her face. She'd left the front door open, but not the screen. There was no draft now, but as she stood there, she felt the same movement again, this time a nudge at her hip, the little hairs on her arms rising. As though someone else were in the hall, had passed by her a second time, too close; a child or even an animal, whisking at her ankles. She whirled around to look behind her, but the hall stood long and dark and empty, trailing off toward the back of the house.

— Dani?

She whispered the name. Could he be here, hiding in the shadows? Hiding, maybe, from Eric? She felt her way along the wall panels and stood at the entrance to the white room, then stepped cautiously in. The garden outside sank back into blackness, the room itself ashy and mute. Moonlight caught on the window glass, the polished lid of the piano, a flicker here and there through the film. Heike's eye followed the glint. She whispered the name again:

— Dani?

Nothing moved.

The French doors were closed and locked. There was no breeze from this end of the house. She turned to face the front door again, half-expecting to see Eric waiting for her in the hall, but that, too, stood vacant and still. The office door closed tight. She stepped forward and then pulled up, her breath catching in her throat. Something brushed again at her side, harder now. Scratching at her. She glanced quickly down, looking for evidence, some thin gash, a pinprick line of blood. Her skirt swept against her thigh, first on the right and then on the left, then on the right again, as though whatever it was, surely now an animal, something come in from out of doors, were moving around her in a swirl. For a moment she heard the sound of it, silvery. A wind through the leaves. A whisper.

She drew her fists in tight, unwilling to turn in circles or to look behind her again. Someone standing by, just beside her. A soft breath at her ribcage, her elbow's crook.

At the end of the hall, the door to the front garden gaped on its hinges, and she stepped lightly toward it, moving quickly now, her eyes low. At the last moment, some movement in the mirror caught her eye, and she turned her head wildly away, afraid, looking instead toward the wall and the armoire. The drawer still open as Heike had left it, a white glint of moonlight catching there.

Everything in her to keep her movements steady, to quiet her breath in the dark.

SHE CAME OUT OF THE HOUSE at a pitch and aimed for Eric's car; steadily, not running. From there she beckoned to Arden to come join her, but stood with her back against the car door, watching the house. The sound of Arden's quick step down the driveway made her stomach tighten.

— I thought you were gone, Arden said. I thought you were caught for sure.

Heike looked over her shoulder and reached for Arden's hand, her elbow, this contact grounding her.

— He's there. Eric. Knocked out cold. He didn't see me.

They had to be quick, she told Arden. She glanced at the house again, but there was no movement from the doorway, and she closed her eyes and took a breath and started over, trying to shake off her nerves. It would be better to buy time to get away by hiding the car, rather than taking it. Something she'd thought of, watching Eric slumber away in the chair. She could imagine him taking a stabbing pleasure in calling the sheriff himself, allowing her to be arrested, then generously dropping the charges. Or not.

This was on her mind, she told Arden, and she preferred that Eric look foolish when the cops discovered the missing vehicle only a few yards from the house. She did not start the car but popped it into neutral as Arden braced herself against the front bumper.

They eased it past the garden, walking backwards downhill, their hands firm on the hood to stop the car from slipping away from them. Toward the stream and into the treeline. The ground levelled out, and they switched sides to push from behind. There was a woody scrape as the car nestled in. Heike pulled Arden into the bush.

From where they stood, you could see the front garden only in pieces. A rough trail led up through the trees to the road. Heike tried to still her fingers, unpicking the pronged tip of a twig where it had caught in the crocheted trim of her skirt.

— Should we push my car along a bit, too, so that he doesn't hear the engine start?

This was delivered in one sharp, exquisite breath. Arden held on to her dress with both hands, as though it were an apron filled with crusts. It was dark, and her face was open, wiped clean. Everything was new. Heike dropped her hem and listened.

She'd felt something, she told Arden now. Inside the house, just as she was getting out. It had given her a scare, she said.

— Right here, right beside me. Like I wasn't alone. They were speaking in whispers. I don't remember how I got to the front door, Heike said. That's how fast I was moving.

She'd still had the notebook under one arm, and turned her head to the side, the way you do in the street when you don't want to be recognized. But it was the mirror she wanted to avoid.

— I had this notion that if I looked in the mirror I might see something, you know, behind me. Someone. Whatever was in there with me.

It was in turning away from the mirror that her eyes had fallen to the armoire drawer, still standing open from when she'd retrieved the key to the car.

— And there she was, she said.

It was not a large drawer. The handkerchiefs had been pressed out flat and folded neatly. But this time something else was laid out on top of them. The Dresden doll.

— But it wasn't there when you first went in?

— There was almost nothing in there the first time I looked. I reached right into it. I would have felt her there.

— Perhaps in the dark you missed it somehow.

Heike did not think she had missed anything.

— You're only giving yourself the willies, Arden said. Come on now. She turned to hike back to where her own car was hidden, up on the road.

Heike looked back at the house. She'd shut the door behind her, and it was still closed now. There was no longer any wind. The kitchen windows were open, their yellow curtains hanging still and slate grey in the dark.

Arden was already out of sight; from the road, Heike heard the dull thunk of a car door closing. She tucked the notebook back under one arm, but held the figurine safe in her hand, where she could see it. The porcelain was smooth, and heavier than she remembered. She forced herself to breathe out, relaxing her face and turning the corners of her mouth up.

There was a little skittering in the underbrush. For a moment she jumped, then shook it off, laughing at herself. All that lurking around, and Eric dead to the world. He had not followed her out. She was safe; he did not know she was there at all. This was only something small: a mouse or, if she was unlucky, a mink. She could feel its movement along the ground near her, through the leaves, no more than a few feet away. She looked down. Where her skirt brushed her knee, there was a stain. She pulled up the fabric, revealing a long scratch down the length of her thigh. The gash she'd felt inside the house, the blood all but dry now.

Above her, the thin branch of an aspen creaked in the wind. And then something closer. More than a whisper: someone speaking, just beside her. The words plain in her ear:

I remember you.

Heike's body stiffened at the sound, and she whirled around, but there was no one there, no one in the shadows, next to her or behind her. She'd been so afraid of Eric—that he'd come out of the house, that she'd be caught. But the voice, high and clear as a bell, belonged to a little girl.

12.

The door swung open and Dolan stepped inside, scanning the place, one hand already on his hat. Heike didn't look up but signalled to him with her empty glass. She was in a booth to the waterside, where the diner car hung over the river, absently thumbing the edges of a notebook in her hand. The only patron in the room.

Her hair was loose in a way that might have suggested foreignness, or the movies, something contrived; in fact, there was a leaf in it, from the escapade with the car in the woods. Out the window was the river, black-looking, and no moon—it was sunk now behind heavy clouds—but there was a streetlight that shone a kind of arrow streak reflection on the water, and a little lamp at the table, and a table jukebox. A woman's voice, Ella Fitzgerald.

She'd put a nickel in the machine.

—You're in no rush to see me.

Heike straightened to look at him, and the crease between her brows smoothed out. Dolan stood tall enough over her that he cast a kind of shadow where the beam from an overhead fluorescent was blocked.

— I'm glad.

— Not every day I get a call from a maiden in distress.

— Or every night?

— At night, slightly more often.

— I'm sorry I woke you.

— Didn't anybody give you trouble, sitting here all alone?

It was two in the morning. Arden had parked the car and waited while Heike used the phone, and they'd burnt their tongues and the roofs of their mouths eating hot french fries, the first thing Heike had eaten all day, maybe the first thing for many days. After that, she'd sent Arden home. The diner was empty now, save for the cook and a scrawny waiter sitting at the counter. The waiter's hair was thin and receding, but he wasn't old. He was a young man losing his hair. The cook was bent so low over his plate you could only see the fur on the back of his neck, the loop of his apron caught on his shirt collar. They were eating what was left of the dinner special. There was a basket of bread in front of them, plain sliced bread, and the cook shovelled cream gravy and peas onto a piece of it and folded it closed like a sandwich.

— They gave me a beer. She held up the empty glass, and he could see a trace of foam curling around the bottom of it. And one free phone call, like in prison, she said.

— End of the night for everybody.

— Middle of the night. Why don't you sit down?

— Don't you have any things?

— What things should I have?

Dolan stuck his lips out and gestured with one hand, a circular motion with just the fingers.

— *Things*, things. Like a suitcase or something. Your things.

Heike let her head sway back and forth. The beer had been Arden's idea: she'd said Heike was in shock.

— I just left. I didn't take anything. No, wait. Just this.

She patted the black-covered exercise book, and then pulled another item up from the bench next to her. Dolan was still standing over her. He parted the wrinkled newspaper to take a cursory look at the figurine. Heike had rewrapped her.

— You know, another woman might have brought her night-gown. Some clean underwear.

— I didn't have time. Or even a bag to put it in. What would I put it in?

It seemed to her then that she used to have a suitcase once, a white case with a latch and a pearled handle, and she worked for a moment trying to recall where it had gone.

— It's an interesting selection that you did bring.

— The book is Eric's. His research journal. Or one of them. I don't know why I took it. Except that he will miss it, and know that I was there.

— He may not guess it was you.

— You don't think?

This disappointed her. She took the Dresden shepherdess out of its wrapping, unfolded the paper and smoothed it out flat against the table.

— Daniel is gone, she said. Missing.

Dolan slid into the booth.

— What'd the police say?

She shook her head.

— But you called the police?

— Eric did.

— And?

— He won't help me. Eric only wants to be in charge. He says if I go to the police myself, he'll have me arrested for infidelity.

— Infidelity! And here you are now, red-handed. Red-lettered, Dolan said.

— Or committed. It would be so easy.

— Who says easy?

Heike put out her thumb and pointed it inward, at her own sternum.

— I'm just an unidentified foreigner, remember? Like in your story. The town will circle their wagons.

— Who says easy?

— Arden says. She says try finding Dani from the State Mental.

— Arden who?

— She thinks Eric has him. Eric has Dani, that he's not missing at all.

— That's an interesting theory.

— I'm not sure I believe it.

Dolan looked up and flicked his chin toward the men at the counter, but the cook kept his head down and concentrated on mopping his plate. The waiter held his eyes on Dolan, then called across the room.

— No beer after midnight.

This came out forceful; pre-emptive, even. He twisted his body back toward his dinner with steady resolve.

— You gave one to the lady.

— No beer after midnight.

Dolan turned to Heike:

— You've been here all night?

The waiter stuck a forkful of shredded turkey in his mouth and yelled out around it:

— Maybe she has and maybe she hasn't. What's it to you?

Heike went back to thumbing through the notebook, one hand pressed to her ear, as though she needed to concentrate. Dolan swivelled on the bench until he was sitting just at the corner of it, feet wide and flat on the floor.

— What's it to me? How about a beer for a paying customer?

— You can have a soda.

— So who wants a soda?

— Buddy, I don't gotta give you nothing at this hour. How about a tall glass of nothing?

Dolan stood up and walked over to the counter, lifted the swing latch and ducked behind it to the kitchen side. Heike took the hand off her ear.

— Hey! Do I gotta get the cops in here? The waiter jumped off his stool.

Next to him, the cook laid down his fork and sat tall. He was a big man, but not what you'd call fat. Not really. His bones were solidly set.

On the other side of the counter, Dolan regarded his surroundings. There was a clock with three hands, two black and one red, hanging on the wall over the cash register. He reached up and dialled the clock's long hand back a few turns, then lifted the swing latch and passed through to the restaurant side again. The waiter was on his feet but didn't make a move as Dolan walked by.

When he was sitting down, he called back:

— I see it's only ten o'clock. How about a beer for a paying customer?

He drummed a little tune on the tabletop.

Heike looked up from the book and folded it shut.

— Either Eric has him, or I don't know what.

— He's hiding him someplace? His own son?

— Dani's not in the house. Arden didn't even know he was missing.

— Arden who?

The waiter was fussing with the clock.

On the jukebox, the record had changed and changed again, and now it went dead. Heike picked through her purse and set down three nickels in a slim row at the chrome edge of the table.

— I can't stand the quiet, she said. She dropped the nickels in one after the other and turned the dial. A wail blew through the silence, Ray Charles cutting in sly and reckless.

A tall glass appeared on the table in front of Dolan.

— There's your soda, the waiter said.

Up close, you could see how short he was. A kid with a comb-over. Dolan pulled a long spoon from the glass and sucked the whipping cream off it.

— Cherry and everything.

— You're a paying customer.

— You got good ears.

— So how about the paying part?

Dolan opened his jacket. The waiter took a half-step back. He had brown shoes on that didn't match his pants, with a lace-up. Dolan peeled a dollar bill off a fold and laid it neatly on the table. He turned to Heike.

— I expect these gentlemen want to close up.

The waiter hadn't moved.

— But you didn't finish your soda, pops.

The cook stood up from his meal and pushed the empty plate toward the kitchen side of the counter. Dolan made a move toward the end of the bench, and the waiter grabbed up the money and moved off in a hurry.

Heike wrapped the figurine back in its paper. Dolan stood up to leave.

—What's with the doll?

He plucked the maraschino off the top of the soda and offered it to her. She put the cherry in her mouth and sucked on it a moment, then pulled it out again by the stem.

—The doll is for you.

—I don't know if it'll match my decor.

—Not for your decor. The doll is a story I will tell you.

—Your ghost story.

—Yes. But only if you are very nice to me. She tucked it back into her purse.

—I'm always nice, Dolan said.

Heike snapped the purse closed.

—Eric says it's my fault. He says I lost him. Me. She said this without looking up. How's that for twisting the knife?

Dolan put a hand out to help her up, but she didn't notice and stood up on her own.

—I stole it, she said. The doll. From a little house where no one lives. An empty house.

—You've got a hell of a thing for abandoned houses.

—Only one. The same place I wanted you to see that night. Only it was too dark.

—Why'd you take it?

—I took it, and then later I went back again with Daniel. To that house. I can't explain why. She stopped. No. That's not true. I went back because I felt something there. I felt like the house . . . I don't know. Like it should be seen.

The waiter had crossed the floor and was standing in the entrance, holding the door open. He cleared his throat.

— Time, lady.

— How'd you get here, anyway? Dolan said.

— Arden.

— Of course.

— I thought if I came all the way to Auburn you couldn't possibly turn me down.

Then:

— You really don't remember Arden? She brought me to your house that first time. When I met you in the greenhouse.

— I remember the greenhouse.

They passed through the doorway, and there was the *thunk* of the deadbolt behind them. Through the glass, the waiter turned away and moved back toward the counter. His shoes were cheap, and from here Heike could see that one sole was hanging half loose. It flapped a little as he walked. She watched him draw himself a beer.

Dolan was already a few steps away and backtracked to where she was standing.

— I meant, why'd you take it just now? Why bring it along?

She turned away from the door. Inside the diner she'd felt light-headed, unreal in the brightness and the music from the coin machine, Dolan's pinging argument with the waiter. The parking lot was unpaved and smelled of loose earth, and the air felt almost damp enough to be called mist. Too warm to be mist: steam, then. The clouds held it down around her, the night heat and the stillness pressing into her shoulders, the back of her skull. There was a pulse to the silence, and she realized Dolan was speaking, had spoken to her.

She looked down for Daniel, to take his hand, a habitual thing.

— I keep thinking he is right here, she said. Just here beside me. I can feel him, his little shoulder, his hand against my leg.

A kind of tinnitus.

— What kind of person could do this?

Heike looked around for the car. She held both the purse and the notebook close to her chest, behind crossed arms. Dolan held her elbow to guide her.

He opened the door for her, and she slid into the front seat. The top was up. She was glad of it: the wetness of the night air pricked at her bare legs, a few spitting raindrops. Inside the car, the air was close, but at least there was no rain. She had shoes on, but her feet were grey to the ankles: the adventure in the bush with Eric's car. Dolan shut the door and walked around to the other side and got in.

— Your place or mine?

She looked at him, and it was like she'd had a knock to the head and was slowly coming around. He was trying to bring her back and kept trying:

— No? And here I thought you were interested in a nightcap.

— I think you're drunk already, she said.

— I'm perfectly sane.

— That's not the same thing.

Dolan turned the key in the ignition, and the car lit up. There was no radio at that hour. Ahead of them the traffic signal went dark, then blinked red.

She pulled out the figurine in its wrapping and tucked it between her knees and held it there for safekeeping, then changed her mind and put it away again, and reached the purse over the back of the seat and let it fall to the floor behind them.

Her wrists felt hot and swollen, and she touched the insides of them together, massaging them lightly, artery to artery. There were no other cars on the road. Dolan didn't talk now but pulled a pack of Lucky Strike from inside his jacket and lit one as he drove. He offered the box to Heike, but she just looked out the window and shook her head.

Dolan lit a second cigarette, and a third. She was quiet. They were close to where he lived now. He flicked the wipers on and they streaked back and forth across the horizon. The house-keeper would be asleep when they got there. This was not the same as going to a man's house for a party.

The mechanical sweep of the wipers as the rain picked up, the rubber-on-glass throbbing, *shh-wump, shh-wump*. She closed her eyes.

For a moment she was back in Eric's office. He was slumped in his chair, and she backed away from him, only this time his eyes were open, watching her go. She tried to pull the door shut between them, but something held it back. Eric rose out of the chair and began to push toward her, heavily, as though he were coming through water. She pulled and pulled at the door, but it would not shut and she abandoned it, running down the hall to the front entrance. She turned to look into the armoire drawer, but this time it was empty, and she realized she already had the little figurine tight in her fingers. As she laid a hand on the front screen to push it open, the voice came again. So close. As though the girl, Tessa, were right next to her, could whisper in her ear. She turned back and Eric was gone. Now it was the girl coming down the hall behind her, her body shimmering as though she'd just burst out of the pond into bright sun. Her lips curled back, teeth bared and shining as a dog's.

The flush of her own pulse woke Heike suddenly, a searing pain at her temples. She held her hands crossed in her lap, her fingernails digging hard enough into her palms to leave marks.

Dolan had turned south down the lake while she slept. There were boats in the water, moored and waiting like big-eyed animals. She pressed her wrists against each other again, and it was as though she were applying a tourniquet. Like some part of her was throbbing out, beat by beat, and she had to stop the bleeding. He pulled the car around the side of the house and killed the motor.

The girl's voice still resonating in her mind, *I remember, I remember you.*

THERE WAS A TRAY of sandwiches under a glass cake dome on the table in the back kitchen. Left by the housekeeper, Heike supposed, but Dolan clutched his heart when she said this and swore that he had made them just for her.

— Cucumber sandwiches? Or tuna and mayonnaise?

— Liverwurst, he said. That's almost the same thing.

Heike clutched her own heart. He had a few brown beers in the icebox, and they drank them cold out of the bottle. Heike said she couldn't possibly eat liverwurst sandwiches for breakfast and Dolan assured her that what they were eating was supper, or maybe lunch.

— Right now I'd say you need some sleep.

— All I've done is sleep, Heike said. Sleep and sleep and sleep. For years.

She took her bottle to the window and stood there, looking out. The faint glow from a string of patio lanterns along the rail of the back veranda, somewhere off to the left of where she stood, provided a smudge of grey light: the outline of a few garden hedges, the rosebushes nearest the windows. Farther back, the lawn sank into darkness. Heike pressed a hand against her belly, fingers stretched out. Daniel's face as she had left him, tucked into bed, a thumb resting against his lips.

She could see the kitchen sink in periphery, and the edge of the table, and she remembered the cook, Mickey, sleeping there while the guests played cards on the lawn. For a moment she felt she'd made a terrible mistake. It was still the night of the clambake, she hadn't returned home, Daniel wasn't missing: a blip, a kind of anxious daydream. So afraid of what Eric might do that she'd made this all up and lived out her nightmare wandering around alone in a strange house. It was suddenly brighter in the room. She felt for a moment as though she were waking up.

She turned back to the kitchen but found it empty, the beer bottle warming in her hand. No cook or kitchen crew. Just Dolan at the table, sitting back, one ankle crossed over a knee.

— I think I might go mad, Heike said.

He'd pulled out a pair of reading glasses. There was a stack of mail in his lap, and he set it on the table.

— We won't let that happen.

Heike stood there with her hand still pressed against her belly. The hand was holding her together. It was keeping her from spilling out, from doubling over, from screaming. Everything stayed quiet and inside. Where her hand was, there was only a hole.

The hum of the refrigerator started up. Dolan put the glasses on.

She stepped forward and plucked them away and folded them.

— You're crippling an old man.

— Not so old.

She set the glasses gently on the sandwich tray.

— So you say.

— There's no one else here?

— Worried?

He went to stand up, but she laid on a hand on his shoulder and he stayed where he was. She picked her skirt up and strad-dled him, the skirt swishing all around. His arms hung loose at his sides, and she wished he would take hold of her somehow, her waist, press the flat of his hand into her back and draw her in. The hole at her centre an icy thing, expanding out.

— It's like I woke up in a nightmare, Heike said. But there's no monster. Only emptiness.

She set her hands against his chest. He picked a leaf out of her hair.

— Tell me you were climbing trees.

— I was climbing trees.

— But really.

There was a pause. She could see their reflection in the window glass, blanched in the hard light.

— I want to feel something else, she said. I need to feel some-thing besides this.

He began to pick at the buttons on her dress. When he was done, Heike slid it down off her shoulders and it fell to her waist. Her hair had fallen away from its pins for good and she brushed it back, away from her neck, and pushed at the straps of her bra until they slipped loose, down toward her elbows. Dolan ran a finger along the lace trim and then tugged the band until it gave, the hook pulling the eye out of its stitching.

The kitchen light shone down from overhead and made her skin glow, pale and bright. He did not touch her but his hands hovered between them, palms out, as though it were a holdup.

—What do we do now?

She pushed his hands down flat against her thighs and he leaned in and put his mouth on her collarbone, her shoulder. His hands were cold from holding the cold beer bottle and his mouth was cold from drinking it and when she kissed him she saw that her own mouth was just as cold and it felt good and clean and hard to kiss him like that, with the rain outside and the July warm night. She cupped her own breast and pushed closer.

He dug his teeth in so that she gasped. She had one hand wrapped around the back of his head; with the other, she fumbled for his belt. Her skirt was in the way. Her skirt was everywhere, light and gauzy and tangling up in her fingers, and she started to laugh but it came out like a kind of crying. He slipped his hand into her waistband and the button broke loose but even that wasn't fast enough and she gripped it herself, tearing the fabric away in a long strip, the dress falling back onto the floor and her hands on him now, guiding him in, the awful brightness of the ceiling light and the shadow of them moving on the kitchen table and in the window, their reflection, pastel and glossy against the black.

WHEN THE SUN WAS COMING UP, he poured a bath and she sat on the edge of it and drained the water out and scrubbed her dirty feet first under the running tap, then plugged it up again. She lay back and showed him how you can use a bar of soap to blow bubbles from the palm of your hand. The housekeeper arrived,

either from an outbuilding or her own house or a room somewhere; Heike didn't know and didn't see her, but there was hot
coffee. Dolan brought it to her on a tray.

She counted the corners of the room before she slept. This is
a way to have a wish granted. His bedsheets were the colour of
oyster shells.

13.

Tell me about him.

— Eric?

They hadn't closed the curtains. The rain that had begun in the early hours came down in a soft sheet now, marking off the boundaries of the house. The house its own country.

— Not Eric. Who cares about Eric?

She'd been dozing, half bound in the bed linen, her feet and legs sticking out. Now she drew them high under the covers and hugged her knees in.

— Daniel, then.

When she said the name, something cold needled through her and made it hurt to breathe. As a child she'd had pneumonia, the bacteria edging its way between membranes until every breath was a blade in her back. Pleurisy, the doctor had said. (A lady doctor from the university; her son lived in the apartment above. She drew the fluid out with a long, hollow syringe, and Heike's mother held her still.)

Now Heike's gaze sharpened, but she didn't turn to him; she

stayed on her back to quell the ache. She'd hardly slept at all, but had lain quiet and let her breath come in the little huffs she associated with sleep. Once or twice her hand had drifted to the side of the bed, as though the empty tumblers she'd lined up in a neat row on her own nightstand at home might be there— the tumblers with their powdery residue, along the rim or pooled to one corner of the bottom of the glass—the tonic she'd poured out into the carpet. Her mind coming back to them in a repetitive way, not unlike dreaming. She'd heard at some point a noise, some kind of banging, and her body tensed, imagining Eric at the front door. Beating his way past the maid to get in, Eric's heavy step on the stairs. But the sound only the backfire of a neighbour's car motor; this time, at least. She let her breath soften again into the sheets. A few hours of stillness as good as sleep, almost.

The rain outside was constant and thin, near invisible. She kept her eyes on the window. There was a single steady, fat drip from above the frame. A crack in the eave.

He was asking her about Daniel.

—What do you want to know?

—Anything. Draw me a picture.

She could feel that he wanted to hold her hand; or rather, he wanted her to want to hold his. To reach for him. She laid her hands flat on her own belly and rubbed at her hipbones.

— He is like other small boys, she said. Dirty. Warm. Curious: he has always his hands everywhere, looking to see what's here, what's there. Sometimes tired. Sometimes angry. She let her head tilt back and stopped talking and counted the corners of the room quietly to herself, and then again. There were six. Then, revising: Not angry, she said. Tired. Maybe sulking, a little bit. Her cheeks lifted. Hungry! Always hungry.

— You didn't have brothers.

— No.

— You'll find you go through a lot of sandwiches.

— More liverwurst, yeah?

Heike let her gaze fall away from the window, but she didn't look at him or even down at her own body, focusing instead on some point in the tangle of bedclothes, as though they were a puzzle to be solved. She played with the sheet, loosening it where it was wound too tightly around her waist.

— At night, when we are sleeping, he curls right here. She lay a hand softly against her breastbone and turned on her side to face Dolan. And his little hair. His hair is always just a bit damp from sleeping so warm, close in together. And he smells of soap, and sweet milk. His breath.

She was quiet then and lay on one side with her arm tucked under her head like a pillow. Her hand wrapped the back of her own skull, and she felt herself rocking slightly. Her jaw was tight.

Dolan pushed back against the headboard and reached for his cigarettes.

— I'll light my own, Heike said. He shook the box at her, and she picked her favourite. She put her hand out for his lighter and let her tongue run along the seam of the cigarette, quick, before sparking the flame.

— How do you speak to him?

She exhaled a little curl of smoke.

— What do you mean?

— In English or German?

— The two together.

— Both?

— German when we are alone. Or when I tell him stories. Or when I sing. But some English, too.

— Tell me a story.

— In German? I think you won't understand it.

— Tell me your best story. Dani's favourite.

She looked away.

— I don't keep track. Every story can be built a hundred ways. All you need are the bricks: a castle, a dark wood, a beautiful child. A clever little animal.

She left it there. After a moment Dolan turned his face to her.

— You think it will make you sad. He flicked his cigarette into the ashtray and set it down and let it burn there, resting on the edge of the nightstand, and rolled toward her and crooked his elbow so that he could lean up on one hand. I think it will make you feel better, he said. Not worse. I think it will make Heike feel more like Heike.

— You're making me nervous now.

— Whatever for? Go on.

His free hand slid along her hip and nudged at the inside of her thigh.

— Alright. Yes. Once upon a time . . . She pushed the hand away and drew her knees together, rolling away from him with the cigarette between her lips, an arm folded under her head like a woman lying on the beach. There was a queen, she said. Now don't distract me.

He lifted an eyebrow.

— I'll nurse my own wounds, shall I? He cast a hand toward the ashtray on the nightstand and took his cigarette back.

— Okay, Heike said. So where am I? This queen. Every day she sits in the window, doing her needlework, and every day there is a raven who comes to perch on the windowsill beside her. The queen scatters a few bread crusts for the raven, and the bird tells her stories of what is happening out in the world, outside the castle. There is only one thing the queen loves more than this pet, and this is her small daughter, Gretchen.

Heike sat up, cross-legged, and drew the sheet up over her breasts and held it there with one hand.

— The little girl sits at her feet, she said, and catches the crusts that the raven drops, and the ends of thread as her mother snips them off her embroidery.

She settled herself in her new position, and then leaned in to Dolan, her face instructional.

— Now, she said. The king is a jealous and resentful man. So much so that even this raven is a source of competition for him, and one day, upon finding the two of them there again, he threatens the bird and nails the window shut. Every morning the queen comes to the window to do her needlework, and every morning the raven joins her there, but they no longer share bread or stories. He is confined to the other side of the glass.

Heike stubbed out her cigarette with a series of small jabs before continuing.

— At this time, the king is hunting every day in the forest, hoping to find once and for all a magic hind.

Dolan's brows came together. A little ash toppled onto the sheet.

— A what?

— Like a lady deer. A magical one. Heike brushed the ash away, off the bed. Evening falls, she said. The king corners the animal and draws his bow, but the hind is really a powerful witch, and although he begs for mercy, she falls upon him with her wickedness. The king is a coward, and he cries and pleads for his life. The sound of the crying is so terrible that the witch decides to let him go. He is instantly transported back to the castle. But at that very moment, Gretchen is taken ill; when the queen goes to check on her, she finds the bed empty. The little girl has disappeared. Heike leaned back on a hand. Of course, you know what has happened.

— I suspect the witch.

— The witch has stolen Gretchen in place of her whining father. Heike's eyes softened. But do not be afraid, she said.

(Here Dolan had to swallow a laugh, and she smacked his shoulder.)

— Do not be afraid, I said. The raven, who was all the time sitting outside the window, disguises himself as a beautiful golden bird and allows the witch to capture him. Day by day, he and Gretchen plan their escape. When the king returns to the castle, he is embarrassed by what he has done—I told you he is a terrible coward—therefore, instead of pleading for his wife's forgiveness, he locks her up in her sewing room and tells all the servants that it was she who killed their daughter. But the queen does not despair. Day by day, she sits and stitches in her window and waits for her raven to return.

There was a pause, Heike shaking her head slowly.

—Alas, she said. The raven in his disguise is killed. But! There is his voice to guide Gretchen out of the forest, and together they finally manage to slip away. Locked in her room, suddenly the queen feels a firebrand go through her, a flame running from her crown right down to the tips of her toes, and in this very moment, Gretchen's feet first touch the soft grass of the meadow. This is how the queen knows that her daughter is free.

Heike stopped and adjusted the bedsheet and took a moment to smile a little. Dolan stubbed out his cigarette.

— And? he said. And?

— The queen lays down her embroidery and goes to the window where her raven used to sit. There she sees a thousand black birds descend upon her husband. And tear his body to pieces.

— Gruesome.

Heike thought about this.

— We Germans really tell the best stories, she said.

SHE DIDN'T HAVE A DRESS TO WEAR, and she put on a pair of his work pants and belted them tight, and a shirt with a collar. With the sleeves rolled up: she didn't want to lose his cufflinks, she said. She had to hold still and stand on a chair while he sheared off the bottoms of the trousers with a pair of black-handled kitchen scissors. Afterward, she creased them sharply up into floods, to hide the ragged edges. They accomplished all this in his office, a long room on the second floor of the house.

The way he reached his arms out to help her down, the physical gesture, made her falter. How many times had she helped Daniel jump down from a bench in the park, or a chair pulled up next to the kitchen counter? She realized she'd gone a little time without thinking of him, and this made her panic. She didn't look for him here, around every corner, as she would have at home. This was in some ways a reprieve. The thought unnerved her.

Dolan waited, his hand held out.

— You'll get him back, Heike.

— I feel like I'm doing nothing at all.

— You're coming off a pretty heavy dose of tranquilizers. It might take a day or two to come up with the right plan. That's not nothing.

— It feels it. It feels like nothing.

She took his hand and jumped down. The only windows were at one end, facing south, and they gave a vague, steady light. There were no curtains. He must have thought she needed a moment to steady herself and kept his hand in hers until she noticed and shook it off, embarrassed. She walked over to the other side of the room, and busied herself with looking around the office.

— What's this?

— What do you think? Take a look.

He'd pinned a length of twine along one wall like a clothes-line. Hanging from this were fifteen or twenty pegs, each peg pinching a stiff white page the size of a poster. She reached out to touch one and held it away from the wall, the corner firm between her thumb and forefinger. It was plain card, well made, the edge raw and soft as torn fabric. He'd scrawled on them all in pencil, each sheet divided into boxes and in each box a kind of scene: stick figures and bits of text. Description or maybe dia-logue, or even just a single question, repeated:

Going my way?
Picture a woman.
Street scene, summer, man on a sidewalk.
The time is now. The place is here.
Walking distance.

Heike moved along the row, examining each sheet in turn

and letting them fall back in place as she went. The clothesline bobbed.

— These are your stories. She turned to him slowly, one sheet still held loosely between her fingers. Her face shone in the afternoon light, wide open and pleased. Your stories for the television. *The . . . The Mind's Eye.* Isn't it?

— These are them.

— There are so many.

— I'm not a guy who gets bored.

She turned back to the page she was holding and ran a hand over top of it, as though trying to clear away some fine debris that had settled there.

— Tell me about this. What's happening in here?

Dolan moved forward to where she was standing.

— You call that a storyboard, he said. Mitigated. Like a sketch. So each sheet is one story. He unfastened the peg and pulled the page away from the wall and held it out to the light. I'll have to write a script for each one of these.

— Yes, yes, I know this. But what is *happening* in it?

— What, the story? There's this man, see him? Call him Jones. See, here he is. (Dolan pointed to a rough figure, head and limbs, and next to it, some low thing. A dog. A cart? A car, Heike thought, she could see the circles now, for wheels.)

Dolan kept on:

— Ad man type, he said. Out for a drive, looking for a day pass from Madison Avenue, and his car breaks down. Wouldn't you know it, the service station needs an hour or so to do the job. But he looks up and sees a road sign pointing to his own hometown. The thing is, Jones hasn't been back there in years, and it's only a mile down the road. So he decides to give it a shot.

Heike took the sheet back.

—Walking distance, she said. The words were repeated at the top and bottom of the page. She tapped at them with a finger.

—You got it. It's walking distance. Only when he gets there, he hasn't just walked down the road. He's walked back in time. He sees himself as a kid. Dolan stood a few feet from her now, bouncing with energy. He goes to the soda fountain and orders an ice cream—a triple scooper—and the jerk only charges him a dime. And here's Jones, he's thinking, This is great, this is wonderful, nothing's changed. Nothing's changed, not even the price of ice cream. There's a calliope and a merry-go-round, and he can watch himself ride it, his kid self.

—What does the child do?

—The kid? You mean the kid Jones?

—The kid Jones. When he sees the man.

—I haven't got to that part yet, he said. Here's the thing: this man, Jones, he's idealized his childhood. He's rhapsodized the whole place, the whole town.

Heike pegged the board back on the line. It was fastened there, but she held on to the bottom corner anyway, regarding the rough panels for a moment before turning back to face him.

—So, it's that childhood was so wonderful? Or because he is so unhappy as a man?

—Neither. It's like a dream. No, not a dream. Dolan was moving around the room again. The opposite, he said. It's the opposite. It's like waking up. He stopped. Like you wake up from a night of hard dreaming and you have that moment, this is my bed, my pillow, that's my yard out the window. My car, my shoes, in the kitchen the same coffee is brewing in the same pot. You can smell it brewing. You know what that is?

Heike opened her mouth and closed it again. He wasn't taking a breath.

— It's grace, Dolan said. He sank his hands into his trouser pockets. That's what it is. Grace.

He quit talking for a moment and stood there with his hands in his pockets and nodded to himself, then looked over to where Heike was standing.

— So you must also yearn for this, she said. For Leo Dolan, the child. For the merry-go-round.

— Don't you?

Heike stared at him.

— I mean, isn't there some time you'd like to go back to? What if your first husband was never killed. Wouldn't you like to live that other life?

— With Harry?

— With Harry.

— I only remember little things.

— But you remember the feeling.

She looked at the storyboard again, frowning.

— It's funny, what I remember. I remember the coffee percolator, the way that sounded in the morning. And his cologne, the smell of his cologne. She dropped the sheet back into its place on the line. We wanted a baby, she said. Or I think we did. She brought her hand to her belly and looked down at it, her fingers grazing the borrowed shirt. Her brow furrowed. But then I wouldn't have Daniel, she said. She shook it off and looked up. So I can never choose to go back like that, she said. Even if I could. Even if it wasn't just a nice story.

Dolan stepped toward her.

— Nah. You hit the nail on the head. That's the whole problem right there. Our man walks down his old street to his old house, but then he sees his folks. And his folks don't recognize him. Why would they?

— Hasn't he been back to see his parents in the meantime? Or his parents are really dead?

— His parents are dead.

— Aha. So. Now he is an orphan, and this scares him. That's why he is out driving. And why he wants again to be a child.

— All grown men are orphans, Dolan said.

Heike tilted her head.

— Everyone has such fears, she said. *Orphan* is another word for *lonely*. That's all it means. It means *alone*.

She turned away and started to move down the length of the wall, tracing the line of pages with her fingers. She hopped the fingers over each peg.

— You should write another one, she said. You should write one where instead of the man going back in time, the child comes forward. You know what you call that? A phantasm.

— You mean phantom.

— No, I don't. Phantasm. Not a ghost; more like a projection. She looked up and gave him a little shrug. You're surprised I know these things. I used to read some of Eric's books in the evenings, after Daniel went to sleep. When Eric was busy working.

— An armchair psychologist. Just my luck. I'd better watch my step before I get a diagnosis of my own.

Toward the far end of the clothesline she stopped.

— What's this? she said.

Dolan was silent, still lost in thought over the Jones story. Heike slowly unpegged the sheet and took it over to the window. For the first time, she used his given name.

— Leo.

There were only three panels on the page. In one, a woman's face, rough-drawn, and in the next, a smaller figure, pigtails, something tucked under her arm. A blanket. A teddy bear. Something in the drawing of the little girl. Indefinable, the angle of her face, the eyes. Her name, a loose scrawl across the bottom of the page. Heike felt a quick wave of nausea, the rise and fall of a boat churning in the ocean.

She let her arm drop to her side, and the page with it. She was small against the window and felt smaller dressed in Dolan's clothes. Like a girl who'd been into the dress-up trunk. The light coming in washed through her, her face pale and tenuous, crystalline.

She held the page out to him.

— Where did you get this?

Dolan took his hands from his pockets and crossed the room in a few long strides. Standing next to him, Heike had to tilt her head up more than felt comfortable. She wished for a small stepstool, or that he would sit down. Instead, she stepped back. Dolan took the page and looked it over.

— This is my third-grade teacher. Miss Healey. I came up with a whole story about her. This little girl appears out of nowhere, see? She just shows up one day, on the apartment steps. Says her mother is missing, she can't find her. And Miss Healey has a soft spot for lonely kids, on account of her own mother being killed when she was a girl.

— Is this a real story?

— Is it true? Nah, I made it up. Like an apple for the teacher.

— You kill her mother and call this a gift?

— It's a real shiny apple, I promise you. I don't have much yet. Fiona comes home from work one day—Miss Healey's first name was Fiona—and there's the girl, sitting on the steps outside her door. A new girl, she thinks, and she invites her in. But then an old friend of hers drops by from out of town, and the kid makes a break for it, she doesn't want to see him—

— What about this . . . this part? Heike pointed to the text at the bottom of the page. Where did you get this?

— What's the matter with you?

— I just want to know how you came up with this.

She'd taken the sheet back and was examining it steadily.

— I don't know. I was looking at a list of names and I saw that one. Lisa. So I gave it to this kid here.

— Lisa.

What's with you all of a sudden?

— I thought it said Tessa.

— I never was any good at penmanship.

Heike looked back at the sheet and then let it drop in her hand. There was a pause before she spoke again, as though she'd lost interest but had to make polite conversation anyway.

— What else happens in your story?

— The kid keeps visiting Fiona, dropping these clues about her own mother being gone, until finally Fiona is convinced that the kid is a ghost: they were both murdered, the mum and the tot. But whenever she tells her old pal about it, he just blows it off.

— Why doesn't he believe her?

— Because if he believes her, it's not a ghost story. Dolan held his hands wide, as though he were describing the size of something, but it was just his way of getting excited. What you need for a ghost story is two things: a ghost and someone who doesn't believe in 'em. You need a good strong skeptical voice of reason, so the guy sitting in his living room can believe in the ghost and feel smarter than the guy on TV who doesn't.

— How terrible.

— It's the way of the world. Dolan tipped his chin and made a little click with his tongue. If you want this ghost over here to be real, then that guy over there has to deny it.

— Give me some paper.

— You look like you've seen some kind of ghost yourself.

Heike looked up at him.

— Give me some paper! Please.

Dolan regarded her a moment before throwing an arm out.

— Plenty over there, he said.

He pointed at the green-topped drafting table in the centre of the room. Underneath the table, Heike could see a carton of paper, the same cardstock he'd been using to make his story-boards. She started toward the table, then stopped and came back to where Dolan was standing. He hadn't moved. She grabbed his wrist.

— Come on.

She pulled a single sheet out of the carton and laid it flat on the surface of the desk. There was a fat hole drilled in the top of the angled tabletop, and Dolan had lodged a jam jar into it and filled the jar with odds and ends: a letter opener, a few plain brown pencils with empty chrome tips, the rubbers all worn down to nubs, a bone-coloured folder, an awl. Resting on the table itself was a Pink Pearl eraser, one side used, the other end immaculate. Heike took up a pencil and started drawing.

— Here we are, she said. Here is me and here is Daniel. Here is the cabin. And here, in the pond, there is a raft, see? We sit on the raft like this, and suddenly there is a girl in the water. She sketched out the scene quickly: Daniel's interaction with the girl, the clapping game, the way the girl dove down and vanished. Heike's attempt to rescue her, and Daniel's own near drowning.

— This is the cabin you tried to show me.

— There was nobody there, Leo. No family. No mother, no father looking for her. Nobody in the woods.

— And in the house?

— Nobody.

— You went in?

— No. Not together. I couldn't take him in, she said. Daniel. I had a bad feeling, so we stayed outside.

She described the doorway, wildflowers strong and bright and tall, aside from the few crushed by her own footfall on her earlier visit, and the thin burn mark, a fire line, across the threshold.

— I pushed the door open and called out, she said. But there was no one. And then this, look at this. She still had the pencil in her hand, and it seesawed back and forth between her fingers as over a fulcrum. She tapped the page. A day later Eric took us to the Willard. Daniel was talking and playing in the bushes, just the same, a clapping game. Only this time no one else was there. He was playing by himself. Like this: Heike dropped the pencil in order to clap her palms together and then slapped them lightly against Dolan's chest. She pulled back and held the hands out to him, fingers wide.

— When he stopped, his hands were all bloody from the thorns. It was the same game he played with the little girl on the raft, but this time he was alone. She looked up at Dolan. It scared me, she said. But now . . . now I feel like it was an omen. It was a sign.

— This is a real thing?

— Yes, of course it's real. I'm telling you it's real. Only a few days after that, he was gone.

Dolan took her hands and folded them together.

— But Heike, we know where Daniel is.

— I don't know.

— Of course you know. He's with Eric. He's got to be. Didn't you tell me that yourself?

— How can you be so sure? She pulled back, wrenching her hands away. He's gone. He's missing, she said. Disappeared. Just like that little girl, just like Tessa.

— And just like your sister.

She didn't answer, and Dolan closed his mouth and looked over what she'd drawn out, her own rough panels. Heike laid a hand on the page, as though he'd been trying to take it from her.

— You think I'm being foolish.

— You don't need a detective, Heike. Your son is with your husband. He leaned in as he said it, catching her eye and holding it. What you need is a damn good lawyer.

Heike took her hand off the desk, lightly, and shook out her cuffs so that her wrists disappeared into the sleeves, just the fingertips showing. It was hard to keep her breath even. She had the urge to run and keep running as long as her legs would hold her up.

She looked around the room, the muscles in her neck and shoulders taut.

— You told me you wanted a ghost story, she said. So. Now you have one.

He took the pencil from her and began to doodle a border around the edge of the page. She watched him for a moment, his smooth lines curling in and out of each other. He was either trying to stay calm himself or trying to distract her. He lifted the pencil, thoughtful.

— What does this have to do with Miss Healey?

— Who?

His own page, the one Heike had been looking at when she'd called him over, lay to one side of the table. He pushed it toward her.

— This, Dolan said, stubbing at it with two fingers. It must have linked up in your mind somehow. What's the connection?

Heike fingered the edge of the page.

— Because I saw your little girl, your ghost girl, and it reminded me so much of Tessa. That's what Dani called her. Tessa.

Dolan's drawing of the girl with her teddy bear seemed sharper now. She fought an urge to lay her hand over the image, to cover her up. She brought the hand up to her eyes instead and gave her temples a rub.

— Or I think so, she said. It all seems crazy now. Crazy and very far away.

Dolan kept his attention down on the page, but his face lightened.

— So that's why you thought I'd written *Tessa*. Instead of *Lisa*. You're right, that would be creepy. But no such luck. Truth is, I don't believe in omens.

He went back to his drawing a second or two longer, then set the pencil down and caught her eye again. The light in the room had changed a bit; he looked older.

— I can tell you right now, he said. You have nothing to worry about. If you saw a little girl, she was probably from around there. There are rich kids and poor kids in your neck of the woods, and the poor kids are good swimmers because their parents just let them roam around outside. That kid was probably halfway home by the time you ever dove after her.

Heike stayed where she was but leaned toward him.

— I think about her all the time.

— You're a mother. You can't help yourself.

She looked down at her own page, the raft and the children drawn simply, a few gestural pencil lines. Dolan sketched something else in now, another figure.

— Your Dresden doll. He gave the figure a few punctuating taps with the tip of his pencil. Now, see, for the TV show, that's what would be causing all the distress.

— The figurine?

— There's the money. The doll is haunted. Not the little girl.

Heike looked away to the window and then back again.

— And she has a voice, this doll. Don't you think? A voice that seems to come out of nowhere.

— You're a natural. I knew it as soon as you started telling me your raven story. We'll call it "Living Doll."

Heike folded the page sharply in half, and then in half again, the drawings now hidden away inside the crease lines.

— I'm not making up stories, Leo. I'm telling you. I heard a voice. Last night, just before I left the house for good. Just after I found the doll. She pushed up on her tiptoes, holding his shoulder for balance. Right in my ear, she said. Like this.

— An animal. Or trees creaking. Or nothing. You were half out of your wits.

— I was full wits. It wasn't a tree or the wind or anything else you can think of. I heard it, just as I hear you now. Just as you hear me. A child's voice. A girl.

He hesitated.

— You've been through a hell of a week.

But she didn't let go of his shoulder, and he stooped a little and his ear came closer.

— *I remember you.* That's what she said. *I remember you.*

— Who said? Dolan straightened himself a little. Heike came down off her toes, her hip striking the edge of the table. The impact jarred the two pages, Dolan's and hers, and they shifted downward, one sliding into the other as a hand might go into a pocket.

Heike rubbed at her hip.

— Tessa, she said.

14.

In the evening they sat out on the back veranda, looking down the long lawn where the clambake had been a few nights before. There were still divots in the grass, Dolan said, from the card tables. Their sharp-turned legs. The table was set for dinner, and Heike played with the flat of her knife, pressing her thumb into it and then watching as the print faded and disappeared. The sun was low, and it caught in the glass of the greenhouse and glinted there like odd shards, sharp against the eye, flame orange. There were still a few more weeks of true summer; the light had not yet begun to thin. Dusk settled in, and the garden went a little bit blue. Dolan had a rolling cart pushed up next to the rail and he made Manhattans, dropping in sour cherries from a glass jar. Imported: his friend Azzopardi had brought them back from France.

Heike could see the willows on the other side of the yard reflected in the greenhouse panes, the draping branches distorted by the light. Their movement almost animal-like, undulating in a way that suggested meditation, not weather. The glass itself was liquid and lawn green, and grew darker as the sun slipped off. Heike was still wearing Dolan's sawed-off trousers. Her feet were bare. The housekeeper served the soup, the toe of her shoe needling up against Heike's ankle bone. Heike flinched in alarm. A little electroshock.

— Sorry, she managed, although as she said it she knew it was not her fault, and in fact she was the guest. I'm sorry.

The housekeeper squinted at her as though she was not familiar with the word and tipped the ladle into Dolan's bowl.

— Sorrel, ma'am. Sorrel. That's why it's so green.

She was an older woman and well used to Dolan's bachelor proclivities. She'd worked for him a long time. Heike wanted to thank her but trailed off, and the woman disappeared into the house, smoothing her apron once her back was turned. The soup was left in a red ceramic tureen between them, Heike and Dolan. The ladle had its own plate.

— I don't know her name, she said.

— What's that? Oh, you mean Susan. There was a bit of cress floating in the soup as a garnish, and Dolan pinched it up between his thumb and forefinger. Mrs. Hammond, he said. You should call her that: the Mrs. name. She's fussy at times, with, you know. He flicked the cress over the railing into the garden below. Well, he said. She will be fussy with you.

— With your ladies? Heike leaned forward, filling her spoon and then tipping it so the soup ran out in a thin stream, rippling into a circle within the larger circle of the bowl. She was cooling it down. Tell me, she said. Do you always chop off the legs of your pants for a new lady friend?

Dolan was eating. Next to the tureen was a little dish of oyster crackers, and he tossed a few of these into his bowl the way you'd shoot dice.

— Most of my lady friends manage to hold on to their dresses, he said.

He'd pegged her storyboard, the sketches of Tessa and Daniel, to the line in his office as though it were one of his own, Heike's ghost story falling between a man condemned to prison on a far-off planet and an aging movie star desperate to disappear into the screen and escape her own redundancy. When she'd pressed him again about the story, though, he'd only brushed her hair back away from her face and taken her jaw in his hands.

— You're anxious. You want to find your boy. Of course you do.

— But we don't know, we don't, that Eric has him. I don't know.

— I think we know that.

The Dresden figurine stood on the table now, with the soup and the crackers. Heike reached out and touched it from time to time, laying it flat, then standing it up again. Some other position always felt safest. Inside the house the phone rang, a jarring sound. The housekeeper did not pick it up straight away, and Heike looked at Dolan, alarmed, and dropped the spoon in her hand.

— He doesn't know you're here, Dolan said.

— It's only a matter of time.

The ringing stopped and she waited, her eyes on the house, to see if Mrs. Hammond would arrive with a message.

— Tell me again, Dolan said. How you managed to wind up with him in the first place. He was eating in a brusque way, but did not slurp.

— Eric? Heike tipped up her bowl a little, trying to distract herself. I met him in Switzerland. I don't know. 1950, I'd say?

We came to America in 1951. He has the paperwork somewhere.

It occurred to her that the empty file drawers she'd seen in his office meant that this paperwork must now be stashed away at the Willard, or in some other place as yet unknown to her. A bank box, a safe with a key.

— And you were unwell?

— I was staying at the convent. After my first husband died. There was the accident, and they brought me back to the convent to recuperate. Because I had no family, you see. She stopped. She set her bowl down and lay the spoon flat on the cracker plate, pushing the leftover crackers to one side. He was so terribly tall, she said. Harry was. And with big hands. She folded her own hands together, resting them on the table. He could never keep still, she said. You can see why you make me think of him a little.

— Always bouncing around, am I?

— You're not a guy who gets bored. See? I remember.

Dolan pushed his bowl away and the spoon left inside it made a sound against the china. The effect was more like a Christmas ornament than a mess kit. He said:

— And you don't remember the accident?

— I don't remember being hit. But I must have been, because there I was, back at the convent, and they sent an American doctor to look after me. Because of Harry, because he'd been in the army.

— And the doctor married you.

— Eric? Yes.

— The convenience!

— Very quietly, I think. In a small room.

Mrs. Hammond came back to remove the bowls. There was no telephone message, she said, when Dolan asked her. Only a wrong number. Heike, newly relieved, tried to pass along the tureen. The housekeeper carried a tray with her and set it down on a side table and took the used dishes and replaced them with what she'd brought: whitefish, pan-fried, and in a sauce; some potatoes in butter and parsley; tiny green peas mixed with smoked ham and sautéed whole onions, little ones, the size of your fingernail.

— I wish I could tell you more, Heike said. I wish I could remember. I try. But it feels like work. And then I don't know what I'm making up and what really happened. She turned in her seat: Thank you, Mrs. Hammond. Thank you.

The woman nodded as she picked up her tray, but did not seem to be nodding particularly at Heike, or in response to anything that had been said.

— And then we came to New York, Heike said. We lived on Eighty-Sixth Street. But by that time, I already had Daniel. So.

The fish was a more delicate thing than she would have imagined Dolan ordering, and she wondered if Mrs. Hammond simply chose everything for him: the flatware, the menus, the linens in the bedroom.

— The girl you saw at the pond, Dolan said. The little girl who disappeared. I upset you earlier, when I said it sounded just like your sister.

— You wonder if I'm losing my marbles. Seeing Lena in the woods?

— You've been through your share of hard times.

— No. No, this girl is quite different. She could almost be Daniel's sister, not mine: blond and with such light eyes. Lena was dark, with dark hair. My father used to say she was the gypsy coachman's daughter, but he only laughed half the time. There was a basket on the table, and Heike reached for it and twisted a piece of bread in her hand until it tore into two pieces. I used to look for her, she said. Lena. On the crowded train in Europe, and then here: in Central Park, or Rockefeller Center. Anywhere there are a lot of faces. I used to comb through, checking always for her dark eyes. But I stopped looking. I had to. She picked the puff of soft crumb out of the middle of the bread and let it rest in the flat of her hand. Some people just stay lost, she said.

— You're afraid now that Daniel will stay lost.

— I feel a little bit lost myself.

She shifted her plate to one side, and Mrs. Hammond came along to clear up.

— Do you eat sweets?

Dolan followed the housekeeper into the house and came out with a bottle of champagne and a silver-wrapped box, smaller than a deck of cards.

He said he wasn't one for pastries, so Mrs. Hammond was unlikely to have done any baking. But he had some chocolates for her, just in case. She said she would eat a chocolate, just one, if it were very simple and very sweet.

Dolan pushed up on the cork with both thumbs and let it fly.

AFTER THEY'D EATEN, he wanted to walk down to the water. A few extra moments of calm; to Heike, the time felt stolen, breathless. The grass had gone damp with the cooler evening air. Dolan took off his shoes and swung her up onto his back, and they charged the willow trees. Heike clapped a hand over her mouth to keep from shrieking. She hadn't had a firm hold on his shoulders, and the sudden speed had nearly capsized her.

— Some decorum, my dear! He clicked his heels together and she jounced on his back, the long strands of the willow trailing down and playing with her hair like dumb fingers.

— Yes, of course. Mrs. Hammond is watching! But the moment she said it she felt it must be true and made him turn in a circle so that she could make sure they were quite alone.

Where the lawn turned to sand, he let her down off his shoulders and politely asked her for his clothes back.

— Right now?

— I'm afraid so.

— But the pants are no good for you anymore! You cut them, *snip snip*! She tipped her head to one side and made a scissor motion with two fingers.

— All the same. They are mine, and I did pay for them. Perhaps I can use them as shorts someday.

— These are really deplorable manners. She was working away to untie the knotted belt that held the pants to her waist. The knot gave, and she stripped the belt out clean and handed it to him. Don't think I am ever coming back to one of your parties, Mr. Dolan.

The pants, unbolstered, slipped down off her hips of their own accord.

— There are limits, Mrs. Lerner, to a man's generosity. Even as concerns guests. He folded the belt and tucked it into his own back pocket. Now. My trousers.

She stepped out of the pants and left them on the sand, and he crouched low to retrieve them, then, stopping there instead, he pointed to their shadows, one hand resting high on the inside of her leg.

There was a little glow coming down from where they'd been

sitting on the porch, but the true light now was the moon. The sky had cleared. In shadow, he was not much more than a mushroom. Her loose man's shirt hung straight off her shoulders like a box. Standing tall over him, Heike might have been a giant.

A giant on high, wooden stilts: the line of her bare legs stretching long and straight to meet the ground. A heron-maid. She had the silly thought that the shadow matched up more exactly with her true self than a reflection ever had. She straightened, raising her arms high over her head. Suddenly she was amplified, her diaphragm filling and her body—limbs, torso, her neck upon her shoulders—unfolding, link by link, lengthening out like rope.

A breeze came up and whipped along the surface of the lake. There was a ripple at the shore. She unbuttoned the shirt and it fell away like wings, leaving only her bird's skeleton behind.

SLEEP WAS NO LONGER the prison it had been, but neither was there any comfort in it. Heike lay in the dark, neither fully awake nor restful. She was thinking of a glass. She was thinking of the cut-glass tumbler in which Eric might mix a tonic, crushing the powder fine with a pestle, sometimes two or three colours together, the liquid cloudy, the bitterness at the back of her throat. It wasn't that she liked the feeling, or even the taste. Her head was empty aside from these thoughts. Powder, pestle, glass; powder, pestle, glass. A high ache sang in her skull, piercing, just beneath her hairline. She hadn't even fully known that she was awake.

Dolan slept, laid out on his stomach, a thin pillow flat under one cheek. Heike slipped out of bed, reaching down and patting the carpet to find her underwear, then pulling on Dolan's undershirt as though it were her own. The room was warm. She could hear the steady pace of a second hand somewhere, and set off to learn the time.

In the hallway, the dark was less complete. She went down the stairs to the kitchen, following the tick of the wall clock, louder now and oddly shifting, erratic. But when she got there, she saw that it wasn't that sort of clock at all. The time showed on the stove: five past five. The sound seemed now, in fact, to have disappeared altogether. Heike moved toward the pantry door and then back again to where she'd started, listening. Perhaps it hadn't been a tick after all, but the creak of a door. The click of one latch after another. The sound of someone moving from room to room, searching the house.

She'd left Dolan sleeping upstairs, the bedroom door closed. Whatever it was, creeping about, it was nothing that belonged there.

The faucet gave a sudden flurry of drips, and she whirled and caught herself against the counter, her voice caught in her throat. The sound tapering off to a staccato ticking.

The noise she'd heard from the stairs. The faucet almost shut off, but not quite.

She turned the tap on full and let it run cold, holding her wrists under the water to calm down, to wash away her nervousness. When she felt better, she filled a glass and drank from it, slowly, sip by sip. She did not think she could get back to sleep—by now, little tendrils of light were sneaking into the sky; she could see them from the kitchen window—but neither did she want to be alone in the kitchen, the weirdness of the last moments lingering in her. She brought the glass of water back upstairs with her and stopped outside the bedroom door, leaning there, listening for Dolan's breath. A thing she was used to doing for Daniel, when he was sleeping and she worried that the sounds of the house might wake him.

Daniel in his bed, waking at night now and calling for her. His voice rising sharper and sharper when she did not come.

Thinking of him like this pulled a tight stitch in her body. Somewhere deep in her ribs. She worked away at it anyhow, picturing him safe and warm, in clean sheets, looked after, wherever he was. An invocation. And then closer: she imagined him here, listened for his breathing along with Dolan's on the other side of the door. If she'd never married Eric, if Daniel were Leo's son.

Safe at home in this house. His hair against the pillow, small fist curled and resting next to his mouth, lips parted, his breath sweet and damp.

The idea settled her, left her calm and even. She could almost hear him, his exhalations coming soft and light. Sometimes, the nights he told her he wasn't tired at all, she'd lay his hand on her diaphragm to let him feel the measure of her own breath. His head on the pillow next to hers, a few moments enough for his body to match the steady rhythm, her belly filling, then releasing, a kind of kinetic lullaby. This was not much different, what she did now. Listening for him. A soothing exercise, even if imagined.

She brought the glass to her lips and sipped, turning back to face the hall. The sound still carrying from the bedroom. A gentle panting. And then stronger. Not Dani, of course, not really. Just Dolan's own murmurs. Some people talk in their sleep.

She stepped away from the door.

But no. It was here, too, and stronger again, the farther she came down the hall. Perhaps there was a ceiling fan in another room, something she hadn't seen, the sound of the blades catching against the walls and echoing. She moved carefully, tracking it, then turned abruptly. It seemed to come from the other direction again. She peered into the bathroom, but there was no fan there.

She found herself moving back toward the staircase. If the sound was travelling, then it couldn't be just an echo. There must be something here, a cat maybe, something almost silent but alive. She peered into the dark but nothing looked back at her.

Following it. Low to the ground. A steady beat, not leading her now, but pulling her along. At the top of the stairs she stopped, her toes curled over the edge. Leaning out.

She felt it then, next to her—not Daniel's breathing at all, but the girl's. Tessa's. As though even thinking of her son had summoned the other child instead. A rasp at the back of the throat, more animal than human. Faster now and shallow, hot against Heike's bare legs, the small of her back. The stairs running steeply down, and the floor far below, swimming before her, and the exhalation rhythmic, almost one long gasp. Pushing at her. Edging her forward.

Heike stepped back quickly, gripping the top of the banister. The hallway was empty.

A trick of the imagination. Wasn't it? A trick of the ear?

The door to the office stood open, and she stepped inside, shutting the door behind her and pressing back against it, the glass of water, still cold, held to her breastbone. What had Arden called it? The willies. But even here, she could feel it following her, throaty, a throttle. The sound of someone desperate for air. A drowning breath. She turned and moved away from the door, walking backwards past the open secretary, and came to stand with her back against the bookshelf that ran half the length of the room. She lay a hand against a stack of spines for balance. The long hiss of breath still there, always there. She moved down the line, so intent on listening that she barely noticed at first the little tug at her side. The fabric of Dolan's undershirt rubbing at her. She flexed her shoulder to shake it loose.

Then, roughly, the edge of the shirt lifted from her waist and pulled her back, hard against the shelf. When she tried to push forward again, she found she was caught there. Something held her fast. She pushed away again with a hip, the seams pulling and grating at her skin. A small hand, grasping, gripping her clothes. Tugging her down. The pressure great enough to make her bend at the knees, and she struggled to stay upright.

She took hold of the shirt herself and spun around against it, breaking free suddenly, water from the glass in her hand splashing over her neck and chest. The sound gone, all at once, swallowed up into silence. She stumbled against the wall.

Heike twisted the garment around her waist. The fabric was torn now. Not merely the seam, but a hole ripped in the cloth. She looked around. There was nothing on the shelf, anywhere, no nail or hook that could have done such damage. She set the water glass down to one side, inside the secretary, her hands shaking.

There was a creak from the doorway and she started, falling back into the corner of the desk, water from the glass sloshing again and papers flying. Half on her knees, she looked to the entry, but the door sat snug in its frame. This seemed too much; she rocked back on her heels, almost crying. Making herself small in the room.

It was from there that she saw it: a splintered place in the wooden shelf. She stood, slowly, to touch the jagged edge, just under the lip of a bracket. There was only the sound of Heike's own breath now, and even that upset her. No thread knotted through the wood. Could this have been what caught and held her?

There was a mess of papers on the floor, and Heike took a wary step away from the shelf and bent to retrieve what had fallen when she hit the desk. To try to restore order, for herself as much as anything. Receipts and jotted notes, blank postcards. A Venn diagram of discarded elastic bands: at its centre, a silver charm, meant for a lady's bracelet. Not a pillbox, but a tiny San Francisco streetcar. She could see the white border of a photograph where it had been swept by momentum almost entirely underneath the desk. More than that: a small stack of photographs. She crouched, looking just once over her shoulder, and slid a hand into the spot to draw them out.

There were three.

In the first one, Dolan cuddled up to a dark-haired woman, his arm tight around her shoulder. The fingers of his left hand curled into view. On the fourth one he wore a ring: a wide, plain band. An old photo, then. His Spanish wife. Their honeymoon. Heike leaned slightly against the desk, low on her haunches, one hand still pressed against her side where the shirt was torn.

A tall palm in the background, Dolan squinting against the sun. The woman did not wear a hat. They'd been shot from below, as though the photographer were crouched somewhere ahead of them. She remembered then that they'd met in a television studio in California, so perhaps this was not a holiday after all, but any day. The woman's black hair swirled against one side of her face. There had been a breeze. She wore sunglasses.

The other two photographs were family shots, posed and taken at a studio: Dolan, the wife, two small children. A little girl in a party dress. The baby in a sailor suit and held for the camera in his mother's arms. In another, the family lounged together on a long chesterfield, the girl's party dress a size bigger now, the boy wearing shoes. The children were both as dark as the mother, but their eyes were arctic pale, large and fringed with lashes. Dolan's eyes the same light grey, setting only the mother apart.

He'd never mentioned the children.

For a moment, Heike imagined things differently: if the wife were not dark, but fair. What Daniel might have looked like with an Irish father.

From behind her, the slightly wet sound of a throat being cleared.

— They say the early bird gets the worm, ma'am. Now I see that it's true.

Heike stood up, banging her shoulder and dropping the photographs, the lid of the desk cracking at the hinges.

— You start your day very early, Mrs. Hammond.

Heike wrapped an arm around her belly and crossed the other over her chest, her hand flat and high against her collarbone. She had not meant to be seen like this, mostly naked and snooping about. She dropped her arms and threw a hand on her hip instead.

— As do you, ma'am. The housekeeper stood in the shadow of the doorway, her own hands folded in front of her apron. She inclined her head slightly. But I have had the time to dress.

Her voice was low enough to be a man's. Heike lifted her chin to feel taller.

— Does Mr. Dolan usually require his coffee at this hour?

Mrs. Hammond stepped forward. Heike realized that she intended to pick up the photographs from where they lay at her own feet, and quickly bent down herself to get them. When she stood up, she found the other woman suddenly quite near. She stumbled back, the sharp corner of the desk jabbing her thigh.

— You found Mrs. Dolan.

— The children, Heike said. I didn't know. She sorted the pictures neatly and lay them back inside the desk where they'd been hidden. Mr. Dolan must miss them terribly, she said. Then: I understand she's run away to Europe.

— With a jazz musician? Mrs. Hammond did not quite smile. Or perhaps you've heard instead that Mrs. Dolan took up with a prizefighter.

— There was a man, Heike said. It's what he told me. The other night at the clambake. The name came back to her in a rush: Renny Paulsen, she said. We were standing on the lawn.

She stopped. Paulsen had, in fact, talked only about Dolan's fight with the network over some script or other. The drama hour about the Till case; the sponsor ripping the Coca-Cola bottles off the tables on set. It had been Arden who'd told her Dolan was a divorcé. That first night, gossiping in the corner by the kitchen and spooning up caviar.

There was a silence between them, the housekeeper saying nothing more, but waiting.

— It's not true, is it? Heike crossed her ankles and uncrossed them. She was cold, her hands and feet especially.

— Jealous people tell jealous stories.

Mrs. Hammond stepped up to the desk and straightened the little piles of receipts. Heike could see their bill from the Auburn Dinerant two nights before, sitting on top. The waiter had charged them for one egg cream; her own beer had been gratis. The housekeeper picked up the photos from where Heike had set them down.

— I'll put these away for you, she said. She paused, looking at the photo on top: Beautiful, isn't she? She stays at the California house now. What with the children in school. Mrs. Hammond slid the photos into one of the desk's little compartments. She turned to face Heike. Mr. Dolan prefers a less sedentary life, she said.

She reached a hand into the pocket of her apron and produced a set of keys. The smallest of these went into the lock at the top of the desk, the little key turning until it clicked. She slipped the keys into her pocket.

— He is quite devoted to her.

Heike gave a slow nod. Her nakedness now seemed extreme, as though she'd been caught, not simply without a dress in what had felt to her like the dead of night, but rather in the middle of some more purposeful act. As though she'd been hired to jump out of a cake, and now the job was done and Mrs. Hammond would be paying the bill on the household's behalf.

— Yes, she said. Yes, I suppose he is.

The housekeeper kept a hard-nosed vigil at the top of the stairs while Heike toed her way back down the hall. It was unspoken between them that Heike was to return to the bedroom and was not to come out again; or, at least, not without Dolan. She could see now that her introduction to the house—packed to the rafters with guests and hired staff both times—had not given her a dependable impression of the place. Empty, the house was half Mrs. Hammond's.

Dolan was still sleeping. There was some evidence he'd thrashed about the bed. Heike had left him lying calm and straight on a thin pillow, and now he was diagonal, corner to corner, with his own pillow folded in two and tucked under his neck and hers pressed sideways into his face. The strangeness of the dark house, only an hour or so before, the breath she'd felt against her skin—this all seemed very far away now. A story in a book, a tale for children, a fancy. The room smelled slightly of onions. She wondered if his pillowcase seam would leave a mark.

Heike nudged the curtain aside and cranked open the window, shivering a little in the new breeze. Tearing her dress the other night—how brazen, how bohemian in the moment!—now left her in a cage. If only she'd thought to take anything else from the house, any bit of clothing, when she was riffling through her drawers, looking for the figurine. It wouldn't have taken much. A negligée. A slip. If not respectable, she might at least have felt older, which was almost as good.

She pulled back the sheet and slid in next to him, pushing at his shoulder a little so that he'd move without really waking. There was true daylight burning through the curtains now. Dolan ceded a small part of her pillow. He moved in his sleep and pawed at her, pulling her closer and curling up, his forehead lodged against her breastbone.

How long had Mrs. Hammond been aware of her? Not just at dinner, surely, but yesterday morning, when Dolan had brought her coffee to the bedroom. She would have noticed then, the extra cup. Would, in fact, have arranged Heike's cup on the tray herself, the little bowl of sugar cubes with a silver spoon, the light blue pitcher of cream. She may have been the one to carry the tray up the stairs, Dolan following behind her in his housecoat, the belt loosely tied.

And earlier? The night of the clambake. Even at the first party, Heike slinking about the coat racks. It was Mrs. Hammond who had retrieved the chipped mask, glaring, after Heike had knocked it down.

The stitch that tightened in Heike's diaphragm whenever she thought of Daniel was no less sharp now as she imagined Dolan's children, his wife; the wife also sleeping at this hour. Perhaps a dog at the foot of her bed in his absence. A malamute. It was almost as though she could not swallow, and she pushed her tongue against the roof of her mouth to prove to herself that she wasn't choking.

He curled against her but held her with an indifferent arm. Already her body felt dependable to him. She lifted a hand and stroked his hair. She could move. It was a conscious gesture. Not like a lover, or even a wife. Her fingers worked at his brow, as though he'd had a bad dream. She had the sense that she was salvaging something of herself, piece by piece.

Of course Mrs. Hammond had known, as servants always know everything about a house. Rita must have seen so much in Heike's home; Rita, the kitchen girl, the part-time maid, scrubbing the stove while Eric crushed pills and stirred them into a glass.

Heike's hand stopped, a piece of Dolan's hair caught between her index finger and her thumb. It had not been only Eric, alone in the house, the night Daniel disappeared. Rita had, of course, been there, too. Heike remembered her in the kitchen early that morning, her stuttered replies and the dishcloth dripping water all around. The way she'd answered stuck in Heike's mind. The edges of her mouth pulling her whole face down long. As though she might cry.

Afraid of something.

Dolan, hot or else moving between dreams, wrested his head away. He threw an arm out and flipped around, his back to her.

Heike swept her hair out of her eyes. She tugged at the pillow, gaining more of it for herself, and also turned on her side. Suddenly she was sure that she would not tell him what she knew. They lay back to back.

This decision did not make the knowing any less. To his children, Heike thought, Dolan was the missing party. A story their mother told them at bedtime, a kind of prince who might someday return to the castle. A golden bird that flies away.

15.

At first, he could not understand her hurry.

She was wearing his pants again but had managed to find herself a smaller shirt, the top half of a set of silk pyjamas he'd once received as a gift and never worn. (She made some internal decisions about the giver, but did not go looking for confirmation.) Having administered a few knots in the right places, Heike now looked almost as though she were a woman wearing women's clothes: Dolan's words. She went about the house gathering up her things, the torn dress, her stockings, the bit of newspaper she'd wrapped around her Dresden doll.

The china figurine itself had gone missing. They'd left it on the table at dinner and gone on to other distractions, the little charge down to the water's edge. He told her not to worry. Mrs. Hammond had almost certainly tidied it away with the rest of the dishes. The figurine was probably washed and polished and set safely in storage in the kitchen, Dolan said.

— Then where is it? Heike made an exaggerated motion of gently closing a cupboard door. He'd asked her not to slam.

— Ask her yourself.

Mrs. Hammond, also, could not be found.

They'd been through every cupboard. Heike began a search of the back pantry. When he asked her what the rush was about, she told him to go find his car keys. She wanted to find Rita, the maid. She wanted to have a talk with her, she said, at her own house. Someplace the girl might feel safer, more honest.

— Don't get your hopes up, Dolan said. Most maids are little fools. Are you sure she was even aware she was babysitting?

Heike said the servants always know everything about a house.

— Secrets are all they have, she said. It's what gives them their power.

Dolan half-turned to the doorway to find the keys, then turned back again.

— If you want me to be nice and drive you places, you're going to have to stop smashing things.

She clinked her way through the jam jars. On waking, her long night had seemed only part of a strange dream, but the discovery of the figurine's absence left her uneasy. What she wanted was to find it someplace banal, set aside as you might any dusty trinket, in a way that would somehow prove that her feeling of dread the night before had been only that. Jitters.

There was nothing hidden away in the pantry; the shelves were open and stacked with canned peaches, tomatoes, pickled beans. Even the stamped glass jars were clear and plain, incapable of deception.

— Maybe she put it upstairs, Heike said. Do you have a display cabinet, anything, someplace you keep such things?

— I have a liquor cabinet. I don't buy "such things."

He followed her at a safe distance, watching as she made a

quick inventory of his dresser drawers, the baskets of towels and bedding in the linen closets that lined the upper hall. When they came to the office door, she paused.

He'd been up and out of the house before she'd woken the second time, late in the morning. There had been a tray with a thermal carafe of coffee waiting for her in the bedroom, but no note or indication that he planned to return. It had taken her the better part of an hour to get up the courage to go looking for him. No way of knowing if he'd seen Mrs. Hammond down in the kitchen, or what they might have talked about.

She found him standing in the middle of the lawn, reading *Variety*. He wanted a bit of sun, he told her. He didn't seem any different; that is, he seemed, if anything, warmer to her, letting his arm with the magazine drop to his side and watching her approach with a golden affection. The possibility that Mrs. Hammond was a liar danced at the fringe of Heike's mind, and for a moment she allowed it in. Her bare feet in the grass, and she shifted her weight back and forth nervously until he kissed her.

Now he went into the office ahead of her and leaned up against the high stool at the drawing table, his legs long enough that the seat did not offer him a boost. There were no drawers or hiding places in the room; just the bookshelves, easily searched, and of course the desk. She stood in the hallway, the heat rising in her body. Anxious, or embarrassed, or ashamed. She hated him for it.

No. This was not quite true. It was more removed than that. She understood in the moment that she was supposed to hate him for it. In fact, she hated Mrs. Hammond. She hated the desk itself; she hated the dark-haired woman. She hated her sunglasses. She hated the girl she'd been the night before—herself, Heike. The foolishness of that girl, spooking so easily, accidentally putting a finger on answers to questions she had not meant to ask.

She went over to the storyboard wall and pulled her sketch off the line.

— This isn't yours, she said.

Dolan's brow lifted. He glanced around the room, as though hoping to find some other person who might commiserate with him. But there was only Heike.

— There wasn't a question of it being mine. It's your story.

— I won't leave it.

— Are you leaving, then?

She didn't answer but stood there.

— Because I thought you wanted me to drive you places.

There was a beat as Dolan waited for her to speak, but Heike said nothing.

— Wherever it ends up, he said, for what it's worth, I'd rather you stayed.

She stood there with the storyboard in both hands, holding it in front of her body like a shield. He pushed off the stool and went over to the desk and rattled at the lid, surprised to find it locked.

— Listen. Let me just find my notebook here.

He was going through his pockets now, looking for something. The key to the secretary. As he pulled out the little key on its ring, Heike remembered her water glass. She'd put the glass down inside the desk, and Mrs. Hammond had sealed it in there.

— Wait, she said.

But he'd already turned the key in the lock. Dolan flipped the lid down with one hand; with the other, he took hold of the drawer underneath, pulling it out as a support for the desktop.

— Well, hey. Here you go!

Inside the desk, the water glass was gone. Heike's Dresden figurine stood in its place.

— Why do you suppose she hid it away in here? Dolan said. He handed the figurine back to Heike, and she stepped forward to take it. He didn't turn toward her. He had the notebook open already, a pencil moving in his hand.

THE GIRL, RITA, sat sullenly on a kitchen chair while Heike drew closer and closer, pulling her own chair along with her as she went. With every question she inched forward, as though she could eventually eliminate the gap between them and dive down the girl's throat and into her heart. The chair's wooden feet rasping against the linoleum floor each time. Dolan winced at the noise and also at Heike's naked, earnest look. Scraping along with her chair.

She kept her eyes on Rita. Dolan was there in her periphery, a shine to his black shoes, his back leaned up against the kitchen counter. When he'd had enough, he came around behind her and sat down in his own chair and pulled it close with one long scuffing sound. He took out his cigarettes and tossed them onto the table and spun the pack first toward Heike and then toward the girl. It was an offer.

Rita said she did not remember when Eric had come home that night, or if he'd gone out again. She did not remember any visitors coming to the house. She had not thought to go upstairs: why should she? Heike had said she'd put the little boy to bed before they left. With every one of Heike's questions, Rita shot Dolan a pained look that he did not fully understand.

— I need your help, Heike said. Tell me everything. Tell me what you *do* remember.

It HAD NOT BEEN Rita who'd opened the door when they arrived. The drive had taken longer than necessary, since Heike knew the route only vaguely, and only from her own place, with Eric, on Cayuga. In the car, she'd crouched on the floor of the front seat as soon as they were close to Union Springs. Dolan looked down at her instead of at the road.

— Don't get too close, she told him. What if he sees me?

Dolan told her she looked like a two-bit gangster groping for her lost shotgun, hiding like that.

— Not a moll? I'm coming up in the world.

He said the molls were taking over the asylum. Heike brought her eyes up to the level of the window and tapped on the glass with a knuckle.

— Here, here! You make a right, see?

Rita had almost always walked to and from the house alone; Heike hadn't had much opportunity to see where and how she lived. Once, or maybe twice, she'd been in the car when Eric dropped her home. Only if they were headed out someplace together as a family, and even then, it wasn't the sort of thing Heike was likely to take note of. It's easy enough to find a girl to do the dishes, especially in summer, when the schools are out for vacation.

She told Dolan to slow down in front of a long, low house, a new construction in a town of old properties. He stopped the car and tugged on the brake.

— This one, she said. I'm almost sure of it.

— Why do I have to come?

— They might not let me in without you. Look at me! You make me seem more respectable.

She climbed out of the car. He watched her brush off her pants and the knotted silk pyjama shirt.

— That's a fact.

But it had been the wide-lipped waitress from Dolan's party who answered when Heike knocked at the door. There was a moment of silence as all three stumbled through recognition and worked to place each other in time. It was Heike who made the connection first, but for a moment she was too confused by it to speak. The girl beat her to it.

— If you're looking for Mickey, he don't live here.

This was aimed at Dolan. His brow lifted slightly, and he turned to Heike. *Mickey?* He mouthed the name without actually speaking. The girl kept going:

— What, does he owe you money or something?

Heike said:

— She's the girl from the greenhouse. You remember? Your cocktail waitress.

There was a silence.

— You took his keys, Dolan said finally. You made a big brou-haha.

— I always take his keys when he's been drinking. My old man used to get blitzed and that's how he died, driving himself home from the tavern. She hadn't stepped back to let them in, and kept one hand firm on the doorknob. But like I said: Mickey ain't here.

— We're not looking for Mickey, Heike said. I was looking for a girl, a little maid who used to come and do a bit of kitchen work at my house. Just down that way. She jogged her elbow back in the direction they'd come from. Rita, she said. But we must have the wrong place.

The girl's mouth came together like she'd tasted something sour and didn't know how to get rid of it.

— What do you want Rita for?

— Do you know where she lives?

— Sure. What do you want her for?

Heike told her she'd lost something precious, and the girl assumed Rita had stolen it.

— She's my sister. The girl took a wide step backwards, as though it was herself and not the door that operated on hinges. I'll get her down here for you. She took a breath and bellowed up the stairs.

Dolan and Heike followed her to the kitchen. She pointed at a couple of wooden chairs: first one, then the other, then back again. It was her way of inviting them to sit. Dolan leaned back and pulled out his cigarettes. Heike remained standing behind her chair, one hand resting on its back.

— Your face is looking much better, you know.

The girl didn't respond, but they stared at each other. Heike came around to the front of the chair but still did not sit down.

— You never told me your name, she said.

There was a dishtowel lying on the kitchen counter, and the girl leaned sideways to grab it. She moved over to the stove and fussed with the towel, hanging it over the oven door handle and smoothing it out. She was no taller than Heike.

— It's Miriam.

— I'm pleased to meet you, Miriam. You must forgive the way I'm dressed.

Heike stepped toward her again, hoping to relate in her expression a gentle reminder of their first meeting, that night in the greenhouse, Miriam hiding out with her swollen eye.

— I need Rita's help, she said, reaching out to touch the girl's arm.

— My sister's not bad, Miriam said. She's going through a rough patch since our old man died. You know what kids are like. Anyway, I don't know what she stole from you, but it's not because she's a bad kid.

There was a thump, and Rita appeared at the bottom of the steps. When she saw Heike, she froze in the doorway. Miriam walked over and cuffed her in the side of the head.

— What'd you steal from this lady?

It took Heike half an hour of convincing to get her to answer any questions after that.

DOLAN STUBBED OUT HIS CIGARETTE, pushing aside the others he'd already left in the ashtray.

— Either she doesn't know anything, he said. Or she won't tell.

Rita had answered every query with a shrug. Heike narrowed her line of questioning further and further, hoping that even a simple yes or no response might push open some door, lead them off in a new direction: Did anyone come to the house while we were out? Did Mr. Lerner speak to you when he returned? Did Mr. Lerner go upstairs at all? What time did he get home? Did he stay at home after that, or did he go out again?

— Why don't you just tell me everything you do remember about that night, Heike said. From the moment you arrived at my house. Okay, you came to the front door. You took off your coat. What happened next?

Rita slouched in her chair.

— It's July, she said. What would I have a coat on for?

Heike brightened. She'd finally gotten through.

— Okay, no coat. Then what?

The girl stared at her as though Heike might be simple.

— I put on my apron.

— Wonderful. What did you do with your apron on?

— Mr. Lerner told me to stay the night, she said. So I went into the laundry room and put my bag in there with my night-gown. There was some ironing in the basket, and I did that, and I took the duster and went over all the books and things in the main room, like I always do. Then I watched the television for a while: it was *Ozzie and Harriet* and *Our Miss Brooks*. And I was gonna watch *Schlitz Playhouse*, but I fell asleep.

— But you were awake when I got home in the morning. And when Mr. Lerner got home?

— Sure, I got up early to get breakfast on. There was a load of dishes left over in the sink. There was a roasting pan from the day before, and nobody soaked it or nothing. I had to scrub it with the cloth, and old meat got under my fingernails.

— You didn't like that.

— Would you?

Dolan drummed on the table with his matchbook. Heike leaned to one side and swiped it out of his hand.

— What did you do when the dishes were clean?

Rita stared at her.

— I put 'em away, she said. Her voice was flat and final.

Dolan leaned forward in his chair, knees wide and his elbows resting on them.

— Rita, do you like trinkets?

The girl turned to him, fish-eyed.

— If you can tell us anything about what happened to the little boy, the lady's little boy, we'll go straight to town and buy you the prettiest necklace in the costume jewellery display. The very prettiest, he said.

The girl looked first at her sister, then back to Dolan. She seemed suddenly nervous.

— Any one I want?

— You name it.

— Leo, Heike said. Don't bribe the girl. I don't want her making up lies.

— There's a red necklace at Platt's, Rita said. With a daisy pendant. It's in the front case. Red glass beads and a daisy pendant.

— It's not a bribe. It's motivation. Isn't it, Rita? Dolan got up from where he'd been sitting. Daisy pendant, he said. Got it. Now let's cut to the quick here. Tell me what you saw. Did Mr. Lerner take the little boy someplace?

Dolan had his car keys out and they jangled about in his hand.

— I never seen him, Rita said.

Heike pushed back in her seat.

— Of course you did. He was there when I got home. You were in the kitchen. Mr. Lerner was right there.

Rita turned briefly to look at Heike, then back to Dolan.

— I mean I never seen him. *Him.* The little boy she wants.

Heike's shoulders dropped.

— But surely you looked in on him? He was sleeping.

Rita didn't respond; Heike's interruptions seemed to irritate her. She twisted her body in the chair so that it was clear she was talking only to Dolan. Now that she had his attention and the promise of a present on the horizon, her story had become a detailed account.

— Like I said, I fell asleep watching the television. When I woke up, it was almost morning anyway, so I thought I might as well get up. First I scrubbed the dirty pots and put 'em away, and then I had to clean my hands. It was real early in the morning, and I wanted to have my cup of tea, so I did that. I made the tea and I drank it in the kitchen, and then I washed up my cup and I put that away, too. Then I went upstairs.

— What time was this? Dolan said.

— How should I know? I'm not a clock-watcher.

— Before Mr. Lerner came home.

— It was early, like I said. I don't wash dishes too fast. And they were messy, and I didn't like the dirt getting under my fingernails.

Heike stood up.

— You didn't go upstairs at all before that? All night long, you just left him there?

Rita turned toward her now. She gave her a hard glare.

— Don't think you can talk to me like that. I know about you. You're just a patient, too.

Miriam stepped in and boxed her ear again.

— You be nice!

— It's alright. Heike crouched down by Rita's knee: That's true. I was Dr. Lerner's patient. It was a long time ago. Right now I'm trying to find my son.

Rita kept one hand on the side of her head and rubbed her ear. Her eyes stayed on her sister, but she was talking faster now.

— I didn't see anything and I didn't do anything, and he fired me anyway. He's got a new maid now. Why don't you ask her about it?

Heike looked at Dolan and then back to Rita.

— No one wants to blame you, Heike said. I only want to know what you saw.

— When you went upstairs, Dolan said. The kid was already gone?

— I came downstairs and Mr. Lerner was there, and a cop with him. He was in a state, asking me if his wife had come home, and when I said I didn't know, he took me by the arm and shook me so that I got scared and didn't say nothing else. I didn't want to upset him more. And then the lady came in after that. I saw her walking down the drive.

Dolan turned to where Heike stood, leaning hard on the back of her chair.

— But you see? It's possible, then, that he came in while she was in the kitchen. So maybe she didn't notice. He could have gone upstairs while she was drinking her tea.

Heike shook her head.

— She never saw him come in.

— Or maybe we've got the timing wrong. Maybe he came in while she was sleeping, and went out again.

— I know you want me to believe this.

— Nothing else makes sense.

Miriam dropped down and set her hands on Rita's knees. The girl flinched.

— I'm not gonna hit you, she said. But you gotta tell the lady what happened to her little boy.

Rita lifted her head to look at her sister, and then hard at Heike.

—You tell her I never saw him, she said. There was never any little boy there that night.

HEIKE SPENT THE NEXT DAY ALONE in the house—stewing, Dolan said—while he drove off to handle the sale of a radio station in Syracuse. She mostly found herself perched on the high stool in his office, trying to tinker at his story about the third-grade teacher. Her stomach turning in on itself: the meeting with Rita felt like a dead end and had left Heike secretly frantic. Dolan had suggested she come along with him. Syracuse, he said, was a very optimistic locale. She told him she preferred to stew.

Now and then she looked up, or over her shoulder at the bookcase. Glad of the bright sun flooding the room, nothing hidden in daylight. At one point, a noise at the door surprised her: Mrs. Hammond, with a tray of coffee and sandwiches, although she hadn't looked for the housekeeper or asked her for anything.

—Mr. Dolan said I should never let you starve.

The sandwiches were cheese and tomato, or salmon and lettuce with mayonnaise. Mrs. Hammond set up a folding table next to Heike with a snap of one wrist and set the tray square on its surface.

—You're certainly attached to that figurine, she said.

Heike reached out to touch the shepherdess. She had it balanced against the lip of the angled desktop, safe from falling.

—I don't have many things from my home. From my childhood. So perhaps I find it comforting. She covered it with her hand as though it needed protection and turned to face

Mrs. Hammond more fully. I suppose it also makes me think of my son, she said.

— Ah.

There were a few linen napkins, and the coffee with cream, and Heike had to ask her to take the cream away and bring some milk instead. When she came back, Mrs. Hammond said she'd known a woman who lost her son, swimming in the Owasco River. They'd been collecting stones, she said, and the woman found a ring. Something someone had lost: a ruby in it, and a row of tiny diamonds. All still there, even with the river current washing at them. The same day she found the ring, her son was swept away.

It was springtime and she should never have let him play like that, Mrs. Hammond said, so close to high water. She said:

— Nothing's so haunted as a wedding ring.

They never found his body. The woman fell to weeping every hour. Two weeks later, she slid the ring onto her finger and went back down to the Owasco and hurled herself into the current. And wouldn't you know, they found her boy the next morning.

— He was drowned, of course, Mrs. Hammond said. And his mother as well.

— My son is not dead, Heike said.

— Of course not, ma'am. And I'm not saying to put yourself in harm's way. But I wonder if you don't have something you could return, she said. A fair trade?

She stood by and watched Heike eat a sandwich, the salmon too dry and sticking in her throat. When it was time to clear away, the housekeeper told her there'd been a man around earlier in the afternoon. Perhaps Heike had heard him at the door? Didn't want to take no for an answer.

Heike set the food down and drew back in her seat.

— I sent him away. Took some convincing. When Mr. Dolan's not at home, I don't let anyone in the house. She folded up the table and hefted it under one arm. At the door she paused, and turned back to Heike: I expect he'll be around again. He said Mr. Dolan has something of his. Something that belongs to him. He seems very anxious to get it back.

16.

Heike was sitting out in a lawn chair when Arden arrived. She had her back to the house and did not turn and look over her shoulder right away, her legs slung sideways over the arm of the chair and kicking a kind of rhythm as she looked out at the lake.

The housekeeper made no announcement. There was the murmur of voices and then Arden in her striped sundress, already coming down the lawn. She was heavily burdened and it made the walking precarious: a mud-coloured carpetbag held out in front, one hand wrapped around the bag's handle and the other supporting it from underneath.

— Look at you, slumming it in boys' clothes.

Heike kissed her cheeks. The effect was more unbridled than familial: Even for a European, Arden said. She squeezed Heike's arm and set the bag on the seat of the lawn chair.

— I got you a few things. It wasn't any picnic, but I managed.

Heike glanced down at the bag.

— You were in the house.

This came out broken—almost, but not quite, a demand.

Arden looked around for any other person, but the lawn was flat and empty. Mrs. Hammond had not followed her outside.

— I didn't even see him. He's got a new maid, and that's who let me in. She looked around a second time. I keep expecting him to show up, banging at my door. I'm half-nervous all the time.

Heike took a breath.

— But no Daniel?

Arden shook her head, so tight and quick it was almost a twitch.

— I wish I'd found him for you.

The sky was both grey and bright. A sky that makes you squint. Heike thought of Daniel hiding on the stairs the night Arden and John had been over, the first night they'd come here to Dolan's house; Dani's fingers gripping the spindles of the banister, the whites of his knuckles. Arden would not know where to look for him. Heike could imagine him in all his best hiding places, stealing sugar cubes to suck on in the low cupboard under the kitchen sink, crouched in the bean teepee out back, flat on his belly under the bed upstairs.

When she looked up again, she had recovered herself, although perhaps not fully. She reached for Arden's hand:

— I'm glad you're here.

She was used to forcing a kind of smile if she had to break a silence.

It wasn't only boys' clothes she'd been wearing, she said. She smoothed her trousers: the raw line of fringe had fallen down where Dolan had sawed off the pant legs, and now she bent to cuff it back again, leaving the edges crisp and purposeful, and stuck a leg out to admire her own work. She said he'd gone to a meeting in Syracuse and brought her back a trunkful of frocks, and they were all the wrong size.

— They never know what to buy, Arden said.

— I haven't had clean underwear.

— I just tried to grab an armful of anything. Gloves. A slip. She paused. But no hat; there wasn't any room for a hat in that bag.

— I'm hardly having tea and sandwiches at the club.

Heike's purse sat on the chair, and the carpetbag next to it, like a bloated twin. She sprang the latch with a finger.

Then:

— He was here, you know. Banging on this door.

— What, Eric?

— Looking for me, I guess. She pulled a brassiere out of the bag and turned her back to wrangle it on under her shirt, an attempt at modesty, pulling only one arm at a time out of its sleeve. Mrs. Hammond sent him away, she said. The housekeeper.

Arden stepped in instinctively to shield her from any prying eyes, the way girls do when they're getting changed under a towel at the beach.

— Ugly. Or so I imagine. Was it?

— Maybe it's nothing, Heike said.

She gave a dismissive shrug, but it came off wrong somehow. She had a wary look.

— No. No, you're right. Now he knows you're here.

Heike flipped the shirt up, exposing the little curve where her belly dipped into the waistband of the trousers. She wrapped her arms around her back to fasten the bra and then pulled the shirt down against her hips again.

— I can't hide out here forever.

— Finesse, Arden said. She reached forward and straightened

the bottom edge of Heike's shirt with a little tug on each side. *He's making you anxious on purpose. He has to think he's winning. He has to think he's the one in charge.*

Heike looked over at the greenhouse. She felt for a moment that if she tried hard enough, she would see Daniel inside, the outline of his small body in shadow on the glass.

— Sometimes I feel I made a terrible mistake. Running away.

— You didn't run away. Don't say it like that. You needed to clear your head. There was a pause, and Arden tried to catch her eye: Are you going back, then?

It was a tentative question.

Heike took a few steps toward the water. The shadow in the greenhouse, Daniel-sized, was gone. Some tall plant that had caught the light somehow, or else she'd just imagined it, some other reality in which it was this lawn where Dani played, that stretch of beach where he dug with his spade and pail, this lake where he learned to kick his legs like an egg-beater to stay afloat.

Arden followed her gaze.

— It's a big place if you take all the party out of it.

Heike said it was remarkably quiet. She came back to where Arden was waiting.

— I rather enjoy my country-mouse life. In another world, it would be quite perfect.

— I guess he can't very well throw a shindig with you camping out in his cast-offs. Dolan, I mean. She rocked in her pose, off-balance, her driving shoes and the soft lawn working at cross-purposes. Maybe it's a good thing I never landed that society column. Is this a liaison or an intrigue, do you think? For the copy.

— An *affaire de coeur*, Heike said. But not an affair-de-column. She dropped her purse into the carpetbag and clicked the latch.

Arden shook her head in a vague way.

— Successful men always have affairs, she said. One just never thinks about the women, who the women are. She broke out of her reverie, suddenly contrite: I don't mean you! Of course it's alright for you. You get all kinds of leeway, on account of being European.

Heike took hold of her chair and folded it up tight, the legs and back clapping into place.

— You were wrong about him, you know.

There was a rim of shade around the perimeter of the willows where a couple of similar chairs stood waiting. She led Arden in that direction and snapped her own seat back into shape in the new spot. She did not sit down, but motioned for Arden to take it instead.

— In what way?

— About the prizefighter.

— Oh, that. Some people say it was a jazz musician. A trumpet? Or a maybe a clarinet. She reached up and adjusted her hat. The sky was overcast, but now and then a streak of sunlight came shining through the clouds. Arden stepped farther under the branches. I suppose the truth is much more banal. His accountant or something. Someone with steady money and a flyweight imagination.

Heike blinked at that for a moment and then left it there. She said the version with the prizefighter was a good story. Arden nodded.

— Where is he now?

The door to the greenhouse stood half open, and Heike gestured to it.

— Tending his greens, Arden said, almost to herself. Her face grew meditative. You're his mistress. Like in a book.

Heike drew a little taller, but she looked away before answering.

— He can't very well throw a shindig, she said.

A KIND OF WILD CLATTER came from the house, and both women turned to face it. For a second or two the porch stood wide and empty, and then the back door flapped open and two dogs rushed out and onto the grass, in dangerous proximity to where Heike and Arden stood talking. Sheepdogs, their bangs in their eyes. The dogs were barking and rushing around in overlapping circles, and Mrs. Hammond stood at the back door, holding a broom across her body with two tight fists, like a fighter. It was a defensive position. Another dog appeared at her feet, an elderly terrier. The small dog made its way between her legs and lowered itself to a respectable seat at the top of the porch stairs. On the lawn, the sheepdogs had begun to tighten their circle. Heike stepped in toward Arden despite herself.

It was Paulsen who'd brought them. Renny Paulsen: the man from the party. Heike could see him now, shooing the housekeeper away from the door. He had the bar cart out in front of him, and the glasses stacked on it jangled as the cart made its little hop over the threshold. He made no effort to call the dogs in but rolled the bar up against the porch railing and added a few ice cubes to a glass.

— Blondie! He raised the glass in Heike's direction. You still hanging around? Didn't anyone tell you the party's over?

Dolan surfaced from the greenhouse and started toward the house. In his left hand he held a pair of pruning shears. Seeing Arden, he snipped them in the air.

— Hello, he said. I am the gardener.

The dogs ran down the lawn to greet him, and he stopped a moment and swung his arm overhead, as though he were pitching a fast one over home plate. There was a race, and the dogs splashed down into the water, snapping at the lake's surface for the mysterious ball.

Dolan gestured to the unused lawn chairs, offering them with a hand to Arden.

— Madam.

Heike swatted at his hand.

— This is Arden, of course.

— The famous Arden!

— Don't be so ridiculous. Of course you've met her before.

Arden put out her own hand and allowed herself to be guided into the chair.

— The famous playwright!

— Gardener, Dolan said. You've got me all wrong.

— Career change, Arden said.

— It's a natural mistake. I've had me all wrong for years.

Paulsen came strolling down toward them with his glass in one hand. He was wearing a tuxedo with a silver smoking jacket and no flower of any kind in his buttonhole.

— You wouldn't believe the week I've had. He said this to no one in particular and looked down to the lake and the wet dogs somewhat fearfully.

Heike remembered her purse where she'd left it in the sun and turned back to get it, the cuff of her pantleg unrolling again and falling against her ankle. Paulsen said:

— You're the kid from the clambake, right? He looked her up and down: Honey, it's possible you've had a worse week than even me.

She dropped into her seat. Dolan pulled his own chair closer.

— Three's all I got, old man.

— Sitting is terrible for the back, Paulsen said. I'd rather stand. All I do is sit. Would you believe I just got back from the city? I had my driver bring me directly to you. Francis, I said. Francis, I need a drink and my friend Dolan is sure to have one.

— Lucky us, Dolan said. Especially Blondie here.

— Drove all night, Paulsen said. What a night. I went down for Pitch Week, with that redhead you had at the party here. You remember her? In the polka dots. I thought she was some kinda chorus girl, but lo and behold she's the real thing. I've never seen so many deals. Amazing. Then, last night, I'm getting ready for one last blitz, and there she is rolling all over the floor. Says the room is full of bugs.

Arden tugged at her earring.

— You mean like Russian bugs? What was she, paranoid? Paulsen wheeled around to look at her square on.

— Nah! Bug-bugs. Ants or something.

— What hotel were you at? She made a face.

— Kid, you're not listening. There were no bugs. What kinda bugs are gonna be in the room at the Ritz? She's rolling all over the floor, trying to sweep the creeps off her arms. I said what you said. I said, Baby, what bugs? He waved an arm as if dismissing women altogether and turned back to Dolan: Just another dope fiend, can you believe it? Where do I find them? Popping pills the whole week. I never noticed.

Dolan gave a long, slow nod, and it was just what Paulsen had come for.

— But she ran out, Dolan said. She ran out and she got the shakes.

— Shaking it all over the floor at the Ritz! I didn't even pack a bag; I just called the desk and told them to send me my car.

— Did you have the dogs at the Ritz? Heike said.

Paulsen looked at her and he was pained.

— Of course not. I got the dogs from my lawyer's place. Dolan, I'm done with the city. Find me a property out here, and I'll be a country gentleman. No more hotels. No more glitzy dames.

Dolan went to pat Heike's hand but found her chair just far enough away that he couldn't reach. He turned back to Paulsen instead:

— Go on and tell Hammy you're staying a few days, he said. Get her to give you a room and some eggs on a tray. Wash your hair, why don't you?

He waited while Paulsen trundled up the lawn to the house in his silver jacket, then yelled after him.

— For God's sake, don't let those dogs back in the house!

THE TWO WET DOGS ran up from the lake too late to slip in the door behind Paulsen and stood whining at the screen for a few minutes before giving up. They shook out and paced along the porch, lifting a nose to cruise the edge of the table for scraps, then flopped near to where the terrier still sat, august and arthritic.

Arden leaned forward as if she was going to say something, but only coiled a piece of hair around her finger and then let it spring back.

— Arden's been to the house, Heike said. She found me some underclothes.

— Thank God, Dolan said.

— But no Eric.

— No loss.

— And no Daniel.

He didn't say anything then, and she stood up and took the shears from him and trimmed the ends off a loping frond of willow that had been teasing at her shoulders. She handed the shears back, passing them like scissors, handle out.

— Daniel is safe, Arden said. I feel it. Eric won't keep him from you forever.

— That's what I keep telling her, Dolan said. He took the shears and stabbed the sharp end down into the lawn for safekeeping.

— No, Heike said. There was a little silence. No, I don't think so. She turned to Arden: We found the maid. Rita. You remember her? The little house girl we used to have in.

— The sourpuss.

— She says it wasn't Eric. Eric didn't take Daniel.

Dolan jerked toward her:

— Is that what she said?

— She never went upstairs to check on him, not once all night. And then Eric arrived, and then me.

Arden let her eyes catch Dolan's for a moment. Heike went on:

— If Eric took him someplace, she should have seen it.

— Of course she didn't see a damn thing, Dolan said. She went to sleep and never stirred all night long. It could have been Ali Baba and the Forty Thieves and she wouldn't be able to tell you how many gold earrings they were wearing.

Heike crouched down to rummage through the carpetbag. She dug out her handbag again, and from there the Dresden doll, wrapped in its bit of newspaper. She swivelled, low on her haunches, to look Dolan in the eye.

— You keep telling me Eric is lying, Eric is hiding Dani

somewhere. Both of you. But what if that's not true? What if it's backwards? Maybe he isn't lying, she said. Do you see?

— No.

Dolan was sitting back in his chair with his legs stretched out straight in front of him. Heike put a hand on his leg.

— What if you're wrong? What if he doesn't have Daniel? She was down on the ground, and it made her feel like a supplicant. Dolan went to touch her hair, and she pulled back: I can't make it fit, she said. I lived with Eric. I know him. I know him better than anyone. Daniel made him impatient. He couldn't look after a child.

— So what? Then he hired someone.

She pulled away. Dolan told her she could go ahead and worry herself to town and back again if that's what she needed to do.

— But your boy didn't wander off in the night all by himself, he said. That's what doesn't fit.

She had a flash of Daniel by the stream in the darkness, his light hair and white nightshirt like a flare against the black of the forest floor. His feet cutting through the shallow water. A heavy breath: something leading him through the trees.

— Maybe this is something I did. Like Eric said. Heike still had the figurine in one hand, and she held it out to them. This thing, she said. I want to return it.

— To the cabin? Arden shifted forward in her seat. I thought you liked it so much.

— He gave me an idea. She tipped her head in Dolan's direction.

— Me? I'm not in the idea business. He'd drawn his legs in to sit up straighter in the chair, and they bent high at the knees like cricket's wings. I gave it all up for the garden shears.

— Remember? Heike said. You said it yourself the very first

day I was here: What if it's not the little girl that's haunted? What if it's the doll?

Dolan leaned over and touched the edge of the china apron, rubbing it between his thumb and forefinger.

— Heike. That was only a story. We were making it up.

— Leo, don't argue with me. I took the figurine, and Daniel disappeared. Maybe if I return the doll, the house will give him back.

Dolan didn't say anything but flicked his eyes to Arden. She was still in her seat, hands clasped in her lap.

— I see you've been conversing with my housekeeper, he said finally. That old chestnut about the river and the ring.

— No chestnut. None of it happened, Leo: not the raft, not the girl—not Tessa. None of it happened until I took that doll. I went into that house, and everything changed.

Dolan stood up.

— You spooked yourself but good, he said. Look at you.

Heike rose up to meet him.

— If Eric doesn't have him, all I've done is waste time!

— Eric does have him, Heike.

— There's something in that house that wants me back. She held the figurine out in one tight fist and shook it. Wants this, this thing. It's this, don't you see? I don't know why I wanted it. It looked like home, so I took it. And that wasn't enough: I went back there; I brought Daniel back with me. And so the house took him. She turned to Arden, pleading: You were there. You saw me that day. There was something wrong. You *know* there was something wrong.

Arden sat up smarter in the chair and leaned in, one hand on a knee.

— There was something wrong, sure, she said. Except, look.

Hate me for saying so, but Paulsen's girl isn't the only one around here who's been popping pills.

— You think I was sleeping. That it was a dream.

— I wouldn't go that far. But couldn't this be something else? Some effect of whatever he was dosing you up with? Or else some kind of withdrawal. Like the redhead at the Ritz. When did you first start dumping those tonics, before that day at the pond or after? Before or after you saw the girl in the water?

Dolan pulled the shears out of the ground where he'd stuck them and turned to go back down to the greenhouse, and Heike shouldered the carpetbag and chased after him.

— Take me there.

— Where?

— Back to the house. Where I got this.

— A story, Heike. Dolan reached out and took her by the elbow. It's a story you told me. You know that. I know you know that.

— How long do you think I can stay here? Wearing your clothes and never seeing anyone?

— You're afraid of him is all. Of Eric. It's understandable. You're afraid that he won't give Daniel up.

She pulled her arm away but then stepped in closer. If she hadn't been holding on to so many things she might have shoved him.

— Listen to me: Eric has already been here once. If he had Dani, he would be using him, holding him out like to me like a magnet, like a lure. I know him, I know what Eric is like. This is my last chance. I have to try every tiny possibility. Ask yourself: If this were your child, wouldn't you do the same?

— I know what's likely. Between the good doctor and a ghost, I'll put my money on the doctor. He sank the shears into the ground again, nose down. No matter what my old housekeeper and her loopy stories have you believing.

Heike said she didn't need him to drive her anywhere. She was just fine to walk. She said she'd walked farther in her life.

— I came here to figure out how to get Dani back. Remember? To clear my head.

— Clear your head? What you're talking about isn't clarity. It's a bunch of hocus-pocus. You're going to take that doll and put it back on the kitchen shelf where you found it. And then what? Do you expect to find him curled up in the kitchen cabinet, too? A puff of blond hair in with the pots and pans? He stepped away from Heike to catch Arden's eye: Arden, what colour is the kid's hair? I want to get this right.

Arden stiffened in her lawn chair. She'd been listening without interjection.

— Arden, you gotta help me out here.

— I can't say.

Heike stood up straight. Her shirt sleeve had slipped down off her shoulder, and she pushed it roughly up.

— You see, she said. Even Arden is not on your side.

Arden pulled one knee up high against her chest and hugged it there.

— No, that's not what I mean, she said. I mean, I can't tell you what colour his hair is. I don't know.

Heike had been about to turn back to Dolan, but she stopped, looking hard at Arden instead.

— I've never been over when Daniel was up and about, Arden said. Hardly surprising, really. He kept you hidden, too, at first. Remember? Eric's always been that way. You think no one knows Eric better than you do, but that's not true. I know him at least as well. I grew up with him.

Heike's chair still sat on the lawn between them. She seemed about to leap over it. Arden only shook her head.

— The more I asked to see Dani, the more Eric seemed to delight in refusing me. Disappointing, but you know: that's Eric for you. You didn't bring him to the wedding, either.

— You don't bring a child to a fancy dinner—

— It's just his way. Easter, remember? You came to that charity party with us. At the Ambassador. Frank Sinatra was there, and Gloria Vanderbilt, and Lyon de Camp. You remember. What a bore de Camp turned out to be. And then Eric took you home halfway through dinner. You hadn't even put your fork down and he was berating the poor coat-check girl.

Heike nodded vaguely.

— But this summer, she said. Dani.

— He was always napping when we came over, or off to bed. He was always upstairs. Don't you see? Eric enjoyed keeping Dani hidden. He enjoyed keeping him in a box—the same way he likes keeping you in a box. The same way he's enjoying keeping Daniel from you now. Why use Dani as a lure when he can control you just as easily like this? Arden motioned to Dolan with her chin. It's like he said. Eric has him somewhere.

— You're on his side. You're trying to make me crazy.

— There are no sides. It's what I've said all along: I don't think Daniel is missing. I think he's with Eric.

— But why?

— I don't know. Meanness.

— Not good enough.

Neither of them said anything then. On the porch, one of the dogs began to scratch at the back door.

— I think it *is* good enough. This was Dolan: he'd been quiet for once, and now his voice cut over the two women. I've watched

Eric with you, he said. Come on, Heike. What happened before Daniel disappeared? Not your ghost story; come back to real life.

— I should have known better than to come here, asking you for help. I should have taken Eric's car when I had the chance.

— Daniel disappeared the night I drove you home. That's what happened: you came home with another man.

Heike stepped forward.

— Will you drive me or not? I took something from that house. I just want to return it. Either you drive me or I go without you. You can stay here with your drunk friend and his stupid dogs.

As if on cue, the door opened and closed. The dogs slipped inside, one after the other.

— I'll take you. Arden pushed slowly out of her seat and moved her body in behind the chair, as though she wanted a barrier between herself and the rest of the action. Dolan flipped his attention toward her:

— This is your brother we're talking about? I've got that right?

— He's my brother.

— I'm sorry.

Arden just looked at him.

— To be honest, I'm not sure what this has to do with you. Sorry or not. She turned to Heike: Look. There's no harm in returning the dumb dolly. But let's say you at least need a backup plan. In case it doesn't work. Bear with me, now. In case Eric really does have Daniel. A bargaining chip.

Heike looked at her.

— The only bargaining chip for Eric is me, Arden. I told you: I can't hide here forever. It's only a matter of time before he comes around again. Banging down the door.

— He wants you home with him, Arden said. That makes this a damn good moment to ask for something in return.

Dolan gave Arden a critical glare.

— Weren't you the one who helped her get out in the first place? What's the backup plan to get her out of your backup plan?

— Finesse. Arden said this in a clipped way. She turned her focus to Heike: You remember I said that? Finesse. With Eric, you have to pick your moment.

Heike seemed not to have heard them. She wrapped the doll carefully in its bit of newspaper and moved off toward Arden's coupe, where it sat at the end of the drive. When she got there, she looked back at them over her shoulder. The wind had picked up. She could hear the lake licking at the shore now, quick little cuts against the wet sand. A darkness sneaking into the sky. She stood close to the car, her eyes resting on Dolan and her fingertips curled into the door handle. She sprang it without warning and got in.

17.

She left Arden up at the end of the road and climbed down the ridge in her bare feet, the sound of the car's motor fading as she began her descent, heels digging into the ground and fingers grasping the strongest of the weeds, low down, where the stalks were woody. The air was still and close, the ground damp but not slick. When she reached forward to the next handhold, her fingers sprang back. Thorns. Something she'd thought was a dandelion but turned sinister: its yellow stars shooting three feet high on stalks that nettled and stung. Heike rubbed her hand against her thigh for relief.

At the foot of the slope she stopped. The light was low in the sky, but there was enough time before evening. The little house had not changed in look, its back windows high and grey with age. The wind chime no longer hung outside the kitchen, but she could see where it had fallen, tangled in the grass. The storm must have brought it down. She walked around to the front.

There lay the pond, calm and greenish in the haze. She hadn't made it up. The raft on its tether seemed to her uncommonly still, and she leaned against the wood slats of the house to look at it, as though she could be witness to some other world and will something to appear on or near it: Daniel, safe and cross-legged in the sunshine, or Heike herself, paddling along, benign in a red canoe. She did not try to imagine the little girl, Tessa, but the feeling of her came. The child's absence was a tangible thing. Thick. Heike turned to scan the treeline, as though the girl might be stretched along a high branch, watching her from above. The woods on the other side of the water fell deep in shadow; every shape, the sprawl of high fern, the muscular reach of paper birch, seemed to conceal the girl's wide grey eyes, her ash-pale hair in their shade.

The door sat slightly open on its hinges. Where she'd jimmied the latch that first day, it no longer caught properly and unhitched in any breeze, although there was no breeze now. She pushed it with a tentative hand. The thin burn mark across the threshold was neither wider nor narrower than it had been. There was no difference, nothing to allow her to change her mind. Instead, she stepped inside and shut the door behind her, leaning back against it.

She expected a kind of nausea. The air was heavy and stale, and with the door shut the room was cast in false twilight. Heike was struck by an urge to lie down on the floor and weep, not out of fear, but from relief. The quiet was absolute. She was alone. Whatever had made her anxious just outside the door no longer existed.

She set the bag on the floor and crouched beside it, pulling the figurine out of its wrapping. In the low light its colours brightened: the little shepherdess had a happy look. Her quick smile and unchanging eyes. It was the first time Heike had thought of her that way, or, at least, the first time since Daniel was lost. The sooner the thing was back on its shelf the better.

Heike crossed the room and tugged on the cupboard's glass door. Inside, a few presentation dishes leaned up against each other like young men on a street corner, each plate with a green feathered edge and a cream and crimson rose pattern in the centre. There was a silhouette marked out on the shelf paper where the figurine used to stand, and she traced it with her finger. A bleached place. A stain outline, a solid vacancy, a hole. No dust at all inside the cabinet: its doors closed, maybe for years. She set the thing back where she'd found it, matching the line exactly. It stared back at her, cold and cheerful. Rather, it seemed to look beyond her, over her shoulder at something else in the room.

Heike suppressed an urge to turn and look behind her and pushed the door back into place. The magnetic latch clicked. She stayed there, her fingertips against the cool porcelain of the cabinet knob.

— Now, she said. Now you can give him back. She spoke quietly at first, and then called out loud, giving the cupboard door an extra shake: I brought you your trinket. Now you can give me my son.

There was no movement in the room. No sudden tugging at her waist, no small arm wrapped around her leg. No chiming child's voice, calling to her from the hallway.

Of course there wasn't. The thought came to her all at once: how ridiculous. A silly pilgrimage. The idea of it embarrassed her. This realization like a sudden wake-up, a kick to the ear, her stomach dropping.

Then, almost a howl:

— Daniel! Give him back to me! Give him back!

Her voice filled the cavern of the house but did not echo. It sucked away into the walls. In the cupboard, the little figurine smiled at some unknown, distant point. Faithless. Hard behind hard glass. Heike let her shoulders drop. Outside, the sun moved into a bank of clouds or sank below the tree line, and the light in the cabin fell. A thin stream of cold air moved past her; she felt it against her neck, lifting her hair, and she shivered slightly and looked to the door, expecting to find it ajar in the breeze, but it had not moved and rested inside its frame where she had leaned against it. A window somewhere, then. Warped through the years of wind and rain, some crack in the frame that allowed the weather in. She wrapped her arms around herself for warmth. No sense staying here any longer. She bent to gather up her bag.

There was the smallest of sounds from behind her: the quick patter of a mouse. A start, and then a stop. Heike lifted her head. A moment of quiet, a three-count, and then she heard it again. Not far away, scuttling against the wood floor. She turned.

The sound had come from the opposite side of the room. Louder now: something bigger than a mouse, surely. She could hear it, running along the baseboard. The thing must have followed her into the house, come in with her when she'd opened the door. Heike peered into the grey corner. A squirrel? She'd once seen an opossum, dead on the highway, its weird white belly and long pink tail splayed out, but it was true that they also had sharp teeth. Where the wall met the floor, the light failed and made a dark corridor. She followed it beyond the boundary of the kitchen, edging her way through to where the house opened up, the bedroom door standing wide. The sound came again, this time over to her left.

A scrabbling. She was still, listening, then quickly stepped into the bedroom after it. The braided rug felt almost greasy with dust under her feet, and she used it to wipe away the grit she'd picked up coming down the ridge. She had a knot high in her stomach and one at the base of her skull. The room was silent.

— Who's there?

The words were out of her mouth before she'd had a chance to think them, and she almost laughed but it came out stilted, a stifled breath. Her hands were shaking. She went to the closet and yanked it open, the accordion door squealing on its hinges. A few empty wire hangers jangled against each other helplessly with the sudden draft. There was a shimmer of white: a nightgown left dangling from a hook.

Nothing. A bit of foolishness, but her head buzzed with it.

She pulled the folding door closed again, the hinges sticking, and as she did so she felt the same current come through the place, cool and cellar-damp against her shoulders and the backs of her arms. There was a long, slow creak: the bedroom door swung shut with a bang.

Heike laid a hand on the doorknob to open the door again, but found it was now somehow locked. She rattled the knob and then pulled at it with both hands.

— Hey! Who's there? Hey, let me out!

The futility of hearing herself call out loud in an empty house frustrated her even more. She turned slowly and pressed her back against the door, the knob tight against her spine. There was nothing in the room with her. The noise had stopped; the animal, whatever it was, must have run out, somehow bumping the door as it went. She wished now that she'd asked Arden to come with her, but Arden would by now be long gone, back home to greet her husband as he got off the train from the city. Heike crossed the room to take a better look at the window. She'd have to jimmy it open and jump out into the high grass. She began to work at the metal latch. The moving parts had been painted over.

The pattering came again, just behind her. This was a surprise. She half-turned her head; she'd thought the thing gone, out on the other side of the door, but now it seemed to be in the room with her after all. It crossed from one side to the other. Then back again, faster, it seemed, this time. The sound of it was difficult to place. Many-legged. Something feather-light brushed her calves.

She spun around and caught the flit of a shadow disappearing under the bed. Out of the corner of her eye. Then from the bed to the corner of the room. Some dark little figure, low to the ground.

The light failing outside, her eyes adjusting, playing tricks.

Almost a flicker. Always just out of her frame of vision. Heike pushed away the thought of her own nervousness outside the cabin, the presence of the girl there, watching, her wide stare concealed in the trees. The girl seemed to be there always, close by. Even in Dolan's house, a breath leading Heike down the hall. A hand pulling at her. She shoved hard at the window and it gave, sliding to her left, but only a few inches. The air outside was fresh with mist, and she gasped at it. The opening too small for her to squeeze through, but perhaps just wide enough to let the thing escape.

She lifted the coverlet and folded it over and sat down on the corner of the bed, the sheet underneath protected and clean and plain white. Her back straight, her fingertips against the mattress, but only lightly. A compulsion to draw her feet up onto the bed with her, off the floor. She talked herself out of it. She was being foolish and had locked herself into a strange room with something that belonged outside, in the wild. A steady, rhythmic scratching now.

Just some little animal. It didn't want to be in the house any more than she did; it wanted to be out in the forest. The scratching sounded almost deliberate. Digging, Heike thought. Except slower, more thoughtful. She remembered Paulsen's red-haired girl, the itch of a million ants crawling over her. The sound a kind of irritation in Heike's mind, and an image came to her: a black insect, long as your hand, carving out its burrow. Its mouthparts working like shiny knives.

A child's sharp fingernail, etching her own image deep into the plaster of the wall.

She blinked hard. Of course not. Stupid. It was digging. It was just an animal, trying to get out. A raccoon. All those sweet photographs in the nature magazines, their masked eyes and hand-washing. Although it struck her that a raccoon might not move so quickly. She gave her head a shake to loosen up her neck. She shook out her hands.

This animal's pattering rush. Almost a flutter. A jay, then, or even a small owl, especially if its wing were broken. An injured thing. She waited, listening, it seemed to her, for its breath. The sound came again, a rasping, from behind the highboy.

Enough. Heike got up to push the dresser away from the wall.

It was a heavy piece, and she braced against one side of it to try to swing it out in an arc. The animal behind it, whatever it was, picked up urgency, scratching away. Maybe it was trapped. It occurred to Heike that it would be easier to move the dresser without the weight of its drawers. She took hold of the middle section and pulled. The drawer stuck and then jerked out into her hands. It was filled not, as she had imagined, with moth-holed clothing, but with bed linens, still almost crisply folded, and on the other side of the drawer, only a few scattered papers. She drew it out slowly, taking the weight of it onto her legs, and set it down on the floor next to the bed. She reached in to neaten the little pile and found the paper had gone soft as cloth over time. In a corner of the drawer, there was the sticky white resi-due of an ancient egg sac. She pushed the papers to cover it, and they slipped against each other, the top one flipping in her hand. A child's drawing, the colours faded: a scatter of letter *m*'s, bird wings in a sunny sky. Heike recoiled and dropped the paper. Hadn't Tessa's drawing also been of such a sky, such birds? The page soaking through and the girl diving down to retrieve it.

Behind the dresser, the scratching went dead. Heike looked back toward the door. The silence was not quite a relief.

She stood up and took hold of the dresser again but found she was nervous of her feet, her legs, where her body met the ground. The highboy was wedged in tight, but this time she felt it budge, and she could hear the animal become anxious again, the scrab-bling spiking as though the thing were running up and down, up and down, along the wall. Was it afraid of her? She braced for one last shove, and the dresser gave with a long scraping noise, sweeping out from the corner, the remaining drawers pitching forward and the top one shooting out and hitting the floor.

Suddenly the sound came from everywhere at once: the thing scrambling over her feet, scratching up the walls on either side of her, above her, the rush of its wings in her hair. She covered her head with her arms and screamed, trying to spin away from it, but it was all around her. There was a high-pitched whis-tle, a shriek that might have been her own voice; she didn't know. She could feel the prick of its nails in her skin, against her thighs and the back of her neck. Dizzy, she rocked back and banged hard against the closet door, grabbing at the handle for balance, the accordion squealing open. The noise of it echoed off the walls.

Heike found herself on top of the bed, folded over, her arms protecting her head. The room swirled with dust. She came up slowly onto her knees, hands clasped behind her head, her elbows drawn in tight against her face. The folding doors to the closet still trembled from where she'd fallen against them. Her pulse surged in her ears.

Gone as instantly as it had appeared. Heike herself the only thing moving.

No. Daylight filtered in through the window and cast a dull ray through the dust. She could see it drifting slowly down, down, back into place. Pinpricks. This listless movement adding to the still. She let her hands come down to rest on her knees, breathing out. It was almost a sob. She had not realized she'd been holding her breath. Through the window there was the high, piercing trill of a toad, and Heike flinched.

Outside, the leaves lifted in the trees; the air seemed warmer. From the next room she heard the low groan of the front door to the cabin and its subtle *thud-thud-thud*, the broken latch bumping against the frame.

There was a residual tingle left on her skin, and she fought the urge to grate at herself with her own fingernails, the prickle on her scalp almost unbearable. She got up instead and tried the door, pressing hard enough on the set screw for it to leave an impression in her thumb. The knob that had refused to turn in her hands now twisted smoothly; the slim creak of the bedroom door as it opened, the difference between a locked door and a jammed one. Heike put a hand to her forehead as though checking herself for illness, a fever, and then squeezed her temples. There was a little stool in the corner of the room, and she dragged it over and wedged it against the door to prop it open. Nothing now behind the dresser, the drawers splayed over the floor at the foot of the bed.

She hefted the first drawer she'd removed, the linens inside it sliding with a graduated *thunk* to one side, and fit it neatly into the middle of the highboy, then the top drawer. The bottom drawer had not fallen completely out, and she tapped it into place with her foot before sliding the dresser back against the wall. An impulse to leave everything the way the house wanted it, as though she were its maid.

The closet door stood open on one side where she'd fallen against it, and she scrabbled her own fingernails against the frame, as a test, then recoiled a little at the noise despite herself. She fingered the nightgown, the empty hangers. A few cotton dresses hanging to one side, a dark crinoline on a hook at the very back. As she went to pull the door shut, something caught her eye. She was looking up into the closet, at the shelf over the rod. The Dresden doll smiled down at her.

Heike stepped back. She'd put the figurine back where it belonged in the kitchen. Hadn't she?

She raised a tentative hand and took it down, the tips of her fingers also bumping against some other thing up on the shelf. A soft-covered sketchbook, what the doll had been standing on. She rippled the edges of the book with a thumb and tucked it under her arm, then passed through the door to the main part of the cabin, back to the kitchen.

The little figurine cut into her hand. She let her eyes drift around the room, unable for a moment to look at the cabinet. Unable somehow to get her breath. She thought again of Paulsen's red-headed girlfriend; Arden's theory that Heike hadn't shed the effects of the drugs. Seeing things. But she was sure she'd put it back.

She looked up. Behind the milky glass, an identical china figurine stood politely, her apron held in the tips of her fingers. Heike let her arm drop, her own fingers still wrapped around the second doll. All of its gravitas had disappeared; it was weightless in her grip now, and she approached the kitchen cabinet sidelong, as you would a stray dog, cautious and curious all at once, and brought the figurine in her hand back up to eye level for a better look.

They were not quite the same. The pattern of the skirt, a fleur-de-lis, was a little more stylized on the original doll; her shoes a softer pink; her buckles fine and narrow where on the new figurine (as she thought of it), the buckles were squat. She turned it over and found no double sword, no Meissen stamp. The one a copy of the other. A curiosity. She peered through the glass, childishly unwilling to open the cabinet and move the figurine again. The face on the doll in her hands was just as delicately rendered. She turned her back to the cabinet and held the new doll to her chest, her face to the window.

The pond greying in grey light. A soft breath ran through the trees now and along the water, its surface rippling like a skein of old silk.

She had not thought of the place as lonely when she first found it.

SHE HAD NOT WANTED to go back into the bedroom but found herself wandering through anyway, checking the dresser, the closet, arranging the bedspread neatly. Not quite able to bear leaving without replacing the replica figurine. In the closet she methodically untangled the hangers and set the replica in its place, then suddenly remembered the book, still tucked against her side with one elbow.

She turned it over in her hands. It surprised her; she had lost track of it there, immediately used to the feel of it close against her ribs.

The *shush* of her thumb against the paper. The book filled with drawings. Not the work of a child this time, but sketches of the woods and the water. A window that looked familiar, set high, near to the corner of a house with a winding morning glory vine coiled at its base. The front door with its window box: drawings of this house, then. The pond, its horseshoe shape unmistakable, snapdragons at the water's edge, the wood-plank raft, lead grey and hidden in the high reeds.

And then the little house itself, or some little house; a path leading to it, a girl. A doe; a hunter's quiver full upon his back. The watercolour head of a bird, lying nestled in a bed of wildflowers, and then a full page of birds, page after page: black birds descending madly from the air and down upon a body. The body coming apart as easily as if it were made of straw.

The artist working up a study, eight, ten pages' worth. Heike flipped to the front of the book and back again, and to the front, the movement of the pages causing the birds to move: diving and disappearing and diving again. On the inside front cover, in black ink, just a number: *06.1950*

— Anyone's story.

She said this out loud, quickly, shutting the book, reaching it high onto the shelf where it had come from. She set the figurine back on top of it and paused, her hand resting for a moment on top of her head.

There are so many stories about ravens. A fable. A fairy tale. Perhaps she hadn't made it up, after all: this story one she'd been told over and over again in childhood, her mother doing the telling, and her mother's mother. Just another thing she could not remember remembering.

She reached up and moved the figurine to one side. The book just sitting there, up on its shelf.

Heike took it down again.

THE FIRST HALF MILE OF TRAIL was the darkest—down to the mouth of the stream, where it burbled into Cayuga. As she got closer, she knew she'd hear the sound of it, the water braiding itself around the rocks. She snaked along the ridge, Eric's book in her purse, strapped now like a postman's bag tight across her chest, and the new sketchbook in there, too, both spines slapping heavy at her ribs. There was a spitting rain, but it was not cold.

Either Eric would be home or he wouldn't be. Heike tried to steel herself for the negotiation. Best to let him think she was coming back, to appear contrite, allow him the upper hand: a snide reveal of Daniel's hiding place or, better, a dismissal. Perhaps he'd had enough by now, would send them packing—Heike and Daniel together—out into the night.

The sun was not completely gone. If it had not also been raining, she would have been able to follow the light, moving west; as it was, she kept on steadily, her arms a little raised to guard against branches, and held the quiet lap of the water to her right.

The air was warm and a mosquito dogged her, landing again and again behind her ear. She thought of the girl, Tessa, as she had when she was standing just outside the cabin, but the shadows were deeper now, and her image, the wisp of her hair, receded farther into the trees. The little house back behind her, alone and somehow broken, stripped away.

Where the woods descended into stillness, Heike stopped, waiting for any splash, a notion that the stream was still there. She could not see but imagined the dragonflies at their evening dance along the surface. The trees black around her—not a watercolour black but made of something thick, unguent, something you could put your hand into. She'd swallowed her heart and it was choking her. No sound but the buzz of some larger thing at her face, a horsefly, and it drowned everything else out.

She'd reached the pool, the place they'd stopped for a rest the day she brought Daniel in the canoe. That's why it was so quiet. The leech on his finger. She listened. The sharp report of a beaver's tail off the surface. Then a softer sound: not so much a splash, but a heaviness, a displacement, water turning over to fill a space. Flip of a fat brown trout. A duck, diving. She went on a few steps and heard it again.

Something in the water, swimming down to the lake along with her. Heike moved faster. She felt now not only the girl's presence as she had in the woods near the cabin, watchful, half-hidden among the trees, but the other, wilder Tessa. Tessa as Heike had dreamed her, the night she left Eric, in Dolan's car: small and pale, her long hair loose, with a jaw that hinged wide as she rushed closer. Her feet almost not even touching the ground as she came.

Head tilted back, a cur's grin.

The horsefly was still at her, and Heike waved her hands

around her face to fend it off, trying, too, to rid herself of the girl's image. Her shoulder smacked hard against a tree. She had to be close to the lake now. In the stream beside her, a quiet splashing, and then something more. What she'd thought of as the lap of the current now clearly the dive and surfacing of some creature pacing her, step for step.

It had been there all along, waiting for her as she came down through the dark woods. Not quite a voice. A harsh exhale, a warning. Teeth bared, something breathing in the dark.

ES WAR EINMAL
EIN MÄDEL

*[At Edgewood,] Ketchum's specialty was a family of molecules that block
a key neurotransmitter, causing delirium. The drugs were known mainly
by Army codes, with their true formulas classified. The soldiers were never
told what they were given, or what the specific effects might be, and the
Army made no effort to track how they did afterward.*
— Raffi Khatchadourian, in "Operation Delirium,"
The New Yorker, December 17, 2012

*The symptoms which are considered to be of value in strategic and tactical
operations include the following: fits or seizures, dizziness, fear, panic,
hysteria, hallucinations, migraine, delirium, extreme depression, notions of
hopelessness, lack of initiative to do even simple things, suicidal mania.*
— L. Wilson Greene, scientific director at Edgewood Arsenal, in his
1949 classified report "Psychochemical Warfare: A New Concept of War"

Look back, look back: there's blood on the track.
— from "Cinderella," as recorded by Jacob and Wilhelm Grimm

LODI 242X Trial Journal, July 1956

Ongoing long-term trial.

July 1, 1956

Extended trial of LODI 242X, 180³.

July 2, 1956

Extended trial of LODI 242X, 180³.

Supplement: CANOGA 4622, one-time dose 190¹.

Patient displays stable mood and abnormal thinking consistent with drug history. No notable somnambulance. Increased confusion with supplement. Compliant.

July 3, 1956

Extended trial of LODI 242X, 180³.

July 4, 1956

Extended trial of LODI 242X, 180³.

No supplement.

No change in behavior. Stable mood and activity; minimal anxiety. Compliant.

July 5, 1956

Extended trial of LODI 242X, 150².

July 6, 1956

Extended trial of LODI 242X*, 120².

Patient unchanged: Some continued experience of abnormal thinking, especially when led. Limited confusion. Stimulant effects unremarkable. Lack of initiative, controlled somnambulance. Unusual weakness/tiredness dissipating with decrease in dosage.

*Research chemical's availability in sharp decline. New supply so far unstable. Enforced reduction program begins here.

18.

Heike came up from the trail and stood at the edge of the property, her breath shallow and uneven. A long scratch tracked from behind her ear down across her shoulder where she'd scraped against the bare limb of a tree. She waited.

The driveway was flat and empty. Unusual to find Eric away in the evening. In the old days, he'd had a routine: leave the house at eight, return at six, two drinks before dinner. On Cayuga, he'd begun to keep odd hours, and she'd found him less predictable: awake and working late into the night, sleeping half the day in his linen suit. His work, whatever he'd been doing at the hospital, had knocked him off his schedule but also galvanized him. Heike had never known him to use a sleeping pill in the city, but remembered now the little eyedroppers, the paper tab he'd slipped under his own tongue. Where he'd once held to his own rigid standards, here he'd begun to seem fearless, too dynamic to need any rules at all. Heike herself a detail he could contain.

She skirted the grass that ran along the driveway. There was a light on in the kitchen. Another light, or the hint of one, upstairs somewhere, one of the back rooms. No sound from the house.

Then, just at her feet, a long, low rattle.

She stood fixed in place. Eric's birdhouses hovered overhead, propped on their stilts, like strange puppets. Holes instead of eyes. She turned toward the sound. From beneath the feeders, a single crow clicked its comb call at her again, the same percussive roll. Head cocked in warning. The noise grew, and Heike stepped back: not one crow, but dozens. An occupying force. A few peanuts lay scattered over the lawn, still in their shells. Closest to her, the sentinel stepped forward and ruffled its wings.

She went in the front door, arms brush-scratched in the light and the cuffs of her pants dragging, like her ball gown had turned to rags. There was a new girl in the kitchen. She was bent over the sink and jumped back at Heike's voice.

— Is Mr. Lerner at home?

The girl put a hand to her mouth.

— I must look a lot worse than I think. I'm scaring you? I am his wife. I'm Mrs. Lerner.

The girl still said nothing, and Heike moved in closer.

— Do you hear me? I'm Mrs. Lerner. Is my husband at home?

— I'm sorry, ma'am. It's just that . . . I thought Mrs. Lerner was dead.

Heike blinked.

— Who told you this?

— No one. It's just . . . Mr. Lerner, he seems so . . . She faltered. He's in his office, she said.

Heike stepped back and leaned out into the hall, looking for a crack of light under the office door, but there was none.

— Oh, no, ma'am. Not here. At the hospital. Mister almost lives at the hospital. Sure I almost never see him home at all. The girl wiped her hands on her apron. Sometimes he don't come home overnight.

— But you stay here? Heike looked back and forth between the hall and the girl, not quite trusting in Eric's absence. What does your mother say to this?

The girl couldn't have been more than fourteen. She had a country face. Her hair was not really red, but close to it.

— I do what's needed.

She sat down suddenly at the wooden table, as though the wind had been knocked out of her.

Heike moved close.

— And what about the little boy?

THE CAR WAS STILL HIDDEN AWAY in the ditch where Heike had left it. The girl told her that Mister had a hired car, that his own car was immovable: something had befallen it, the muffler was detached, or the gas tank had a bad puncture. He said he needed a tow truck, but never seemed to remember to order one. He mostly lived at the hospital. Lived for his work! Had she already told Heike that? Almost never home. It was why she had imagined him sad.

Heike walked around the place, flipping switches on every wall, the whole house lighting up stark and lonely. Like she was the janitor on a movie set after all the players had gone home. The house was strange to her: a place she'd heard described once, or read about in a magazine, while waiting for an appointment or sitting on a train. She opened the closets and the cupboards.

In the white room, she found a picture in a lacquered frame. For a moment she didn't recognize herself. A half-glance over one shoulder. Taken how long ago? Two years? A prop. The bright sunlight off their Manhattan fire escape. She'd been wearing a dress the colour of heather.

The girl had never seen any little boy, and Mister had never mentioned one. He came home at odd times, took short showers and asked only for cold sandwiches. The groceries arrived by delivery, left on the porch: bread, apples, onions, a chicken she was told to cook and leave cold in the icebox. When he was home, he could not keep still, she said. She hadn't had to make up the bed once.

Heike thought of the last time she'd seen Eric: unable to stay conscious, much less move around. His eyes rolling in their sockets. This version of him seemed unreal to her now, like something she'd once dreamt that had wormed its way into real memory.

What she did understand was that he was not coming home often enough to tend a living thing. Nor had the girl been hired to look after one. Almost two weeks now since she had arrived home in the early hours to find Daniel missing. She had a sudden image of Eric striding through the forest, Dani's small body slung over his shoulder as a woodcutter carries his axe. A spade in his hand. She shook her head in an effort to banish the thought and searched the house.

The hardest places. The woodbox, wide and empty aside from the dust of last winter's kindling. She cracked open the porthole of the dryer, just big enough to fit a child's body. In Eric's office, she rolled up the carpet, looking for a false floorboard, a wall safe. The room felt tight as a secret, and she set the carpet back neatly, everything in its place. The root cellar. The chest freezer at the back of the pantry. Whether Eric came home in the middle of the search no longer mattered. The girl followed her, room to room, and did not ask anymore what she was looking for.

Everything gone, wiped clean. The toy box in the garage where she'd kept his ball, the yellow-painted dump track with its rusty axel. No trains, no toys tucked away; nothing hidden, put aside, as Eric had told Heike, to protect her. The house had an antiseptic feel. Eric's razor and shaving brush laid out on the bathroom sink, meticulous. His toothbrush dry.

No small body, alive or otherwise. No trace.

In the bathroom, her eyes drifted from sink to mirror to vanity. Something caught her eye down in the tub, and for a moment she thought it might be a towel, some colourful thing, tossed aside, but when she leaned in to retrieve it, she found instead the blue boat, the boat with its wind-up motor that Eric had given to Daniel. Her heart caught in her throat; for a moment she thought she might vomit. A piece of him, the only piece left. She turned it over in her hand, recalling Eric's delight as he pulled the surprise out from behind his back, the way he'd shown her the little rudder, playing at it with his finger and his thumb.

The feel of the wind-up gear where he'd pressed the boat into her hand—and Heike who'd wound the mechanism for Dani, who'd pointed as the boat cut its path along the surface. The water warm against her skin. Heike watching the boat. Eric watching Heike.

She set the toy down on the edge of tub and peeled her hand off it, unnerved somehow, her hand slightly trembling. She went back to the white room and the photo on the shelf, then combed through all the pictures she had: two albums' worth, summers and springs and Christmases. Page after page, Heike's hair so pale that it appeared almost white in the photographs, and a thin white band framing every picture. She'd glued the little black corner-holders in herself, written captions. *1954, July: Staten Island Ferry. 1955, December: Manhattan wedding, Jack Wyland and Arden Lerner (Eric's sister).* Her fingers moved automatically. The corners dislodging as she grew rougher, more frenetic, the stiff photographs sliding out of the albums and onto her lap, then down onto the floor. Heike in the window of their apartment, Heike on the beach at Atlantic City. *1954, April: Balcony, 86th Street. 1953, August: Coney Island boardwalk.* Heike in every picture, so thin in the beginning that her collarbones cut a line from shoulder to shoulder, so tiny in a bathing suit on the beach that you could see the jut of her hipbones, like sawed-off horns, pressing out against the fabric. Always Heike alone, as though she were merely a doll, a mannequin for Eric to catalogue and pose.

A few of the photos lay scattered across her lap, and she brushed them off onto the floor. She left a hand pressed hard against her belly, trying to remember the long-ago pulse of Daniel's movements inside her. What's lost to the mind is not lost to the body: a baby rolling and twisting and pushing out, a sharp heel wedged between her ribs. She could feel it there now, as though something had kicked her open.

Heike asked the girl, still lurking around, to leave her then; she climbed the stairs alone, ran a bath and sank into it, her skin reddening. A clean white dress and a thin belt draped over the clotheshorse, waiting. She imagined Daniel's body, could almost feel it there: the pruning fingertips, smooth, round belly, scooping little thighs. Her hands slipped away from the sides of the tub but found only her own thighs, her own belly. The water hot enough to steam at its surface.

Daniel wore cotton pyjamas after a bath, liked to pour the bubbles from one empty shampoo bottle to another, asked her to plug his nose for him when it was time to wash his hair, wrapped his arms around her neck and held on tight. He fell asleep curled against her chest or with his head in her lap. His breath, the little rasp in his voice calling to her early in the morning.

The day she'd run up to this room, taking the stairs two at a time, sure of Eric's firm hand on Daniel, pushing him under: Dani thrashing below the surface and then still.

Now Heike pushed herself under the water and screamed. Pressing the air from her lungs; the pitch of her own voice, shrill and violent. Her hands slipped against the sides of the tub as she forced herself down. Eyes wide open, hair streaming. Her throat constricted. Water rushed in and she held it there, kicking out despite herself. Her ankle broke the surface, smacked sharply off the faucet, and she used it, bracing the foot against the tap to try to sink her body lower.

She was choking. Her head felt light.

Daniel, quiet and breathless and half-hidden behind the door in his hooded towel when she'd arrived to save him that day. She'd imagined him drowned. So far away now: Daniel safe in a hooded towel.

And Eric, watching, his notebook in his hand.

She pulled up suddenly and shot forward, coughing, leaning hard over the side. She couldn't hear herself, and she couldn't get any air. She kicked at the plug. The bath began to drain out, and she hauled herself against the side of the tub until she vomited, water spraying the floor, and she heard her own gasp, almost a shriek of breath. Her ankle was bleeding where she'd kicked the faucet, struggling against herself.

The blue boat still sat where she had left it, placid, next to the tap. She had somehow missed it with her leg. When she could sit up, she grabbed it and hurled it at the wall. A sound sharp as a pistol—the boat's plastic case splitting down the hull—the echo of metal mechanism and rudder hitting the ground and spinning out in different directions.

The room was steamy. She sat sideways in the tub, her knees pulled in against her chest, and rested her forehead there and cried. The last of the bathwater sucked away, leaving her cold and naked and shaking in a warm room. A thin stream of blood ran from her ankle to the drain.

After a while she lifted her head. She pressed the heels of her hands against her eyes for a moment, then wiped them roughly, slicking away whatever trace remained of tears or bathwater.

Through the open window, the scrape of tires on the drive.

BUT THE FUSS the girl kicked up. What a lot of squawking and foot stomping. Heike curled in, combed her wet hair back with her fingers, wrapped her arms around her knees. With the door closed, she could hear only so much. There was volume. The words were missing, but the vehemence carried. She should jump out of the tub, cover up, dress, protect herself. She did none of these things, but only crouched there, her breath still shallow.

The foot stomping gained sudden fervour, and the bathroom door swung into the room, its interior handle smacking off the wall. But it was Dolan, not Eric, who came in, and the girl after him, frantic, arms waving.

— It's alright. Heike took a hand from around her legs and gestured to the girl to go back downstairs.

The girl paused in her discomfort, treading from one foot to the other out in the hallway, and did not leave but backed up to watch from a safer distance.

— I know: it's unusual. But I know this gentleman. Heike gripped the edge of the tub and pulled herself to sit upright, leaning out with her head and shoulders. She coughed.

Dolan stepped in a little farther, glancing down only for a moment at the wet floor.

— I didn't expect to find you here, he said.

— You thought I was eaten by a wild wolf?

— I came to see Lerner.

She stood up in the tub.

— I am afraid you're out of luck, Mr. Dolan. Only Mrs. Lerner is at home.

The water had made her hair curl, and the ends of it lay damp, stuck to the hinge of her jaw. Her arms hung at her sides, and she stood with one knee angled out like a street urchin, the cut on her ankle throbbing. The maid, half-forgotten at her hall-way post, looked down in a modest way and then up again when she thought no one was watching. Heike held a hand out. Dolan went to take it, but she waved him away.

— The towel, of course. Give me a towel.

When she was wrapped, she stepped out of the tub.

— I figured I could choke the truth out of him, Dolan said. Man to man.

— You long to be needed.

Heike stepped to the mirror and polished a steam-free circle with the flat of her hand. She wanted to take a good look at her face. Dolan was there behind her, a rough silhouette.

—Woods were wolf-free, then?

She turned, gripping the towel just under her collarbone.

— There was something there. In the water. Barking at me almost. Not a bark. I don't know. She looked away for a long moment before coming back to him. Snarling, she said finally. Not barking. But after a time I wasn't afraid of it. It wasn't chasing me. It's like we were travelling together.

Dolan watched her.

—An otter can make quite a noise.

—If you say so. She went back to her own reflection. I'm tired of arguing with men.

The fog was slowly losing its territory in the mirror, the counterpart version of Heike widening out and gaining in detail. She fingered her earlobe, the tiny nut-brown skin tag that had grown there in adolescence. One of her eyes was strangely bloodshot, as though a capillary had burst.

—You won't come home with me, then.

Dolan stood over her shoulder, his reflection in the mirror still obscured by steam. She straightened.

— I will find my son.

There was a long silence, Heike examining her eyes, her jaw-line, her lips. Dolan behind her. He reached out to touch her waist, and his hand stayed there. Heike turned to the doorway. The girl, still waiting in the hall, arranged herself.

— I really must ask you to go downstairs now, Heike said.

They could hear her feet on the steps, shuffling her way down, and then the long creak that was the middle stair. She'd sat down to continue listening. Heike let the towel drop and began to dress.

— I needed a place to go; you gave me one. I won't forget that.

She bent at the waist to fasten her bra, then straightened, adjusting the straps in the mirror. Dolan watched her pull the white dress over her head, cinch the alligator belt in. Her fingers with a slight tremor. She threaded the buckle through.

— Is that all this was?

Heike grabbed his elbow for balance as she slid her feet into her shoes.

— This? This was nothing. A distraction. Everything in me is for Daniel. Surely you always knew this. She stamped her heels lightly, a final adjustment, and looked up at the reflected Dolan, the mirror clean and clear. I have no more time for distractions now.

He stepped back and away from her, out into the hall, and she followed him. They crossed into the bedroom. She dragged a stool over to the closet and pulled down a wicker laundry basket from the top shelf.

— Here, she said. She motioned to Dolan to put it on the bed, then climbed down herself. She started pulling clothes out of the wardrobe and layering them in the basket.

Dolan stood quietly, waiting for whatever she was going to say next, but she said nothing and kept packing. He sat down in the rocker, legs splayed.

— Where will you go?

Heike turned away from the wardrobe, gripping a handful of underclothes in each fist.

— If I want Daniel, I have to find Eric.

— Alone? I'm not sure that's wise.

— What would be wise? You want to go instead?

She shoved the clothes in her hands down one side of the basket and stayed like that for a moment, her arms hidden in the pile of clothing. Almost packed herself, folded over.

— I'm saying you might need a little backup.

— No. She looked up. No: with Eric, everything is about power. You see that, don't you? So I can't send a man to do my work.

She picked up the basket and hefted it onto one hip.

— You remember what I told you about stories? You begin with a girl, alone in the woods. So now it's time for the end of the story, and it has to match the beginning. Some things you have to do by yourself.

THEY FOUND THE NEW MAID sitting pressed up against the wall halfway down the stairs, her hands on the step behind her, as though she'd been lifting herself stealthily, step by step, back up to the second floor. She'd been listening, or trying to, head down, and didn't see them behind her. She seemed oddly fixated on the front door, staring at it even when Heike spoke to her.

— Were you able to hear everything, or shall we make a dramatization for you?

There was no answer, and the girl did not turn her head until Heike repeated the question. They were above her, at the top of the staircase. The girl got to her feet.

— I'm sorry, ma'am. It's just that . . . She paused and turned her body to face them, her eyes turning last. I was listening in, it's true. Only a little bit, ma'am. But then I heard something else, from downstairs. Like there was someone there. I thought it was Mister, come home. I could hear him in his den, ma'am, opening and shutting things. But then it stopped, just like that. And then . . .

She trailed off, turning to look at the front door again.

Heike moved to pass her on the stairs, but Dolan held up a hand. She pressed the basket on him and slipped by the girl anyway, her shoes sliding as she reached the wood floor at the bottom. She peered down the hall.

—And then what? I don't see anything.

The girl hadn't moved, and Dolan herded her down the stairs now, carrying the basket out in front and using it to move her along.

—It was the strangest thing. There was a gust of wind through here, as though the door had opened and shut again. But I was right here. I would have seen him, ma'am.

Heike took the basket from Dolan and set it down on the floor near the hall closet. The front door was firmly shut, the dead-bolt engaged. She leaned in through the kitchen doorway, but everything was as the girl had left it: dishcloth hanging off the handle on the stove, a single pot left to drip in the rack. There was no evidence anyone had come in or out, but there was a scent throughout the place, something mossy and familiar. Rot, the underfoot smell of the woods, earth and crushed plants and something else, too, something heavier.

She turned and looked toward the back of the house. The office door was still shut, but there was now a trace of light around its edges. Not just through the wide crack at the bottom, where the glow spilled out in a thin crescent, but along each side. She edged toward it, one cautious foot in front of the other.

Dolan turned to the girl, now perched on the steps.

—You should be ashamed of yourself. Can't you see you're

giving her the shakes? He caught up to Heike with a few easy strides. You probably left the light on in here yourself, he said.

He took hold of the knob and pushed the door open with a sweep of his arm. Heike, next to him, stepped back.

In the office, every lamp was lit. The little desk light, and the standing reading lamp at Eric's chair; overhead, a single bulb flickered in its polished brass fixture, casting a trembling glow. The room quivered with it.

—Who did this? Heike said.

If the place had been searched, it had been done with a precise hand. Each desk and file drawer stood open just two or three inches more than the one above it, turning every cabinet into a set of ascending stairs. The floor was carpeted in loose paper. A few sheets still fluttered slowly to the ground, as though they'd been released in bundles from above, or thrown like confetti by some invisible reveller. A hiss and pop from the fireplace; sparks shot out from an open flame.

Heike stepped into the room and pulled the fire screen shut. In the hearth, a solitary log burned, without paper or kindling wood. Even the ash had been swept clean.

The room was warm and almost sultry; there was a musky softness to the air, the forest smell amplified by the small space or the fire. Heike had the feeling she was underground, the den not wood-panelled but rather dugout, walled in damp earth.

She turned back to face Dolan in the doorway.

—No one would leave a room like this by accident.

Dolan turned and moved off to the back of the house. She could hear him rattling the doors in the white room, his steps heavy as he searched for other exits, any way for an intruder to escape. Heike came out of the room and found the girl still cowering by the stairs and took her roughly by the shoulders and shook her.

— Why would you do this? Who brought you here? Eric? Did Eric tell you to do this?

But the girl cried and did not try to wrench herself away. She was young, younger than Rita even, not so much a girl as a child. Heike let go of her with a shove and then felt sorry for it. She walked back down the hall and into the office again. The ceiling light flickered. She reached up and turned off the switch. On the desk, the little lamp burned a steady, downward beam. Heike paused, staring.

The wood beneath the light gleamed. There was nothing of Eric there: no fountain pen, no stationery, no pile of letters to be sorted or read. No files, no papers. No notebook.

The notebook she'd taken herself, the last time she'd been in the house. In its place, a trace wetness, uneven: the beads of condensation left from a cold glass, or a few drops of moisture from someone's hair after a rainstorm, after a swim. Heike touched her own hair, still damp from the bath, then pulled the tip of her finger through the little puddle. It was murky, a remnant of grit against her skin.

She wiped her hand on the hem of her dress and backed out of the room.

— Everything's locked tight, Dolan said. From the inside.

He'd come back to the front of the house and found Heike in the entryway, gathering her things. He was holding a photograph, a younger Heike with her hair under a summer kerchief, leaning against a rail.

— I found these spread out all over the couch. A real mess of them.

She didn't seem to have heard him. She was riffling through her handbag. The girl sat wiping her face with a handkerchief on the bottom stair. Dolan glanced at her and turned back to Heike.

— He's come in with a key, that's all. She missed it somehow. She admits she was eavesdropping. Here he looked hard at the girl, sitting so low she was almost on the floor: Don't you? You must have looked away and missed something.

The girl didn't answer but dabbed the handkerchief against her nostrils.

Dolan said:

— That's all that happened. He came in and out with a key. He's trying to frighten you, Heike.

He stepped close, his face tipped down toward her, but he did not try to touch her.

— Heike, you see that, don't you?

She looked up as though his voice had come out of nowhere.

— It was me who made that mess, she said. The pictures, just me.

She straightened and adjusted herself in the hall mirror, then turned to Dolan and took the photo out of his hand, stopping to look down at it. She stroked the line of her own cheek, gently, with a thumb.

— I look almost too young to be a mother, she said. Don't you think?

She tucked the picture into her purse.

19.

She had not driven so far by herself since just after the war, when she'd driven the truck—as she'd told Dolan, packed with vegetables—over the border to where she knew families were starving in their early penance. And even then, never at night. Sunlight, a plain novice's veil over her hair to lend authority, the dirt smell of raw potatoes. At the border she swung open the back doors and drank chicory while the *Grenzwachtkorps* dug through the bushels with the butt ends of their rifles.

Now she was heading north. The sweep of the headlights as she came around a long curve, the top end of Cayuga, where the lake turned to marshland. She caught for a moment the shadow of a bird, wings spread and lifting, but this must have been an illusion. Shallows on either side of the road mirroring in the glint of moonlight or the erratic light from the car. It was long past dark. Even the crows she'd seen down in the lawn outside the house had been quiet when she left again, only one of them batting its wings at her from the top of a birdhouse, the others sunk deep in the grass. An odd place for a bird to rest.

The bumper had snagged in the brush at the last moment as they excavated Eric's car—still nestled away where she and Arden had stashed it, and entirely serviceable after all. Dolan with his jacket off and Heike gunning the motor from the driver's seat: he'd only just let go pushing and then came the crunch. As a result, one light beamed forward as it should, a long, convex warning signal to those ahead; the other pointed slightly down and to the centre, like a crossed eye. There were almost no other vehicles on the road. Once she passed an army Jeep with one of its own lights burnt out, cyclopsing its way toward her. Once she passed a deer, dark and splayed at the side of the road. She thought it was a downed branch. Just the top half: antlers, head, spindly front legs. The haunches taken home by the driver for easy chops.

Coming out of the marsh, she saw it again: a night heron, rising black over the deadwood. A wingspan the length of a child. She turned south again and lost sight of the water. Farms on either side of her, the road a thin passage between cornstalks, their leaves held out in a scarecrow shrug: What can you do?

THE DAMAGED BUMPER had begun to make a rattling sound. She dropped her speed and cut in along the edge of Seneca. It was not the way that Eric had approached the place the day they'd come with Daniel. To her left there was a rise, the earth cutting away dark and pronged. She could see the run of tree roots coming down through it like burrowing veins. The road turned away from the water abruptly.

At the axis of the curve there was a brick house with an electric light fixed over the entrance. The light shone down the length of a wooden dock that extended like a long tongue into the lake. She followed the road around until the lake was behind her. Ahead, the grounds sprawled out, the residences with their high dormer windows, punctuated at regular intervals by slim smokestacks rather than chimneys, and the smaller shapes of outbuildings growing on all sides, errant, like mushrooms. Farther down the road, the town itself, called not Willard but Ovid. Heike did not know which had been there first: the village around the asylum, or the asylum at the centre of the village. She knew there was a post office, a diner, bungalow houses where the nurses lived with their families, a creek, a schoolhouse. She enumerated these things to herself, the lives of others in the shadow of the place.

She pulled the car to one side and cut the engine. The asylum's main building rose up like a great curved hand, grasping, set on its edge in the middle of the lawn. There was light there, too, from its centre windows, the offices, but not from the residence windows to either side. She could see the outline of the dentils along the high trim and above those, more dormers on the third floor. A turret sat dark and geometric at the building's centre. If he were there, Eric would be in his office. One of those lit windows beneath the high turret, and Daniel with him, hidden away.

Outside the car there was the insect sound of any summer night, jaw against leaf, wing on wing. She pressed the door closed rather than slamming it. On the road she'd at least had the breeze made by the vehicle's motion, air rushing through the open windows. Now the heat held her down. Sticky, waiting for the storm.

There were no buildings on the other side of the road, but a wide path cut through the trees to a meadow or some other clearing: it opened out round and full beyond the tree line, dark as open water. The woods she'd seen from below, rising up over the road as she came in.

Heike squinted. At the edge of the path, the shadow of a tree swayed forward, and then kept coming.

She shrank back against the car. Not a tree after all, but some creature. A stag. No: some other thing, one head piled onto another, seven feet in the air. A man. Some monstrous version, grown large. The way she had imagined Eric, cutting a path through the forest, Daniel's body slung limp about his neck.

A loping arm swung purposefully at its side as it came out into the road. The moonlight caught him then: the old man, Marek, a long spade high across one shoulder, its blade making the shadow of a second head. He'd seen her right away, as she stood there in the night heat, listening to the cricket song. Long before she'd noticed he was there. He came across the road to meet her, the soles of his shoes scuffing against the tarmac.

— *Na, schau mal. So viel Glück hab' i', so ein hübsches Mädchen wiederzusehen!*

Lucky to meet up with such a pretty girl again.

There was a clod of earth stuck on the rim of the shovel blade, and Marek brought the spade down off his shoulder and let it fall, blade first, into the lawn. He was wearing the same striped shirt, buttoned to the collar, the same jacket as before, hospital issue or his only possessions, and he held on to the top of the wooden handle with both hands, flexing them gently, like he was wringing out a wet rag. His eyes stayed fixed on hers.

What had Eric told her about him? That there was nothing wrong with him; he'd become trapped in the asylum. Her eyes flicked up toward the path he'd come through, the clearing.

He dug the graves. That's what Eric had said. No way out once you're in.

When she looked back, she half expected to find him closing in on her, shovel raised, but in fact he had not moved at all. He did not smile at her, but seemed as though he would have liked to. His eyes watered, especially the left one. An old man. She gestured to the shovel:

— You've been hard at work tonight.

— The dying and the dead. They have no respect for a man's bedtime! He tapped the spade into the grass. Tonight, the earth is soft. Tomorrow, who knows? Old men, we have no choice about such things. We must dig while we can.

— There. It's the cemetery? *Friedhof, ja?*

— *Friedhof.* Marek looked skeptical, but then he surprised her and laughed. *Friedhof!* His moustache lifted and she could see all his teeth.

The car was still close behind her. At the main building, a light flickered out. Heike caught it from the corner of her eye. When she turned to look, there were still a few windows lit and she counted them. She was running out of time.

— You are looking for someone.

Marek shifted, facing the darkness. She spun back to look at him.

— Yes. Yes! You remember.

The old man had seen them, the day Daniel scraped his hands against the thorns. He'd seen them together, Heike and Daniel.

— The last time I was here. You remember? I had a child with me.

For a moment he said nothing. His expression was hard to read in the low light, his features half-shadowed, but it seemed to Heike that the little fan at the corner of his eye deepened. Then:

— Come, he said. *Kommen Sie, kommen Sie, bitte*. I will take you. He moved the spade from his right hand to his left and grasped the handle lower down, firm, like a walking stick. Then, holding out his arm: Young ladies should not walk around in the dark!

Heike looked at the elbow, its wide crook offered up. She moved stiffly, still deciding whether to take his arm as she slipped her hand through. The thought that this was a lonely man's ploy occurred to her. They began to move forward through the long grass, Marek favouring his right side a little and the shovel making its dull noise against the earth, something Heike could feel more than hear. An absurd agitation seized her: she could have been across the lawn by now, inside, going from door to door.

— We met you in the garden. Yes? Grasping now at optimism, and she knew it, but the words came anyway. We were playing hide-and-seek, she said. She held a hand out at the level of her hip: Just this tall. Very little still. You remember?

The old man nodded and spoke in response without turning his head. Heike struggled to understand. She'd caught only *Kindlein*, little child. With no one else to speak to, he seemed to have made a dialect of his own, a twin German, inflected both with archaic structures and bits of English thrown in when it suited him. He was leading her away, in the wrong direction, the light from the main house behind them now.

— *Ja, kleines Kindlein*, she repeated. A little child, my Dani. Have you seen him again? By himself? Or with the doctor? *Vielleicht mit dem Arzt?*

They passed between two small outbuildings, one close by and the other at some distance, the grass between them worn away over time.

— *Schauen Sie her.* Marek stopped and pointed toward the little house closest to them. He pulled away from her and mimicked turning the doorknob. In here. *Herein.*

An ache inside her, her heart twisting and dropping.

— In here?

She stepped up and set a hand on the knob. Tentative. It didn't turn. She tried again, slamming hard at the door with the flat of her hand, her shoulder. Marek stood watching her.

— Give me your spade. Here, here in my hand, your shovel, give it here.

Heike lodged the blade into the crack by the strike plate and let her body fall forward against the handle. The frame splintered. She pushed the door and walked through.

A series of small, high windows lined the ceiling along both sides, and these were the only source of pale light. Heike stepped away from the door to allow whatever moonlight possible to come in behind her. The shadows rose up on either side of her as though she were standing in a tunnel. A dull smell of ammonia. The fidget and murmur of birds. Pigeons, she thought.

— Dani?

There was no answer. As she stepped forward, her shoe slipped a little against the floor, a layer of grit making her slide.

There was a sputter of light and the room warmed. Marek had come in behind her; he'd had a flashlight in his pocket. What had seemed like tunnel walls were bracketed shelves, racks five feet deep on either side of her, stretching from floor to ceiling. Each shelf stacked with travelling cases: trunks and duffel bags, hat boxes. Suitcases. Her stomach dropped, and she had to swallow against the impulse to gag. If Daniel were hidden away here—if such a thing were even possible—he was not alive. She cycled through the same set of images: Eric with a hand over Daniel's mouth to keep him quiet. Daniel's body, limp over Eric's shoulder as he cut a path through the woods.

She turned to Marek.

— He's here? Is that what you're saying? She crouched low and began to crab along the floor, checking the lowest shelves first. Marek stood over her, and she saw that he was trying to hand her the flashlight. He wanted to go to bed, he said. She leaned a hand against the floor; it was rough and filthy, and she pushed up instead, standing with her face in Marek's, and brushed the hand off against her skirt.

— Why did you bring me here? You said you saw him. You saw him!

— *Na sicher.*

— So where is he? *Wo ist er denn?*

— I saw a child with you. *Kleines Kindlein, ja?* A little child, sometimes far, sometimes closer. You were following her. Then you turned suddenly, and you washed your hands at the pump, like this. He stooped over and rolled the flashlight between his hands, then straightened again. A little girl, he said.

He held the flashlight out to her a second time, and this time she took it, bringing it in close to her body and stepping forward to catch Marek's face in the light.

— Not a girl. A boy, a little boy.

— *Mädel, mädel, es war einmal ein Mädel.* A girl. Pretty hair, long hair. So blond like you.

— You've made a mistake. There is no girl, do you hear me? A boy! A little boy! Old man, your eyes must not be so good anymore.

Marek only looked at her and turned to go.

— And then your hands were clean and you wandered away.

He said this with his back to her. He was leaving her there. He switched to German again: *Allein.*

Heike had her tongue pressed hard against the back of her teeth. A cruel trick. There was the threat of the first prick of tears, and she refused them, drawing her forehead back and yelling out instead, her voice rough.

— Hey! *Was sagen Sie, allein?*

— *Allein, allein!* She was frustrating him. He batted a hand in the air, waving her away: You were. Alone.

Heike let the arm holding the flashlight drop a little. Above her, the ceiling stretched high. She was back in the tunnel, the light dropping out. She spoke, and it was a child's voice, unsure and recalcitrant, an apology for something she'd done but could not understand.

— I wasn't alone. He was always with me. Daniel.

Marek's eyes hardened, but it was not an unkind look. It was as though he were pushing her words around, through heavy weather. He gestured around at the trunks and cases.

— There is a lot for you to see here, *ja?*

Heike glanced down at the shelf closest to her. The place was a storage facility, unkempt and unthought-of. A mess. The room may as well have been filled with straw.

— I don't know why you've brought me here.

She would have liked to lie down somewhere and sleep for a long time.

Marek turned to go, pausing to look back at her over his shoulder.

— You washed your hands, he said. He had cloudy eyes, very pale, the pupils visible even in the low light. When he spoke to her, he moved between languages, and there was grace in that.

He said: *Dann waren Sie allein*. And then you were alone, walking away. But she followed behind you, of course. The little girl. Not right away, but slowly; slowly she followed behind you.

He slung his spade back up onto his shoulder.

— Just like today, he said.

MAREK'S FLASHLIGHT IN HER HAND made a disc of bright light at her feet, then another, wider ring around it, mostly shadow. He was gone; Heike was by herself. Her jaw was tight enough to make her head hurt. The old man's glance shifting just beyond her, over her shoulder, when he said it: *Just like today*.

For a moment she had almost called to him not to leave her.

She thought of the girl, Tessa, as she had appeared on the raft in her blue bathing suit. Then again, Tessa, no longer a child, jaw set open and shining. The thing she'd heard in the water, keeping pace as Heike came down through the woods. Teeth bared: how Heike herself had described it.

The air was still and warm, and the longer she stood there, the more she was aware of the smell. Dust and wet wood, and an animal smell, too, the birds high in their roost. She could feel her pulse, the surge of blood in her wrists, the back of her neck prickling with the heat and the space behind her, empty or not. She spun around suddenly, the light playing over the shelves and the blank floor between them.

There was a flapping up near the ceiling; a little raw sawdust floated down from the beam. She'd disturbed the pigeons. Her breath came short and fast, and she worked to slow it down, to make a plan.

What the old man had said: *Es war einmal ein Mädel*. The way her mother had begun every story. *Once upon a time there was a girl.* He was crazy, after all; or else he was trying to frighten her. There's power in scaring a woman, whether or not you know her, late at night. Heike let the light fall to the floor and followed it with her eyes.

For a moment, everything she'd seen at the house rushed in: the albums of photographs of Heike alone; Eric with his notebook, keenly watching as Heike set Daniel's blue boat afloat in the bath. And then Marek's words, sharp enough to make her catch her breath.

She dropped to the ground and began beating at a raised nail with the end of her flashlight, then another, and another. The action felt like control. A little shock shot up into her elbow and shoulder every time the rubber-coated end of the flashlight made contact with the plank floor.

Mäd'lein. A little girl.

He'd made a mistake. What he'd seen was just Daniel's blond hair, grown a bit too long, the little curls licking around his ears. He thought he'd seen a girl. But there was no little girl. There had only ever been Dani.

She stopped hammering, leaving a ringing stillness in the place. From the back of the room, a soft ticking started and then stopped again, a sound like something moving, the creak of wood expanding with heat and pressure.

She squatted there and shone the light to the back of the room.

— So. Are you there? Come out, then!

There was the hum of silence, like a high whine. Heike shifted onto the balls of her feet. The flashlight's beam arced across the door, still open, an old white lab coat hanging from a nail on the wall.

353

That first night, standing in Dolan's greenhouse, how he'd come in with a lantern and groped around at her feet for a bottle of booze, the light flickering at her knees. An easy moment. She'd still been somebody's wife, someone's mother. This seemed very long ago now. Dolan offering a quick flush on her cheeks and in her fingertips, his light flicking at the hem of her skirt. She'd thought he was trying to embarrass her.

Catch and release. She longed for it now, the safety of fluttering down out of the greenhouse.

She stood up again, and her ear popped and cleared, as though she were coming down from a great height. The pigeons' downy underfeathers were glued to the floor all around her. There could be only one good reason for Marek to have brought her here. The little house was not much more than a storage centre for old garbage, the cases and trunks coated in dust and untouched, maybe for years. There was no little girl.

SHE BEGAN AT ONE END, shining the flashlight first at the high upper shelf and jerking it down without method, shelf to shelf. The light trembling. Looking for any trunk large enough to hold a child. A child's body. She did not want the image, but it came to her anyway: Daniel, curled tight inside a latched suitcase. His eyes closed, cheekbones high and pristine, rosy enough to make you believe in sleeping spells.

There was a burgundy case half the length of Heike's own body, with brass fixtures, and she dragged this out, but it refused to open even when she kicked at the lock with her heel. The centre beams that held the place up cast shadows as she moved around, the flashlight in her hand. She moved back and forth, looking first at the shelves, then wheeling to shine the light behind her again, the light revealing nothing, empty space, each corner darker than the last.

She grasped the top rail and pulled up, stepping onto the low shelf as she went. There were fewer cases to look at here, and only the smallest ones. She ran a finger along the edge of a round hat box with a loop handle, trying to find the catch, the dirt coming up thick as a curl of apple peel. The slight ticking sound again. She stopped, frozen. At the other end of the row, the cases suddenly collapsed down on themselves, falling like rocks into a trench. Heike's hand slipped on the flashlight and it fell, too, ringing off the floorboards. The sound and sudden darkness pushed her into a kind of hysteria, and she jumped down, swinging the hat box by its loop and smashing it against the floor to break the clasp.

The light had rolled away from her and now shone back over the floor like a wide and solitary eye. She crouched low, quiet and panting so that she would not cry. The falling cases her own fault, Heike's doing, an accident.

She gathered up the contents of the hat box, spilled out: no hats, but pins, and a photograph, and an old envelope, addressed and torn and missing the letter inside. The pins were what she'd been after. She went to work on the lower shelves, each one stacked with more and heavier-looking baggage, using the hat-pins to crack the hasps and prying them open, one after another.

Some were nearly empty. In one there were only shoes: black dancing slippers with ribbon straps and dull leather strips stitched onto the soles, and a pair of farm boots, worn at the insides. A wooden crate held a stack of shellac records, the paper sleeves clean and thin, with a greasy feel. Fred Astaire and Jack Payne, and Billie Holiday.

The racks were labelled, where the label wasn't too filthy to read, by letter: *A* to *Z*. Everything she found on the upper racks was coated silvery white in pigeon droppings, and she wished she had a kerchief, anything clean, to tie over her mouth and nose. She worked faster and faster, not replacing the open cases but shoving them away from her and in her rage smashing everything, boxes too small to hold a child, breaking everything open, ruining it all.

A black doctor's bag filled with tools from an abandoned practice: a blood pressure cuff, the glass gauge with a hairline crack and the rubber of the bulb dry and crumbly at the join. Heike jarred at the flash of her reflection in the head mirror—a sudden memory of sitting in the roadway after the accident, Harry injured and bleeding in her lap, the first doctor who arrived to help with a light and a mirror like this one. The very fact of remembering, this thing that had been out of reach for so long, felt sharp as a kick to the gut. Razor wire. It almost made her double over. She crushed the thing under her foot.

She was sweating and pushed the hair off her face. She was tired now, so tired. The flashlight shone down from where she'd lodged it, tight on a shelf; the trunks and broken boxes grew up all around her, casting their shadows. It was hot.

He wasn't there. It was a relief and it also wasn't. She understood now what Marek had wanted to show her: that the bags and his graves were related. What they had in common were the patients locked up, working their days away in the cookhouse or smithy, or long dead and gone. This house the holding place, where they put your things when you had come in off the dock. No way out once you were in.

ERIC HAD BROUGHT HER to the Willard three times. If anything, he preferred to keep a barrier between his home and his work, although each time he allowed Heike just that little bit closer. A weird delight in his eyes as he pointed out the buildings, the patients at their exercise. The first time, she had sat in the diner up the road, drinking coffee at the counter and watching the proprietor layer together a row of hot turkey sandwiches on blue-rimmed dinner plates. White bread, brown meat, green-flecked dressing. Brown gravy. The owner's name was Lucinda; this was embroidered on her long apron, at the place you might pin a carnation on your jacket. She'd asked if Heike had someone in the asylum, a mother or brother, and Heike had said, no, her husband was a doctor there. Lucinda had made a face.

— There's a reason folks choose to go to work at the mental. Them doctors and nurses. Not like there ain't other good work out there. Drawn to it, that's what I say.

She'd finished each plate with a scoop of mash and refilled Heike's cup.

The next time, Heike had waited more or less in the car, parked at the far edge of the grounds. Eric striding off to the asylum along the road and waving to a limousine as it rolled by. She'd opened her door for air, then taken a few steps away from the car into the long grass of the field, where a few young men were planting apple trees. Teams of three: a wheelbarrow and two spades. They measured the eight feet between trees by walking, toe to heel. There had been two teams; one moved faster down the line than the other, but it was because on the slower team the digger had a deformed arm. He knelt in the dirt to dig, the useless arm half the length of the other and withered. This was before Eric told her it was the patients who did all the work.

And then that last time, with Daniel.

She stepped out of the storage house onto the grass. Marek was gone. Heike tried to shake off the feeling the suitcases had given her, the weird guilt and nausea of looking for a body instead of a child, as though it were her best hope, and becoming instead a silent witness to many lives, left to the pigeons and the mice. All their little things: petticoats and hair ribbons and photographs of children. She felt around inside her own bag and withdrew the photograph she'd pulled from the album at home.

Heike, the kerchief over her hair, leaning on a third-floor railing. How many times had she looked through those pictures? Heike sitting on a bench in Central Park, or posing near a Christmas window, or holding a stuffed bear at Coney Island. Eric documenting each moment from behind the camera.

The flashlight's beam spread out wide, and she let it move from tree to tree, turning a full circle. The gardens where they'd been at their game of hide-and-seek were far on the other side of the property. There were no roses here, no lilacs to hide in. She turned again.

At the base of a young oak, the light caught something globed and spongy. Slick. A cluster of mushrooms broad as a kitchen sink, tan and wet-looking, a glint of violet at their edges. She kicked at one with her toe, thinking it would be rubbery, but it broke immediately at the stalk, the cap flipping up to expose its scored underside, the furrows deep and tufted. A sound like breath all around her, warm and sweat-damp as silk.

Soft in the throat: the lenient pant of a wild dog. Black and huge as a bear. Heike's heart pounded against her back. She tried to summon the calm she'd managed along the stream, some creature pacing her in the water as she'd moved down the trail in the dark. What had Dolan said? An otter.

Madness, Eric had told her once. Madness follows you like a dog.

There was no stream here, no woods, no sharp sound. Just her own rough breath. She flexed her wrist, allowing the light to sweep the yard in an arc.

Up in the main building there were only three lights still burning. There was nothing behind her at all.

THE FLOORS INSIDE the entry were polished stone. She bent down and took off her shoes so that she would not make any noise, then slipped the flashlight into a shoe and carried it along like that, a glow coming through the leather at the toe. There were a few steps up and then a door off the landing. As she came through, she heard the sharp tap of another woman's shoes, but it receded into the distance, heading away from the residence. Halfway across the lawn, she'd imagined Eric, up in his office window or his lab, looking down at her, but there had been no shadow there and no curtains. There were nurses, she supposed, awake at all hours, but not many.

She was at one end of a wide hall.

Long doors lined the left side of the corridor, each with a transom window overhead, a half moon, now darkened. Every door open, at least a crack. The hall was broad enough that Heike could have lain down three times between one side and the other: fifteen feet across or more. She'd come up the side stairwell, and from here she could see the stairs from the main entrance where they opened out to a central foyer, and a light from a doorway there, on the right-hand side. The nurses' station. The tick-tack of shoes she'd heard must have ended up there.

She moved down the hall in her bare feet, her shoes and flashlight in one hand and a bit of her skirt wound around the fingers of the other. The thin drone of a radio made a tinny echo against the stone floor. The night shift, sitting in their lit room. They were listening to Benny Goodman to stay alert. Heike stopped briefly before each threshold to make sure that inside there was no nurse completing her rounds, no one about to pull back the door and surprise her.

She crept closer. Something else now over the sound of the radio, a steady pounding. She would have said a hammer, or the dull butt of an axe. The stump of footsteps, if the stepper were a giant. She pressed against the wall. The air inside the building was no less oppressive than outside, and she stopped for a moment, trying to catch her breath. An ammonia smell, cleaning fluid or soiled sheets or both, mixed with the humidity and the scent of whitewash. Her stomach turned, the hall wavering before her. The odour reminding her of something. For a moment she felt surrounded by a different sound, sheer, a papery rustling. Shuffling. She shrank into her bones, working at her breath, each inhalation cutting out shorter than the last.

Nothing: the moment passed, lifted away. She took in a long, deliberate pull of air and let it out again, counting to five in her mind. An odd sort of déjà vu.

Down the hall, the pounding continued. No voice cried out. She remembered Eric saying that in the old days they'd kept the inmates chained to the basement floor. They did not do that now.

The thump grew louder as she moved along, and Heike leaned just slightly left, enough to push the next door a crack wider.

The room held six beds, each with a curtain strung around it, although not all the curtains were pulled shut. An old woman lay in the bed next to the window, restless. Heike waited to hear the sound again. The room was darker than the hall, and she let her eyes adjust.

She blinked. She could see now that she was wrong: the woman was in fact not much older than Heike herself—perhaps thirty—but ragged around the mouth and eyes, and it gave her a hard look. Her arm lay at an odd angle, and Heike realized that she was restrained by a wrist to the bed. It was her leg that was making the noise: not because she was seesawing restlessly against the frame, but because she was kicking it, solidly beating at it with an ankle, harder and harder.

A wooden cross hung on the wall over each mattress, suspended there with a loop of twine.

Heike was standing just inside the doorway now, the door pushed wide on its hinges and her back close against it, the spell of vertigo from the hallway coming back to her. Where the ambient light from the hall reached the white walls, they swam. It was as if there were an animal just beneath the paint, and it had run from one side of the room to the other, making a weird ripple. She would have liked to sit down.

The place was not strange to her.

The curtain at each bed, the little cross, the room's tall, skinny windows: all of it so much like the room she knew from her last stay in the convent. After the accident, when they'd placed her with the elderly nuns for lack of a room among the noviciate. A thin perspiration at her brow, her lip, on the back of her neck.

Her knees buckled and she put a hand out, catching herself against the door. She wondered for a moment if here, too, there was a garden just outside the window, if there were chapel bells at first light and in the evening.

From another bed, someone moaned and snorted, and Heike jerked to one side, her heart kicking up, but the patient was asleep, her hair cut short and bristly against the pillow. Her wrist also tethered to the frame of her bed. The women's floor.

When Heike lifted her eyes again, a child stood staring back at her.

She froze, dumb with surprise. Too small to be a nurse, the girl stood maybe ten feet away from her and did not move. She was gauzy-looking, her hair untidy and luminescent. A little bride, all in white. No, of course not. In her nightgown. A capped sleeve slipping at the shoulder. Behind the girl, the room stretched back, larger than Heike had originally thought; she could see the posts of a dozen beds now. She drew in her breath. It couldn't be a child. A patient, then? Next to her in the bed, the first woman pounded her leg again and then again, faster, the sound of it coming on like a warning. An alarm, pealing out.

It was a moment before she realized her mistake. The row of tall windows lining the exterior wall of the room, the glass lit by the same ambient glow coming down the hall from the nurses' station. Against the black of the outdoors, the girl in white was just Heike herself. A mirror image, slightly unfocused in the dark. Her own white dress slipping off her arm; she raised a hand to fix it, watching the girl in the window do the same. When she moved to the left, her body blocked the light and the girl in the glass disappeared. In her wake there was only the after-image, shadowed deep grey and expanding out like a dark star.

It was here that she'd recovered, after Harry's death. Not Switzerland, not the convent at all. In this room, or one very like it. She remembered now, lying on her side, a stain on the wall by the window where water had seeped in after a storm, a long, deep crack in the paint that snaked its way almost to the floor. The paint peeling back, lifting away around it. Instinctively she brought a hand to her chest, expecting to recoil or find the contact strangely painful, but her body was her own, compact and easy and soft.

She stepped out of the room. Even the hallway was now familiar. She looked down at her bare feet, her shoes still in one hand, and flexed and curled her toes. They'd given her slippers. Paper slippers, strung with thin elastic. The sound of her own feet an echoed whisper, a sheer rustling, as she'd walked down the hall. A nurse at her elbow, pushing her along. *Miss. It will be good for you to walk, miss. Walking helps you heal.*

Heike pressed her cheek against the cool of the wall. She tried to take in air, long and slow. The light, the smell, everything working together. She was dizzy with it.

It was here she had been a patient, here that she'd first met Eric.

In bed, the woman kicked her beat, trying to do damage. The radio kept on. Heike heard the slide and slam of a heavy file drawer in the office. She pushed off the wall before she'd really regained her equilibrium and moved away from the noise, afraid. Up the central stairway before anyone should come out in the hallway and find her there. More sure than ever now: she'd come here looking for Eric, not knowing she was only coming back to the start.

At the head of each banister, the wall rose like a column, the plaster carved with vines and fruit, a false Continental opulence that must have been popular when the building was designed. At the second floor she stopped and peered down to where light spilled out the open door below. The radio cut out for a moment, and she heard their voices then: only two nurses were sitting up overnight. Heike waited, breath held, but no one entered or left the room. She turned and kept going, trailing her hand over the plaster decor, up to the next landing. The ceiling stretched high above her, the tops of the doors arched as though every office were a ballroom.

On the third floor, the radio could no longer be heard. Eric leaned in the doorway of the one lit room. He'd seen her coming, after all.

20.

I've been waiting for you.

Eric stepped toward her. He'd been leaning in the door-way, and the new movement seemed to throw him off, his body weaving a little, almost as though they were stand-ing on a boat. Heike froze at the top of the stairs, unsure of whether she'd really seen him falter, or whether it was her own light-headedness at work, a visual trick. She wondered for a second if he'd been drinking.

— Eric. She took a breath. Please, Eric.

He was wearing something on his arm, a new watch. The shiny face of it flashed at her. She flicked off her light with a thumb.

Eric shook his head.

— There aren't any children here, Heike. No children at the asylum.

There was a low groan from somewhere behind her, or over-head. For a moment she allowed a thought: some heavy-jawed animal, whatever she'd felt outside on the lawn, slouching up the stairs behind her before dropping back to wait. Dogging her. She glanced over her shoulder, but the stairwell behind her narrowed into vacant darkness: the turret she'd seen from the ground.

When she looked back at him, Eric was standing straight and tall, his strange unsteadiness gone.

— Doesn't that upset you? You won't find him here. Daniel. He paused, looking at her curiously. Or have you found him already?

She'd crept closer as he was talking, her hand resting now on the wall near where he stood. A smell of bleach through the place, and underneath it something else, a body smell, sweat and urine and staleness, stronger down on the ward but laid down even here like a soft, wet film, like skin. The plaster almost sweating beneath her fingers.

— Maybe I came here to find you.

Eric's face twitched, just for a second, as though there'd been a flash of bright light.

— What about your friend Dolan? He is still your friend, is he? You haven't fallen out?

He rubbed at his wrist.

— Let me past you, Heike said.

— Am I your friend again?

— I said, let me past.

Eric gestured for her to move by him. The shift made him falter again; she was sure of it this time, his eyes wavering and then landing, refocused. This disequilibrium unsettled her: could he be doing it on purpose? He braced himself against the doorjamb but did not allow her any more space. When she tried nudging her way through, he swung back so that her body brushed against him as she went, and he caught her waist and held her there and ran a hand down along her hip.

Her breath skipped. Standing close to him, the heat seemed to double over on itself. Her scalp prickled with it, a fine sweat breaking at her hairline. She pushed against him, but he didn't move or let her go, and she stiffened and turned her face away, trying to give herself some air. There was no smell of booze on him.

— Daniel. He shook his head. Daniel, Daniel.

He was trying to rattle her, every time he said the name.

Heike glanced back at him and then away. On the other side of the door, the room was spare and open. A wide desk, the chair with its back to the window, and another chair as well, rose-coloured, the upholstery threaded and worn. No curtains, but a set of thin-slat wooden blinds, pulled all the way up, the toggle dangling from a cord. The windows were all closed.

— You have no time for anyone else. It's amazing that you ever let him out of your sight at all. He was chiding her, both affectionate and mocking, the way a child might poke at a pet. Something very small.

She pushed against his arm again, and this time he released her so suddenly that she almost fell into the room.

— Your songbirds miss you, he said.

— Do they?

She recovered herself and tried to put a little space between them. Eric followed behind her. She could feel him there.

— The crows came and set up shop. They chased them all away, all your pretty birds.

She turned to face him:

— Sometimes things go wrong.

For a moment she heard the same creak again, from over-head. Something padding across the floor in the turret, heavy and quick. Pacing. Heike looked at Eric, but he did not seem to have noticed the noise. She held her face still, listening. If she was anxious, she did not want to make a show of it.

He was fussing with his wrist. She saw now that it was not a new watch he was wearing, just a glass watch face taped down against the skin.

—What have you got there?

He held the arm up, and she could see a thin sheen of liquid floating just below the glass, the rainbow blues and greens like an oil slick.

—There's a tremendous market for drugs that need only cur-sory contact with the skin. Or there will be.

Heike frowned. He said:

—Doesn't seem to have much effect: so far I don't feel a thing. It's a shame. There's a general I know who controls some very interesting purse strings.

—You're testing something.

— Something to drop from the sky that's not a bomb. You should like that idea.

She remembered waking up after Eric's mistaken doses, her limbs lax.

—It sounds like a bomb that you strap to your skin.

—I only take a little taste. It wouldn't make you sick, anyway, not physically. Make you see things. That's the idea: a nightmare drug. In wartime, we could make it rain down like water. Imag-ine, whole cities, every person with the thing they fear most come to life—they'd gouge their own eyes out before we ever got a soldier on the ground. He shook his arm out, dismissing it.

But like this? Perfectly safe. It's candy. I might see some bright colours, if I'm lucky. He liked her attention. Think of my work like a candy factory, he said. I have to be able to describe the flavours, don't I?

Heike turned her back, trailing her fingers against the spines on the bookcase as she moved away.

— It's just that enemies can change so quickly, she said. And friends, too. Of course, I suppose you lost your best guinea pig. She looked back at him, nodding toward his arm. I hope you are being careful with yourself.

— I thought it was Daniel you wanted.

— Stop saying that. She turned to look at him: Stop saying his name. Her voice shaking, despite herself.

She stepped toward the window. The air was close and heavy. She wanted to pull up the sash, but the window's height stopped her, the gravel walkway below swimming back and forth, three storeys down. Eric must have watched her from here, she realized. The flashlight beam playing ahead of her as she came, a firefly's path in the dark. It embarrassed her to think of this, how easily he'd tracked her approach. Her gaze widened, searching the ground for whatever she'd felt there, beside her in the shadows.

A dog, she'd thought, or something bigger. Something black and wild.

Outside, the weather pressed down like a hand, clouds dense and almost green against the night sky. She felt feverish. In the silence, the ceiling groaned again overhead.

She pulled up the window all at once.

There was no rush of fresh air. The humidity rolled in like soft tar, and the scent of mushrooms, a forest smell. The heat would not break until the storm did. The heat playing tricks.

She turned back to Eric.

— I felt it, you know. That day we went to Dolan's, the first time, with John and Arden. You were shaving, and you filled the bath for him. I felt you were capable of something. That you were dangerous.

She set her bag down on the desk and clicked the catch, drawing out her cigarettes. When she tucked them away again, she pulled out both his journal and the photograph she'd taken from the house, of herself leaning on the rail in back of their city apartment on 86th Street, the metal steps of other people's fire escapes zigging and zagging off the buildings behind her. The cigarette made her head light and clear.

Eric hesitated and then jerked a hand toward the journal, where it lay on the desk, but the movement was strangely clumsy. Heike swiped it back.

— At first I thought you'd stolen him from me. That you had him hidden at the house, or else here, locked away. She took a step toward the window again and began flipping through the pages. But that doesn't make sense, she said. Because you'd have to look after a child, and a child cries and is hungry and is cold. A child needs too much. She stopped and pressed the book against her belly like a shield. I even thought maybe you'd killed him. Daniel, she said. To punish me.

Hard work to keep her voice steady, and it came out raw and stubborn, low in her throat.

— Tell me. Tell me how you were studying in Switzerland and found me at the convent.

Eric moved toward her, measuring his steps.

— You've never understood how very sick you were.

— I was hysterical. Isn't that what you like to say?

—You're hysterical now.

Heike held the book out to him, and he snatched it.

—Take it. She stubbed her cigarette against the window ledge and left it there, looking out at the darkness. It was in the night-time, she said. Wasn't it? My accident. I don't remember every-thing, but I remember that. I remember the dark. She picked up the crushed end of the cigarette again and rolled it between her fingers, then tossed it through the window, out onto the lawn below. My accident, she said. The car hit us both, not just Harry. The car hit me, too. She turned to look at Eric: You thought I'd never remember. But I do.

From overhead, a creak in the joists, a sound like pacing, and she looked up, distracted, then shook it off. Eric stood as though he were about to lunge forward. His grip on the journal tighten-ing so that his fingertips went white.

— There was a doctor, Heike said. Shining a light and a mirror at my face. But I think that wasn't you, was it, Eric? You don't have the stomach for such emergencies. Too much gore. My hair was pink in the mirror, there was so much blood. She leaned back on the ledge. You found me here, she said. That's right, isn't it? That's why you never brought me inside with you. Because I might recognize something, and that would ruin your experiment. I lived here, downstairs. Didn't I? In a bed with the curtain pulled around it. When you were my doctor.

—You're a very interesting case. He turned back to the desk and opened a file drawer, then slipped the book inside.

—You let me believe I was home, at the convent in Switzerland.

— I did nothing at all. You had a kind of shell shock. From the war, and then you'd married and come to America. The truth is, I don't know much about it. He pulled his own cigarette case off the desk and lit up, waving the match vaguely in the air to extinguish it, as though to emphasize the insignificance of her history. When you said you were in Switzerland, I went along. It seemed the kindest thing to do.

— And the boat?

— You must have some real memory of your crossing. All I did was let your mind fill in the blanks. He inhaled sharply and held the smoke for a moment before exhaling again. His arm dropped. You are so fascinating, Heike. Your mind is plastic.

He nudged at the file drawer with his knee until it rolled shut, slow and heavy on its runners. Heike was quiet. Listening. Then:

— So the accident happened here. Not in Austria, but in America. Where? In New York? Or some other place?

Eric let a shoulder rise and fall.

— You were a transfer patient. I don't know where you lived before they brought you here.

— What about my papers? Or Harry's? There must have been a funeral, an investigation, something.

— I never saw papers. For all I know, your name isn't even Heike. He half-turned to the desk, leaning on it for support. But it doesn't sound made up, does it? You seem so sure.

— You went along with it. Very kind.

Outside, the stillness was absolute: there was no night bird calling or insect sound. Heike waited for a faraway roll of thunder, but it did not come. The air bristled with electricity. She pushed away from the window.

— I looked for his body, you know. Dani. Hidden in the attic. I berated that poor girl, your girl, Rita. I blamed her.

— Rita can't help you. She can't help anyone.

— Maybe. But she said a peculiar thing to me. Heike looked up at the ceiling, then moved to face Eric again. She told me: "There was no little boy there that night." Not, "I didn't see your little boy." *There was no little boy there that night.* And I thought this was so strange. Don't you think? Isn't that a strange thing to say to a mother?

She was standing in the very centre of the room. They were close enough that if she'd held her arm out straight, she would have touched him.

— And then Arden. He was always napping, she said. She said you kept us too close. That you were cruel, or trying to control me. All those tonics! She pressed a hand against her side, along the lowest ribs, where Daniel had curled in against her. Do you know I can feel him, just here. She let the hand fall and brush her leg, then tugged at her own skirt. You remember how he used to do that? Always at my feet, you said. Always pulling me away. It drove you crazy. She shook her head and it was a tiny motion, controlled and dismissive. It's somehow so hard to recall exactly how he looked, she said. When I see him now, it's like a dream. I get the feeling of him, but I can't remember the details.

When she looked up, she saw that Eric had stepped away from her. She closed the gap.

— Tell me, she said. Tell me about the day he was born.

He didn't say anything at first, and she kept on looking at him. His eyes a little unfocused now in the dim light. He moved back against the desk.

— Surely you recall that yourself, Heike. An important day. Are you saying you don't remember?

— No. I don't remember. She stepped forward, following him. In all those years, she said. Not a single picture of him. Just Heike alone. Heike on a ferryboat, Heike on the fire escape, Heike drinking a coffee. I went through everything, Eric. She reached out for the photo of herself in the kerchief, where she'd left it on the desk behind him. Not even you are in those pictures, she said. Because, why? Because they weren't meant for an album. Were they? They were just a document. A record. She pushed the photo at him, at his chest. That's all we ever were to you. All I ever was, Eric: an experiment. It's true, isn't it?

She held her fists high and clenched, as though she was about to beat down a door.

— Say it, Eric! Say it. Tell me I'm right: There is no Daniel. Say it! There is no Daniel. There is only a tonic. There is only a little pill.

Eric was silent, looking at her. Then:

— There is no Daniel.

Her arm swung out.

— I want him back!

She threw her weight at him, her fist connecting hard with his throat, and he coughed and stumbled long enough for her to pull back and hit him again, cutting into his shoulder before he caught her. She was screaming, almost a shriek, to keep herself from weeping.

Her arm twisted. She wrenched away from him, but he had his hands on her already, and she felt the crack of her head against the wall. They were close to the open window—the darkness spiralling down to the walkway below—and she caught the frame with one hand, pushing herself away. Eric stood over her, his hand at her collarbone, pressing her back into the frame so that she could feel the open ledge cutting at her thigh.

The blow to the throat had left him breathing hard. He spat, staring at her.

— Pull yourself together.

She smacked his arm away and spun sideways. Whatever the drug was, on his wrist, it slowed him down. She moved across the room, putting distance between them.

— I can remember, she said. I remember carrying him inside me. I know how that feels. A baby kicking you, a baby pressing down hard. She spread her shoulders wide, her arms unfolding to either side like wings. I thought he might tear me in two, she said. You could see him when I lay flat, see the shape of a foot, a shoulder, a little bum, where it pushed out. She brought her arms in again and came a step closer. That's the only part I couldn't explain, she said. But then I think of the accident, of course. And things make sense. Don't they? Tear me in two. All that blood. My skirt was soaked with it.

Eric drew a hand back as though he might hit her.

— I saved you.

He was still breathing hoarsely. His hand curled slowly into a fist, the muscles in his arm twitching. After a moment he let it drop, watching her steadily, but moved instead to fumble for his cigarettes.

— Do you think you would ever have gotten out of this asylum if it weren't for me? People don't leave this place. Look around. No one leaves. Not men, not women, and not foreigners. Some city hospital transferred you here. That's what happens: you've got a woman who can't stop crying and has no next of kin. Nothing wrong with you that they can fix. You had no papers, no identification. You could barely remember your name.

— But I did know my name.

He was struggling to get the smoke lit, his movements weirdly incongruous, almost lethargic—the match in one hand and the cigarette in the other, as though he were comparing them. When he spoke again. his voice had regained its edge.

— You didn't want your memories.

— So you gave them away.

He wheeled around and flicked at the file drawer handle with an open hand. It rolled open and stopped with a rough bang.

— You want them back? Take 'em.

His voice was sloppy. He hauled five folders up onto the desk, throwing them down one after the other, each of them stuffed full and the papers spilling out across the surface and sliding to the floor. Heike stepped back despite herself, nervous of him.

— This is all you: Patient K. He lurched toward her. That's what I named you, he said. Because that's what the nurses called you: the little Kraut girl. *K* for *Kraut*.

He picked up a sheet and held it away from his face, then closer again, tromboning it back and forth and narrowing and widening his eyes before throwing the paper down in disgust. He rubbed his face:

— Must be dark in here or something.

Heike approached the desk cautiously, keeping her focus on Eric. She retrieved the sheet.

— Patient K. *Psychogenisch*—

She paused, aware that she was pronouncing the word in German.

— Psychogenic amnesiac, Eric said. The words ran together a little as he spoke them. It means your brain looks fine from the outside. It's not just a bang on the head, like in the cartoons. Biology can't explain your amnesia.

Heike tried to scan the paper in her hands, her finger running jaggedly down the margin.

— I could tell you everything about your case without looking at a single note, he said. Pathology: Trauma, automobile accident—

She held up her hand in an effort to silence him, but he kept going.

— Next of kin: Deceased. Concussion. Contusions to left side. Eric rhymed the terms off, his own hand in the air, as though he were conducting some invisible orchestra.

— Please! Heike's arm jerked, and the paper in her hand with it. She brought it closer.

— Massive hemorrhage, late-stage placental abruption—

— Stop, Eric! I can read.

So much blood. Her dress soaked with it. Harry's head in her lap, and both of them lying in the road.

— Stillbirth, she said.

When she looked up again, she couldn't focus and her eyes wandered from one side of the room to the other before coming back to Eric. He was talking to her. She squinted at him, as though that would help her hear him.

— Hysterical with milk and pregnancy. They didn't know what to do with you! Put you to sleep, and when you woke up, you couldn't remember a thing.

Heike sank back against the desk. Her hand slid against a file folder, the pages inside it shifting: the sound of paper slippers on the hall floor, a nurse urging her on. *It's good for you to walk, miss.*

Her body felt very far away, a thing that used to be connected to her. She brought a hand to her heart again, as she had downstairs. Her breasts swollen, hard and burning.

She turned to Eric, her voice low and blank.

—When did he come along? Daniel. Was it right away? Or was he something you invented for me later? Sometime when you were bored.

She wondered that she was not crying. Instead, she could feel her jaw wiring itself together, tooth against tooth. The ceiling, or whatever she'd thought she could hear moving there, pacing her, was mute and dull now. Eric close by her, half-sitting on the desk.

A slouchy look to him. He seemed drunk.

— You were absolutely lovely. Like a china doll. When we were alone, he said. When it was just me and you. A beautiful doll with only one crack—one crack!—and I knew I could fix it. I knew I could, he said again, talking more to himself than to Heike. I knew I could fix it. He tried to take her hand. You would have been happy! I saw it in you.

He was pawing at her now, a hand at her face, her neck, her waist, pulling her in close. She tried to twist out of the embrace, but could only free herself halfway, his fingers wound tight around hers.

— Why, then, Eric? Why invent a child for me if you were so happy.

He didn't look at her but scratched at his wrist, rubbing the glass watch face against his leg.

— All I invented was a tonic, he said. You said it yourself. All I invented was a little pill. You invented Daniel.

He pushed her away suddenly and picked up his abandoned cigarette, seesawing it over the fulcrum of his index finger. This seemed to take all his focus. He flipped it over the finger and caught it with his fist. The trick pleased him, and he looked up at her:

— Lodi. That's what I call it. *L-O-D-I*. Supposed to calm your memory, take it away, make you feel good. Healing without trauma. He nodded to himself. The thing worked better than I'd ever imagined, he said. Even when you started to remember things—

— My mind filled in the blanks.

— Seeing is believing, Heike. And you saw that kid for years. Who expected that? He opened his hand, and the cigarette spilled out onto the desk, in pieces now. Without that hallucination, I could have managed, he said. Even when the chemicals ran out. I tried everything: switching up drugs, rotations. No way to tell you. It would have broken your heart. It would have broken you.

— That's why you agreed to come out here. To leave New York. In case things went wrong.

For a moment he didn't respond.

— It was time to go. He said this more softly than she expected. Then: I thought I'd get better stuff. A steady supply of test drugs. Between the Willard and the college, he said. Wouldn't you think? He walked away again, his voice rising higher and higher. But no. Damn chemists. Jealous. Jealous! They could see I was on to something. And then you, dumping your meds on the sly. Instant withdrawal! How could I have predicted you'd do such a foolish thing? He wheeled back around to face her. I would have had the Nobel. His finger pointed in accusation: The Nobel!

She could feel her face constrict, stony.

— Your experiment is over now.

— Maybe. He stopped and turned his head decisively to look first over one shoulder and then the other. Loss of peripheral vision, he said. That's the first symptom. He tapped the watch face. Don't let me forget to write that down, he said. When he managed to focus his gaze, he leaned forward, pointing at her again. Hard to say how a drug like this might mess up a weaker mind.

Heike nodded, just once. She stood up and moved toward him.

— What does the hospital think of this experiment of yours? And at Cornell, what do you think they'll say when they find out?

His brow creased and then relaxed.

— When they find out? About you, you mean? He craned his head to look out into the hall beyond the door, as though checking to see if anyone was listening. I'll tell you a secret, he said. I saw you coming across the lawn. I saw you coming. My experiment doesn't have to be over. I transferred you out of here, and I can transfer you back in. He glanced toward the hall again. Then, reaching for a new cigarette: I already called for the nurse.

There was a moment of stillness as the weight of what he'd said lodged itself in Heike's mind.

— I'm not crazy.

Even as she said this, she caught her reflection in the window glass: her hands and nails ragged from digging through Marek's storage room, and the white dress, dirty now, slipping off her shoulder like some cast-off bit of charity. She could feel her breath shorten. A kind of prickling in her wrists, the back of her neck. The dress damp against her skin. She looked at the doorway herself, gauging the distance, how fast she could get out.

— Aren't you? You turned up here, raving! He cast his hand about the desktop and held up first a fountain pen and then, thinking better of it, a pair of scissors. You tried to kill me, Heike. What could I do?

The sound she'd heard on her way up the stairs, what seemed to come from above them, in the turret: just Eric's nurse all the time, following her at a distance. Waiting for his signal. She thought of the woman in the bed downstairs, her ankle and calf bruised and bloody from the way she kicked at her own tether. Relentless.

— I only came here to get my Daniel back.

Eric set the scissors down and struck a match instead. The tip of his cigarette flared.

— That's a funny thing to say.

— It's what I came for.

He exhaled a little smoke, watching her. Then reaching for her hand and missing, his fingers closing lightly around a bit of her skirt.

— There is no Daniel, Heike. You just told me yourself. He tugged at the fabric. You had what we call a long-standing compound hallucination, he said. A medically induced delusion.

Heike stood quiet, looking at him. She stepped closer, and then again.

— Then you can give him back to me. The tonics, Eric. Or a pill. She reached for his hand, intertwining her fingers with his. Some tiny capsule, she said. I know you can.

— Is that all you want?

His other hand lay high on her thigh. He was using her for balance. Heike pressed her body against him now, working to keep her voice even and steady.

— That's all I want. I know you can do this, Eric. You won't leave me here.

— Leave you? Heike, the world is just opening up. It's opening for us, don't you see it? He reached for her face, stroking the line of her cheek. Like a flower, he said. I'd never leave you. I'd keep you. Safe.

He had his arm around her now, and he swayed her back and forth against him, as though they were dancing. His breath hot on her neck. She looked down.

— You'll always take care of me.

— Always. He started to laugh. I gave you a son, didn't I?

Heike let him pull her closer. Her fingers light against his chest.

— Then give him back.

There was a pause, his hand tightening roughly on her arm.

— It's too late.

He pushed her away, his mood changing again. Heike stumbled back and a few papers slipped off the desk to the floor. She watched him tentatively, then stopped and looked over her shoulder to the window. The fall was three storeys. If she jumped, they would catch her and keep her here. There was no nurse yet, no sign of her.

— Too late, Eric said again. Haven't you been listening? My supplier dried up. He'd rather play cards with the general himself instead of a middleman.

He turned his head from side to side, testing his vision, then pulled another match from the book and lit his cigarette a second time, the burner briefly flaming up. He shook out his wrist, and the match flame died.

— But you don't have to go with the nurse when she comes. He leaned in again, taking her elbow this time, his weight jarring her. See? You can still come home with me. You only think you came here for Daniel. He took a long drag and offered her the cigarette, shrugging it off when she refused. You really came for me, Heike. We're good together. We're good. Think of it: now that Daniel's gone, it's just the two of us. Out here in the country— didn't you see it, at those parties?—people were absolutely struck by it. Perfection. Those people were dying to be us.

He reached out and patted her cheek, a little too hard.

— And what did you do but run away? Your party trick with that two-bit hack. Small-potatoes television man. I called the police and everything. He paused and dragged on the smoke again, rocking back on his heels. And even that, you managed to make it about the kid! It's not what I wanted.

— And if what I want is Daniel?

— Ha! Let's say I could make that same tonic. You know now that he doesn't exist. You *know*, he said. That's too big a hurdle to overcome. Your brain would just supply a new delusion.

— A delusion.

Dani, hopping from foot to foot on the raft, holding his skinny arms out to her before he jumped.

— Always there, Eric said. Pulling at your skirt. Wanting something. And maybe this time it wouldn't be so nice.

Heike felt herself growing starker, a tight muscle.

There was the vaguest rustle from the hall, a sound of dry leaves skittering across the stone floor toward them. Eric picked up an ashtray and held it to eye level, puzzling at it as though he were taking a kind of measurement.

— The only thing I could never explain was the second hallucination, he said. That little girl of yours. I don't know what caused that. Once the drugs ran low, it was hard to keep track. I missed so much in your withdrawal. His voice slurring over the *r*'s and *l*'s. Tell me, he said. Did you ever see her again?

From the doorway, the same light rustling picked up speed

and then stopped abruptly. Almost the light clatter of footsteps. Heike thought of Tessa, skipping lightly across the surface of the pond, her feet barely sinking into the water as she ran. Tessa, so like Daniel, she could almost be Heike's daughter. Small and blond, a tiny creature. A little bird, with sharp teeth.

She looked at Eric, and his eyes were wide and black. She stepped closer.

— I wish you'd seen her that day, Eric. My little girl. She was absolutely lovely. Just what you always wanted. A Dresden doll.

Eric pulled back, as though he'd momentarily recalled something uncomfortable. Heike moved toward him again and then stopped, her skirt catching on the drawer handle. She tugged at the fabric. Eric let the hand with the cigarette drop, and ash sprayed over the papers on the desk.

— What are you doing there? He had the strange look of a barn cat, only the slimmest ring of pale grey banding his pupils. Stop it. There's nothing there. Nothing. Do you hear me?

But he glanced at the doorway warily. Heike turned again in the direction of the hall, following his gaze. Whatever was out there, a hiss of wind or some other thing, he also seemed to hear it now.

She picked the skirt free. Eric snapped a hand out and grabbed her wrist.

— I said don't do that, didn't I? There's nothing there. Nothing's pulling at you.

Heike froze for a moment, and he peeled his hand off her and took a cautious step back toward the window. His eyes still low, fixed on her skirt where she'd just been fiddling with it. When she spoke, she kept her voice low and steady.

— Such a sweet little thing. The girl in the water. So like me, only smaller. I wish I could have shown her to you. I can almost see her now, Eric. Can't you?

Eric stepped back again, until he was almost sitting on the sill, the window still half open where Heike had pulled it up. He blinked and then blinked again, holding his eyes closed and then opening them again. Three storeys down.

The door to the office tapped lightly against the wall. From just beyond it, the same noise came again.

A skittering sound.

— Of course, she said, these things can take on a life of their own. What did you say? Always there. Wanting something.

Heike looked over her shoulder to the doorway and then back again. Whatever she'd imagined in the turret, heavy and waiting, it was gone. What was coming now was fierce in its lightness.

— I can almost hear her, she said. Coming down the stairs. Can't you? Listen: her steps are so quick. Heike took hold of his arm, gently at first, then tighter. Someone only you can see, Eric, she said. Can you imagine that? You won't ever be alone. Never again. The little fingernails scratching at your arms. Scratching until you bleed.

He pushed her away, aiming back toward the desk, Heike at his heels.

— Always there, following behind you, she said. Just like today.

Eric's leg buckled under him, and he tried to catch himself, grabbing at anything. Heike swung out of the way just in time.

The office door banged back against the wall, harder this time, and they both flinched.

— Doctor? You needed something?

The same breeze as before, from some unknown source, but

now Eric's nurse stood in the hallway. Her cloth cap shifted on her head. Heike turned slowly to the door.

The sound of footsteps still lithe and light, up and down the hall behind her.

Eric stared down, first at his leg, then at his own hand, flexing and opening his fingers.

— I'm bleeding, he said. Just like you said. I'm bleeding.

He held tight to a fountain pen, the barrel cracked where he'd been squeezing it in his fist; a few droplets of ink ran over his hand in a thin stream. The nurse stood frozen in the entryway. Eric's eyes moved around the room as though he were following something with his look.

— Do you hear that?

The sound changing as Heike listened for it: a breath at the back of the throat. A furious panting. Gasping. Faster now. A bird, caught in the chimney, its talons rasping against the stone. Eric took hold of Heike's dress and dragged her in toward him, his voice louder now and low in his throat.

— Keep her away from me, Heike.

She could see where his fingernails dug into his palm, his hand shaking with the strength of its grip, and reached up to grab onto anything, the cord from the blinds, an anchor, however fragile.

As she turned, she caught a flash of white in the glass. Her own wrist tethered to the window frame, and then next to her, some other version: the girl in a matching white gown, lip curled back, the muscle of her diaphragm beating out, pushing air from her lungs in a seething stream. Too fast to be seen. No bird, but Tessa in her moment of changing, muscles taut and ropey along their bones, massive jaw gaping. Her cur's grin:

Heike could almost feel it in her own gums. She wheeled back from the window, looking wildly around her, but found only Eric in the room.

— She's coming. Isn't she? You hear it.

There was the pop and split of thread, the seam of her dress coming apart where Eric tore at her. Ink streamed down his arm from the fountain pen, shattered and glinting where he grasped it still, almost a dagger in his hand.

In his panic, he began to weep:

— I don't want to see her! Get her away. Away!

The window gave suddenly, slamming down into its frame behind them, the chime of breaking glass covering everything. Heike bent at the waist, a pain in her ears as though the pressure in the room had been sucked out all at once. Eric grabbed at her again.

— Do you hear it?

The last shard of broken glass spun to a stop on the floor.

Whatever she had first sensed outside and then high in the turret above them, some strong thing in the dark, came into her now, burning hot and unbreakable. She cast her gaze down, allowing her cheeks to lift as though something there delighted her. Her throat open, muscular in its exhalations. She leaned close to Eric's ear:

— I hear her.

Eric raised his hand. From the doorway, the nurse began to scream.

A DESCENT
OF RAVENS

Two forces create eternity—a fairy tale and a dream from the fairy tale.
— Dejan Stojanović, "A Fairy Tale and the End"

Dear Prince, I must leave you . . .
— Oscar Wilde, "The Happy Prince"

21.

Arden met her out on the courtroom steps, carrying a large canvas bag. She'd been worried that she was still too shaky, she told Heike, to attend the hearing herself. Heike said it was just as well. The nurse from the asylum had spent an hour on the stand, her testimony prickling with detail.

The audience—a larger than usual number of onlookers, and mostly women—had been wedged hip to hip on benches that were in fact church pews borrowed from the neighbouring Presbyterian in anticipation of the crowd. Heike sat unobtrusively at the back of the courtroom, just another curious housewife in a lavender sundress. The heat was cloying: a rivulet of sweat trickled down her back. At the sight of the nurse, she'd pulled her hat just a little lower, but the nurse herself wanted only the attention of the judge and had not looked around the crowded courtroom at all.

There had been only one moment of true anxiety during the inquest: a record existed, the court clerk said, at the local sheriff's office, of police being called to the deceased man's house just a few weeks before his death. Heike froze in her seat, bracing herself to hear that the man's wife was under investigation, or was at least a person of interest. But no report had ever been filed. The judge struck the item from the transcript and moved on.

Now she dipped to pick up one handle of Arden's bag.

— Come on, she said. Before that nurse comes out here and spots me. We are two very average ladies, out for a walk.

The women turned to head east toward the river, and made some small talk as convincingly as they knew how: the quality of the button tables at Lasky's Dressmaker Supply (very good), and that of the vodka gimlet at Saul's (rather wanting, unless you like the taste of ice). They shared the weight of the grocery bag, each holding one handle, the bag swinging between them. Arden had an umbrella with her, and she rapped it against the ground as they went. It made a counterpoint to the sound of their heels striking the sidewalk, and if you were not paying close attention, you might think it was three women walking instead of only two. There was a tavern wedged into a corner at the end of the block, its shutters half down. Heike wondered if Arden wouldn't fancy a cup of tea.

— This place looks pretty.

Inside, there were only three patrons, all on stools, and an old-timey popcorn maker and a defunct slot machine.

— Just for show, the bartender called out when Arden stopped to finger the handle. Imported!

— I'll bet. All the way from New Jersey.

— That machine has crossed water, is what I'm saying.

He was a thin man with long legs and a skinny tie and his sleeves rolled up way past the elbow. There was a tattoo up there, but Heike could see only the bottom corner of it. He had hair on his arms, dark but baby fine, and he carried a little scratch pad in his breast pocket. When he came to take their order, he pulled out the pad like it was lunchtime.

— What'll it be? I got a cold plate with pickles and a pig's knuckle on it.

Heike reached up and pushed at the fold of his sleeve with a finger.

— We'll have a fifth of bourbon, she said. And two glasses if you've got them. But we're not fussy. We'd rather have the bottle than the glasses.

The bartender looked down at her finger. She tipped her head up so that she could see what she was doing from under the wide brim of her hat.

— Ah. It's an anchor you have. I was afraid it might be a hula girl. What would your mother say?

He pushed the sleeve up higher himself to reveal the letters *M-O-M* in an arc above the anchor.

— Perfect. I approve, Heike said. We don't need a pig's fist, though.

— I can't serve you dames liquor without some kind of food at this time of day.

Heike untied the strap of her hat and shook her hair out.

— Haven't you got anything else? Some crackers or some-thing?

— How about a piece of cake? Arden said.

— No crackers. He turned to Arden: And no pastry, neither.

The canvas bag was on the chair next to Heike; she settled the hat on top of it.

— So what do you have?

— I got a cold plate with pickles and a pig's knuckle on it.

— It's terribly austere, but I suppose we'll pull through. She looked at Arden. We'll have a pig fist, please.

— Knuckle, the bartender said.

— Yes, the knuckle from the fist.

— Two glasses, two plates.

— In that case, Arden said, we're quite hungry.

He went back to the bar and poured a double for one of the hard tickets sitting there, and then he ducked down behind the counter and came up again with a couple of plates. There were three big glass jars on the counter, and he unscrewed the lids, one by one, and used a pair of wooden tongs to distribute some onions and pickles on the plates and then the pickled hocks next to those. Heike watched him working as she pulled her gloves off.

When he came back, he had the two plates balanced in one hand and the fifth and the two glasses in the other. He set the plates down first.

— *Schweinshaxe*.

There was a pause, and he put both glasses and the bottle down on Heike's side of the table and leaned there.

— *Schweinshaxe*, Heike said again. That's what we call this at home. She poked at the knuckle with the same finger she'd used to examine the man's tattoo. Only I think we make it better, crispy. And with a cabbage salad. *Schweinshaxe*.

— *Gesundheit*, the bartender said. He went back to his bar and began washing and drying glasses that hadn't been used.

Arden pulled the two glasses into a line and dosed them each with an inch or two of bourbon.

— I suppose we'll have to orchestrate a funeral next, she said.

Heike hooked a finger into the rim of one glass. The mention of a funeral made her blanch. Arden flicked at a bit of pickled onion on the table.

— John says a memorial in New York in the fall will quite suffice, and I'm inclined to agree.

Heike nodded.

In the end, Arden told her, very few people had even known Heike existed. No one would expect her to attend such a service. Arden would not expect it, at least.

— What was the verdict?

— Misadventure, Heike said.

— That makes it easy, then, for the obituary. In that he didn't throw himself out the window, she said. Or hang himself with his own suspenders. Arden lifted her glass to eye level and swirled it as though she were examining the colour and viscosity of the liquid for laboratory reasons. When she set it down again, she looked tired. No need for any extra cleanup, she said.

— I'm sorry, Arden. I am sorry for your family.

Arden took a drink and set the glass down again.

— I'd say it's my family that owes you a thing or two, not the other way around. She spun the empty glass on the table and caught it again. But goddammit, she said. He ruined everything. I don't want to be angry. He was my brother, after all. She lifted a hand to touch her forehead.

Heike pulled her handbag into her lap and picked through it. She needed something from inside.

— I brought this for you. You should have it.

She pushed a little pink sachet across the table. Arden opened the snap and fished through the bag with a finger. A few dry calendula blossoms tumbled out, and then a ring, the gold of it dimmed by a bit of powder, some cardamom or lavender turned to dust.

— Oh, Heike. This is yours.

— It isn't.

— At least melt it down.

Arden laid the ring on the table. It had a dull lustre, even in daylight. Heike pushed it away again.

— No. No, it's part of your brother's estate. I don't want anything to do with it.

After a moment, Arden slipped it back into the sachet and clicked the snap.

— My estate now, though. She looked at Heike once more, then tucked the sachet into her purse. John's been going through the files, she said. He says it looks like Eric got rid of a fair amount of paper in the last while.

— But no marriage certificate, Heike said. That's right, isn't it?

— I guess not. He said there are gaps everywhere, though. Not just in his research documents. The financial records are a mess—funding seems to come out of nowhere, and then the money just disappears again. No receipts for anything.

— There are no wedding pictures, Arden. Not even one. Heike emptied her glass. I wonder sometimes how he managed to sign me out of that place.

— The Willard?

Heike gave her head a little shake.

— I can't even say the name, she said. It makes me nervous. If we weren't ever really married, he must have faked some kind of paperwork. A transfer? I keep worrying that one day I'll hear a knock on my door and it will be the straitjacket, come to get me.

She waved her arms stiffly, zombified. This was meant to be a joke, a distraction for Arden. A decoy. Heike couldn't be sure if she was taking the bait.

Her own questions—the things she could not say out loud—remained unanswered. What had happened to her real wedding ring, for instance, Harry's ring, the ring she'd been wearing the night of the accident? Or her wedding photos? Somewhere there would have to be pictures of them, Harry in his army uniform, Heike in a travelling dress, boarding the train to Vienna for their honeymoon. Easier to focus on these details, lost objects, than to struggle for memories that wouldn't come.

She could not remember what Harry had said to her before he died, lying in the road, or if he could talk at all. What he'd wanted to name the baby. If they'd been hoping for a boy or a girl. She could remember the feel of the baby kicking inside her, but not the feel of Harry's hands on her body, her face. His parents had been dead. Who had buried him?

True memories felt chromatic—a vivid flash—and at the same time, suspect. Hard to trust: she wanted them so much. The first time she'd kissed Harry, a secret, in a passage between houses. She'd pulled him along to show him where a stork was nesting on a chimney pot. The shine of daylight, and high above them a voice calling out: *Kuckuck! Kuckuck!*

A little girl leaning out her window, red ribbons in her hair. Spying there.

Arden spun the bottle cap on the table. The chime as it pinballed from bottle to glass. Heike pulled her glass over and poured again for both of them.

—Well. What do you think? Are we going to drink this whole thing?

Arden stayed where she was, watching. Her fingers wound together in her lap.

— It's inadvisable.

— And yet.

There were two large windows on either side of the door, and Heike turned her head as if to look out onto the street. Where there were no shutters, the sheers hung down in front of the glass, grey with age and tawdry along the edges. On the other side there were only silhouettes moving in turns along the side-walk, as though someone had rigged a slow-moving fan to cast shadows.

— The hospital will keep it quiet, she said.

THE NURSE AT THE INQUEST—Marjorie Halloway—had started her testimony by saying she'd been called to Dr. Lerner's office, but he seemed zonked, out of sorts: she'd been afraid to come in, and then afraid he might hit the young lady, his lady friend, who was with him.

Heike had also thought Eric meant to hit her. He was weeping in fear—*Get her away! I don't want to see her!*—and suddenly raised the broken pen high in his fist, his whole arm shaking with the force of his grip. She was trapped between him and the window and threw an arm over her head to shield herself, the other hand grabbing at the cord from the blinds, trying to wrap it around her wrist like a tether. She was afraid he might push her out the window, the nurse only standing there, stupidly, frightened of him herself.

But he did not hit her. Instead, he brought his hand down to his own eye—the hand still holding the fountain pen—and the action of driving the nib's point and then the barrel of the pen itself into the eye socket was not impulsive or easy. It was a fervid gesture, determined, and the bursting of the eye seemed meant for Heike alone. A kind of final punishment.

This could not be true. Eric was by that time lost to his delusion, she told herself, and Heike's own face hidden away under her arm, bracing for the blow. She did not look up until she heard him screaming, his face already running with ink and blood. Heike felt the room weave around her. Eric's other hand still held tight to her dress, pulling her closer.

He threw himself forward, his face coming down hard against the desk and driving the pen farther into the eye. There was a crumpling sound, eggshells crushed in a fist, and she told herself it was only his nose against the oak desktop. A sound like gristle in the teeth.

The nurse was screaming too, from her place in the doorway, and she did not, as she told the inquest, run into the room directly, but waited for Eric to fall to the ground, dragging Heike with him. Her arm caught in the cord and wrenched back, her shoulder twisting in its socket. Eric's other eye rolling, just the white of it gleaming beneath her, his hand tight in her skirt and her body suspended somehow between the two, the skirt and the window cord, as though she were strung on a line.

The nurse called out for help, and her cries to the younger girl, Harriet Woods—*Harry! Harry!*—jerked at Heike's memory: Harry, her husband, Heike calling to him the day he died. She heard herself screaming the name now. Her vision faltered, the room darkening in little fits. Harry. She was light-headed. As though the room were a jigsaw puzzle, falling away piece by piece.

Eric convulsed beneath her, blood draining from his nose

and ear. She thought for a moment she would vomit and turned her face to the window to breathe.

It was true, as Miss Halloway told the court, that she'd had to tear Heike's skirt to free her, and that Heike herself sat on Eric's ankles to hold him down, but he was mostly still by then. The other girl arrived, breathless up the stairs, and she ran around the room twice before leaving to fetch the doctor. No one thought of the telephone. They waited and did not speak, but the nurse wept and Heike fumbled to unwind the cord where she'd wrapped it around her wrist, the skin coming up in welts where it had cut against her and the whole thing a tight web, pulling tighter. Her hands shaking as she worked to untangle herself. It was only when the new doctor arrived that she realized she'd also been crying. Her fingernails tearing at the cord.

At first he thought the stains on her skirt were blood, but it was only the black of the ink where Eric had grasped at her. This was the doctor, Tate, up from the village in his suit pants and slippers, unprepared for the scene he walked into. The blood was there, too, but in a fine, even spray, across Heike's face and neck and collarbones, as though someone had brushed her with powder. There was blood on the floor, and more of it, as you'd expect, near to where Eric had fallen. A head will bleed, Miss Halloway told the inquest, like none other.

It was Tate who dismissed her. He asked her which village she was from, or if Eric had found her on the road. If she worked on the road, or at a roadside bar, or if she'd come from a house with other girls in it. She froze, understanding suddenly what he thought of her. When she did not answer, he assumed she was in shock, and he told her to run away before the newspapers got hold of her, or the police. Heike was out of the room before she realized she'd forgotten the flashlight, her purse, everything she'd brought in with her, and had to go back in and watch them covering Eric's body with a white sheet. His features appearing slowly, grotesque and exaggerated, staining dark through the cloth.

She left the building, shoes slipping off her heels as she ran down the marble stairs and along the hall, the woman in her cast-iron bed sedated now, her leg calm under a heavy blanket, the bell of bone on metal ringing out for no one anymore.

OUT ON THE LAWN it had been cooler and quiet, and she half-expected to find Marek there, waiting for her. Instead, she was alone. The silence was expansive around her, and the grounds seemed wider and more vacant than they had before, the space between building and tree, or tree and tree, opening out long and deep green. She did not bother to turn on the flashlight. Before she reached the car, she noticed the little storage house, its door still open, and she went in and this time flipped on the light, for the moment unworried about being seen. It flickered and then buzzed to life, a fluorescent trough running down the centre of the structure.

She could see now the disorder she'd left behind, the bags and boxes upended and torn through. The brightness made the place lonelier than ever, an abandoned museum of belongings. With the light burning, the birds in the rafters made daytime noises, and she noticed for the first time a ladder at the back of the room, fixed to an open hatch in the ceiling: the attic access. She left her bag at the bottom of it and climbed up, just high enough to poke her head through the hatch. Here there were no racks, no labels, the bags just jumbled together. It was hard to know if these were the oldest remnants or the newest additions. The light from the main room was present but blocked by her body on the ladder. Heike went all the way up until she was on her knees on the floor, then flicked on the flashlight.

To one side there were crates without lids, as though a rash of people had been stripped down and their things tossed into the nearest container and the container tossed aside. To the other, just more suitcases, mostly well-worn, the leather cracked. She had not asked herself why she was here or what she was doing, but the knowledge sat at the back of her throat. The thing old Marek had wanted to show her: if she'd been a patient here, there was a chance that her own bag was in this storage house, and in it, some clue to what had come before. The life she'd had before Eric, before Daniel.

She drew up high on her knees and began to poke through the open crates, but the contents were dusty and unremarkable. If there was a past Heike in here, how would she ever know? It was the by-now-usual collection of shoes and belts, work pants and embroidered blouses. A tartan shawl. A blanket.

Heike turned to the other side and let the flashlight graze the floor and the pile of leather bags. The sole of her foot pushed an empty tin crate, and it fell, lopsided, off its perch over an old duffel bag and hit the ground with a shudder. The lid broke off, dangling there by a single hinge. It was a dump, a garbage house. She should go down the ladder and switch the light off and get back in the car and be gone, before Tate changed his mind, or the police changed it for him.

She turned back to the crates instead and shone her light toward the wall. It caught on the pearled inlay of a handle, creamy white. Well protected back there. She climbed in and drew the case out. A last whim. She used to ask Eric for a white suitcase, didn't she? Hadn't she been sure, once, that she had lost such a thing? The curve of the handle was cool against her hand, and she crawled backward, watching behind her for the hatch and hitting the tin lid with her foot. The case was heavy enough to make it awkward to lift, and she dragged it along, drawing a furrow through the other bags. Pure white with a white handle. She kicked the empty crate out of the way and drew up onto her knees.

Schneiders it said on the closure. She lit up the brand name with the flashlight. There was no standard keyhole or latch. Heike ran her thumb over the ornament at the top of the case, a copper dragon's head. No, not a dragon: a bird, a swallow; the fork-split of a tail, not a tongue. She flipped the case over. The copper swallow the only possible latch she could see. Her thumb on the swallow's tail, she pushed up, lifting the notch. She did this without thinking, as though she'd opened it a hundred times before. Her index finger flexed; the tiny hammer swung out. The case fell open at her feet. Heike flinched without meaning to, as though there might be a body in the bag.

But there was nothing macabre inside, only the leftovers of some long-ago picnic: three glass bottles, rinsed and wrapped in cloth napkins to protect them; the waxed paper wrappers off a few sandwiches, the paper blue with mould at the edges; a bathing suit. Bundled in a blue cloth she found a folding camera, still clean and, like the case itself, German-made: a Zeiss Contessa with a little hinged door to protect the lens. Its owner just returning from a trip to the beach, something pleasing and sunny, the day the bottom fell out of the world.

The case was lined with gingham. On closer examination, Heike saw that this was just a groundcover, its edges stuck to the true lining, years of being pressed up against each other creating a seal. She ran a fingernail underneath and stripped the cloth out. Between cloth and lining there was a newspaper, folded in half, part of the crossword filled in and smeared with ink. The date on it mid-June, 1950. No pen, but a bit of dry grass, as though the cloth had not been shaken out thoroughly enough, and a sketchbook, the size and shape of the one she'd found at the cabin. Heike opened it, the flashlight shining straight down. Some of the pages were blank, some dense with charcoal drawings. A few simple watercolours, gestural, unfinished. She combed through, letting the edges flutter past her thumb and watching a weird filmstrip of moving images, from the back of the book to the front. Near the centre of the book, a page stuck and she stopped.

Ravens on a wire and diving, the swoop and fall of their wings.

She could see now why the flutter of pages paused here: wedged into the binding was a small photograph, cut with a crimped edge. The style of the time. In the picture were two girls, one light and one dark, hands clasped. Barefoot. Out in the countryside somewhere, posed on the grassy banks of a river. The smaller of the two so familiar: Lena.

Heike traced the dark hair with a finger. Her sister, Lena, about three in the photo. Her thighs still baby soft. And next to her, blond hair in braids upon her head, Tessa. The girl from the raft.

Heike flipped the picture over. Her mother's fine, spidery handwriting: *Lena u. Heike, Meissen an der Elbe, 1941.*

On the inside cover of the book, there was a little sketch of the swallow closure from the suitcase, curlicued, and in the same black ink her own name, her name for only a short while, her long-ago name: Heike Foster, Dresden Pond, Cayuga County.

— Do you think he knew? Arden asked.

She had gone next door to the bakery, and they were eating hot rolls from a paper bag out in the sunshine. They'd left the pickles and hocks back at the tavern, sweating on their plates, but Heike had brought the fifth of bourbon along with them, and she slipped it into the bag next to the remaining rolls. The bottle could now be called at best an eighth rather than a fifth, and this only if the caller had a magnanimous eye.

— He was so sure of himself, Heike said. It was a kind of bragging, to bring me back so close to the asylum. And every time we went, he let me get just a bit closer: now in the restaurant down the road, now close by the building, now right on the grounds. I must have walked there before, through the garden. Every time he was only proving to himself how clever, how divine he was.

— I don't mean the asylum. I mean the cabin, Cayuga, the whole landscape. It's amazing that he ever agreed to come here. It's like bringing you back to the scene of the crime.

— Oh, no. I'm sure he had no idea I'd ever lived here. It's only a fishing cabin; a summer place. The accident must have happened in the city—Eric said I was transferred from a city hospital. He told me how patients come in, on the train, all the way from California sometimes. No way out once you're in—he used to say that. Because you arrive and the connection is immediately lost. Your history, everything. So there is no proof the cabin is mine.

—A person could look up the deed.

Heike swallowed the bit of bread in her mouth. She'd thought of it: the dresser drawer with its ream of papers. The possibility of something official in there, a passport, a marriage certificate that linked her to Harry Foster and so to the house on the pond. She'd kept the white case, carrying it away with her the night Eric died. The photo and sketchbook were in her handbag now, the Contessa camera still loaded with a roll of half-spent film.

They were standing in the middle of the sidewalk. Arden reached into her purse, and then Heike felt the nudge of something against her hand. For a moment she was worried it was Eric's ring, Arden giving it back, but in fact it was a billfold.

— Just to help you get settled. Or get started, however you want to phrase it.

Heike fingered the thin leather, opening it and closing it again. The money inside held in place with a silvery bobby pin. Arden snapped her purse closed.

—You'll take it, won't you? It's just a boost. I didn't even have to lie about the groceries: it's my own money.

— It's more than a boost.

—Well. Take it. I mean to help you, at least to get yourself set-tled. Like I said, I never had a sister. Then, catching herself: Oh, please don't . . . I didn't mean it that way. I don't want to make you sad.

Heike clutched the money in one hand.

— No. You haven't. Of course not. It's lovely, you know. It's very sweet of you. She looked down at the billfold again. I haven't had a sister for a long time, she said. She reached out for Arden, squeezing her arm. At least Lena is someone I can remember.

Long weeks hiking through the countryside, hiding in ditches and stealing bread, or begging for it. Lena repeating a little song she'd learned in school, "*Goldvogel, flieg aus, Flieg auf die Stangen, Käsebrode langen . . .*"

Heike's face lightened.

— It means: "Golden bird, grab us some cheese sandwiches!" Her grip on Arden's wrist, another quick squeeze before she pulled away again. We were so alone, she said. And then one morning, she was gone.

As though she'd been plucked away by some invisible hand, the junipers and late-spring snow around their little camp crisp and untouched. The coat she'd tucked around Lena had still been there on the ground when Heike woke, with a trace of frost along the lining of the hood where Lena's breath had dampened it. A few feet away, the sun had already warmed the earth, and there was no snow.

No snow, no footprints.

She was lost; she'd wandered off. She'd woken in the night, disoriented, and gone to look for some familiar thing, her doll, her blanket. What Heike feared most was what she'd already known was most likely: that the cold had been too much for Lena, the cold or else a steep fall, a wrong turn in the dark.

They walked on in silence for a moment, Arden's paper bag crackling around the weight of the bread and bottle inside.

— There was a dog, Heike said finally. Did I ever tell you that? A dog, loose in the woods. A giant.

Arden stopped, hedging a little.

— And you think . . . Lena? The dog, I mean . . .

— Did it eat her, or attack her somehow? Heike looked up at the sun, her eyes almost shut. No, she said. I don't think so.

It stayed with me for a day and a night, that dog. Not too close, but never far away. It wasn't vicious. Or else it wasn't hungry— but everything was hungry, everyone, so . . . She looked back to Arden again, sunspots clouding her vision for a moment. I almost wondered if it would lead me to her, to Lena.

— But it didn't.

— It was killed, Heike said. In the night. The soldiers killed it.

The dog lying there stiff against the snow in the morning, curled into itself, and the girl, also killed by soldiers, lying stiff in the barn where Heike had hidden away all night, and Lena seven days gone. A wisp of smoke in the sky from the forest on the other side of the village, the camp where the men had come from in the night. She'd turned and run the other way.

Now she caught herself:

— I don't really know how long she was missing. Lena. I couldn't remember, later on, how long I spent trying to find her. So I made it up. I decided it must have been seven days.

Arden stopped and shook out her hand where she'd been sharing the weight of the larger bag.

— Seven is a fine number in a story, she said.

She juggled the bakery bag from one arm to the other, so as to switch sides. Heike waved her away, taking the canvas bag herself by both handles. They walked on together, slowly now.

— I'll be up here for another few weeks, Arden said. I mean, if you need a place to stay. You can keep on with me at our place. John won't mind if you do.

Heike shook her head.

— You've already done too much. But maybe I can have the rest of my clothes.

— Best of the best right here. Arden gave the canvas bag a

poke. Plus a few extras. A good pillow. I thought I'd bring you things in shifts, while you figure out . . . While you figure yourself out. You know, unless . . .

— Unless?

— I figured you might want to leave these memories behind.

— No. I'm not going anywhere else. Where would I go?

— I thought you might run away to California.

— Oh. You mean with Leo? No. He came to see me, Heike said. I think maybe he thought the same thing.

Dolan cutting his way down the path to her door in his travelling clothes. A grey felt Trilby instead of the Milan.

— He found it funny, I think, for me to be there. At the cabin. He said I used to be so afraid of it, and now look, here it is—like a refuge for me.

— I don't know. I'd say just about the safest place you can be is somewhere that used to frighten you.

— I think men prefer not to think about fear, Heike said. But what frightens you is so important. Your whole self is hidden in there.

— So, no palm trees?

— No palm trees.

They could see Arden's car, parked up ahead in front of a white two-storey house with a knee-high garden fence. There was some architecture at the foot of the drive, a construction of wooden milk crates stacked together, and two little boys standing behind it. They had a pitcher of lemonade and another one that was empty and a row of plastic glasses sold to their mother at a Tupperware party. When they got close enough, Heike dug a handful of change out of her purse.

— How much?

— Two cents a glass. We used to have cake, and that was a penny for a square of it, but we ate it all already.

— Arden, we missed it! What kind of cake was it?

— Chocolate. But no icing, just powdery sugar on the top.

Arden let her arms hang down in a droopy way.

— This is just my luck, she said.

— Here. Heike counted out a few pennies. I will pay for two glasses from you.

She took the bottle of bourbon out of Arden's bakery bag and unscrewed the lid. Here, she said. Just put it right in here.

The boy filled the plastic glass, then picked it up and carefully poured the lemonade from the glass to the bottle. He did that two more times and they were out of lemonade. Heike counted out two more pennies.

— Business is very good for you, yeah?

She could see now that the two boys were not quite the same age. The smaller of the two still had her pennies in his hand, wrapped tight, and he opened his fingers slowly so as to put the money into the cash box without spilling any of it out onto the ground. Heike watched him and only recognized how long she'd been standing there when Arden took the bottle and its cap from her, sealing it up again and tucking it away in the bakery bag.

Arden took Heike's hand. There was a breeze, and the boy's hair fluttered, light and soft as a little chick's. He pushed the pennies around in the box, counting them silently. His lips moved as he counted. There was a tiny dimple in his wrist.

Heike turned away.

— Take me home, will you? She stepped closer and linked her arm in Arden's. Everything has been lost for so long, she said.

Or I've been lost. It feels good to have found something. It was my home once: that pond, that little house. Maybe it still is. Besides, no one else is using it. She almost smiled, but it was mostly to herself. It seems a good place to start, she said.

THE LAYER OF DUST that had covered everything inside the cabin was gone. The very first thing she'd done: kettle after kettle of hot water, every corner scrubbed clean. In the bedroom, she'd found a hole through to the outside, just big enough for a mouse, or perhaps even a chipmunk, and filled it in with a torn rag and carpenter's glue. She was waiting for some sense memory to return: the wood floor against her knees, the curve of the base-board, the smell of the damp plaster as she wiped down the walls. At night, she lay in bed and counted the corners of the room. A way to have a wish granted.

Now she slipped her sundress over her head, trading it for a bathing suit she'd left hanging off the arm of a chair. There were some papers strewn on the wooden table, and a makeshift easel pinned with pages she'd ripped from her notebooks: bird studies, pen and ink, or the birds' motion captured with a few strokes of charcoal. A perfect descent of black ravens, spilling down the page like a bright helix, sharp in their relief.

Trying to pick up where the other Heike had left off.

Outside, the ground was warm and firm beneath her, the path clear but banked with wildflowers to one side, under the window, the colours catching the light. Cosmos, like cocktail umbrellas floating high on tall stems.

She waded into the pond with a few long strides, swam out cleanly, then pulled up onto the raft, crouching there with her toes curled over the edge, looking down at something just below the surface.

Her body was cool from the water, her hair wet and away from her face. She pushed up to standing, a hand at her hip, listening—but there was only the low rumble of a car far up on the road somewhere, already fading into the distance, and back in the reeds, a loon. She could hear it calling to its mate and the echo of the call.

The sun was strong behind her. She turned away again to gaze down at the girl, her skin shimmering green and gold just below the surface of the pond. When she leaned out over the water, the girl pulled closer. Blond hair falling around her face, already almost dry in the midday heat. Heike had an urge to reach in and take her hand.

The breeze picked up. Her reflection rippled there.

She sprang forward off the raft, the dive almost soundless. Below the surface, her arms pulled out wide and back in again.

One good kick and she was already halfway to the other side.

Acknowledgements

I'M VERY LUCKY to have had the support of some wonderful friends, family, and colleagues in the writing of this book. First thank you goes always to George Murray, whose keen ear and eye and hours of conversation allowed me to take what felt like a dream and fine-tune it into a proper story. I'm grateful to my early readers, Andreae Callanan, Megan Coles, Miranda Hill, and Bianca Spence, for their time and their thoughtful consideration of the novel when it was in draft form. My mother, Eva de Mariaffi, for looking over the German to make sure I had it just right. My children, Nora and Desmond, Silas and August, for keeping me grounded and for the final-draft-panic high fives and kind words—and Desmond especially for the memory of his childhood adventures with tadpoles and turtles. Financial support from ArtsNL made it possible for me to devote much-needed focus to the project. As always, my agent, Samantha Haywood, provided unfailing support and sharp ideas. And, of course, a huge thank you to my wonderful editor, Iris Tupholme, who loved the book from the start and has pursued it with me rigorously—exactly what I love best.

A Note on Sources

ALL OF THE CHARACTERS IN *Hysteria* are fictional. While I created
the character of Leo Dolan, his body of work is based largely
on the work of Rod Serling, an American writer/producer and
creator of the groundbreaking television series *The Twilight
Zone*. Serling really did write a teleplay for *The United States
Steel Hour* that aired in 1956, originally based on the story of
the lynching of Emmett Till, and it was changed and rewritten
at least twice to suit the network executives—something Serling
only occasionally spoke about in interviews. Serling's experience with network censorship was one of the factors that led
him to write and produce his own series *The Twilight Zone*, which
did not air until 1959. In the scenes where Leo Dolan and Heike
Lerner discuss his work, several real-life *Twilight Zone* episodes
are referenced, including plots and characters from "Walking
Distance" and "Nightmare as a Child," in forms that have been
altered to suit my story. Fleeting references are made to "The
Sixteen-Millimeter Shrine," "The Hitch-Hiker," "The Lonely,"
and "Living Doll"—these are Easter eggs that only a real *Twilight*

Zone aficionado will spot. It was a fun surprise to find that Serling's own production company was called Cayuga Productions.

I visited Ovid, New York, the site of the former Willard State Hospital, in 2015, and also spent time in Aurora, Union Springs, Lansing, Ithaca, Auburn, and Skaneateles. *The Lives They Left Behind: Suitcases from a State Hospital Attic* by Darby Penney and Peter Stastny (Bellevue Literary Press, 2008) was useful to me in imagining the world of the asylum as it existed. The character of the old man, Marek, is based on the real-life Willard patient and gravedigger Lawrence Mocha. The authors of *Lives* gave Mocha the pseudonym Marek, and I have maintained it here. A man can only have so many names.

Among other resources, Ernest Hemingway's short story "A Way You'll Never Be" was useful in my imagining of Heike's experience hiding out in the barn and afterward, as she escaped from Germany in 1945. I was interested in the aftermath of battle not from a soldier's perspective, but as it might be experienced by a young girl.

Where Heike's long solo trek across a whole country is concerned, my own great-great-grandmother, Maria Sieber, left Switzerland on foot in the late 1800s, arriving some time later in Hungary—alone, with only her little brother in tow. She was fifteen at the time. So I know such things can be done.

Epigraphs

Dr. Frank Berger's comment, quoted here on page 9, was made to the Senate Antitrust and Monopoly subcommittee in 1960, and was reported by Joseph A. Loftus in his article "Costs Held Small in Making Drugs," which appeared in *The New York Times* on January 27, 1960.

Rod Serling's conversation with journalist Mike Wallace, quoted here on page 169, originally took place on *The Mike Wallace Interview*, airdate September 22, 1959.

The excerpt from L. Wilson Greene's classified document "Psychochemical Warfare: A New Concept of War," on page 323, was quoted by Raffi Khatchadourian in his December 17, 2012, *New Yorker* feature "Operation Delirium."

The quotation from "Cinderella," also on page 323, is from *Grimm's Fairy Tales*, translated by E.V. Lucas, Lucy Crane, and Marian Edwardes (Grosset & Dunlap, 1965).

Dejan Stojanović's poem, "A Fairy Tale and the End," quoted on page 391, is part of the sequence "Forgotten Place," published in English in *The Sun Watches the Sun* (New Avenue Books, 2012).

The full title of the work quoted in the very first epigraph on page vii is *Niederlausitzer Volkssagen Vornehmlich aus dem Stadt und Landkreise Guben Gesammelt und Zusammengestellt (Folktales of Lower Lusatia Collected and Compiled Principally from the Town and County of Guben)* by Karl Gander. The translation of the epigraph is my own.